Praise for *Cobra* and *Maitreya*

"Severo Sarduy has everything .
bewilderingly apt in his borrowin
his inventions, his findings, he lea   ᴜᴏt of
rum."

—Richard Howard

"Sarduy is the master of wordscapes that dip, shake, and explode. But if *Cobra* is a magical juggling act, of image balancing dangerously upon image, the translation is as remarkable as the book itself. Levine has managed to snare Sarduy's sense of play, all his conundrums and fabulations, and a good many of his Spanish puns, with a gorgeous transference of rhythms from one language to another."

—Jerome Charyn, *New York Times Book Review*

"In Severo Sarduy's *Cobra,* the alternation is that of two pleasures *in a state of competition;* the other edge is the other delight: *more, more, still more!* one more word, one more celebration. Language reconstructs itself *elsewhere* under the teeming flux of every kind of linguistic pleasure. Where is this elsewhere? In the paradise of words. *Cobra* is in fact a paradisiac text, utopian (without site), a heterology by plenitude: all the signifiers are here and each scores a bull's-eye; the author (the reader) seems to say to them: *I love you all* (words, phrases, sentences, adjectives, discontinuities: pellmell: signs and mirages of objects which they represent); a kind of Franciscanism invites all words to perch, to flock, to fly off again; a marbled, iridescent text; we are gorged with language, like children who are never refused anything or scolded for anything or, even worse, 'permitted' anything. *Cobra* is the pledge of continuous jubilation, the moment when by its very excess verbal pleasure chokes and reels into bliss."

—Roland Barthes, *The Pleasure of the Text*

"*Cobra* is in a class of its own, unrelated to any 'serious' genre, whether encoded or codable, to any type except the one whose new genus it events: a bizarre hybrid, a composite of snake, writings, rhythms, of a flight of luminous traces and a series of infinitesimal sparkling instants."

—Hélène Cixous, *Review*

"*Maitreya* [is] a mesmerizing literary mosaic fusing the memories of a Caribbean sense of place with a fluid existential state where transmigration is commonplace."

—Juana Ponce de León, *Voice Literary Supplement*

"*Maitreya* is rich in political and historical suggestions . . . among the most compelling products of contemporary Latin American fiction, as finished and original as *Hopscotch* or *One Hundred Years of Solitude* . . . funny, kitschy, irreverent."

—Roberto González Echevarría, Yale University

"*Maitreya*'s outrageous characters maneuver through endless passages and trapdoors, as if in a *Tibetan Book of the Dead* recited by saucy drag queens. The dialogue can be as sharp as that of divas speculating cock size, but the sentences are sometimes as ornate as the spaces his characters inhabit, rambunctious as their makeup."

—Lawrence Chua, *Voice Literary Supplement*

SEVERO SARDUY

Cobra
and
Maitreya

Translated with a Preface by
Suzanne Jill Levine

Introduction by James McCourt

Dalkey Archive Press

First Edition, 1995

Cobra was originally published in Spanish by Sudamericana (Buenos Aires), 1972. © 1972 by Severo Sarduy. *Maitreya* was originally published in Spanish by Seix Barral (Barcelona), 1978. © 1978 by Severo Sarduy.

Suzanne Jill Levine's English translation of *Cobra* was originally published by E. P. Dutton & Co., 1975. © 1975 by E. P. Dutton and Co., Inc. Her translation of *Maitreya* was originally published by Ediciones del Norte, 1987. © 1987 by Ediciones del Norte.

Translator's Preface and revised translations © 1995 by Suzanne Jill Levine
Introduction © 1995 by James McCourt

Sarduy, Severo.
  [Cobra. English]
  Cobra ; and, Maitreya / Severo Sarduy ; translated with a preface by Suzanne Jill Levine ; introduction by James McCourt. -- 1st ed.
  p. cm.
  I. Levine, Suzanne Jill. II. Sarduy, Severo. Maitreya. English. III.
Title: IV. Title: Maitreya. V. Title: Cobra ; and, Maitreya.
  PQ7390.S28A6   1995   863--dc20   94-25167
  ISBN 1-56478-076-7

Partially funded by grants from the National Endowment for the Arts and the Illinois Arts Council.

Dalkey Archive Press
Illinois State University
Campus Box 4241
Normal, IL 61790-4241

NATIONAL
ENDOWMENT
FOR THE
ARTS

Printed on permanent/durable acid-free paper and bound in the United States of America.

Contents

Translator's Preface

A versatile and prolific master of several genres—a painter as well as an avant-garde novelist, poet, playwright and essayist—Severo Sarduy died on June 8, 1993, of AIDS. His last book, published posthumously, is a volume of poetry which he titled in homage to his imminent death, *Epitafios* (Epitaphs). Born in 1936 or 1937 (accounts vary) in Camagüey, Cuba, Sarduy had been living as an expatriate in Paris since 1960. To be Cuban is, however, already to feel foreign, Sarduy once quoted his mentor, the neobaroque Cuban poet Lezama Lima.

Though "postmodernism" was not a term on everybody's lips when Sarduy's first novels *Gestos* and *De donde son los cantantes* appeared in the sixties, one could say that his work is exemplary of postmodernity. As a pictorial writer and a textu(r)al painter, as a reveler in literal and figurative transvestism, he transgressed genres and genders, cultural and linguistic borders. As an exiled Cuban devoted to baroque poetics, *santería,* Maoism, Tibetan Buddhism, and French theory (among his close friends were Roland Barthes and Jacques Lacan) he deconstructed logo-centrism in witty, lyrical, densely rigorous narrative structures that trace the fragmented subject's relentless self-quest as well as the arabesques of today's cultural and political realities. A difficult and unclassifiable writer, Sarduy characterizes the place of "Latin America" (the French name for South America) in Western civilization perhaps more authentically than the writing of some of his more accessible colleagues in the mainstream. High and pop art, the Americas and Europe, East and West all meet and change places at the crossroads of this displaced cosmopolitan Cuban, this tropical tripper in triste Paris.

Sarduy's last prose works, *El cristo de la Rue Jacob* (Christ on the Rue Jacob, 1987), a volume of short autobiographical pieces or "traces of the ephemeral," and his seventh and final novel *Pájaros de la playa* (Birds on the Beach, 1993), explore, with meticulous yet hallucinatory lucidity, the experience of dying, or the "mal," as he calls AIDS. Despite the playful, subversive irreverence in his life and his writing, Sarduy had a profound commitment to Eastern, indeed to many, forms of spirituality; he spent his last weeks at home in Paris with his longtime companion François Wahl, painting and reading, surrounded by his canvases and his books in meditative withdrawal.

His novels in English so far (in my translations) are *From Cuba with a Song* (*De donde son los cantantes,* 1966; Dutton, 1972), reissued by Sun & Moon Press in 1994; *Cobra* (1972; Dutton, 1975), and *Maitreya* (1978; Ediciones del Norte, 1987), here reissued. *Escrito sobre un cuerpo* (1969), his first book of essays, has been translated by Carol Maier in a collection (including later essays) titled *Written on a Body* (Lumen Books, 1989), and Philip Barnard translated *For Voice,* four radio plays (*Para la voz,* 1977; Latin American Literary Press, 1985). *Christ on the Rue Jacob* (in translation by Carol Maier and myself) has just been published by Mercury House.

Cobra, Sarduy's third novel, which inspired Roland Barthes's study *The Pleasure of the Text,* is ostensibly the story of a transvestite that begins in the "Lyrical Theater of Dolls" and ends with an "Indian Journal." The erotic search for an absence motivates a metamorphic quest that takes Cobra—assisted by her tiny double, "Pup," and a versatile "Madam": they form a dubious Trinity—from Paris to Morocco to Amsterdam and ultimately to an India which may be the Indies—repeating Columbus's error! The book of the voyage is the voyage of the book: in Part II, when Cobra is initiated into a band of leather boys with fetish names, they suddenly turn into a sect of Tibetan lamas struggling, far from their "pristine sources," to revive their rituals. Are we in the suburbs of Paris, or in a Chinese landscape, or in the labyrinth of the text?

The joys and intricacies of reading *Cobra* can be found—for starters—in its title: named after an "actress" who had been killed in a plane crash over Fujiyama, COBRA alludes to the "gestural" school of painters—based in COpenhagen, BRussels and Amsterdam—which had an early impact on Sarduy, and also comes from the Spanish verb *cobrar,* "to collect payment," but also anagrammatically suggests *barroco* and Córdoba—remnant of the Arabian empire in the south of Spain—and, of course, Cuba. *Cobra* most obviously refers to the hypnotic snake that bites its tail, emblematic of India and circular time, which leads us to the novel come full circle, speaking of itself, the vocable "cobra" winding its way along language's slippery, rootless route. East and West mirror each other parodically in the theater of Sarduy's Cuban imagination, as he warns the reader in an interview with Emir Rodríguez Monegal:

we're not talking about a transcendental, metaphysical or profound India, but on the contrary, about an exaltation of the surface and I would say costume jewelry India. I believe that the only decoding a Westerner can do, that the only unneurotic reading that is possible from our logocentric point of view, is that which India's surface offers. The rest is Christianizing translation, syncretism, real superficiality.

Elsewhere (in my book *The Subversive Scribe*) I have spoken about the challenging and creative process of interpreting the many languages in *Cobra* and producing the translation of its babelic surface, adding one more metamorphosis to its spiralling series of transmutations. Suffice it here to say that I am grateful to those who came to my assistance in clarifying the elusive referent, among them Enrico Mario Santí, Emir Rodríguez Monegal, and especially the author himself.

The first chapter of his fourth novel *Maitreya* (1978) is titled, it now seems prophetically, "At the Death of the Master." The search for an absence continues in *Maitreya,* tracing the desire for the future Buddha, a longing that becomes a continuous displacement of scenes from the mountains of Tibet to a pool in Miami, from the Washington Square Park fountain to the North African desert. *Maitreya* can be read as a poem and as a political satire of global struggle, as an elaborate parody—a "spicier" version of Hesse's *Siddhartha*—and as an allusive, hallucinatory, spiritual passage toward revelation—real or imagined but "always already" written.

Translating *Maitreya* has been another journey through varied and difficult terrain, a labyrinth of signs and images, in search of resonances. I am grateful to the National Endowment for the Arts for supporting this project. And again, I am thankful to those friends and colleagues who helped along the way, especially Emir Rodríguez Monegal, whose wisdom and encouragement were an inspiration not only to me but also to Severo Sarduy.

—SUZANNE JILL LEVINE

Introduction

James McCourt

La Prematura (Luis Echegoyen), the drag sensation of Cuban TV in Severo Sarduy's formative years, was famous for the line "*¡Es que tengo tantas cosas en mi cabecita!*" ("Oh, there's such a lot going on in my little head!"). In the decade following Castro's ouster of Batista, *La Prematura*'s offspring, bevies of fleeing Cuban drag queens, made for New York (foreshadowing the journey of *Illuminada* in *Maitreya*) on wings of wild-woman stichomythia and quack and in feathers, finery and costume jewelry we'd never encountered the like of till they hit town, and the reverberation of their landing operation was all there was in my head as I took up *Cobra* and *Maitreya*. Despairing of coherence, I sped up to Yale to speak to the leading Sarduy expert there.

There is no more ardent (or taxing) enthusiasm than that of the newly converted—illumination through shock, as Sarduy puts it—and until asked to contribute this, I'd read nothing of the author. Having now absorbed *Cobra* and *Maitreya* and some key glosses of Roberto González Echevarría (who, prodigal of energy and insight, tended to my first impressions, imparting confidence while allowing me to rely on his expert discourse throughout: all italicized remarks unless otherwise noted are his), I see that in my pursuit of the Latin American Boom, my reading angel has left the best late.

Oscar Wilde wrote that no man may become like his mother, and proposed that as his tragedy. What this means of course is that in the inverted Wildean view, characteristic of the homosexual melodrama, no man can (without breaking the taboo and the home too) become his father's lover. He cannot bear his father's children: a man cannot in fact bear himself. The drag queen (a creature I reckon a kind of Essene, each with a purse containing her own Dead Sea scroll), by crossing every nerve wire and breaking every incest taboo, bears in her brain her/himself, and gives to the world that chimerical monster, the travesty androgyne. Each becomes a Tiresias. This is why writing about them is so difficult; one is sadistically inclined to make them suffer, to pay for their insolent wisdom, and in *Cobra*, Sarduy does so. Cobra is broken like breadsticks and distributed for communion. In *Maitreya*, the greater book, the author has come by way of his own shock treatment to the bliss of a higher wisdom, and can grant his hero(ine) like access.

Of course my excitement over Sarduy begins with the fact that he ran away from Cuba and made it in Paris. Was this any kind of *political* decision? I can only ho-hum a chorus of whatever Cuban equivalent there might be of "How're you gonna keep 'em down on the farm." (Down on the collective, in this case.) In any case, there are only two places in which such a literary soul as his could have flourished, New York and Paris, and just as no Anglophone need become installed in Paris (Gertrude Stein and Samuel Beckett notwithstanding) virtually every other phone should for a time, and particularly exiled Hispanics, both literary and histrionic, who have a history of refuge there. Think of Lola Montes (who, granted, was Irish, like Beckett, and is buried in Brooklyn, but it's the principle of the thing). Paris made her, Max Ophuls remade her there, in French, in color and Cinemascope, and what *Cobra* really reads like is a treatment, in the dialogue-scenario stage, with story boards evolving like a game of *chemin-de-fer*. A treatment for a *Lola Montes*-like picture that will play at the Cervantes cinema (p. 54), where upon entrance the ticket explodes. A film shot to climax in an apocalyptic vision crossing stylistic elements of Thomas Hart Benton's *Hollywood* and James Ensor's *Entry of Christ into Brussels* in terms of an apotheosis of a lost drag Havana, fabled Eden of my so fondly remembered *Cuba Libra chicas*. One that celebrates the absolute ascendancy of *mise-en-scène* over montage, an Ophulsian tracking extravaganza in which the walls of logic dissolve the better the eye may widen in amazement. (Meyer Shapiro assures us interpretation is only interesting when extreme.)

Moreover, in addition to re-invoking the older Spanish glories of both the picaresque and the clandestine forbidden (Fernando de Rojas's notorious *La Celestina,* from whom, as González Echevarría points out, he appropriated the whorehouse as Arena of Initiation) Sarduy is surely impersonating Scheherazade, wish-fulfilling in the seraglio a tale to succeed in putting off night after night the original executive decree: extinction.

Running away to Paris and getting involved with the apache dancers at *Tel Quel* (and soaking up the atmosphere, the literary rubrics and the ventriloquial theatrics exemplified by Genet's *Notre Dame des Fleurs, Haute Surveillance, La Balcon* and *Les Paravants*) was perhaps a foregone conclusion for Sarduy, a rail-road station keeper's son from Camagüey, a backwater in the island nation. (I like to think of him gathering voice impressions and stories there from the waiting passengers and assessing their aural dramatic possibilities—for Sarduy's art is the art of the ear, much as is Beckett's, that daily commuter from Foxrock station to Harcourt Street station in Dublin, who organized his overheard voices into the radio play *All That Fall*). His arrival into a literary and philosophical milieu that immediately succeeded Existential-ism enabled him to exercise his blasphemy and profanity in a congenial deconstructionist atmosphere. (For blasphemy is spe-cifically the *utterance* of profanity, and profanity is that which places the user existentially outside the temple walls.) There on the Left Bank, night after night to the echo of jazz *boîte* trumpets, Sarduy perfected his riffs against Jericho. I liken his advent to the arrival in New York from Tulip, Texas, of Holly Golightly, who fell in with the Upper East Side high life, and with the Mafia. (Cubans are a lot like Texans and the *Tel Quel* crowd is such a mafia.) And all the while he listened to them rattle on in their way stations, sporting their postwar *hautes écoles* literary *prêt à porter,* he was calling on not only the characters from the railway station in Camagüey, and on the radio soap operas played in Havana, but of course on *La Prematura* to supplement and counterpoint the chattering savants and their fashion-war *evenments de '68.*

For *in Sarduy language is always an enigma, against which each culture or discourse makes violent but inescapable decisions.* (Such as those made for example by Chanel and Yves St. Laurent when they rumbled around Paris in their Rolls-Royce during the uprising, scooping up the wounded and taking them home for bandaging. Talk of appropriating revolutionary discourse for bent ends.) A sadomasochistic enterprise, dually driven: the eros of the inescapable and the aggression of willed impact implied in every decision. And so, spurred on by that most industrious pawnbroker of literary criticism, Jacques Derrida ("If one calls *bricolage* the necessity of borrowing one's concepts from the text of a heritage which is more or less coherent or ruined, it must be said that every discourse is *bricoleur*"), Sarduy became a master appropriator or recyclist. González Echevarría's take on this is succinct and elegant: *For the fragment, as it expands and becomes a new text, is larger than the particle whence it originated.* This is cognate to the use Holly Woodlawn makes of quality garbage in Paul Morrissey's *Trash,* although Sarduy's arrogations, consonant with his stylistic ambitions, are hardly in the trash line—more on the order of what T. S. Eliot does in *The Waste Land* and of Lezama Lima's novel *Paradiso,* cited by González Echevarría as a primary source of *Maitreya* (as the spiritually rotten, albeit kinetically exemplary *The Ticket That Exploded* is of *Cobra*). (*Paradiso is the text to which* Maitreya *appeals in order to acquire authority for its prophetic tone.*)

But before *Maitreya, Cobra,* whose name means for me not only the derivatives *cobrar,* to collect, to feel desire, also *abra, vocablo:* breath, life force, also *obra,* work, *braco,* arm *abrazo,* but ultimately, as Mother of the Muses, not Mnemosyne, but that cruel high priestess and Kali figure ("Young men, young women, children . . . all must go!") Cobra Woman aka the legendary, tragic (died in the bathtub) and salvific Maria Montez, an only somewhat lesser Lola. (And how these names reverberate through the nineteenth and twentieth centuries: Lola-Lola, Maria . . . Virgin, Mother, Whore. All products of the male Unconscious, provoked by the thrust of that Introject the drag queen bests by getting into Daddy's pants.)

Sarduy's Cobra *attempts to embody nothing less than the subconscious of the Latin American narrative.*

Likening his art to that forensic examination of the corpus

delicti, Sarduy declared, "I practice a kind of linguistic psycho-analysis, but obviously the unconscious mind of Spanish is very different from the unconscious of the French; in the theater, or rather in that *factory* as Deleuze and Guattari put it, which is the unconscious mind of Spanish, we find the baroque, with its residual basis which it implies; its excesses, its extravagance, its gold/excrement and above all its continual *flux.*" It is perhaps not good form to correct the dead (especially if, as Maeterlinck thought, there are none) but I can perhaps illuminate one point by doing so. Strictly speaking, the Unconscious (and Freud, who used both the Subconscious and the Unconscious at first inter-changeably, later settled on the latter term) is not a *mind* as such, and so the Spanish and the French cannot differ either the one from the other or from any other. Although *access* to the Unconscious in aid of making its contents a utility for the conscious mind is (or ought to be) in therapeutic praxis strictly verbal, and thereby grammatically informed, the putative entity is itself wholly undifferentiated, and consequently unthinking. However, Sarduy was on the right intuitive track, since it is the principal attribute of the Unconscious that *it knows no negative.* Thus, for example, if we wish to conceive of the Unconscious negotiating love and hatred, we must not style them as opposites, but as two *parallel streams.* This is particularly useful when we think about what writing is, and why, for example, it shrivels when drenched in politics (whether *phallogocentric* or not) like the male member in a cold shower. Cobra (who, if she knows any nega-tives, certainly tolerates no prohibitions, *goes all the way*) sacrifices herself to the higher good, amid many thrusts and setbacks, whereas Maitreya *attempts to achieve a textual nirvana that corresponds to its title. This is the reason for the absence of sacrifices and violence.*

It might be noted here in passing that just as the Unconscious knows no spatial, or impinging negative, neither does it know a temporal one. (I equate, for the writer, fictional present with nir-vana.) If the past is what isn't here anymore and the present what isn't here yet, the strenuous present of *Maitreya* recognizes the demands of neither. There are no contretemps, no setbacks. *Those large plot units repeat a single message: circularity, repetition.* (Freud wrote, in *Beyond the Pleasure Principle,* that stronger even than survival and gratification is the compulsion to repeat.)

The action moves toward a difference that winds up being the same. In the end everything looks like everything else. Nothing is sufficiently distinct to be declared unique.

Except of course the totality, and Sarduy himself

Even the French all want to come to New York, and so *La Tremenda* in *Maitreya* succeeds in doing so. The metropolis, for Roland Barthes, is always an enigma, against which each culture or discourse makes violent but inescapable decisions. And so Sarduy must send his drag queen cortege there in his mind to forge a milieu which only existed in the world enough and time (time out of mind) at Max's Kansas City, the freaky Vatican of the Cosmopolis. I see a gigantic Ensor-inspired mural, done on the side of a wall in the back room: *The Entrance of the Author into Max's.* I like to think Sarduy might have found his spiritual *monte,* his Tibet among us, grooving to Lou Reed and Nico upstairs at Max's and later to Holly Woodlawn at Reno Sweeney's, and toured with us all the Cuban-Chinese restaurants on Eighth Avenue, even if *the Orient in Sarduy is a false chimerical origin, a sort of veiled death. Its presence through* Maitreya *is constant, from the real Orient to that of the Cuban-Chinese restaurants in Manhattan.*

The Orient, figured by Sarduy in his earlier *From Cuba with a Song* as Shanghai, is the emblematic whore's capital, where his adored Marlene was bound on the express, where Wallis Windsor learned her tricks. (The very word *shanghaied* signifies rape.) "And yet," Wilhelm Reich wrote, "the Orient did see one aspect correctly—namely that living matter is not a machine capable of being constructed." So neither for Sarduy was fictive matter, which out of the detritus of episodic experience must be *engendered.*

Death of the father, revolution, black hole, Maitreya *is engendered out of those moments of dispersion and their recuperation in the fictional present of the text. To do so, Sarduy's novel takes recourse to a hermeneutical process as old as Biblical exegesis: figural interpretation.*

Since I take no interest in Buddhism and consider the much vaunted spiritual agon between East and West something best resolved by a summer evening's pavanne (of inescapable decisions, night after night) in Central Park, I read *Maitreya* categorically intrapsychically—an exegesis of the Book of Self—and the inside of the head of Severo Sarduy is a place where wild things in perpetual conflict rumba to a kind of dead calm.

Two conflicting prophecies issue from our reading of Maitreya: *the figural one that signals the end of time and the textual one that proclaims the possibility of meaning in the fallen present, in exile.*

If *Cobra* owes a debt to *The Ticket That Exploded*, *Maitreya* is a little like Nathanael West's *A Cool Million* and *The Day of the Locust*, two earlier pieces of whacked-out American vision literature. Here in an early passage I see the melodrama of the writer's head *toute étourdie*. As Paul Ricouer (a genuine literary mediator) puts it, "the notion of emplotment, *transposed from the action to the characters in the narrative*, produces a dialectic of character which is quite clearly a dialectic of sameness and selfhood." Imagine *La Tremenda* in cabaret upstairs at Max's, holding the mirror up to her own image (nature reworked) and singing "I get a kick out of me!" To me her song is the sound of the night (*la noche entre en calor*) at the Mais Oui, the legendary West Side cha-cha bar of the late fifties (its name echoed in *Maitreya* by the chant "*¡Sí, cómo no!*") or indeed of a night at Cherry Grove on Fire Island, or later in Key West. And it is both the *Dies Irae* and the *Lachrymosa* of a requiem for the sacramental celebrant of sex and drugs that Sarduy was (as signer of the text: I know absolutely nothing of a biographical nature concerning the author's habits). Sex and drugs; about the rock 'n' roll dimension, I'm unable to infer much, but if we replace it in the litany with those fabulous Afro-Cuban jazz forms whose power and sophistication, known and felt by cognoscenti as something every bit as potent as either acid rock or Wagnerian opera, I think we're in business.

From *Maitreya:*

The head, like a planet torn from its course and which upon falling would turn back into lava, lime or mother-of-pearl, in a luminous, spiral unwinding, became a giant iridescent conch which when blown by the wind emitted a muffled, unchanging sound, the charred vibration of a remote explosion. A sound that became deeper until, followed by a rain of tiny bones, a hoarse hailstorm, faded in the circle of an OM.

Maitreya achieves finally what I take to be Sarduy's glory, the achievement of the *serenity* pitched by Eliot in the Quartets. (Or is it just the Atavan or its equivalent? I am aware that if malt does more than either Eliot or Milton can to justify God's ways to some, then someone who grew up amid the strenuous exoticisms of *Santería* might require something a little stronger. Miltown rather than Milton.) Or the feeling you get when you stop banging your head against any wall (just as the wall dissolves: see above).

Maitreya *attempts to achieve a textual nirvana that corresponds to its title. This is the reason for the absence of sacrifices and violence in this novel as opposed to* Cobra. Whatever the reason, I prefer it; it exhibits a progression from the purgatorial to the paradisiac. At the still center of the whirl: the primal sea sounds in the ear/brain conch shell, or the eye/brain registers its serene purr in the contemplation of the north rose window at Chartres.

Finally, of the two drives, the aggressive and the erotic, one or the other is always dominant. (*Measured* as such; in this I liken them to particle and wave in quantum theory: the erotic as particle, the aggressive as wave.) This imbalance, as in Plato's parable of the Charioteer, requires correction. Writers have this in common with drag queens: in order for the aggressive drive to dominate, erotic energy must be transferred to it or the ego will go under. A writer drag queen has the condition in spades. Only in the late work of a strong poet (Eliot, Stevens, Schuyler, Ashbery) is serenity achieved. Sarduy didn't live to leave old bones, but I do think he made it to the moment in the rose window.

Cobra

Part I

Lyrical Theater of Dolls

She'd set them in molds at daybreak, apply salt compresses, chastise them with successive baths of hot and cold water. She forced them with gags; she submitted them to crude mechanics. She manufactured wire armors to put them in, shortening and twisting the threads again and again with pliers; after smearing them with gum arabic she bound them with strips of cloth: they were mummies, children of Florentine medallions.

She attempted scrapings.

Resorted to magic.

Fell into orthopedic determinism.

COBRA: "My God"—on the record player Sonny Rollins, of course—"why did you bring me into the world if it wasn't to be absolutely divine?"—she moaned naked on an alpaca rug, among fans and Calder mobiles. "What good is it to be queen of the Lyrical Theater of Dolls, and to have the best collection of mechanical toys, if at the sight of my feet men run away and cats start climbing on them?"

She took a sip of the "pool"—that pitcher in which the Madam, to compensate for the rigors of summer and of the reducing operation, served her a raspberry ice cream soda—she smoothed her tangled glass hairs, with a metric ruler she measured the rebellious ones and again launched into the "My God, why . . .," etc.

She began to transform at six for the midnight show; in that crying ritual one had to deserve each ornament: the false eyelashes and the crown, the pigments, which the profane could not touch, the yellow contact lenses—tiger eyes—the powders of the great white powder puffs.

Even offstage, once painted and in possession of their costumes, they obeyed the queen, and at the mustached apparition of a devil the servants would flee through the corridors or lock themselves in the cupboards and come out plastered with flour.

Swift, disheveled, the opposite of the pageantry onstage, the Madam would glide in Wise Monkey slippers, arranging the screens which structured that *décroché* space, that heterotopia—tavern, ritual theater and/or doll factory,[1] lyrical bawdy house—whose elements only she saved from dispersion or boredom. She'd appear suddenly in the kitchen, in the orange smoke of a shrimp sauce, she'd run in and out of the dressing rooms carrying a plate of oysters, she'd prepare a syringe or lacquer a comb to twist an obstinate curl.

So the Go Between came and went, as I was saying a paragraph ago, through the corridors of that snail shell of kitchens, steam baths, and dressing rooms, crossing tiptoe the dark cells where all day the mutants slept, imprisoned in machines and gauze, immobilized by threads, lascivious, smeared with white facial creams. The network of her route was concentric, her passage was spiral through the baroque setting of mosquito nets. She would watch over the hatching of her cocoons, the emerging of the silk, the winged unfolding. The Guggenheim Museum, with its centrifugal ramps, was less dizzying than this place which, muddy, reduced to a single layer, the Procuress animated with her daily roving: flattened circular castle, "labyrinth of the ear." With cotton soaked in ether she would calm the suffering, give gin tonics to the thirsty, and to those who grew impatient with the wait among compresses of burning turpentine and poultices of crushed leaves,

---

[1] Yes, because the swains would arrive in such embarrassment that you had to push them to the place where all saints help: which the Madam did with Cosmetic's aid. The dolls would leave their cubicles in full splendor of yin, crackling with jewels like Coccinell; or on the contrary, minted like Bambi, with brown bangs and in ready-to-wears, aggressive out of pure discretion. At each show a new wave of converts would appear, another sopranoed chorus of transgressors: "Soon we'll fall into Stakhanovism!"—the Madam would protest. "We must correct the errors of natural binaryism"—she added, Benvenistean—"but *per piacere*, gentlemen, this is not like shooting fish in a barrel!"

her favorite advice: be Brechtian.

She ruled, braiding buns, reducing with ice massages, here a belly, there a knee, smoothing big hands, tuning husky rebel voices with cedar inhalations, disguising irreducible feet with a double platform and a pyramidal heel, distributing earrings and adjectives.

Cobra was her greatest accomplishment, her "rabbit-foot." Despite her feet and her shadow—cf. chapter V—she preferred her to all the other dolls, finished or in process. From daybreak on she would select her outfits, brush her wigs, arrange on the Victorian chairs Indian cassocks with gold galloons, real and velvet cats; among the cushions she would hide toy acrobats and snake charmers which on being touched would set off a *Skater's Waltz* on a tin flute, with baritonal shrieks, so that they'd surprise Cobra at siesta time. Then she would surrender to the contemplation of the color poster which, framed between red pennants, presided over that chamber.

Dear Lady Readers:

I know that at this point you don't have the slightest doubt about the identity of the character presented so disproportionately here: of course, it's Mei Lan Fang. The octogenarian *impersonator* of the Peking Opera appeared in her characterization as a young lady—a coif of rattles on her head— receiving the bouquet of flowers, the pineapple and cigar box from the virile president of a Cuban delegation.

And when each ringlet was in its place, then the Mother would arrange rendezvous, fulfilling the petitions of the most persistent and the high rollers, spacing out the schedules of the most solicited ones, plotting chance meetings in the cells of the least solicited. To these she'd give her best advice and reveal the weakness of each customer, to once again correct the laws of nature and rescue the always uncertain balance between supply and demand: the poor wretches knew who was foot adorer and for whom one had to do a Javanese dance in a Mata Hari costume, while having an enema.

Writing is the art of ellipsis: in vain would we point out that of all the agendas Cobra's was the most crowded. Dior was a close second with her bouquets of orchids received anonymously, Sontag for her Cartier jewels and reserved tables at Maxim's, Cadillac for the number of hours Caddy convertibles and their black chauffeurs dressed in white had waited for her and for all the other friendly presents which, before he sends his card, have already introduced a South American ranch owner.

What is really worth mentioning is that Cobra's fervent admirers rioted only to adore her close up, to remain a few moments in mute contemplation of her. A slight, pale London tea importer brought her three tambourines one night so that at their rhythm she, laden with bracelets, cymbals, torches and hoops, would prance on him, like Durga on the demon turned buffalo.

Some, coolly, would ask to kiss her hands; others, more perturbed, lick her clothes; a few, dialectic, would surrender to her, supreme derision of yang.

The Go Between would concede appointments by order of certainty in ecstasy: the contemplative and lavish would obtain her for the same night; the practitioners and close-fisted were put off for weeks and only had access to the Myth when there was no better bidder.

. . . the Mother, suddenly, would fall into a chair, fatigued. They'd fan her. Even from there she would continue directing the mise-en-scène, the traffic of movable platforms and trappings in the visible show—where Cadillac was already singing—and in the broader theater of consecutive rooms.

Writing is the art of digression. Let us speak then of a smell of hashish and of curry, of a stumbling basic English and of a tingling trinket music. This signalectic file card is the Indian costume-maker's, who three hours before curtain time would arrive with his little box of brushes, his minutely precise bottles of ink and "the wisdom"—the same turbaned one would say, in profile, displaying his only earring—"of a whole life painting the same flower, dedicating it to the same god."

And so he'd decorate the divas with his arabesques, tit by tit, since these, for being round and protuberant, were much easier to adorn than the prodigal bellies and little Boucherian buttocks, pale pink with a tendency to spread. The hoarse divinities would parade before the inventor of butterfly wings and there remain static the time to review their songs; devoted, the miniaturist would conceal *in vivo* the nudity of the frozen big-footed queens with silver fringes, eye hieroglyphs, arabesques and rainbows, which came out thinner or thicker depending on the insertion and watery brew; he would disguise the shortcomings of each with black whorls and underline the charms surrounding them with white circles. On their hands he'd write, in saffron and vermilion, their cue lines, the most forgettable, and the order in which they had to recite them, and on their fingers, with tiny arrows, an outline of their first movements. They would leave the minister of external affairs, all tattooed, psychedelic, made for love from head to toe. The Madam would look them over, stick on their eyelashes and an OK label for each, and send them off with a slap on the backside and a Librium.

Writing is the art of recreating reality. Let us respect it. The Himalayan artificer did not arrive, as it was said, bejeweled and pestiferocious, but in a newly ironed and virile cream-color twilled suit—on his silk tie an Eiffel Tower and a naked woman lying on the *Folies Chéries* caption.

No. Writing is the art of restoring History.

The dermic silversmith fought in the court of a Maharajah, near Kashmir. He was master of holds and grimaces—which demoralize the enemy; he could, sketching a cartwheel, land on his hands and fell an aggressor with a double kick in the stomach, or whirling him around, he could thrust into the nape of his neck the very dagger with which the assailant attacks.

Waving a large madras shawl with his right hand he could hurl a javelin into the left side of a Cambodian tiger.

He believed in suggestion, in the technique of surprise and in victory being irrevocable if one succeeded in frightening the adversary with appearance; he would deform himself with patches and falsies, he'd arise before the gaping opponents with two noses or with an elephant trunk, red like a pimento, hanging from his forehead by a spring. He learned from his daily incarnations into devil the art of tattooing and the ventriloquist's foils, which make the rival look over his shoulder.

He had escaped the Kashmir revolution with a suitcase of jewels that he squandered among rouge-painted whores in flowered barges—the lake brothels of the north—and in fixed tournaments—they proclaimed him Invincible—against the champions from Calcutta; he had revived a wrestling school in Benares, and in Ceylon a tea concession on whose boarded floors, which overlapped in a spiral like those of a tower, obese paint-smeared matrons came to lie at nightfall, among little sacks of tea.

He was a spice importer in Colombo. He fled one night, after losing a boxing match. From the ropes that secured it to the earth, the flames reached the circus tent that sheltered the winners.

His last feat was a bluff in a Smyrna pancratium: without allowing himself intermissions he reduced to cripples six Turkish champions. So erect, so imperturbable was he when they dealt him a blow, when the giants, climbing with a jump on his belly, pulled his hair, like one who scales a cliff grabbing onto lianas, and then such was his thrust in the cathouse (he celebrated his trophies by laying eunuchs and broads) that the matron—an obese Greek, mounted on heels and with a flower in his hair—won over by the philological itch and to evoke all at once his verticality in the arena and his licentious thrust, nicknamed him Eustachio.

He went over to the West then, carrying that name which was all he preserved from his gymnastic wanderings.

He concealed beneath a benign transgression—bottling coke without a license—his real infraction.

He was an ivory smuggler in the Jewish flea markets of Copenhagen, Brussels and Amsterdam; he cultivated to obsession an Oxford accent and black, shiny hair which, sticking out of a green suede hat, ended in an officially Oriental, combed, straight beard.

A convex mirror and another dozen smaller ones which surrounded him multiplied his image when with a puff-cheeked servant he entered a house of white walls and white doors closed by black knockers.

Through the Gothic arched windows rings of opaque glass filtered a grey and humid day. A Flemish tapestry stuck out of a Sienese trunk. Smoked herrings and silver clusters of garlic hung from the rafters. On a table there was a scale and an open Bible whose initials were hippogriffs biting their tails, sirens and harpies. Reflection of a glass of wine, a transparent red line trembled over the tablecloth.

On a shelf, behind bottles of cherries in *aguardiente,* the servant hid a bag of florins.

Writing is the art of disorganizing an order and organizing a disorder.

The Madam had discovered the Indian amidst the steam of a Turkish bath, in the suburbs of Marseille. She was so amazed when, despite the prevailing vapor, she distinguished the proportions with which Vishnu had graced him—all those hieroglyphs inscribed there, used by destiny to astonish us without revealing their nature—that, without knowing why, she thought of Ganesa, the elephant god.

Let's take advantage of that steam to fade out the scene. The next one is more in focus. In it we see the fighter in full possession of his writing skill, "which veils without dressing and adorns without hiding," preparing the models of the Lyrical Theater of Dolls for the show.

With so many cocoons in flower, so many golden locks and Rubensian buttocks around him, the cipherer is in such a state that he no longer knows where to knock his head; he tries a brush stroke and gives a pinch, he finishes a flower between those edges most worthy of guarding it and then erases it with his tongue to paint another with more stamens and pistils and changing corollas. The Wide-Eyed Girls would crowd around him and with the opening of ink bottles the hustle and bustle would begin. Half-dressed, yawning and soaked, the Adam's appled fairies would await him playing anxious card games and drinking cans of beer. The jamboree that reigned in the twisting corners of the Shrine was such that the Madam no longer knew how to intimidate the ladies-in-waiting so that they would not lose their control as soon as Eustachio the Luscious appeared.

They began organizing naval battles in the bathtub, which were splashings and submerged penetrations; the "wars of flowers" ruined the Matron's art nouveau furniture.

Till one day.

The Madam appeared with a palm-leaf broom in her hand and so yellow with rage that she looked like an Asiatic stewardess. Three playful jokers, in their underwear, had wound themselves in a red bedcover: "And Priapus rose red out of wine"—caroused Eustachio. Cadillac, who was going over her bel canto lesson in the midst of the frolic, pretended not to notice: she pressed the alarm button and continued vocalizing.

The bilious lady rushed against the spasmodic bundle as if she were putting out a fire; she launched forth with the devotion of one who flagellates a penitent brandishing a cat-o'-nine-tails with ball-bearings on the tips.

She heard a *saeta*. She felt in her mouth a spongeful of vinegar. With an open hand she hit her forehead.

She went / barefoot, dragging incensories,
　　　　/ smeared with crosses of black oil,
　　　　/ in a Carmelite cassock, a yellow rope at her waist,
　　　　/ wrapped in damasks and white cloths, with a wide-brimmed hat and a staff,
　　　　/ naked and wounded, beneath a dunce cap.

She crossed / whitewashed corridors, with wooden ships hanging from the ceiling and silver lamps in the form of ships,
　　　　/ high-domed octagonal chapels, whirlwinds of plaster angels whose walls supported shelves filled with crowns, arms and hearts of gold, opened heads revealing a wafer, small glass tubes with ashes.

In a monstrance a funeral amulet shined; in its middle circle, protected by two pieces of cut glass, surrounded by amber beads, little porous bones with filed edges were heaped—baby teeth, bird cartilage—bound by a silk hatband, lettered in black ink and Gothic capitals with German names. In the sacristy the altar boys played cards. On a wooden pantry, among opaque pitchers and breads wrapped in white napkins, three silver glasses glistened.

She found herself in a town square.

The ground sloped. Over a stone arch, golden eagles, yokes, fasces of arrows, intricate knots.

She was surrounded by the entranced devotees, praying, lashing themselves, shaking wooden rattles.

SEVILLIAN MUSIC

THE MADAM—wrapped in raw silk, Torquemadesque, as in a morality play: "Half-converted!"—and a blow with her broom— "Possessed!"—she crossed herself three times, spit on the bundle of red corduroy, beat her chest. "Poisoned leeches!"—she sprayed the hooded trinity with *aguardiente:* she couldn't find alcohol. "Burn, boiling bodies of worms!"

The three-cornered dunce cap: . . . .

When the Madam regained consciousness, she let the ashamed and swollen threesome come out of the bundle: the Indian, of course, Zaza and Cobra: "From this night on"—she managed to articulate panting, addressing herself to Cadillac, who then interrupted her trills—"you will be queen of the Lyrical Theater of Dolls. You have shown with your example that in art, if you want to get places, you've got to work even if optimum conditions are not assembled. And you"—she flatly ordered the Indian— "put on your clothes and leave. My God"—she added sobbing— "Eustachio's tube has brought down this house."

Which, a few days later, did not prevent the perverse fellow from communicating his nirvana to the dolls: he penetrated floral arrangements, he contemplated them frolicking before a Venetian mirror, spraying them with ginger he spread their legs open on a bison rug, naked but crowned with towers of feathers—that's where the decline of the West will lead us!—and he lay down on the beast, face up, his hips flanked by the horns, making them beg for it, sniffing them, prolonging the preambles. Slow, parsimonious, with sophisticated attentions he drew them onto himself: while the middle horn penetrated, the side ones scraped.

You couldn't tell what was making them moan nor, when they begged for more, what more to give them.

A broken-down net of wires and cables hung from the ceiling; from the net, lamp bases, red cellophane circles, and a broken, sparkling light bulb were suspended.

Writing is the art of patchwork. From what precedes one infers that:

if the Indian is as priapic and pleasure-prone as you have heard, he will never finish concealing with his signs the nudity of the chorus girls nor will they be able to submit impassively to the tormenting contemplation of his gifts, which is greater if you keep in mind the unbuttoning that prevails in show biz.

NOW THEN:

1) without body painting the show cannot go on; this, and even if you bribe them with increasing gratifications, is the minimal pomp, which the agents of the "orgy patrol" demand; it would be worthless to resort to other coverings, nobody's interested in them;

2) without "tableaux vivants" there are no customers, nor without them can the doll factory subsist, since only when subsidized by the interested, surely, but generous, can it live;

3) without a doll factory, without a theme—*the Madam:* "Ah, because literature still needs themes . . ." *I* (who am in the audience): "Shut up or I'll take you out of the chapter"—this narrative cannot continue.

ERGO:

The Indian has to be as in the first version. And in fact that's how he is.

Only a moron could swallow the obviously apocryphal comic strip of the fighter who, out of the clear blue, appears in a Flemish painting and renounces his he-man strength only to fasten tight his green hat and start trafficking in florins! Come on, man!

It is true that Eustachio entertained the court of a Maharajah, but, as was to be expected, in his capacity of naked dancer and ritual choreographer; it is true that he combs "silky horse hair": he adorns it with carnations—which stay on with Scotch tape—

in order to dance a lively flamenco.

Nor do we lack data on his travels in the West. I will register only one: he was identified on board "The Neutral," an establishment of rubbers and gadgets in the red light district of Barcelona. He would sample condoms and douche syringes; he would manufacture, in painted rubber, vomit, excrement, and worms jumping out of a cigar. The emblem of that house, likewise cacophonic, could be his life's: WONDERS OF CA-COMIC VOMIT.

If he strolls with impunity among the dolls it is because, as usual, he has placed his somatic vehicles between parentheses. Although for pleasure your edges are sufficient—Lacan explained to him one day—little does the king of bouquets enjoy his.

Order re-established in the department of pictograms, the Indian has just covered the chorus girls with silver pistils, wings of Melanesian butterflies, branches of birdlime, peacock feathers, gilded monograms, tadpoles and dragonflies, and on Cobra—who is again queen—birds of the Asiatic tropics, iridescing the phrase "Sono Assoluta" in Hindu, Bengali, Tamil, English, Kannada and Urdu.

He tests new tints on his own face, he lengthens his eyes, to be more Oriental than the real thing, a ruby on his forehead, shadow on his eyelids, perfume, yes, he perfumes himself with Chanel Eustachio and he vanishes, dancing, down the corridor.

A bell.

The curtains open for the show.

Of which I shall return to tell you anon.

II

Flat anchors fixed her to the earth: Cobra's feet left something to be desired, "they were her hell." She'd set them in molds at daybreak, apply salt compresses, chastise them with successive baths of hot and cold water. She manufactured wire armors to put them in, shortening and twisting the threads again and again with pliers; she forced them with gags; she submitted them to crude mechanics; after smearing them with gum arabic she bound them with cloth: they were mummies, children of Florentine medallions.

She attempted scrapings.

Resorted to magic.

Fell into orthopedic determinism.

At noon one day when, down at the heels, she was looking through the files of the National Library, she thought she found the solution in the *Méthode de réduction de testes des sauvages d'Amérique selon l'a veue Messire de Champignole serviteur du roy* (Method of Head Shrinkage among the American Savages According to the Testimony of Sire Champignole, Servant to the King). At the burlesque it was rumored that she had chartered a platoon to investigate the method *in situ,* bribing ethnologists, mortgaging her soul; it was alleged that the CIA was paying for everything, but that was only a machination of her double—Cadillac—to pull the rug from under her and replace her forever in the Lyrical Theater of Dolls.

A greenish vapor, of camphor, emanated from Cobra's dump, an arabesque which expanded into a nebulous spiral band, into a spreading snail shell of mint. Trapped in transparent flasks, boughs sprouted everywhere, wide and granular leaves, pestilent dwarf shrubs, sick flowers whose petals minute and shiny larvae gnawed at, crumpled ferns in whose folds small translucid eggs lodged, in constant multiplication. From stylized vegetal art nouveau the cubicle had moved on to weed anarchy—relentlessly she sought the saps, the elixir of reduction, the juice that shrinks. In a chest of drawers and on a divan robust artichokes opened, a white down gradually covering them; in Lalique glasses formaldehyde preserved crushed roots and sugarcane knots, bagasses in which large red ants were caught. Earthenware vessels and round lamps, upside down, protected the germination of cotyledons from light; a mother-of-pearl vanity case preserved seeds in alcohol, others, of tortoiseshell, snake butter, mahogany resin and nux vomica.

The bathroom supplied that laboratory. In porcelain wash bowls, where spontaneous generation had already propagated fly larvae, tadpoles and—Nature boasts of her miracles—even toads, a black watercress proliferated, with thick branches and sensitive purslane that closed its leaves at the slightest contact and whose clusters were already covering the bidet, a white Knoll seat—gift of Eero Saarinen—and the soap dish.

The bathtub: a field of tubular reeds, a flowery and concave Nile. Under the sink, in a Mozarabic plate pomegranates fermented, and beans that already had shoots and spirally striped grains, shagged like almonds, whose milk, upon souring, carpeted the smashed polygons of a yellowing hide.

Invaded by vegetal scabs the bells of the door and the telephone filtered all signals from the outside, all calls to order.

At night one heard a continuous murmur: it was the vibratory movement of the fly larvae.

—"Soon there'll be crocodiles!"—the Madam exclaimed (she'd cover her nose with cotton soaked in *Diorissimo*) and fled down the corridor whose rug the green scum of the jungle was already threatening.

They accused her of witchcraft,
of weed dealing,
of breeding a wild boar in her room.

She did not care. She'd spent the day deciphering herbariums; the night boiling pits. She had initiated the Madam and the green alchemy gave them no peace: they lived amidst Latin mumbo jumbo, root squeezing and cooking branches; Cobra's feet endured the daily extract, in rigorous poultices—sure of possessing the juice that shrinks. When getting up in the morning they'd uncover them with the caution of one who digs up an Etruscan toy. According to the fissures in the plaster and the ruling astral configuration— which the Madam calculated with an ephemeride whose firmament presented mushroom signs—they would decide the next brew. Neptune in Pisces, the Madam had stated one evening, fosters shrinking, the contraction of the base, the take-off.

They were rolling easy, the astral way. But impatience is bad counsel. One morning screams were heard in Cobra's cell. The makeup man—an Indian ex-champion of Greco-Roman wrestling—knocked the door down with a shove. The Madam came running. What they saw left them dumbstruck. The queen had hung herself, from the ceiling, by her feet, an upside-down hanging: slave chains hung her by the ankles to the base of a lamp. She was an albino bat among opalescent glass balloons and quartz chalices. Forming meanders, her hair fell among ceramic reeds, scorching themselves on the transparent gladioluses of the lampshades. The clinking of the hanging fruit was that of a Japanese mobile at the entrance of a monastery in flames.

"Daughter of Poppea!"—was as much as the Madam, ulcerated, managed to exclaim.

"The lymphatic flow"—the overturned angel answered panting—"invariable if we remain on our feet, nourishes and strengthens the ankles, hardens the tarsal sponge, circulates through the phalanxes and ends up developing the nails, toughening the toes, supporting the arch and consequently enlarging the square surface of the sole and the cubic of the whole member."

When they managed to extricate her from that floral scaffold, the poor thing was in such a state that she touched one to the quick. She had lost her sense of balance and, it seems, the balance of her senses as well.

As with all revolutions, this one received a regime of Draconian mustard plaster. The feet gave little way: they responded to ointments with swellings, to massages with welts and eczema. Cobra moved painstakingly on stage. It is true that the role of queen was mostly static. The fallen angel sweated her head off. Her own steps resounded right to her head. The floorboards were drums upon which dead cranes fell.

The itch gnawed at her—"pernicious leprosy"; as soon as the canned applause would explode she'd run to the wings—she had sunk to those therapeutic depths—to splash in a bowl of ice. She would put on the imperial cothurnuses again and return to the stage, fresh as a cucumber. To these thermic surprises the invaders responded with great maneuvers: from her nails a vascular violet burst out which smacked of frozen orchid, of an asthmatic bishop's cloak: beneath a crumbling refectory he eats a pineapple.

That Lezamesque purple was followed by cracks in her ankles, hives, and then abscesses rising from between her toes, dark green sores on her soles. One morning, while changing the nocturnal poultice, the Madam pulled off scabs. Then they left them in the open air, night and day, to the very gravity of their textures.

Seeing that this didn't make them worse, they began to believe in Nature and forebade its perversion and meanness: Science.

They burned the *tractatus,*
threw out fetid seeds and herbs,
washed the vases,
scraped the bathtub,
cleaned the furniture with lye.
They opened the windows.
They made each meal "a banquet of fresh vegetables"—Helena Rubenstein; they avoided coffee and absinthe.
They drank six glasses of water each day.

Soon they understood her presumption. The evil was corroding from within. A white eruption invaded them, a hoarfrost, arborescent scab which formed Coptic designs on her ankles, ascended. Malarial flowers, perforated ships: Cobra's feet were slipping into chaos.

The Madam hid in hampers, fled from the living room with her face soiled, and sat on the bidet to cry for hours. The two took turns crying; they began to lose color, wearing away, pickled lizards, lilies of the gospel.

They comforted each other:

"God squeezes but doesn't strangle"—Cobra.

And the Matron, very relaxed: "Have you seen, my dear, what a darling right heel?"

But they knew that they were lying, that the disease ran rampant, that the pustules proliferated every night.

The gods do not skimp on irony: the more they deteriorated, the more Cobra's foundations rotted, the more beautiful was the rest of her body. Paleness transformed her. Her light blonde hemp curls fell—pre-Raphaelite spirals—revealing only half her face, an eye enlarged by blue, purple lines, tiny pearls.

They capitulated.

The two of them, finally, gave in to passive resistance. They practiced non-intervention, the *wu-wei.* Like the ancient Chinese sovereigns they adopted great hats from which a curtain of pearls fell, destined to cover their eyes. They wore earmuffs. Plugging those openings they closed themselves to desire. They no longer touched or mentioned the sick ones; they exiled them with baroque periphrasis: they became the Nile—for their periodical floods—the Occupant, the Unsinkable. Unperturbed by the new symptoms, they came closer and closer to ataraxia by means of internal alchemy and embryonary respiration.

When they freed their senses it was to dedicate themselves to the study of the tables of correspondence. If Cobra nourished herself with dew and ethereal emanations from the cosmos, if she covered her nose with formaldehyded cotton between midday and midnight, pit of dead air, it was to evict the cadaverous devil who had taken over her third field of cinnabar—beneath the navel and near the Sea of Breath—malevolent being, stationed in her feet, who emptied her of essence and marrow, dried her bones and whitened her blood.

The error they had committed was foreseen by Taoist hygiene: the "worm" fed precisely on malodorous plants.

At night, while the Mother slept, Cobra "walked the homunculus." Thus had she visualized, following the *Materia Medica's* advice, the breath of the Nine Heavens. The dwarf would enter through the nose and, led by the inner vision that not only sees but illuminates, would wander all over her body, stopping for a pause in her feet to reinforce the guardian spirits; then it would withdraw though the Palace of the Brain.

Seeing that she grew pale, the Madam surrounded her with stronger drugs. Around the circular sofa on which she lay, white like a crane, she placed red enamel saucers filled with vermilion, gold, silver, the five mushrooms, jade, mica, pearls and orpiment. On a bamboo tablet, which they divided in two, they wrote out a contract with the gods: they promised to respect gymnastics, sexual hygiene and dietetics; in return they demanded immediate cure and reduction. With this writing as a charm, the Madam would go up the mountain; standing on a tortoise and rising from among the jujubes, an Immortal would hand her the product of the ninth sublimation in a lacquer case; this, duly applied, would produce the miracle.

The Unmentionables were not totally insensitive to that mysticism. They became damp, tame, porous. They sweated a colorless liquid, rainwater which upon drying left a green sediment. In it appeared denser little islands, thick colonies, breathing conglomerations of algae. The pores dilated. The perspiration ceased. Cobra had fever.

One night, her senses plugged, closed to external distraction but alert to the space of her body, Cobra felt that her feet trembled; some days later, that something was breaking in her bones; her skin stretched.

They abandoned hats and ear plugs.
    They spent the night observing them.

At daybreak flowers sprouted.

White Dwarf

"A white dwarf is characterized by a very small luminosity and a very small radius; the radius, in fact, is comparable with that of one of the larger planets, Saturn. Because of this very small radius the density with which material is packed inside a white dwarf is extremely high, so high that nothing at all comparable is known on Earth.

"One well-known white dwarf is Pup, companion of Sirius. So densely packed is the material at its center that a single matchboxful would weigh several tons.

"Clearly the white dwarfs are stars that have reached the end of their evolution."
—FRED HOYLE, *Astronomy*

The copartner and the Madam—grey all over, lace mantilla, closed fan, bows on her toes, high heels, pink pompons—got so worn out, so tuckered out,[1] that they ended up finding the juice that shrinks. But alas . . . poor Cobra! All that effort for nothing. Learn, bullheads; cry your eyes out, pigheads. Splashing, sloshing, thus does all daring and vigilance go down the drain.

Read well, you who strain
(or your necks will be cramped),
meditate, self-sacrificers
and kidney mortifiers,
Put things right, you pigheads
who didn't enjoy, while you can,
ball away, O continent,
the Toothsome Reaper waits for no man!

---

[1] tuckered out/played out/fagged out/bushed/pooped . . . I owe these expressions to *Roget's International Thesaurus*. Glory to its author, Peter Mark Roget! He's the one I can thank for being a "millionaire of language."

(Sorry.) As always with fags, invention turned into a restless toy; abusive, irresponsible, they rubbed the Damned with it, without restraint, morning, noon and night; for an if and/or a maybe they surrendered to the diabolic reducing exercises.

The rubdowns weren't enough for them. First in drops which they would count a dúo, in soprano, then in furtive teaspoonfuls, they began to drink of the brew, finally they declared it "plain water."

In bed, wrapped in jute sacks—a buttonhole at mouth level— silent and parallel, almost mummified, they would spend the night sucking.

Through the buttonhole a tube entered: a black rubber tube, connected to a glass pitcher hanging on the wall. Through the mosquito net they would watch the milky potion, the mashed leaves, descend the red scale. They'd smile, close their eyes in pleasure, look at each other, and again absorb from the chin, their mouths heartshaped, in their nirvana, up in the pale clouds.

When by noon they'd already feel that they were drifting, "hollowed boats descending the Amazon," they would interrupt the swallowing beatitude, heavy and damp, soaked like blotters, to urinate—they were so detoxicated it came out pure opal—and to refill the containers with the broth that by now they were manufacturing wholesale, macerating trunks and reciting exorcisms.

"Exactly, reciting them"—the Madam—"but thinking always about something else. Without a doubt"—and she split open a pomegranate—"absent-minded invocation is the only efficient kind. The more you empty out"—she crunched her teeth into one of the halves—"the better your formulas."

Audio: a *fado:* Cobra sings, disheveled and yawning, at the end of a majolica corridor—sifted bluish light; on a wall a map— leaning on a mortar pestle.

"He who believes does not believe"—she continued, Sancho style; "sense, dear tadpoles, is a *product,* the result of a milkshake"—and she waved a fork sketching quick circles in the air—"like any of these watery brews."

She clattered her clog and continued praying and scratching her head. Hanging from the ceiling, clusters of onions surrounded her. The bulbous reflections painted her green.

Cut by the reducing bacillus, the milk curdled. At dawn the basins, and even the washbowls were overflowing with translucid curds, shivering gelatines; in the yellowish sweat that emanated from the curdlings, blown over the emery edges of the pots— rapid sulphurous forkings—and in the arborescences of the casein, the Venerable Lady, a milk reader, deciphered the day's schedule, the density of the nocturnal doses.

To conquer the uncontrollable proliferation, at dawn something was cast out of that yogurt into the tubes; down the drains went little contracted fetus hands. But as if those residues were offered to the gods of the ancient Chinese cultivators, who reward the spendthrift and give doubly to those who waste their gifts, the following morning surprised them with another assault of little compressed jade trees, which spread open upon the contact of water.

"Soon we should go out and indoctrinate!"—howled Lady Dean—"let's see if we can give a little of this custard to the converts!"

And so their fortunes fared.

Till one morning, doped, out of it, they awoke in a sandpit of fringed edges. Rows of braided bundles of cotton, strings of lint, wool octopuses; in successive waves of pink thread they swam beneath a wavy tent.

Grabbing onto the ropes, panting, with her little froglike hands Cobra tried climbing. She would fall, slip down the jungle of cotton, turn head over heels into the bottom of the valley. She was now white, calcareous, made of chalk dust, she was tiny and lunar, frozen, humpbacked, and compact, she gave off powder. Down there, among folds, fighting hair and nail—wild boar in the burning thicket—rebounding against embankments of fibers, reduced to the absurd, Cobra glittered. The light that emanated was ashen, lacking igneous strips, like a flooded crater.

She rested, leaning her elbows on her knees, fists closed; her eyes were two bulky spheres, each divided by a slit; her navel had grown; her skin was cracked.

When finally, grasping her blanket, swallowing plush—she was breathing through her mouth—twitching and going to pieces,

Cobra was able to peer over the edge of the bed, she found herself
nez à nez against a little shrunken head, wrinkled and disheveled,
that made faces at her from the next bed.

They squinted at each other with customs officer eyes.

"We are diminished"—murmured the Madam, first looking all
around her.

"It's not only that"—added Cobrita—"before we were pretty
and round; now, frightsome and ugly."

"What?"—the other inquired.

"Frightsome and ugly."

They took each other's hand.

They cried, though tearlessly.

"Let us avoid"—the Mademoiselle uttered, separating her
locked jaws syllable by syllable—"like the Alpinists, the contemplation of our nothingness, the fear of the void, the ladder complex."

"The plane of the plain"—Cobra; her teeth were rattling.

"Let us desist from disaster. We must go down to the rug.
There the cats will keep us company."

"The cats?"—Cobrita bit her blanket.

"They are friends of dwarfs."

"And men?"

"Whoresons and giants."

The fringes were lianas; the girls, monkeys trained in the sabotage
of fortlets, capable of escaping when the shoes of the gunpowder
guards in the tower are already burning and the lookouts are fleeing along terraces covering their faces with cloth caps.

They slipped, it is true, they stumbled a bit, they covered
themselves with scratches—they were dense and rocky, but had
fragile nodules, sand spots. Providence took care of them: when
one was falling the other's well-planted foot would inevitably appear, and for the other vice versa, plunging headlong, she would
have the one's savior hand, to bite.

They landed on the carpet, shaking off their dust.

Frantically shaking off their dust. Or flinging it off with invisible rooster feathers. Flapping their hands right and left,
smacking and whacking their own cheeks, to chase gnats which,

attracted by the fermentation of wild weeds, were forming a motionless storm cloud at their present height, and which before, from their enormity, the Shrunken had not thought worthy of chasing away.

The constant buzz, cut by treacherous little whistles—diving insects—stupidified them.

PETIT ENSEMBLE CARAVAGGESQUE

They were dwarfs, but let's not overdo it.

The preceding tale, like all the insidious Madam's stories, suffers from swashbuckling hyperbole, abracadabra rococo and boundless exaggeration. Yes, they were dwarfs, but like any old dwarfs. The Madam, for example, had the proportions—"and also the poise and majesty!"—of a prognathic infanta's lady-in-waiting standing beside a page who steps on a greyhound, watching the monarchs pose. As to Cobrita, let us say that she was exactly like a crowned and rickety albino girl, crossing a company of musketeers on their nightwatch, pulled along by a servant and carrying a dead chicken tied to her waist.

ZOOM

The plunging view gives us the following: along a thick and yellowish rag—a square carpet knit with variant gold threads—among complex unraveled arabesques, into which phoenixes and dragons are woven, following the edges at full speed—newly caged anteaters—the dwarfs are moving. Symmetrical, out of bounds, the one from the black North to the green East, the other from the red South to the white West, both kick along, their ends touching, grabbing demons right and left, now turned into two gauntlets, two autogenous mills, two Burmese leopards catching pheasants; shrieking, terror-stricken, their cracked blind gramophone voices at a thousand RPM.

In bossa-nova rhythm:

"a time of plenitude,
a time of decrepitude,
a time of thinning,
a time of thickening,
a time of life,
a time of death,
a time of collapse,
a time of erection,
a time of yin,
a time of yang."

Yes, they advance, parallel, but in opposite directions. The Mademoiselle—who covers a jacaranda hat with a sculpted Christmas manger—shaking six feet; Cobrita—who, to be brief, is a two-legged Tomar window, accumulates to an extreme anchors and cords, corals and crosses, armillary spheres and Portuguese Gothic bracelets—imploring a rainfall of Fly. Frantic, as if those distances regulated the always uncertain rhythm of the seasons or prescribed the harmony of the kingdom, the dwarfs continue chasing gnats. They do, of course, take advantage of the least insect that brushes the other's cheek to give her a slap. They end up purple and choleric, entering helter-skelter and kicking, unloading sparkling cornucopias of interjections. Disintegrated into hoops of gestures, raised hands and blows on foreheads, they conclude the compulsive rectangular course. They know they're being observed, "and described"—the Mademoiselle, naturally—from above. Slow, ceremonious, too theatrical, they move their repoussé bootees forward, with the tips of their fingers they gather, how graceful, their silk tails, haughtily they raise their heads, one step, another, goodbye, they disappear under the bed . . .

They lived a long time among the cats they had formerly bred, lice-ridden and eating garbage. That cockroachy world, with its chiaroscuros of pissed-on quilt and creaking springs, that grotesque arthritic-styled dampness and those stalactites of dirty shreds, soaked their bones, filled them with bagasse, caused rings under their eyes: life *underbed* depressed them.

It is known that of all the stars of the Lyrical Theater, Cobra was the Madam's greatest accomplishment, her "rabbit-foot." Despite her feet and her shadow—cf. chapter V—she preferred her to all the other dolls, finished or in the process. From daybreak on she would select her outfits, brush her wigs, arrange on the Victorian chairs Indian cassocks with gold galloons, real and velvet cats; among the cushions she would hide toy acrobats and snake charmers which on being touched would set off a *Skater's Waltz* on a tin flute, with baritonal shrieks. Used to these surprises as she was, Cobra almost didn't react when one midday, upon bending down to pick up a shoe, she discovered under the bed two rather melancholy miniatures. They were wrinkled and stiff, had solid eyes, with moldy hinges. The amazing part is that they emanated a dimmed light, of glowworm eyes.

Cobra picked one of them up from the floor, flipped her over, and raised her dress looking for the mainspring.

"How dare you!"—the Shrunken One uttered furiously, and smacked her. And then, automatic, as if she had a record inside, she added in the same tone: "We're hungry."

Cobra never found out—don't bother to tell her now, what for—why she had become partial to—body and soul = precious double-entendre—the two dwarfs to such an extreme, and, if one may say so, to the dwarfier of the two. Thanks to the queen, that pumice stone fetus, that vermin found under the bed, cracked and basaltic, "as if she had ice buried within her, the damned thing," completely dumbfounded, whom one had to watch over to make sure she wouldn't keep eating dirty shreds, began to transform into an articulated and quite human toy. Into a doll, bilious and surly it's true, and in all that regards her midnight toilette cranky and pesty, for which one had to tape her mouth at times so as to paint her in peace, but when she became more familiar and they allowed her to go among her cats she was quite witty and gabby.

Yes, by a phenomenon of *i.p.s.*[1] which this is not the place to analyze, no sooner would Cobra finish her first show of the night—she'd sing a samba; the Brazilian band had by these hours reached delirium in high; she'd look at her nails—that she would run to her dressing room to look for her favorite pygmy, among cushions and in trunks of wigs and even in the drawers where

---

[1] indefinitely proceeding sequences, of course.

she'd often hide—her surname had been abbreviated from La Poupée to La Pupa and to the tenuous explosion of Pup. The other one would blow a police whistle and kick and point to her, as soon as she heard Cobra's footsteps in the corridor. They would pull her out from among synthetic pompons. The jumpy kid would slip away through hairy wigs, under sticky corkscrew curls and double buns, among armors of concentric braids and Antoninus hair chains. To hide, hair in hair, when she felt pursued and heard the informer's shrill whistle, she would put on luxuriant horsetails, hats with Marlene locks and even scabby, bald skulls which the miserable poor would use in crowd scenes.

When finally, in spite of her squeaks and fainting fits—she creaked around, like a lobster in a bottle—they managed to save her from the tangle, they'd immediately submerge her in a basin of warm water.

The old dwarf would run around the room, building rapid towers with hatboxes, to climb up and reach for bars of soap.

After a good smudge removal, the grasshopper looked *white, the dashing white of the new and impeccable, even in her collar and cuffs,* as if washed with Coral, the modern detergent for the modern woman.

With Pup clean, the ceremony, the gibberish of the redoubling, began. We could, formalizing it in mathematical terms, represent the relationship between both characters as follows:

$$Cobra = Pup^2$$
$$\text{or else}$$
$$Pup = \sqrt{Cobra}$$

An equal correspondence between the Madam and her reduction.

All that she received, all that they said to her, all that they did to her, Cobra restored, repeated, or did in turn to the dwarf. While the Madam—they, true disciples of Derrida, did consider her the original of her reduction, though not for pre-existing: they called her the Expanded Lady—was traveling in India with the choreographer of a Kashmirian Maharajah, seeking red paint for the *Féerie Orientale,* the coming show, the $\sqrt{}$ of Madam sponsored, as an accomplice, that Borgesian shifting of mirrors.

If flowers, flowers; if shields, shields; if anamorphosis, anamorphosis; if affected symmetries with flying birds, affected symmetries with flying birds: all that they painted on Cobra, Cobra, as well as she could, it's true, repainted on Pup.

"Peroxided giant"—shrieked the one too luminous for her mass, fed up with such bungling—"I'm going to turn into your drooled-on decal!"

One night Cobra lammed into her: she had received the same, when the curtain fell, in a bombastic row with Cadillac—they tore off each other's false eyelashes and nails, they rolled on the floor; became absorbed in themselves: two witches—Cadillac, the hussy, with her sensationalist and cheap mimicry, had monopolized the ovations. Another night Cobra presented Pup with a three-storied cake in the form of a tower of Bethlehem.

After her midnight toilette and while Cobra stripped off her own attributes, Pup received, grumbling inevitably, the attributes of her character of the day. They divided her into squares before painting her. They enlarged on her skin, or repeated *au pochoir* along a spiral beginning at her neck and ending on an ankle, the *motifs* of a fleur-de-lysed cartoon which formed combinations according to the "optic contrasts" of a HARMONICOLOR disk.[1]

The $\sqrt{}$ of Madam—lying on the carpet, looking up: "Cobra, put more gold on her."

COBRA: "Prepare the soup while I paint her another angel."

Sundays and holidays—Cobra would get depressed—instead of painting her, they'd disguise her. Pup was a little black rumba

---

[1]Harmonizing colors is a difficult art. A skillful florist, a dressmaker of proven taste, a talented interior decorator, all find, almost without looking, thanks to a kind of instinct, the combinations that enchant the eye; but those who are unaware of the rules that govern color relationships, struggle with overwhelming difficulties.

Harmonicolor allows one to conquer those difficulties, automatically, if one can use the expression. This is based on the following fact: color combinations are always reduced to fulfilling either a *harmony,* or a *contrast.* Cf. *Harmonicolor,* Disque d'harmonie des couleurs, by Luis Cabanes, Inspector of Design in the Schools of the City of Paris, and C. Bellenfant, Professor with a degree from the City of Paris.

dancer, a Dutch girl from Edam with a cheese in her hand, a medieval astrologer—a dunce cap on her head; she displayed two fishes biting the same line, she'd push them by the tail, in opposite directions—a cross-eyed Burgundy queen, a dwarf—the humbled maid of a Bengali burlesque . . . but almost always a little boy.

It was in this disguise that Cobra wished to preserve a memory of her; in oil, so that people would see it was a lasting memory. They portrayed her, then, stiff, in a simplistic setting, an original by the √of Madam, among cats and other cunning ornaments.

The painter was a devotee of the Lisbon school.

He had been born in Macao, then a Portuguese colony, and skilled in the art of the portrait which does not admit subterfuges—he painted the interior, the invisible—he went over to the West in circumstances blurred by a pious chiaroscuro; he had given up his sharp styled calligraphy and his mastery in stamps barely dampened in red sealing wax and writing dedicatories on landscapes of winter plum trees, to adopt a thick and vainly authoritative brush stroke, tending toward pitchblack and the grotesque. He enameled his flourishes with great embellishment, showy little phrases of the tenor "Time also paints," "Technique is not enough," "He who knows does not know," etc. With such theoretical stimulation, and also that of generous fizzes, they managed to carry out an honest entertainment.

When finished, Pup's likeness could almost talk.

PORTRAIT DE PUP EN ENFANT

The canvas in unevenly illuminated; the Shrunken One, standing, balanced despite her big bean, looking at us.

THE MASTER—with a silly giggle, sucking with a straw his supposedly vervain infusion and introducing *l*'s all over the place: *a river that dries up, a hill that collapses or a man who turns into a woman foretell that the end of the dynasty approaches* . . . He blinks, puts down the cup, and dashes off delicate cherry red strokes, like one who paints macaw feathers, philosophizing all the time, with a dry cough . . . He coats the brush thick white, some light touches right and left: the pleated tulle collar, the silk girdle, completed by a great transparent bow. He wets the brush again: satin shoes, like little gloves with bows, lace sleeves . . . *Swallows cease to be swallows when they go through winter: they hide in their aquatic refuges . . . and turn into snails!* He throws in oil, mixes it, with a few strokes he makes the bangs . . . how well-combed poor Pup looks now! he changes brushes, with a fine one, of rabbit hair, he makes her a perfect little mouth, flawless, symmetrical, Faiyumesque . . . *When the radiant days end the hummingbirds dive into the sea or into the Houai River; during the winter, which they spend in hiding . . . they are only clams! The magpie*—from Pup's right hand, he draws out with a single line a cord which, tipped by the Monster girl's left hand, falls to the floor to tie around the claw of a black and white magpie—*is a mouse which spring transforms; when it has sung the whole summer it burrows and turns into a rodent until the good weather returns . . .* More dye concoction s'il vous plaît . . . And with a malicious giggle he hands the celadon semblance to the Madam, who listens gaping . . . *Everything depends on signs*—he put a white card in the magpie's beak: *men do not become hunters until they change emblems and in the sky the cipher of the sparrow hawk does not substitute the wild pigeon . . .* Throw in sugar . . . Ah, but what was I doing? Let me add some cats, for your entertainment.

And at Pup's feet, for her entertainment, three cats appear; *Calderonian, fluidly sententious,* they look with astonishment at the ugly bird: a spherical, mouselike calico, with dilated eyes; a thoughtful, more definitively bewhiskered grey, and in the back, fusing into the black, a black cat.

PUP: "May I scratch my nose? And since we're pausing I may as well tell you to put in some birdies, they're always cheery."

And at Pup's feet, a few cardinals, which are always cheery, appear languid and red-headed among the bars of a Churrigueresque cage.

Now, among her favorite animals, as if from a funeral stele, Pup looks at us.

THE MASTER: "Be still. Return to your pose"—how mother-of-pearly he has made her face and hands! Pup is neither sickly nor frightened: it's the style.

He retouches her eyes. A white dot on the iris.

And on the card which the magpie holds, in carbon pen, and in a hurry, he draws a few brushes, a palette, and perhaps an inkwell.

With his steady script and flowery hand he stamps, below and to the right,

his signature.

II

> *"The American astronomer Allan R. Sandage revealed, at the astrophysical congress now taking place in Texas, that in June 1966 astronomers at Mount Palomar witnessed one of the most prodigious explosions of an astronomical object ever detected by man.*
>
> *"The astronomical object in question is a quasar that bears the number 3C 446.*
>
> *"Quasars, discovered in 1963, are young stellar objects, extremely distant—several billion light years away—and very luminous.*
>
> *"The explosion, which multiplied the surface brightness of quasar 3C 446 twenty-fold, could have been produced some billions of years ago, perhaps shortly after the initial explosion which, according to Professor Sandage's theory, gave birth to the universe such as we know it today."*
> —Le Monde

There wasn't an inflatable Buddha, nor a life-sized celluloid elephant with two archers on its back, no silk, sari, satin, wash and wear Indian silk nor electric sitar that the Madam, incited by the obsequious choreographer—an ex-boxing champion in Macao, and today, how things change, a devotee of Portuguese Gothic art, that's where it all comes from—did not haggle, pillage and carry off at auctions, pleading with hagglers, bribing dealers and cheating auctioneers in the seedy bazaars of Calcutta.

For the *Féerie Orientale*, the dream of every doll in the Theater, she returned to the West bent under a mound of Indian junk where each piece of tripe claimed a fantastical adjective which the diligent metteur en scène pronounced with ornamental phonetic relish, spattering it with sickening Brahmanic references.

What a surprise was in store for her when, cluttered with rummage, she made it to the Lyrical Theater: she found herself shrunken and rather pathetic, toothless and showy, giving

affected orders to another ugly and big-beaned little dwarf, as anemic and buffoonish as herself but dressed as a male, on how to sit
for an oil portrait among meowing calicos and three plucked and
drooling turkey vultures—*Cathartes aura*—who chirped in a
cage.[1]

To realize what follows is, in appearance, only yielding to the
common mania of mirrorlike plots. But what can you do: life likes
those crude symmetries, which placed in any novel would appear
as unbelievable melodrama, as ordinary, for being too plain, cunning. No sooner had the Madam arrived, Cobra, with the pretext
of copying for the *Féerie* certain festooned Khajuraho *motifs,* left
for India in the arms of a slanty-eyed boxer, leaving in the
stunned procuress's arms the transvestite with the very small radius who had reached the end of her evolution.

The Landlady soon got used to Pup; what she couldn't do, un-
like Cobra with hers, was to coexist with her ducklike miniature.
The Madam and her concentrated double took on a mortal hatred
for each other. For the Venerable Lady to look at her square root
which was already fermenting and becoming liver-colored and
badmouthed . . . So that to humor her—and so that the idle
reader may enjoy the turns of fortune which await the characters
of this tale—we are going to eliminate the Mademoiselle, inscrib-
ing on a memorial gravestone with inverted plump angels, marble
bows and flower vases which would have made even Dolores
Rondón envious, beneath Latin scribblings, her withered posthumous monogram:

$$\sqrt{\text{Mme.}}$$

THE MADAM—looking at Pup from above, screwing up her face
piously, like someone who looks at a rotten black bean: "Now we
have to make you bigger."

PUP: "Stop blabbing."

[1]Anyone who, upon getting up in the morning, has seen himself enter
the bathroom and sit on the toilet, just as he was when he still had hair,
or has said good-bye to himself, between two subway corridors, older
than a faded postcard, will not be surprised at this coincidence.

THE MADAM: "Well, you rickety thing, you asked for it by consuming garbage, so now, accept the consequences, because nowadays nobody wants a dwarf, not even in the circus, and in the shape you're in, dissipated and ugly as sin, you'll never become, and I won't even say queen, even only second weeper in the last row on the left at the Lyrical Theater of Dolls . . . So get back again for the change . . ."

PUP: "And why don't you change, toothless misbegotten creature, procuress, witch?"—she stepped backwards to gather impulse and took off like a rocket toward her hiding place under the bed.

THE MADAM—catches her in mid-air and flips her over, shaking her by the feet and slapping her backside: "Clod, devil, mischiefmaker . . . Now you'll see how the Master will make you grow with four punctures. Servant! Servant!"—the maid came, she was none other, as was to be presumed, than Cadillac herself in a Mozartian housemaid's cap. "Tie her up and call the Master. You're going to be transformed, you repellent dwarf, you reeking abortion"—Pup spits at her, ripraps her skirt by clawing it, howls inaudibly, like a bat, to kill her with sounds, looks at her without blinking to hypnotize her . . . "Yes, you stinking waterworm"— and taking heaven as her witness—"you're going to be transformed!"

so that: TRANSFORMAÇÃO!

Sound of oiled metallic hoops sliding along a rod. Purple velvet curtains open: my shrunken cockroachy home-movie screen grows larger . . . it is already a vast and very white surface, subtly curved. Yes, my black and white 16 mm—I know: it's really sickly violet and yellow—with worm-eaten edges, interrupted now and then by porous numbers, upside down heads and shaky letters, is transformed into a Cinerama screen in full MetroColor. Stereophonic hymns. On the screen a landscape comes into focus . . . The outline of the streets thrusts something like a black net over the uniformity of white houses, in which hay markets form green bouquets, drying yards of dyers, splashes of color, and the gold ornaments on the frontispieces of temples, bright dots. Grey walls encircle it all, beneath the blue firmament, beside the motionless sea. A great copper mirror, turned toward the bay, reflects the ships. On that reddish orb there appears, in glazed, printed letters, naturally:

Scenery and Costumes
by

—and with the same print, but in capital letters, while the landscape and the hymns fade out—

GUSTAVE FLAUBERT

From the center of a porphyry bowl a golden shell full of pistachios bursts open.

In the palms of their hands, along tile walls, generals offer conquered cities to the Emperor.

Everywhere columns of basalt appear, silver gates in filigree, ivory trunks and carpets embroidered with pearls. Warm perfumes. Sometimes the silent creaking of a sandal. The light sifted by the domes reveals, in the background, a succession of salons. Passing through them the Master approaches, in a violet tunic, wearing red buskins with black bands. A pearl diadem frames his hair arranged in symmetrical curls. Slowly he enters the room: in his right hand, hanging from a black thread, a copper cone.

Fascinated by the oscillating reflection the Madam draws near. Pearl, jade and sapphire furbelows divide her golden brocade dress at regular intervals: a narrow sash adorned by the colors and signs of the zodiac girds her waist. She wears high-buttoned shoes, one black, covered with silver stars and quarter moon, the other white, with drops of gold and a sun in the middle. Her wide sleeves— emeralds and bird feathers—reveal her arms; ebony bracelets curl around her wrists; her hands, loaded with rings, end in nails so sharply filed that her fingertips seem like needles. A thick gold chain, passing under her chin, rises along her cheeks and curls in a spiral in her hair covered with blue dust, then, descending, it brushes her shoulder and ends at her chest, tied to a diamond scorpion whose tongue thrusts into the flaccid flesh of her breasts.

Two great ruby pearls lengthen her ears. On the rim of her eye-lids, black stripes.

To protect her from the brilliant glare that comes through the windows, a raggedy maid—but of course! Cadillac again—opens a green parasol; vermilion bells clink around the ivory handle. Twelve frizzled little black boys carry the tail of her dress, the end of which, from time to time a small monkey lifts up.

"There she is, Maestro"—and she pointed to Pup with her nail: "Enlarge her or bust her."

"Where?"

"There . . . It's that white thing moving on the purple-striped sofa."

"My God, if it isn't a lizard!"

PUP ON THE PURPLE-STRIPED SOFA

It is a circular divan, covered in silk; purple and parallel bands follow the curve of its back, mark a green wall with their reflections. Interrupting them, an amoeboid pink bulk spills over them—the pink of English Bacon: guess why—with big knees and tiny poisonous feet: that's Pup, swollen on all sides, the one who already, to be sure, was not what we'd call proportioned, now not as rocky, nor as dense with matter inside her, blistered, hu-manized by force of whacks and slaps. They have tied her with small chains to the legs of the couch, by her wrists and ankles. The unhappy creature barely breathes. And through her mouth, at that.

"Let's see what we can do"—with his right hand, farcical, a car-dinal or *maja* who leaves the stage with the sign of the cross or the final Flamenco tap of the heel, the Transformer raised the plushy tail of his dress and, hoisting it, drew near the little crucified one. His image diminished along the checkered floor.

"Let us see"—he persisted, rounding his syllables. And he be-gan to consider Pup from top to bottom and from bottom to top, sometimes moving back (he strutted affectedly after each step, as if to recover the balance of his already over-abundant and there-fore poorly distributed masses), placing before his eyes his own right hand, rigid and vertically, to study the Runt through an axle, as if he had to copy her in plaster or paint her as the Virgin of the Conversions to then raffle her off in a tombola.[1]

Yes, my dear ninnies, the Transformer is a transformed one, so that upon approaching the little tortured one with his clinical garlic—he feared that the case was one of vampirism—he knows what he's doing.

As was to be expected of her, Pup insults him conscientiously, without a pause and by heart, in alphabetical order.

"What do you think?"—the piqued Madam, who points to her from afar as if she were an upchucked delicacy.

"The whole"—the Magician, after catching his breath, ushered in a Gongoristic clause—"the whole is to puncture the *centers,* I mean those vital, enlargement centers, those of development and expansion . . ."—and here one of his silly giggles escaped him. "If we find them, everything will be fine . . . if not . . . we will have to appeal"—he grew sad and shrank—"to snow."—And opening his right hand, he hurled to the void, with the dignity of someone rolling out a yo-yo, the copper cone.

The radiance of the artifact decomposed the figure of Pup into various prisms. Then, the semiological pendulum slowed down in the air—the Master contained his breathing—stopped still a moment, and began a slow-moving rotation over the chained body.

"What are they going to do to me with that astrolabe?"—grunted the scanty one.

"Clean your insides of all the wild Chinese weeds you've been swallowing, tramp."—And on Pup's thighs, with a belt lash, the scorpion, the scale and one of the Gemini were left imprinted.

THE MASTER—the Madam's eyes, fascinated with the oscillatory motion, moved from side to side: the little black boy in a Venetian clock—: "The body, my esteemed lady, is inscribed in a net . . ."—the pendulum rose to Pup's head—"six flowers mark

[1]Moronic reader: if even with these clues, thick as posts, you have not understood that we're dealing with a metamorphosis of the painter of the preceding chapter—if you haven't, look for yourself how he has retained the gestures of his profession—abandon this novel and devote yourself to screwing or to reading the novels of the Boom, which are much easier.

the middle line . . ."—and he lowered it, solemnly, as if the rotations traced the windings of a snake around the spinal cord. "From the flowers, and in all directions, forking, interweaving, threads branch outward . . . The man"—over Pup's sex organ the pendulum stopped—"is opaque, the skein is golden. A dark fringe, a continuous black line borders the figure, which glowing fibers cross . . ." the shining cone hesitated, began to turn in the opposite direction. "Every one of his gestures, no matter how sudden or slight, reverberates in the entire texture, like the fright of a fish in its flagelli . . . Here, see, now here we must alter a flower, a nervous corolla, we must stimulate a plexus, so that it will live . . . It is difficult to explain . . . certain almost invisible, almost unclassifiable beings, among animals and plants, once pricked, grow . . . Give me the needles."

Swift, becoming entangled in her own rags, ripping off with her heel small beads, pearl rosettes and fleur-de-lysed bows, letting fly flaming flocks of fucks, the Madam disappeared into the succession of rooms—it is not a mirror: starting from a middle and flawless point, on both sides of the corridor, Egyptian claws, moldings, interlaced numbers and Corinthian ramiforms are repeated with rigorous symmetry. She returned shortly after, out of breath, her hair unfrizzled; she brought a convexed and smooth silver case which she displayed with the identical surprise of a Byzantine saint revealing an ossuary.

The interior was laminated in fine cedar, like a cigar box. Dull greens, different knots, opposed bands of the same vein, formed an almost uniform marquetry of empty octagons, dark-edged cubes, a compass and several circles in which the figure of a man with open arms was inscribed. On the other side of the cover a landscape composed of minute inlays sprawled out: a wooden Christ, majestic and dying, was entering a tropical city—in the background one could see palm trees, colonial façades, a sugar mill. —The cabinetmakers' cunning: tiny fragments of mahogany imitated the rotting mahogany. Two broads dressed in black, but with violently painted faces, run toward the foreground, their arms opened, screaming.

At the bottom of the box a serrated support held stilettos of diverse caliber and size in place, but these were not arranged in parallel order and along the length of the receptacle, but rather met in a diagonal bundle which, coming from one of the lower corners, ended in the center. Guessable blasphemy—for its simplemindedness: once the case was closed the darts would nail the Christ.

Pup's scream chases away the digressive devils, who were already starting to pull at me from all sides.

The Little Bound Maja goes out of orbit, collapses against the sofa, grabbing on to the edges with her tiny nails, her stomach sinks, she begins to deflate, becomes thinner and thinner, poor creature.

> she flees without fleeing,
> howls without a sound,
> by now she's just a ribcage,
> an ivory bag of bones.

Ivory with sashes—the purple reflections of the sofa—bones striped like peppermint candies, gay-colored skeleton, yes, even the Wretch's support is pretty, even her primary structure, that's why it's not necessary to change it, but rather leave it as it is, something that the fiendish Master and the Madam might do well to understand. But no way.

From the abovementioned bundle of darts, and with the delicacy of one who selects the best pastry from an overflowing tray, the Transformer—ex-champion of chopsticks—picked up between his fingers a slightly curved copper needle, which ended in a small sphere.

He didn't fall into the easy trap of the voodoo nail fetish; neither did he inflict other cheap analogies upon Pup: he did not transform her into a wax figure pricked with ardor, nor into a pincushion doll, nor into an arrow-pierced saint, no; he limited himself, almost with love, with care, to pricking her rapidly, and sometimes only epidermically—he had always had a good aim in puncturing—wherever the cone, in its course over the body, hesitated, interrupted or altered its rotation. He reserved the deepest punctures for the places where the pendular motion had abruptly changed direction.

"Here, for example." —He squeezed his eyes shut, raised the

harpoon, and nailed it right into the groin. Then he suspended
the pendulum again, and, always at the same height, moved it
over the little hooked body.

Wetting them in a thick curare, the Madam prepared the stilettos.

And so they spent the whole afternoon.

"Have I grown?"—Pup finally asked between two howls and,
as well as she could, turned toward the window.

(Upon a bluff sprawled a new city with Roman architecture,
stone domes, conical roofs, pink and blue marble and a profusion
of bronze applied to the whorls of capitals, to the cresting of
houses, to the angles of cornices. A forest of cypresses overlooked
it all. The color of the sea was very green, the air very cold.

Covering the mountains,

in the horizon,

snow.)

"Have I grown at all?"—she insisted.

"Not at all"—the Madam replied implacably—"actually, you
have withered. Ah . . ." —and she began to pace, hurriedly, from
one side of the room to the other; also wailing, the maid, the
twelve little black boys and the macaque followed her—"after all
that running out of breath, all those breakdowns, all that move
aside you so that I can sit down, from a choreographer and two
tame elephants, painted Sivaic red and saddled with cardboard
castles brought from India, for your caprice of taking things
orally, for your persistence in becoming more and more of a
woman, more and more perfect, in having more and more aluminum on your eyelids, you have left me, on the eve of the premiere,
without a queen for the Lyrical Theater of Dolls. Who, at this
stage, is going to substitute for you? Who will occupy the queen's
blind spot? What jewel shall we put on the lotus flower? What
Cambodian devil shall I dress as you, and among the butterflies of
the *Butterflies and Pheasants* scene, who will have the nerve to be
your double? Ah . . ." —the maid shook the parasol so that the
little bells on the handle would ring—"who made me squander
my savings in order to restructure you, pull out your scalp with
wax and electricity, with a saw cut off your enormous fingers phalanx by phalanx, pay for a platoon of ethnologists, massages and

paraffin, feed you with bitter almonds and snake milk so that you'd be flexible and so that at night your eyes would shine, whose color you wanted to be, rather than burnt opal, brimstone (goldener and goldener!), lynx urine, mandarin orange, double hummingbird . . . until you achieved the imposture: canary yellow contact lenses?"

"Rest tranquil, oh, Madam"—uttered the Master—"the morphological change which we are attempting can be obtained, and without the creature having to abandon Morpheus' lap: we have only to inject snow into her veins."

Pup shook her head no—a rattling of her tiny cervical bones.

"Yes"—added the Physician—"the legendary witch doctors who founded the Sikkim, to combat the white leprosy or *alba Morphea*, a corrosive tetter, or rather a leprosy which attacked cattle, injected the cattle with an alkaloid of coke dissolved in cold water. In the mountains the shepherds used snow. Little by little these shepherds discovered that the animals, after the enema, and at the same time they entered a boundless sopor, grew miraculously, and that this, against all predictions, was in direct relation not to the quantity of the extract, but rather to that of the dissolvent. Thus they formed the breed of the yaks, those buffaloes, tame like horses, which still today roam the plateaus of Central Asia, following the pilgrim monks."

The night of her first injection Pup dreamed that she was a princess of the royal house of Nepal: the Madam, wearing a black hat crowned by a skull, came up to her on a black horse. They were in a town square, facing a palace of golden and conical towers.

Upon dismounting, with bows and arrows forming symbols in the air, the Madam, turned into a magician, performed a dance against the evil spirits.

One of the arrows killed the king.

The magician, galloping, fled.

The Madam appeared on the other side of the river:

white hat,
white horse.

Afterwards, she did not know how much time she spent looking at her feet.

One morning they managed to get her up. Pup asked for water.

She was in the bathroom. Behind an oval mirror, a Mongol peasant woman, opening her eyes, looked out at her, a pink and chubby hand, with short fingers, over her mouth and squeezing a bunch of cherries. Her eyelids were swollen and red; her cheeks: newly washed apples.

"She has grown"—she heard the Master declare, emphatically, in the adjoining room.

"To me it seems more like she's puffed up, dropsical . . . and look at her legs: a little wild elephant's. Rubber doll knees. A fetus in a tube, don't you think?"

Pup drew near a circular window bordered by thick roots. The city from afar was a heap of grey spots; the whites of the snow shriveled; the colors evaporated, seen behind a river of alcohol. Shoots, tender buds which centipedes came to gnaw at, lapis lazuli amulets, mandarin cornea hinges, heads with black signs, as if pushed out from within, sprouted on the roots.

It was summer.

She heard the Noise of the Earth.

Upon returning to her room, she passed the kitchen. On the majolica awning she saw them reflected: Cadillac was coming, cambric apron down to her feet, light grey cap. On a table she placed a pitcher, which she had difficulty holding: "That's all there is. Each day we must climb higher to find it and each day more and more has melted. What we accumulate this week must last till next winter, if not we will have to cancel the doses definitively. After all, with the result they've given: a morbid corpulence . . ."

"If envy were ringworms"—baritoned the Lady Dean—"how many scaldheads would there be around! You can see that without rhyme or reason she has grown, you have proof that, though defying the divine proportions, she prospers, and of course, you feel you ephemeral preeminence threatened; you know that at her appearance you will lose all category and majesty and, inveterate second fiddle, from the queen you will become a bedaubed usurper, a bovine substitute shrieking in the finales of arias. That's why you exult in the omen of the summer. You think that without the daily frost the Shriveled One will cease her expansion and that, the snowdrifts ever higher, we will renounce our plan of enlargement and development. I'm disappointing you: once the threshold of invigoration has been reached, the body"—the Fury burned her with Lezamesque secretions—"is like certain crocodiles from the bottom of the Nile, if they manage to get into the riverbed they may then lose their caudal fins, because the canyon of the running current, in the shadow of funeral barges loaded with the mummies of children and wooden toys, pushes them to the mouth, where the dew of the air and the underwater humidity favor them."

"Well from now on let her navigate alone! the tips of my toes, my knee, my calf, elbows are all a-hurtin', my arms are full of water, my hands cramped and the crown of my head open, I've lost my laughter, I've lost my color, my lips are cracked and my permanent ruined, I look like a hag, a witch of the popular Burmese theater, and all for the love of art, for seeking among the summits, to help a prostrated girl, the hail of proliferation. The more I perfect my Alpinism the more she perfects her ataraxia; the more mountain goat I become, the more ninny she is. No! Down with the latifundium of sleep!"—and she hoisted a French flag which she carried hidden in her front pocket; she took off her grey cap: underneath was a Phrygian cap.

"Transitory queen"—answered the Madam—"how voracious is your leprosy!"

Etc., etc. . . .

Pup continued along the corridor. She didn't cry. She adopted the disdain of a little Gothic Death dragging along her clutter; a twining retinue preceded her; along the glazed tiles, reflecting sandclocks and scythes, her passage was a parade of skeletons, a pageant of macabre allegories.

She locked herself in with two turns of the key.

She undressed before the mirror.

She placed the Marlene wig and two cloth gardenias among her curls. Of course she had grown. She was a haughty broad, somewhat aqueous it's true, and rather ordinary, with the exception of one detail, which she discovered much later, when she was about to stop looking at herself: she closed her eyes from the bottom up.

It was from all that sleeping with her head lower than her feet.

She tried on the queen's dresses one by one.
She sang *Blue Moon*.
She drank a swig of cane liquor.
She went to bed very cocksure.

The Madam, just out of bed, blear-eyed and barefoot, a nylon bun hooked to her grey hairs with a string of hairpins, came to her the next day.

"Cobra"—she said to her after a coffee break—"there's such a thing as too much of a good thing." —And she dropped onto a divan; from among the cushions three calico cats rushed out. "You are as before. Or almost. Winter has already left us and envious Cadillac as well: the rivers and your body have grown. Now get ready for penury. For want. For the frolicsome little monkey on your back."

"Prepare the show"—Pup replied. "Dismiss the Master. Let the summer rain fall though my hat."

She went two days without snow. She drank coconut milk to appease her thirst; she sucked it through a small hole which she opened in the nut with a nail, threw her head back, showed the whites of her eyes. The third night she woke up sweating.
She opened the garden windows.
The trees were adorned with round, red, and polished fruits, so many that one couldn't see the leaves. Among the branches silver roosters slept; from time to time slight tremors shook their tails— a spurt of white feathers, as if they fell from the hats of frightened pages, reached the ground.
She closed the windows. She went back to bed. She heard birds flutter their wings.
Or the creaking of a windmill wing.
She got up again. Opened the windows.
The sea was black.
Among the feathers rabbits frolicked.

From a wicker basket she took out a small pair of scissors. She punched a hole in the Chinese bedspread—with gold trigrams, a gift, dear me, from the Madam. Starting from the edge, quick, voracious, yes, rapid and voracious she cut a straight band, with fringes and all, one strip, another. With the same quick, voracious determination, when she finished the bedspread she attacked the curtains, the cushions, the cute little taffeta hand-embroidered tablecloths with the variegated backstitching in canvas, and the carpet, to be more treacherous she cut the carpet along its own color patterns: from east to west a black band, from north to south a white, from west to east a red, from south to north a green. And while she frantically stuck her puncher into the yellow center, eager birdie with a bifid beak, she clamored with a flute voice:

> "a time of decrepitude a time of thickening,
> a time of collapse a time of death,
> a time of yang a time of yang."

She got cramps in her upper extremities and pins and needles in the lower, hot and cold flashes, chokings and tremors; she blinked with one eye only,

> she laughed without laughing,
> she had no nausea but wished to vomit,
> her only sound was moaning,
> climbing the walls was all she wanted.

> She carved the dress she wore,
> and one by one, the queen's.
> She cut her nails,
> the four tangles she had left,
> the hairs of her genitals,
> her eyebrows and lashes.
> She was choking.
> She breathed though her mouth.
> A thousand reeking demons entered her
> and poisoned her membranes.
> She prayed.
> She urinated on the mattress.
> She bit the leg of the bed.

Searching for the box of snow she forced open the door to the kitchen. She threw all the drawers to the floor. She tore off the shutters of the pantry. With her teeth she split a flask of sugar—along with pieces of glass she spit blood. She flipped the table over. She shattered a fruit bowl with a nutcracker. She found it at the bottom of the garbage can, covered by leftovers. She had the little key on her. Two handfuls were left. She swallowed them in one gulp. She began to sing a samba.

A good thing the Madam found her. She was a Virgin of Fertility proclaimed apocryphal, a fetish cudgeled to expunge the demons that decimate the harvest: on the floor, naked, showing the whites of her eyes, surrounded by bananas and tainted custard apples, lychees and pears. She was crowned by hoops of broken glasses, toppled saltshakers, red peppers, cloves, clusters of garlic, a ham, big copper spoons and a coffee grinder whose handle continued turning.

"I have failed"—groaned the Dean, whose hair in a matter of minutes had turned grey.

She straightened up the table.

She laid the tablecloth and set her down on top.

She rubbed her with an aluminum swab and then with a kitchen rag dampened in vinegar.

She lit a candle.

Spent the night sprinkling her with hot coffee—Pup's jaws were locked—reciting exorcisms into her ear.

At daybreak she was still alive, though—Beauty is ephemeral—she was already shrinking.

When Cobra returned from India she found her as rickety as ever.

Of what they told her she did not believe a thing.

To God I Dedicate This Mambo

Like a goose's neck, the envious Cadillac's arm undulates in the mist, plumed white on the gloomy platform. The three are going away, or the two which add up to three,[1] to Moorish lands in search of a distinguished though hidden Galen, the conspicuous Doctor Ktazob, who in crafty Tangerian abortion houses uproots the superfluous with an incision and sculpts in its place lewd slits, crowning his cunning with punctures of a Muslim balm that changes even the voice of a Neapolitan brigand into a honeyed flute, that shortens the feet Ming fashion, Byzantinizes gestures, and makes two mother-of-pearl turgescences billow upon the chest, mimicries of those displayed by Saint Olalla upon a plate.

Writing is the art of ellipsis. I'll pass over, then, the encounter of our rovers with four mercenary monks—black background, white cloaks—who in Madrid tried to dissuade them, reasoning with ovaled gestures, as if caressing invisible doves who upon a sash, to give the finishing stroke to each argument, brought in the pertinent Latin, from the mutation to which the girls aspired, concluding, though charismatically intransigent, that it was "violence against the *res extensa,* a gift among the many of the Most Holy One, upon whose wise providence all creatures are dependent"—and they pointed to, on a window case (in the distance a convent, a holy man consoling paralytics), a book with an apple on top— . . . "ergo sin."

I record nevertheless, and with such care, the dialogue which

---

[1] [Mme. + Cobra (+/=) Pup = (3/2)]

in Guadalupe the Madam sustained with Father Illescas, an enlightened theologian and Jerome's prior.

Having crossed the Sargasso Sea, docile Indians, naked and painted, showing off their bells and little glass beads, arrived in those times at the mountain convent, coming from distant archipelagoes, to learneth to speaketh, be baptized, and die of cold; they brought the gently smiling convert parrots who recited Salve Reginas, trees and marvelously flavored fruits, little birds with red crystal eyes, aromatic herbs and, why not, among such a gay-colored presence, from golden sands the small fat nuggets which the Churrigueresque faith, cornucopia of floral emblems, would convert into knots and arrow, oscillating Mudejar lamps, capitals of Sephardic fruits, Viceregal altar-pieces and thick Gothic crowns suspended over plump whirling Tridentine angels.

Cobra marveled at such coarse ornaments and many-hued feathers. She wanted to dress herself with cassava, with tortoise-bitten wood sculpt herself cothurnuses, with tobacco leaves, *caimitos* and mangoes build a tall and gaudy hat like a Giralda weathervane, with Taino statuettes, brittle necklaces and fragile fetish wristlets that jumped like coal dust at the surprise of her gestures.

Pup, a regular Phoenician merchant by now, had given herself over to bartering with the guileless: for death masks and ambrosias she exchanged with popping eyes, in alluring little balls, the moth-eaten pages she was tearing out of a damaged Missal.

But, enough arabesques, let us move on to the medullary subject, to the theoretical marrow of the exchange:

"What folly, my daughters! and from what rustic and debauched minds do you inherit such a pitiful invention?"— admonished the Father when he had measured in carats the extent of the enterprise which animated the pilgrim girls and had raised for a moment the quill pen with which he signed a parchment. Pup, under the table, frolicked with a measly hound. "And, once the surplus pudenda is converted into its contrary and duly buried (as the Church orders to be done with one's fingers and even with loose phalanxes), on Judgment Day, under what guise and nature will the ill-fated appear before the Creator and how will he recognize her without the attributes that he knowingly gave her, remodeled, redone, and handmade, like the circumcised?"

"It amazes me that you think in such a way"—replied the Theoretical Lady: "the body, before reaching its lasting state"— and she observed, with showy compassion, a skeleton and an hourglass placed on a closed fascicle, on one corner of the parson's table—"is a book in which the divine judgment is written; why not, in a case like the present one, in which most evidently in *Written on a Body* there has escaped a minor though annoying erratum, amend the blunder and nip the erroneous bud, as with infants, when they bore through, one cauterizes a marginal finger or the soft spot on their heads? And it is precisely in this hamlet"—the Illustrious Lady continued—"where I shall produce evidence, worthy of reverence, though to your eyes heretical remedy, because I know myself to be among dissecting experts, and all this skill, I believe, applies very much to the superfluities which thus I would baptize these inconsequential regalias of nature and malformations of the living."

Tucked up among processional moldings, Cobra followed the discussion lying in a corner of the capitular room, surrounded by burnished Plateresque tabernacles, vaulted reliquaries which among thorns exhibited tibias and rotulas, three chasubles embroidered with tiny gems, panels with casks, breads, pitchers of wine and monks in white, and a book of anthems where sirens plunged into the gold of the initials.

Pup, the Costumed Monster,[1] had slipped away among great naval chests and Diocesan cases: in the area where the thorny theme was being debated, she appeared very smily and in full regalia, squeezed up to her neck in an episcopal cloak, a mitre clapped backwards on her head and the puppy in her arms muzzled with a scapulary.

"What baroque mockery is this, shitass, or what blasphemy?"

---

[1]See her portrait by Carreño (1614-1685) in the Prado (no. 646) with her compliment: "not too pleasing, but majestic, he has painted her nude, although with features of Silenus to diminish the repulsiveness of the figure." F.J. Sánchez Canton, *Guide to the Prado Museum.*

—the Father chided, going at her with spankings nomine Dei to rid her piggish body of the hydrosulphuric demons and vermin which doubtlessly corroded her ganglia and spleen.

Choked up, he continued: "The remedy to which your speech alludes, Madam, has more in common with Leng T'che, the Chinese torture of the one hundred slices, and with the medieval extremes of grafting mongrel animals to lunatics and emasculated bodies, than with the benign post mortem anatomy lessons which here, approved by the Holy Congregation of Rituals and with ecclesiastical license, have been dictated."

"Then you defame me, ponderable prebendary"—the interpreter concluded without composure—"since you seem to find such little sense in them." —And with no sign of vexation: "I will recall for you then, to close this delicious exchange and so as not to keep you in suspense any longer, a precedent which I hope will not embarrass you: that of an Alexandrine saint mortified, in their origins, by the flows due to Luciferian itches of his pudenda, who, in an ecstatic rapture and as if possessed by surgical seraphims, amputated his cockatrice with one fell swoop, flinging it like a piece of tripe to the dogs; thus unburdened he ascended, in a whirlwind of gnostic utterances, to the supreme cupola of the Platonic pantheon." —And between sobs and poorly formed sighs, to Cobra: —"Let's get cracking."

"Then engage yourselves in that manner, my daughters"—the deacon concluded indignantly—"and stir the live coals of this simpleton, since to the same Gehenna and without further preface will you all go, including this dwarf who, though not for being stunted and puny, is more innocent, since it could be said—such ingenuity adds evil to its lubrications—that she is only the unsuccessful and derisive double of the transvestite."

"Put fire, to me!"—the Madam clamored in exasperation, with a neoclassical gesture—"I shall make of this ambiguous one a houri and even of her miniaturized analogy"—and she grabbed Pup, who began to utter niceties, by the arm—"a plump Moorish girl, since you must know, priest, that if I have come to these godforsaken haunts it is to untie Gordian knots, clarify enigmas, and redress all manner of wrongs."

And with that the threesome marched down the hill, not

without first providing themselves with nougat pastes and anise, bread and raisins, blanc-mange, and a few of those meatballs to which Pup had taken such a liking.

In the square, near the fountain, they handed out medlar fruits to the needy and to beggars.

They bade grevious good-byes to the faithful.

They were so good.

Withered, they entered Toledo.

The three of them: with phosphorescent insect intestines, elongated and ascendant like the portraits of Spanish gentlemen—reflections (the learned Madam noted with precision) in astigmatic pupils—with rainbow-hued elytrons, near a windmill met up with none other than Help and Mercy. More than simply textual, they were like parchments and yellowed rhetorics: so Toledan were they that they were Moorish, so dyed-in-the-wool Hispanic that they were antiquarian. Picadors and mule drivers, duennas and maidens followed them in retinue. Their amber silks, their brimstone chattels shined like mirrors. They were made of wings, of white flames.

No sooner had they recognized the duo than they began leaving them for being impossible, so much advice—and all in ballad form—did the Ever-Present want to give them, so many proverbs did they aim right and left at them, since Help and Mercy did not know what a damnation it was not to be able to say reason without rhyme nor rhyme without reason:

that Cobra should trim herself immediately without awaiting further opinions, since in delay there is danger and "better to have than to wish,"

that the Madam should return to the Carousel and there, without further somatic preparations, put on a "Cherchez la Femme" like all others, since there's no place like home and a bird in the hand is worth two vultures in the bush;

that the Changeable would be better painted all in arabesques with an awning of glazed tiles and a stucco dome on her head;

that the customs men at Algeçiras, bloodhounds of greefa, were going to humiliate them and procrastinate and call them to disappear into the elusive hinge of silver that embraces, though fine, the two Oceans;[1]

that, finally, in this still forming infant, in this soft spot—they were referring to Pup—such raving and metamorphosis was going to accumulate into a pathogenic knot which, when she reached development, would string her up, converting her into a doomed virgin, a blunderhead, or a pixilated loon.

They left them upon a minaret, *dressed in wide floating habits, seemingly made of milled wool, and hoods of fine white muslin which were indeed so long that only the hem of the habits were exposed;* their hands slender and white—stuffed herons—waving good-bye; their voices, high-pitched muezzins, scattering auguries, blessings, go with god most holys.

They all cried.

They marveled—who marveled?—at their boldness; though they held them as daring, witty, and bold, not to the point that they would expect them to venture such foolhardy exploits.

At dawn they saw them move off, weary and dusty, their bundles on their shoulders: they were shepherdesses and mule-drivers. To the south, to the south: outlines of black figures, blurs, earth-colored stains which the reverberation duplicates, dots . . . flat country.

How many days did they plow the plains? What befell them in the sierra? What droughts or frosts did they go through, in what wheat fields or olive orchards, and on the charity or lust of what scoundrels, did they live?

Cobra reappeared some months later, in small rotting letters, on the slangy poster of a Tangerian café. She was a platinum blonde tango and mambo dancer, loads of khôl on her eyelids, a beauty mark on her cheek and two lovelocks.

On her right breast a ruby was hidden.

Her feet were big and her heel was crooked.

She sang a mambo in Esperanto.

While the cabaret girl pandered her milongas to a pack of

---

[1] They mistook the Strait of Gibraltar for that of Magellan.

French colonists, groping natives, drug addicts in need and legionnaires, the Madam, disguised as an Andalucian beggar with Pup starving and sniveling in her arms, at the door of a mosque, inquired, under the cover of selling condoms under the cover of selling reliefs with Koranic inscriptions, after urgent signs of Doctor Ktazob, with the pretext of fibroid in the obese one and in herself premature senility, menopausia precox, partial amnesia and undulating fever.

They shook a tin can of coins.

They sang *a dúo* the first sura of the Koran.

Darkened Mozarabic lamps swung with difficulty—so dense was the air. Beneath the ceiling—a star-filled and gyrating sky, with sudden noons and purplish twilights—their paths mixed together smoke strata, slow whorls of mint, raw rum and hashish breath, tea with peppermint and absinthe.

Before a vaulted window which faced onto a covered street—striped figures beneath wicker roofs—and further away onto a grove of palm trees with its camels and domes crowned by the crescent, a squalid Sudanese with an imitation tortoiseshell pocketbook and a magnolia in his hair, presented, to boot, "the zaniest show in the whole province," Cobra: background of accordions, fading light which thickened over chlorophyll green footlights.

She sang with tremolos—there wasn't a night without a knife-fight—wasted and falsetto.

She sold apples during intermission.

From cock-teaser waitress, she stepped onto the stage again for the last mambo.[1] She was preceded by the Dolly Sisters, hormoned twins, a Moroccan boy inured in Indian dance, the Cherche-Bijoux and Vanussa, gigantic and prognathic Canadians who among endless red spotlights and soap bubbles dubbed, never in time, their own records.

[1]The chorus included the Divine Her—a slanty-eyed Cuban launched yesteryear by Juan Orol—the Diviner—who at intermission tossed the tarot, the cards, and the conch shells—the Di Vine (. . . er . . .)—Neapolitan dancer from Caracas, of Austrian ascendance and born in Puerto Rico—and Lady Viner—so-called noble English lady come down in the world after the loss of her tea plantation in Ceylon.

While Cobra wiggled her hips to a Perez Prado mambo, the Madam, pillar of the Small Marketplace, was not idle. Following the trail of the transformer she went ever deeper into the maze of the Medina, descending into an abyss of smugglers and drug traffickers. In exchange for news she even made deals with slave mongers. She fell into the white slave trade.

(LISTEN TO UMM KALSUM)

Four long-haired boys from Amsterdam, distillers of drugs in search of raw material—they hid cocaine in hollow-headed Buddhas—murmured to her in a smoking room on the port that the Doktor had been found in a bawdyhouse strangled with a Korean mask, doubtlessly the victim of a sailor left unfinished, in transformation.

A Marrakech tanner, a good-natured fellow with saffron-stained hands, showed her, in the side room of a ramshackle café, his member, and thus seduced and dragged her off to the Medinian cemetery; next to a marabout tomb, smiling, he took out the erect aforementioned and also a curved dagger with an inlaid handle, demanding her pocketbook without further ado and pleading with her in the name of the Prophet to immediately abandon her obstinate search.

Beneath the whorl of a mimbar a Mohammedan priest sang her the praises of the ex-therapist repentant of his jugglery and converted to the faith.

A fag of the "Festival" insinuated to her that Ktazob did not exist and that he was an invention of the painted "dames" who cruised Pigalle.

In a rococo bar—vermilion plush and gildings—against a wall of pink shells—its air charged with a repugnant and maleficent smell of stale honey—William Burroughs wrote for her on a ticket, in hieroglyphs, the exhaustive biography of Ktazob: enriched by the configuration of new Evas and the disfiguration of old Nazis, the artificer was today a first class "traveler": in the cellar of a flattened earth hut, near the Sahara, dissembling an Alhambra which in turn dissembled a Polynesian brothel with blue-lined screens, red-striped lamps, nude waiters and floor level tables topped with kif pipes that never went out, narguiles of opium and overflowing bottles of mescaline, harmaline, LSD 6, bufotenin, muscarine and bulbocapnin. Given over to the latter, which he activated with curare, the former expert alternated his days between the catatonic syndrome—he represented this notion to her as a little man sleeping under a great black bird—and automatic obedience. *"Son cosas de la vida"*—he concluded orally, with a Colombian accent.

Count Julian conducted her: stands, storage sheds, bazaars, jingling of water carriers, groups of curious loafers, aroma of couscous, sausages and brochettes: a moor preceded them tiger-marked in his striped hooded robe, shiny feline eyes over the handlebars of his pointy mustache. They walked faster to catch up to him.

In a box at the Cervantes movie theater the Visigoth count assured her that the Doctor, a stingy demiurge jealous of his own fabrications, had ended up by exercising his magic on himself: today he was a neo-Liberty midwife with a starched bathrobe down to her ankles, a touch of Rudolph Valentino in her eyes, devoted to her uterine activities and household chores.

Finally, when she no longer searched for him, fanning herself at home with a pulpy palm leaf and helping herself to a daiquirí, minding her own business—what a farce life is—the Madam met head-on with the long-sought informer: in a street quarrel over caramel earrings Pup lopped off a little girl's ear. An intern came to sew on the severed pinna, but discouraged by the difficulty of the first stitches, it makes no matter, he preferred to dispense with it altogether. The surgical prodigy completed, and a few drinks later, the expret commented that he had reached such extreme mastery as the right hand man of a renowned cartilage specialist—Doctor Ktazob.

Without further insistence and gratified by a few dirhams, the second man promised, in front of Pup tied to a chair, that the next day, after the show, the Physician would appear in person before Cobra herself.

They made a pact not to think about the date. Behind each other's back they took Librium. So that she would sleep the whole day, they put a pill in Pup's soup. They knitted. They talked about the bad weather. They confessed a lack of energy. At six P.M. Cobra began to put on her makeup. At eight, in front of the mirror, she was waiting in the dressing room. At ten the bell rang for the first show. She sang a "Cumparsita" without enthusiasm. When her dance number came up she felt weak in the legs. Dragged on by the Diviner and with the help of cognac she went on stage.

"To God I dedicate this mambo"—she muttered when the drums started playing.

She went back to the dressing room lulled by aguardiente, caressing a cat.

At one o'clock sharp she heard firm steps approaching. Someone knocked loudly on the door. It was a tall, thin man, with slender hands—a great surgeon. Greased sideburns descended from a wide-brimmed Panama hat. Patent leather shoes. A button on his lapel. Mirror green sunglasses. Light beige drillsuit. Fat as a chickpea, a diamond buttonholed the silk tie. The eyes:

Cobra: a loud scream: the bulldyke she had in front of her was none other than Cadillac.

"Yes, doll"—the newly glossed Moroccan gangster bragged in a heavy anisated voice, and squeezed her breast—"I've double-crossed evil. Allah le Tout-Puissant m'a couillonné au carré: the inversion of inversion." He winked at her—an Al Capone giggle. "I was fed up with my rags, honey. I went to see my buddy Ktazob"—he inhales the cigar, shuts his eyes, puff of smoke; Cobra: little nervous cough: "he took an Abyssinian's dong out of a narrow pitcher"—he comments licking his chops—"and here I am, like a pimp's shoe: long toe and two-toned. With a few punctures and some slickum my hair came back"—he opened his shirt: Whew, what BO!—"Now I'm in the white slave trade. If you want to get rid of the excess, with these rubber tits"—with his forefinger and thumb, as if her were going to unscrew them, he pinched her nipples—"don't lose time in the meanders of the Medina: like a purloined letter that the police doesn't find because it's laying right there on the fireplace, like the name of the whole country, which nobody sees on the map, Ktazob hides in the most visible, in the center of the center. Give that tip to the old lady who cruises for you. Ah, and say I sent you, babe; he'll leave you well creased. But, and don't forget this, reserve the premiere for me."

A big laugh. A slap on the backside. He slammed the door.

Cobra dropped onto the bed.

Her head was in chaos.

The Conversion

THE MADAM: "You're going to Ktazob, my dear, as easy as if you were going to the dentist. You think that in the evening, after the benign extraction, without further torment than a slight indisposition, a Biscayan nurse will bring you, along with a bouquet of Burmese orchids, a glass of sour orange juice and your discharge papers, a hand mirror where, rather than your own image, you will contemplate on a background of twilight, with that pallor of a convalescing consumptive, Greta Garbo in close-up. . . Get off of that cloud: after the butchery and if you can stand it, what awaits you is a rainfall of punctures, tweezings and scrapings, wax in your breasts, crystal in your veins, mushroom vapors in your nose and green yeast by mouth. Cover your eyes with grapes. Your ears with plugs. A yellow dog will lick your feet.

"Rather than into your delirium, look at yourself in the mirror of others: they flee crestfallen, as if they had just lost a ruby on the sidewalk, so that, like Veronica Lake, or like lepers, their hair conceals their faces. By the fire-escapes they enter Negro nightclubs. Furiously they dress as odalisks. They plaster their faces. With blood they paint their eyelids. While the cooks sharpen knives, with squeaks in the background they tire the rabble. Scrofulous and bald like them, an Afghan hound swoons at their side: they inject him to make him sleep. They talk to themselves. They set the table for a dead friend. With their clothes on they shoot up in the subway's urinals. The Indonesian maid finds them seated on an inflatable sofa, in long dresses, covered with flies beneath the poster of Queen Christina: 'Air in the needle, as usual'—and she continues sweeping.

"Or in the operation you feel that the table slopes. You hear a stream falling into an aluminum container. They give you cocaine so that you can stand it. The blood breaks the catgut again. In a transparent nylon cube, they leave you lying naked, in pure oxygen.

"Or you remain perfect, like a statue, until from the wound gangrene starts creeping over you.

"Now then, Cobra, if despite everything and to be divine for five minutes on stage you want to confront this test and commit the ultimate sin, alas, of which man is capable . . ."—she removes the white wig, of weighty years of experience, throws down the ball of wool, from a long jeweled cigarette case lights an ever cooler mentholated Winston, glosses herself with rouge, dons jewelry, sticks a spangle on her cheek, crosses—revealing her genitalia—the legs a surgeon had lengthened Marlene fashion—"then, honey, go down this minute to the avenue on the port, a cognac at the Tout Va Bien, think about something else, take it as if you were going to the dentist, beauty has its price, continue till you get to the docks, you'll see on your left, in the Medina, raised above storage sheds, a decrepit bar: on the balconies enraptured moors and blond boys smoking weed, go up the narrow staircase that leads to the entrance, a vendor of stale sponge cakes, a singing blind man, smell of cumin, a fountain, a flea-bitten movie house: on the billboard a fat lady with gold teeth and a red dot on her forehead, go straight ahead, to a small market, you'll hear the pustulent pupils of a Koranic school sing, a Spanish boarding house: there you'll see Ktazob's shingle." —She becomes a prudent octogenarian again: "Take the dwarf. I'm no longer up to the job: all that stair climbing."

The most difficult part—Ktazob had platinum hair, was a devotee of the florid perfumed Partagas cigars, and to the branching of subordinate clauses. A slight cough, or rather a strained echo, as of one who must dissemble a gnat's goading on his right testicle, culminated the twisting and turning exhalations and syntactical foliage. A tight black sweater no longer narrowed the stomach's little dome nor the rear and rotund hemispheres. His manners: parsimonious, his tone, despotic; glasses; a cock pigeon's pupils—

the most difficult part is not the final formality, a question of minutes, but rather the preliminary apprenticeship, to transfer the pain, and subsequently, to eliminate the sensation of loss.

From a walnut case he selected a cigar, rolled it between his fingers against his nose; closing his eyes, with dilated nostrils he inhaled the fragrance; along the gentle leaves he passed the tip of his tongue: "You must know that I don't use anesthesia. It is essential, or at least my practice thus configures it, that the mutant, in transition, does not lose consciousness.

"If in the intermediate state the knowledge factor of the subject vanishes it is possible that he may founder in that limbo, or that, when coming to, he might not recognize himself in his restructured body. To achieve this wakefulness one must dissipate all signs of pain, which is achieved by algesic transference, a simple exercise of concentration with a distant support, which deflects the neuralgic lightning toward a scapegoat.

"The Sufistic martyrs were invulnerable: their disciples suffered for them."

He picked up a lighter engraved with silver Kufic letters. "If I, for example . . ."—voluptuously he drew the light near the fragrant fibers and, quickly, like a diving kingfisher, or a syringe thrust into the gluteal region, he brought it down to Cobra's hands; the candidate for change bit her lips—"if I for example . . . burn your hand, the burning can pass, shall we say, onto that dwarf in the waiting room. If your concentration, ergo if the transference is correct, I can even pull a tooth out or shred you to pieces without your feeling the slightest discomfort; the receiver, alas, will fall flat on her face, pierced by inexplicable spasms. An Instructor I will train Subject S to learn to emit the caustic darts; another, the scapegoat, to not offer resistance. The Alterer A will be able to practice his modeling force on the Subject to convert him into Subject prime, a force whose stabbing vector will be suffered by, in this case, the altered girlie out there (a), she of course being transformed, by the coaching therapy, into optimal receiver (a) prime. The whole thing can be represented by the graph of the mutation: Diamond."

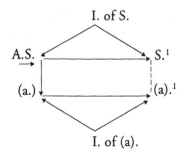

The next day they began their homework. Early in the morning, talcum-powdered and cool, their hair gathered up in a high bun that is so comfortable, Cobra and Pup arrived at the doctor's office, already imbued with lacquered psychosomatic aphorisms, to receive Doctor K.'s analgesic theories. Among tarnished hypnotic pendulums, stained pincers and surgical knives piled in Romeo y Julieta cigar boxes, with a musical background of Koranic strains, he rambled on about esthesia—for an hour Pup, locked in a closet, has been twisting and turning: the point is to verify certain assuaging fundaments of dervishes—spontaneous narcosis, the visions of interregnum and the *episteme* of the Cut. It was not difficult for him to achieve "somatic identification" between Cobra and the albuminous pygmy who served as her base, but the dizzying filigrees—that the Sufistic metaphysics of the fissure intertwine—were not sufficient to "read" in the milky Lilliputian the separate and cold better half of the convert, her double satellized in rotation.

Like everything with her, that's why the miserable wretch has gotten where she is, transference in Cobra worked the other way around: she fell flat on her face, possessed by yellowish vertigo, shaken with vomitous heavings: alas, we'd forgotten that Pup was still twisting and turning in the closet!

"The sidereal emanations of this gyrating weakling are so concentrated"—concluded A—"that she has managed to invert the hyperesthesic arrow. The rotation, doubtlessly"—and he exhaled a whorl of smoke—"has charged her with energy. We are going to have to submerge her for nine days in a barrel of ice and choke her with passive substances, and at the same time hang you, Cobra, from the ceiling with a trapeze artist's gag so that you may achieve the revolutions required, and keep you going with fresh pig's blood, to see if that way we can obtain at least a biunivocal correspondence that will allow us, the moment of surgery having arrived, and if the white dwarf has been sufficiently weakened, welding her to an amianthus sheet, to channel the course of the pain correctly."

Cobra has revolved so many times . . . that tears have come to her eyes. Her tears and that reddening urine—distilled hog blood clots—have left, at different levels on the white walls of the cell that surrounds her, and from the molding up in the following order:

> dripping amber sashes
> opal splashes
> strips of honey
> stains of orange
> twilight strata
> threads tinted purple
> clots of garnet
> once more, blood.

Ktazob looks at the inflamed rainbow. He points out, with the euphoria of one who celebrates the gestural impetus of a Sam Francis, the uppermost, bloody stain: "With maximum acceleration . . . we have here the *red shift!*"—And lowering the lever to OFF he stopped the machine—an autogenous refrigerator motor and two pulleys—which made the socle, fixed to the center of the ceiling, revolve and with it the blood-drained acrobat. He unhooked her as well as he could: Cobra fell, boneless, a bundle of dirty clothes, flat on the floor. She opened her eyes very wide, and her mouth; not even a sigh escaped.

"The worst is over"—the Alterer assured her, knocking her on the nape of the neck with the tip of a shoe—"Now, honey and rest for a few days, to stabilize, with the red indicator, the energy at maximum."

And he went into the adjoining cell.

Charred walls. There, in a sink overflowing with starch where splinters of ice floated, was Pup, submerged to her nose.

Like Allah with dead children, by the lock of hair he had left upon shaving her—hair is a source of energy—the Galen raised her from the Antarctic. Not effortlessly: despite the bath she was still compact. "Magnificent results in (a)!"—he communicated to her along with a few slaps—"What elegant gradations!"—From her nose down, the body of the dwarf, girded from amber to pure white, was a spherical all-day lollipop for big-headed carnival mannikins. An anemic rainbow made a ring around her: fading successive streaks became lighter, dulling their tones to her marble feet.

Pup opened her eyes very wide, and her mouth, she puffed her cheeks, like an Aeolus, spat a puddle upon the doctor's face.

"Remnants of aggressivity"—strained the platinum blond wiping off the phlegm with an embroidered shawl. "Next week"—he added with great cool—"we shall operate." —And he hoisted an overwhelming cigar whose tip he amputated with his sharpened cigar cutter.

COBRA'S DREAM

She was near a cracked mausoleum, among reefs dashed by waves. Stuck to the stones, rags, locks of hair, candles and votive offerings; cylinders crowned with livid turbans, around the lime marabout tombs arose. She made an offering of saffron and flowers and burned camphor in circles, among chalk and snail marks she plucked a pigeon, over the turbans she spilled ointments, she polished the cylinders with a thick milk which, among the rocks, splattered copper-toned crab shells.

At his feet surgical knives and silver lobsters, in his hands eels and stethoscopes, at the entrance of the funereal mound, triumphant big shot, Cadillac appeared, looking like Saint Ktazob. The arch framed him at the midway point of the door; tinted crystal painted his robe like a stained-glass window. Oars. Small boats and fishing nets. Golden sardines slipped away among the garlands that adorned it with marine violets. In that niche, the bull dicker—whose attribute, a cylinder crowned with a livid turban, emerged erect from a nest of lace—was patron of the altar of Provençal fishermen. His wide-rimmed Panama hat → *a hat which adorned* the concave mirror of ear, nose and throat doctors;

his tie → a phylactery—silver caduceus on black felt—; the jewel shines among ruby auricles and wine-colored ventricles—open pomegranates—bleeding garnets.

Minute golden inscriptions emanated from a motionless white sea gull on his head. His bare feet on the coral on the reefs, a rainbow over the mother-of-pearl waves.

With lobsters' pincers Cadillac → Saint Ktazob touched Cobra. Nude, alabastrine, a tall microcephalic, in slow spirals the pricked one ascended. An almond of flames shielded her; among concentric clouds her little feet, over a field of stars, and equally sparkling, her humid eyes; a Prussian blue mantle, shreds of sea and sky, were ready to cover her; creating in the water a whirlpool which sucked in oarsmen and tail-wagging dolphins, a spout of angels revolved around her. In the quietude of the vortex, together in prayer, her lily-white hands; among the reefs, charred and covered with tumors, pupils encircled by rings of fire, a purplish devil croaked in his pulpit. It wasn't an elephant trunk; bleeding, from his mouth, with balls and hairs a prick sprouted.

Three little shepherds were looking for lost goats—the Madam, Cadillac, and Pup—enraptured, fall to their knees on the rocks, forget the *Ave*, gapingly attend the ascension, raise their arms, touch the mantle, receive a rain of roses.

At a distance of 12 km. from Casablanca, going in the direction of Azemmour by the coastal highway, one can see on the right, perched on an accessible reef during low tide, the sanctuary of Sidi Abd-er-Rahman. The rock, beaten by the waves, is considered a sacred place. Stuck against the rough stone are rags, locks of hair and other diverse offerings. Around the sanctuary one can see the tombs of pilgrims who died during the pious visit, and a few yards ahead, commemorating a popular miracle, a group of three shepherds sculpted in marble, the work of the Italian artist Canova (1757–1822).***

DIAMOND

The Alterer's *face is uncovered, smooth, clear, impassive, cold like a newly washed white onion;* a cloth hides the faces of the Instructors, robed in black. Cobra lies naked on the metal table; arms and legs spread out; Pup on an amianthus sheet. On a cart being wheeled in clink test tubes filled with blood. Someone coughs. In the corridor someone murmurs. Receptacles dragged along floor slabs.

ALTERER—"And if we pretended it's a game,"

COBRA'S INSTRUCTOR—"like something reversible:"

ALTERER—"a sound which is repeated?"

COBRA'S INSTRUCTOR—"Man is a bundle: neither its elements, nor the forces that unite them are at all real."

ALTERER—"Cobra, you enter the intermediate state: empty heaven things,"

COBRA'S INSTRUCTOR—"clear intelligence, transparent void"

ALTERER—"without circumference or center."

COBRA'S INSTRUCTOR—"Concentrate. You have learned to deflect pain. Lucidly. I take you to the test."

PUP—"What are they going to do to me with that astrolabe?"

ALTERER—"Take an open-winged bat: nail him to a plank. Have fun making him smoke. He chokes. Shrieks. Give him a light. Take a rabbit: bleed him through the eyes. Take a little man who smiles, tied to a beam. Cram him with cocaine. One by one, bloodlessly—brief cuts in the tendons of his joints—separate him into pieces, one by one, up to one hundred. So that a merchant, smoking a pipe, points at him. A photograph. So that a woman laughs."

PUP'S INSTRUCTOR—"Do you want a doll who opens and closes her eyes, who urinates and everything, with real hair? Do you want a rainbow ice cream treat, in the shape of a pagoda, with a little flag on top? Come on, Pup, what's the matter with you, don't tighten up like that."

COBRA'S INSTRUCTOR—"Think of a very hot sun. You are invulnerable. The windmill wings of pain break against your body. A transparent heaven."

The Master gets ready.

Pup screams. Splashes. Big drops of thick ink flee toward the edges of Cobra's body. Lightning. Rupture. Red branches that descend, forking rapidly along the sides of a triangle—the vertex torn out—over the white skin of the thighs, along the nickel surface, following the contours of the hips, between the trunk and the arms, forming puddles in the armpits, thin speeding threads over the shoulders, matting the hair: two streams of blood, down to the floor.

COBRA'S INSTRUCTOR—"Equally destructive is the exercise of good and of evil. You have eliminated in yourself compassion. With all your strength now, direct the pain toward the dwarf: she is diabolic, needy and ugly, what does it matter what happens to her? She is nothing but your waste, your gross residue, what comes off you formless, your look or your voice. Your excrement, your falsies, how disgusting! body fallen from you that is no longer you. Are you going to care about her, are you going to bother about what happens to her, you who will be perfect, lean, like an icon? Are you going to get blood in your eye for a stinking good-for-nothing? Cobra, the Master is already carving your body. Now he's going to sculpt your nose, design your eyebrows. You will have enormous eyes, crowned by perfect arches, passionate, like those of an antelope who flees in the night, disproportionate: a Byzantine Christ; you will be fascinating, like a fetish. But don't weaken now. Don't let yourself be corrupted by compassion. Overwhelm her. Torture her. I have eaten human flesh and drunk blood. How hateful! You didn't know: with magic she has tried to scar your face in order to take your place. Pins for her: let her bleed. Needles. Coals. Let her burn."

PUP'S INSTRUCTOR—"Rockabye baby. Loosen up. You're getting tight. Don't tense up like that. It will be over soon. Think of a little toy train, red and pretty, it whistles, how cute! do you want it? A bell rings, it takes a fork, it stops at the stations, it goes up a very high overpass, it goes down . . . Do you want to go on a ship? Think of a very funny cat, and now of a baby elephant, bathed and perfumed, who frolics in the sea; they paint flowers on his trunk. Loosen your little self up. Do you want me to tell you a story, sing you a song? Do you want a cake with candles? Oh, Pup, why are you so naughty? Why do you tighten your jaw that way and gnash your teeth? You're going to break them, you bad girl. Why do you cry like that, Pup?"

The little dwarf neither dedicated her curses to nor spit upon the hooded man. She looked at the floor. A smile of resignation stretched her lips; as with a little crushed toad, the hiccups shook her from time to time. *Her head was turned toward her right shoulder, her two thumbs were bent into the palms of her hands; a white dust veiled her eyebrows, a viscous pallor, her eyes, as if covered by a spiderweb.*

Hastily the Instructor moved away. *He came back with camphor, aromatic herbs and benzoin; a glass of chlorine to chase the miasmata away.*

Pup's *chest began heaving. The whole of her tongue protruded from her mouth; her eyes grew paler, the two globes of a lamp that is going out.* A whitish liquid began coming out of her ears, her nose, and her mouth. A lividness came over the strata with which she was tinted, from her little rotten feet right to her head, white sheet.

She was now lifeless, the poor innocent, on the amianthus sheet.

From his black jute hood the Instructor took out a little mirror. He put it in front of the festering nose: "A toy train"—he repeated caressingly—"a little toy train, Pup." And raising the cloth to her forehead, as if rolling up a sleeve, her right hand bejeweled lustfully, a spangle on her cheek, the coquettish octogenarian made a bony signal which the Master understood.

The Alterer dropped a needle.

Cobra's Instructor became silent.

From her eyelashes, piercing her upper eyelids, the horizontal wounds of her eyebrows furrowing threads of blood like broken lips, vertically striping her forehead, two big tears ran down to the clots of Cobra's hair.

The Master went to unnail Pup. *It was necessary to straighten her head a little; a mouthful of black liquids came out, like vomit.*

COBRA—I can't go on any longer. Is there much to go?

ALTERER—The stitches.

COBRA'S INSTRUCTOR—Now, Cobra, you are like the image you had of yourself.

COBRA—How am I?

Se recobra.
Se enrosca.
(La boca obra.)*

She has passed the intermediate state; she now knows she does not dream; she has incarnated: she wonders which bird.

A radiance of copper iridesces the camera obscura. A murmur of overlapping raucous vertebrae, of caudal cartilage: tiny spheres of aluminum with pellets inside.

Limpid starch or semen, a drivel makes the pillow gluey: shining filaments: Grooved, small rough tongues secrete them.

She raises herself.

Blowing and whistling.

Sinuous furrows.

Slow viscous spirals.

Overturn. Swoop. Whack.

She unfolds.

Fearful she touches herself.

She no longer knows if she's dreaming or not. She wants to drink, shout, pull off the bandages, take flight.

Mask of another gloss—lukewarm spangles—eyeglasses of other reptile scales, an iridescent band, narrow in the center, crosses the triangular head crowned by an arch of suction cups; on that vault of slobbering bulbs—his eyes half closed—a young god comes to recline, with the fatigue and serenity of one who has finished a dance: a red U which a plaster stripe crosses, vertically, marks his forehead. With the breathing of a sleeper the striated eye socket contracts and dilates; around him, followed by long white veils, little women with narrow waists and orange breasts fly; silver anklets at their feet.

She vomits a mouthful of poison.

She covers herself with copper hoops.

*She recovers./Curls around./(The mouth labors.) (Translator's Note.)

She is invaded by reddish spots like enlarged freckles, large grease stains identical to cocaine and dirt, yellow fungi of tea leaves in autumn, small Philippine fluvial fish and pus.

She curls around the red columns of a temple of the Asiatic tropics, the ankles of an ascetic, motionless on one foot, the knees and elbows of a corpse abandoned to the vultures in a tower, the neck of a Ceylonese streetwalker smeared with rice powder, the wrists of a dancing god.

She descends into a river—the fault of a rock—from the sky, among chained Fakirs, people in prayer, ducks, deer, and turtles. Toward the waters which bring her to land an elephant draws near with his offspring. On top of the pachyderm, waving, attracted by the coolness, spirits of the air.

She wants to swallow a toad.

The cartilage of her neck dilates—humid ganglionic branches, rings of soft apophysis—poreless skin: her throat expands: oval box where, the sponges of the tonsils squeezed, spurts of corrosive juices and of carbolic saliva will souse the trembling wild dove, the still drowsy hare.

Her tongue splits.

Her fangs fester: green blood.

Without further affliction than a slight fever, with a bouquet of purple tuberoses imported from Rangoon, a grapefruit juice and the medical discharge declaring her out of danger, at twilight, a Biscayan intern presented her with a circular quicksilvered glass complete with a handle.

Cobra contemplated herself at length: "Have you ever seen *Camille?*"—she asked upon handing it back.

¿Qué Tal?*

———

Into the stagnant air of the tunnel, the subway train enters slowly. Greased turning of wheels; gears glitter, the connecting rods overlapping. Vegetal fringes, cars pass in silence, without corners, their edges like lianas. Horns align aluminum edges.

The train stops now. The brittle flowers of the door locks tremble. Long twanging series, from a row of silver cubes, one by one the names of the stations sprout; the echo prolongs them in the tunnel.

Diffuse, behind steamed windows figures deep in black felt seats appear, shrunken behind newspapers. A coat, a hat with a twisted brim, a hand which traces a sign on the glass, someone who laughs, a glove, a wave, become sketched in the grey contour of the car.

The doors slide open. Two well-combed boys appear, wrapped in woolens, they jump toward the platform, feet together, looking at each other. Groping for the exit someone advances along the corridor, faceless, in the dark filtered light of quartz lamps, in the dark again, yellow.

An Indian gets off.

The loudspeakers are silent.

Cobra appears at the back of the car, standing against the tin

———

*"¿Qué tal?" meaning "How're things?" or "What's up?" is also the title of a painting by Goya, on display at the Museum of Lille. The closest to it, among his more famous paintings, is the portrait of the *Marquesa de la Solana y Condesa del Carpio,* at the Louvre. (Translator's Note.)

wall, bird nailed against a mirror. *Her makeup is violent, her mouth painted with branches. Her orbs are black and aluminum-plated, narrow beneath the eyebrows and then elongated by other whorls, powdered paint and metal, to her temples, to the base of her nose, in wide fringes and arabesques like swan's eyes, but in richer, kaleidoscope colors; instead of eyebrows, fringes of tiny precious stones hang from the rims of her eyelids. Up to her neck she is a woman; above, her body becomes a kind of heraldic animal with a baroque snout.* Behind, the curve of the partition multiplies her ceramic foliage, repetition of pale chrysanthemums.

She waits until everybody has left the car, the departure whistle. Grabbing onto twisted handrails, to nickel-plated columns which open into corollas against the ceiling, tottering on her heels, frightened, mute, she reaches the door. She flees along the platform, between the rusty rails, through narrow corridors and staircases with slippery, damp steps.

Between rails and streamers, swaying signal lights, beneath traffic lights with gray fluorescent figures—fur coats—standing on traffic islands the wearers of numbered helmets point to her; beggars laugh at her; enveloping her in their breath, drunks follow her. She walks against walls, wrapped in a black cape, covered by a cardinal's hat, crestfallen, as if she had just lost a ruby, so that, like Veronica Lake or a leper, her hair conceals her face.

On the ground clochards are sleeping on their vomit; they awake to sing an aria. On white canvas chairs, tall, exposed like mechanical dolls—little heads protected by linen hats—blind men play arias on their worm-eaten, wall-colored accordions.

The songs pursue her, and the fluted blowing of the mother-of-pearl inlaid boxes enlarged by the dark.

A filthy beggar woman, tatters strung with trinkets, comes up from behind, on tiptoe, a scream, she tears her cape. They pull off her hat. The cackling resounds in the cavern, interrupting the blind men's monotonous ballad, interrupted by the successive banging of subway doors.

She disappears among mute maps,

> Fused fluorescent tubes,
> stuck revolving doors,
> upside down arrows,

collapsing ramps,
passages with no exit,
puddled urinals,
distributors of stale pastries,
vendors of worm-eaten newspapers,
carnivorous flower stands,
cableless elevators,
telephones without lines,
drugged policemen,
crazy shoeshine boys.

//Behind the fading light sifted by shells of yellow quartz, sketched in the interval left by the grey tops of cars, the street; among branchings of iron and glass, her orange hair: Cobra with the station masters // a purple blinking neon M that is growing // near barefoot beggars—their scorched, humped feet occupy the foreground—an orange light sketches her too neatly among tatters of red cloth and bread baskets. In the dark, one can barely distinguish the profiles, the objects—a glass pitcher full of wine, a lute—the gestures // in the street.

It is night. It rains. Water striking against asphalt. Behind the rain people pass, outlines blurred; beneath the striped halo of street lights, blue rectangle, the store windows frame fruit baskets full of apples, pastry bowls dripping honey, kitchen boys with starched white caps, iron ovens where, stuffed with almonds, surrounded by laurel wreaths, whole animals revolve.

Protected by a nebulous god—the thick smoke coming out of inns—Cobra crosses the street. Behind remains the opening, in the middle of the sidewalk, its stairway sinking down, ceramic reeds that rise, fork, curve around, envelope the sign of the METRO.

The rancid vapor of the chophouses, the stench of burnt meat, sour alcohol and fat: the acid of the rain that works upon her, corrodes her.

She took shelter under the marquee of a theater. On a corner, among stucco pergolas, panels with balconies in bas-relief, gilded merlons and a gondola, there was a photomaton. Inside the machine—having drawn the black curtains the flash had worked by itself—before a mirror flashing light, she was able to register the damage: the severe scaffolding of her hairdo crumbled on all sides, the curls—vanquished springs—dripped bleach, over a forehead tripe bows fell, a large black stain rolled down from her eyes, the blue shadow emerged around her mouth.

She came out crying.

A little boy stared at her.

An old man remembered Theda Bara.

A cat followed her.

A Portuguese bricklayer inhaled her perfume.

Radiating a neon daylight, the transparent cubes of show windows advanced at intervals over the sidewalks. Inside them, inserted into the fixed scenery, in the darkened theaters of their rooms, whores lay naked among purple cushions, on lynx skins, cuddled in vast wicker chairs whose backs formed a circle of Moorish stars around their heads; paper flowers, bottles of crème de menthe, Danish magazines and small monkeys surrounded them. Their servants—Jamaican eunuchs—rubbed the dampened glass of the windows with flannel; the sailors knocked from the outside with their knuckles.

They were the ones who saw Cobra.

People started crowding around her.

They followed me.

They harassed me.

They chased me up against a wall.

Black spangles on her cheeks, lustful rings on her fingers, dart of jewels on the grey-haired pompon, from the group emerged a grease-painted octogenarian. She strutted near, singing, with a nasal twang, in falsetto: "¿Qué tal?"—she asked, imitating me.

Her bony forefinger very close to my lips, she shouted: "It's him."

Part II

The Initiation

He had wandered along the street of show windows—among purple cushions, on lynx skins, cuddled in vast wicker chairs whose backs formed a circle of Moorish stars around their heads, whores lay naked—sipping anise in old bars, beside flower-belled gramophones.

Not daring to enter, he had passed near the little door, beneath the wrought iron insignia—a coach.

DRUGSTORE

He saw himself in a mirror, surrounded by a drawerful of disheveled scarves, a plastic sphere filled with water—in the back, bubbles, several watches—ties with golden branches and another mirror, where he appeared backwards. It caught the image of his hand among the fabrics—attentive to the saleslady's movements—opening the buttons of his jacket, stuffing the black scarf inside, against his chest. He leafed through a magazine. He was sweating. He turned around absent-mindedly, leisurely. He smoothed his hair, with his knuckles he caressed his beard, he adjusted his belt, dusted the chamois leather of his boots. Little by little he pulled out the wool band. He ripped off the price tag. He tied the scarf around his neck. A black sash girded his chest, the other fell from his shoulder to his waist: the saint of a Ravennese mosaic, phylactery of black stones.

He bought a newspaper. He unfolded it, leaning against a column which open hands engulfing celluloid globes joined to the ceiling. Oval shields with eyes and lips for coats-of-arms hung from the walls; on curved-legged tables silver muses danced: the trains of their gowns were flower vases, and their heads, decorated with butterflies, lamp fixtures.

copenhagen   *brussels*   *amsterdam**

Outside, beneath palms of an acrylic green, a mulatto woman dances. Over the sand, orange light; kites over the black bands of the sidewalk.

appel   *aleschinsky*   *corneille*   *jorn**

He put the newspaper, folded, on a pile of magazines. He picked it up again taking one.

Undulating corridor of mirrors.

poisonous snake of India*

Plexiglas flowers open. The same record in English begins again. Vinyl circles overlap. Hum of Japanese movie cameras. Double images. Reflection of symmetry. Multiplication of reflection. Repeated photographs, overexposed. On the whiteness of a book cover, a porcelain head covered with black ideograms. Volumes of Bakelite. Intersection of edges. He knew he was going to find them.

he receives his wages in the paymaster's office.*

Empty sequences.

IN THE BAR

Now he moved along the corridor, over a black carpet which hid a net of tigers and white letters. Almost without realizing, he had opened the little wooden door. He felt his own breathing, his footsteps, the arches of his feet light upon the tapestry, heel to

---

*Anagrams and synonyms (or hypographs) for COBRA: 1) COpenhagen BRussels Amsterdam; 2) appel aleschinsky, etc., a school of artists centered in these three cities, known as the COBRA group; 3) poisonous snake of India = Cobra; 4) he receives his wages in the paymaster's office = the verb *cobrar* and thus cobra, third person singular conjugation of this verb. Cobra is also the name of a singer who died in a plane crash over Fujiyama, and the name of a motorcycle gang that frequented St. Germain des Près. (Translator's Note.)

toe. Near the animals, smearing the white of the letters, the traces of his steps were caught for a moment, in the tangles.

At the end of the corridor, in a corner which received the diagonal precision of the bar, in front of a black chalk drawing projected upon the back wall, TUNDRA appeared. As he moved, black lines fled across his face, across the edges of his body. *A-13470, Los Angeles, Calif. USA. Good-looking man of 33, height 5'10" (photo and particulars available); interested in meeting a good-looking, well-built, education-minded, dominant male, possible motorcycle-type leather fan. Photo and sincerity appreciated (and if in L.A. area, a phone number).* Cracked black leather. His dirty, straight hair fell in tangles to his shoulders. *A-13486, New York, N.Y. USA. Handsome male of 30, of docile nature, well-built, wishes to meet or correspond with boot-wearing men interested in the subject of discipline, levis, boots, belts, leather clothing, uniforms of all types: would like to meet and correspond by letter or tape with dominant men interested in these subjects.* At his waist, welded to a chain of forged links, a tin rosette. *A-13495, Vancouver, B.C. Gentleman of 40, of dominant nature, very sincere and understanding, with varied interests, would like to meet slim man between 20 and 45, not over 5'8" tall, of docile nature and interested in the subject of discipline. Also would like to hear from "Foot Adorer" in issue of November 25th.*

"We were waiting for you." —And he turned around. He wore his name on his back, tattooed in the leather, dull black upon the shiny black of the hide.

In the drawing projected on the wall two men were fighting. Or not. The blanks formed other figures: the same men jumped toward each other, but to embrace, naked.

"It's a good thing you came. Today's the day. Because to be a leader you have to pass through submission, to gain power you have to lose it, to command you have to first lower yourself as far as we want: to the point of nausea."

SCORPION wore around his neck a funeral amulet: in its middle circle, protected by two pieces of cut glass, surrounded by amber beads, little porous bones with filed edges were heaped—baby teeth, bird cartilage—bound by a silk hatband, lettered in black ink and Gothic capitals with German names.

On his wrists, eagles with blue dots. His boots, untied.

/Bleeding skeletons stick to caryatids. Burning bodies. Ashes. White mausoleum. Shrouded in brocades and coarse jewels, toward the towers they escort the dead infant.

From TOTEM's coat dangled little bronze cymbals, bells with broken clappers, dented cowbells, Mexican jingles. His straight eyebrows were joined, his high cheekbones, yellow. Torn pants, mended with patches; in the pockets penknives and glass; from a sweater tied to his waist, sleeves hung down to his knees. A rattling of junk, the rusty creaking which announces a row between Chinese shadows, the apparition of a devil in the Indonesian theater, the tumble of a monkey acrobat, measured his gestures.

/Sudanese soldier. Abyssinian water carrier. Horse rider from Ethiopia. Pitch-black body, smooth and shiny, grape-colored pupils. He drinks from an ox horn and pours over his genitals an opaque and acidulated mead. Face down, he rubs his tense frenum—*masenko* fiddle string—his bulbous, purple glans against a buckskin stained by cum. He turns around. Starchy puddle on his belly. Laughter. A little twangy song. Eating sorghum bread. In the corners of his mouth, and of his eyelids, the sign of monsters.

Behind shelves of bottles, opaque screens, and the curves of Turkish tools, a light filtered by algae emerges from the bottom of the aquarium which occupies an entire wall of the bar; slow shadows—vibrations of tiny wings—blur that neon daylight submerged among stones and white polystyrene coral, beneath motionless sea horses of fluorescent glass and lily-white rustproof flowers, always open.

In front of the light which gushes from the water, where the shadows of fish are black butterflies, TIGER dances, smokes, hits himself, inhales again, impelled by the kif he jumps, bursting Tibetan necklaces, diagonally into mid-air. Now he runs circles around me, looking at me. Underwater transparency. Looking at me. Hothouse light. I revolve too. Glass on the floor. Looking at each other. He bangs on the glass of the fish tank with open hands. Slow, flat, lanceolated animals, open symmetrical leaves with tenuous nerves, hurry back and forth. Streaked with mercury. Mayan faces. Their glowing orange flagelli follow, entangle them.

I am smoking. The weed is blowing through my ears. I am running circles around them. Looking at them. They are revolving too. A glass breaks.

/Behind the bar three naked women appear, gilded.
The fish have clouded it all.
Behind the wall zebras are fleeing.

TUNDRA: "We will assign you an animal. You will repeat his name. La boca obra."

SCORPION: "So that you'll see that I am not me, that one's body is not one's own, that the things that make us and the forces which put them together are passing fancies"—and he cuts the palm of his hand with glass, then rubs it against his face; he sucks his blood (laughing).

/The burning bodies, blue corpses burnt to ashes, brimstone feet and eyes shrouded with mushrooms, fall into the white, still river. Into the river, somersaulting in the air; into the still water the cremated, the leprous fall. Among gurus who pray, gods who give out rotten oranges, and children who beg, bones in flames fly over the astrologer's choir loft, into the water that doesn't move, and also rotting genitals, corroded faces, slashed hands: blood clots. Along the banks, flames, the cries of gongs, the night.

TOTEM paints on his chest, over his heart, a heart. He dances and smears himself with scarlet. A snake shines phosphorescently on him, curled around his phallus. Its soft head sticks on to the glans. Sharp, dripping cum, the little tongue penetrates.

TIGER: "In a dream I saw myself walking past a tent crowded with boots, shoes, mountings and buckled straps, but those objects were not made like ours, and their material, instead of leather, seemed like dry and sticky blood. I told it to the Instructor: 'A total absurdity,' he said to me. Later, when I saw them, I understood that they were objects that westerners use."

And he bangs on the fish tank again. And to the puzzled bartender: "What's the matter? Don't you like it? Do you want me to say a word, a syllable and turn you into a bird? Do you want me to conjure up five thousand minor demons right this minute, to prick you, to poison your precious body fluids? Make me a gin and tonic."

/Behind the aquarium—black stripes ripple when the water moves, through the white, fish glide—zebras continue rushing. Chessboard loins. Viera da Silva loins. Parallel bands spread behind the glass, skulls, necks which cross, tails, manes which open in slow motion, lips discharge strings of silvery drool which dash against the glass; parallel bands which shrink, seen in a concave mirror. The galloping sound, muffled by sand, by water, mixes with the percussion of the orchestra; its rhythm is the banging on the fish bowl. The zebras leap in files, at regular intervals, a file of black zebras striped white, a file of white zebras striped black; they reach the top—the height of the water—they fall, front legs bent, they rise and flee in disorder while another file behind the glass rises, flies.

On another wall in the bar, in black and yellow dots, a blonde cries—her tears are enormous—; in a bubble, gushing from her lips, the words *"That's the way it should have begun! but it's hopeless!"*

We went out.

Everything had changed.

The corridor was white.

On the floor, skull-goblets, femur-flutes, striped scepters, swastikas, wheels, were arranged in an indecipherable order among cubes of a rainbow-hued glass.

The street door opened automatically.

We could barely stand the night's glare, the noises reverberated in our heads. The motorcycles were lying on the sidewalk. It was raining. In the square one could hear the guitar-strumming of the inns, far-off. At the subway entrance a frightened woman appeared. She was wearing a red hat; its ribbons, falling from the brim to her black cape, hid the gold flowers on her face. Her makeup was violent, her mouth painted with branches. Her orbs were black and aluminum-plated, narrow beneath the eyebrows and then elongated by other whorls, powdered paint and metal, to her temples, to the eyes, but in richer, kaleidoscope colors; instead of eyebrows, fringes of tiny precious stones hung from the rims of her eyelids. Up to her neck she was a woman; above, her body became a kind of heraldic animal with a baroque snout.

We're moving now—in the suburban silence the rumble of motors; over yellow bands, black flashes—on our motorcycles, at full speed. No hands, we shut our eyes, we pass—an alarm bell—under the barriers. Zigzag between crossing locomotives: from open train windows handkerchiefs come out, straw hats pulled by wind, a girl shouting. Our wheels don't touch the ground; on the asphalt arrows pass, in enlarged letters, names of cities, numbers.

TUNDRA repeats a formula, flings a bottle which breaks against the pavement: green spot; SCORPION accelerates, takes off his helmet: "the skull is a casket: let my brains spill over the road!"; TOTEM hugs him by the waist, braces his head against his back, TIGER opens a hand and in the air a strip of sulphurous powder remains, spreading, unfolding; orange strata, fluorescent cumulus clouds: chemical twilight. We take off, yeah, we rise, higher, higher: we are flying!

Sounding sirens, in pursuers with ultraviolet headlights, with poisoned arrows and crossbows, bottles of bacteria and ballistas, the greenish agents of the orgy patrol follow us—monstrous syringes—waving night-sticks of war, miniature lasers in each cavity, macromolecules in their ears.

We turn at every corner,
we blow up the bridges behind us,
we turn traffic signs around,
we spray nails and blazing phosphorus,
we make traffic lights red.
Thrice do we paint the raging sea.
With the triptych we close off the street.

To urge them to turn back, TUNDRA delivers a speech to the pursuers. He translates it into every language alive and dead: when he's going through Sanskrit they respond with a tactical atom bomb: the BOOM makes the earth quake.

SCORPION blocks their way with pyramids of skeletons which stir and creak like crabs; he shows them, on a magnificent neck chain, their heads spitting coins.

TOTEM writes on a kite: FATE L'AMORE NELLA GUERRA and flies it high; from the tail condoms and bells fall.

"Stop!"—TIGER shouts—"or I'll stamp my foot three times and make an army of gigantic cats rise up and charge against you!"

And he stamps his foot three times: out of season and place, flowers sprout everywhere: sandalwoods and white lilies bud on the enemy motorcycles; gardenias on the handlebars, white orchids on the exhaust pipes and big sunflowers which paralyze them by becoming entangled in the wheels. The foliage covers the cops, remains of petrified pursuers; the weapons have been caught in creeping ivy, taken, hooked in the green tangles. The vice squad, in its frozenness, is already a snapshot, a photostat copy of the primitive squad, a wax museum, a gathering of cardboard demons, the abandoned props of a cheap circus which are disappearing among the weeds, in the dust, into the ground, which no one remembers and are only visible by the darkest green of their shadows, in certain aerial shots, taken at twilight and after the snow.

THE RUINS

The archaeologists studied them by deciphering the shadows, believing they were from a Roman theater.

Others suggested an Indian observatory with its hourglasses, sundials, telescopes, celestial charts, and astronomers viewing Orion, draped in a tapestry of fossil shells—proof that the sea had once invaded it and that in another era it had been embalmed in a river of lava.

They dug them up.

With the weapons they founded an arms museum.

They filmed them in Cinerama.

Planeta devoted an issue to them.

Coco Chanel engaged them for her winter fashion show.

From everywhere tourist caravans stream.

Straddling the sergeant's head, a little boy eats a strawberry ice cream cone.

PRAISE AND GLORY TO THE VICTORS
TO TUNDRA

Your locks are golden and around your body an orange halo
glows; you sleep upon the tree of Rhetoric: your voice is the unit
of all sound, your body, which rocks the leafy treetop, is the stan-
dard of human form: your height is exactly eight times your head,
your eyes are perfect ovals and around your navel a circle defines
the curve of your hips, the Gothic arch of your thorax, and the
implantation of hairs in the hollow of your pubis;
at your footstep one hears music of the five-tone scale, the trees
bend to give you shade;
you walk leisurely.
By the way you moved your right foot I knew you were a god.

TO SCORPION

To the gems, pastries, and toys with which we have filled your
barge, we add new offerings. To favor your voyage, close to your
body, which the damp adorns with tiny flowers and which is
cloaked, from your feet up, by lichen veils, we place an ibis, a
pineapple, several coins and a chart of the river, a stone fallen
from the moon, another which will make you dream, and another, yellow like lynx urine, which will be clear or cloudy depending on whether you are happy or sad.
We know you will return.
We shall wait for you in the murmur of the night that precedes
the river's flow.
Our emblem shall be the bird you become.
You are the jaguar that springs toward the summer sky and turns
into a constellation.
We lick the pus, the wax from your feet.

TO TOTEM

Your phallus is the largest and on it, as upon the leaves of a sacred
tree of Tibet, all of the Buddhist precepts are written. Without
having been ciphered by anyone, starting in spiral formation from

the orifice, the signs of every possible science are inscribed around the head. Your buttocks are two perfect halves of a sphere; we come to trace purple and gold concentric circles upon them, and to pour ointments over your hands.
Look at us.
We have covered your bed with striped orchids,
the chamber with Persian tapestries, pillboxes, fruits, and astrolabes. So that you come to inhabit them with your laughter.

TO TIGER

Your mother bore you beneath a tree: from her belly you leapt to the ground; where you fell a giant lotus flower, of every color, burst forth.
You pronounced a name:
on your left and on your right two cascades spouted, one of cold water and one of hot; four gods descended to shower you.
Your name, recorded on an aerolite.
You enter the water without wetting yourself, the fire without burning yourself; you walk over clouds and mist.
At the passing of your horse the forest opens.
Sacred monkeys, elephants, and disciples follow you in caravan.
If you command
a rain of stars will fall at once over the earth.

THE PARK

Over the tiles of a poplar grove the motorcycles glide, between gazebos cracked by dog-chewed mint sticks, dry roots. (Through the crevices white lizards slip away.) We accelerate, we brake suddenly: skid, capsize, rapid hoops of mud. Bellflowers close, the dark green tangles around broken capitals, unfinished marble heads, upside down on the ground, tremble. Armadillos curl up beside the whorls; frightened hares flee through stone ducts. From left to right. From right to left. We circle a dry fountain until we're dizzy. We urinate in the mouths of dolphins: the porous stone drinks the yellow stream they vomit, foaming drivel.

We strip a small wood of willow trees.

We rain pebbles upon a ridge.

The park: a burning embankment, beneath the humus.

Pollen in flames. Black grass.

Ashes consume the last branches.

Plain razed by night beasts to sea level, cyclone, napalm.

Over the white even surface, fossil flowers.

We continue toward the outskirts. Identical avenues. On either side unfinished Gothic castles of reinforced concrete pass, a second before collapsing—in the oval windows, ladies of stone—churchless towers whose electric bells toll the Angelus, gas stations, lamp stores, parallel lines of blinking yellow lights, smoked glass crematories. Under the silver-plated signs of Esso and dripping oil tanks, sitting on the ground among wax mannikins, families spread flowered blankets over the mustard grass. "A nice day!"—they comment with their walkie-talkies—they open Coca-Colas and cans of herring.

Naves lie at ground level, the neon brilliance of hothouses.

A dam.

An antelope crosses the highway.

We are going into a forest.

We have left the motorcycles and are walking along a narrow path, sheltered by dry branches. In the distance, the hum of the highway. On the ground, among black feathers and snake scales, mixed with pebbles, perforated, drooling eggs break against the palisaded sides as we pass; biting the rushes, bathing them with their thick saliva—blurred pupils—iguanas, fierce chameleons watch us; in the brush, snakes battle: we hear panting, overturnings in the hay, torn membranes, creaking cartilage, splitting fangs; we hear cooings, seeds rupturing, cottony flowers opening, sap rising, buds sprouting. We hear our breathing, the murmur of the night, the wind.

I am afraid.

We come to a clearing.

Silence. Laughter. A bird passes.

TUNDRA: "Now you pass over to the other side: Look." —And he opened a box in front of his face.

A drooling animal jumped on me, with cold paws, his toes stuck to my cheeks, like suction cups.

The jack-in-the-box jumped on him, sounding its toy croaker. Out of the box came springs, a stream of water, a little key from one of the frog's legs. SCORPION wound it up again. TOTEM wet his lips with beer, helped him undress. With open arms and an unraveling skein of hemp rope placed on his right arm like a bracelet, TIGER started to run around him.

Tied to a tree.

Triangles of bindings on his chest.

Two bloodied furrows swelled his knees and fists, cut into his ankles.

They stepped back to look at him.

"Not bad"—said TUNDRA. "Set the camera."

Flash: icon lacerated by infidels // white fang mask against the white fungi of the tree // ashen actor who bends under the weight of his ornaments and falls over a drum // plaster death mask; conjurings in green ink.

SCORPION: "On your guts, on your rotting liver enormous pale butterflies will come to rest."

TOTEM: "You will drink of my blood"—and he poured a bottle of ketchup over him—; "of my cum"—and he opened a container of yogurt over his head.

TIGER: "I am going to blind you"—a flash, in his eyes.

It wasn't Indian music. It was the Beatles.

It was Ravi Shankar. The tabla served as background for a Shell commercial. TUNDRA repeated yawning, "You have gone through submission, you have lost power," etc. Another raga followed the pause that refreshes.

SCORPION: "Now what, do we kill him?"

TOTEM: "He has to be fucked."

TIGER: "No. Let him loose. He's to get dressed now."

TUNDRA: "He needs a name."

SCORPION untied him pulling the bindings to break them, cutting them with a knife against the skin. TOTEM took his hand and put it on his penis. He wet his index finger with saliva and caressed his lips. He blew into his ear. TIGER stirred a mill of noon prayers.

TUNDRA dipped the paint brushes.

SCORPION sketched on the back of his jacket a vertical arch which opened in the hide, dripping, soaked in by the plush, writhing like a mangled snake.

TOTEM, who slept among the stones—drunken god upon a miniature landscape—jumped up: with a single stroke, expert penman with an angular style, he drew the circle of Divination, twisted over itself and edgeless, the perfect hoop. With a stone seal TIGER stamped beside the circle a square mark: BR. TUNDRA branded into his shoulder an A.

SCORPION: "Cobra?"

TOTEM: "Cobra: so that he will poison. So that he will strangle. So that he will curl around his victims and suffocate them. So that his breath will hypnotize and his eyes will shine in the night, monstrous, golden."

TIGER: "So that he will ooze and blend with the stones. And bite ankles. And with a whack of his sharp scales, strike."

COBRA: "What now?"

TUNDRA: "Nothing."

We took the road back.

The scenery had changed. Through the fog one could see pines, cypresses, and winter plumtrees. We went along a ravine. One of the walls fell vertically, carved, neat like a screen; strains of different sands crossed it—still waves—so polished and shiny that we were reflected in them. The stone corridor echoed our voices, our footsteps on the wet grass, deformed and opaque like the images on the wall.

The opposite slope was not as steep; from its crevices wild olive trees sprouted—*ilex pedunculosa*—whose branches descended to the ground, arborescent peony flowers, lianas and ferns. Among the pebbles dwarf fig trees grew—*ficus pumila*. On the ridge, frost covered a forest of willow trees whose threads, along with those of the frozen water, fell from the summits, cascade of fibers. Among colorless and dry rushes cranes perched; the fluttering of their wings shielded our path. As we advanced the murmur of the water grew louder.

From the highest clefts, skimming the rocks, hemp ropes with baskets tied to their tips were lowered. In those crevices, marked in the cliff by palisades of hay, Buddhist monks lived, naked and alone, mute examiners of the void. The birds knew them and made their nests nearby; hovering around and chirping they guided the few pilgrims, who brought tea and barley meal, to the hampers below the hermits' refuge.

In a corner of the wall *there were several peasant boys who were looking for mushrooms in the grass. They laughed at us, as if surprised at seeing so many strangers in that place.*

We went along a frozen river the hermits always crossed on a blue buffalo when retiring from the world.

Following its winding and ever wider course, covered by white stones, angular and smooth like the vertebrae of prehistoric reptiles, we came upon a meager grotto where the water stopped, crystal-clear; in the white sand at the bottom a dark red grass grew.

The ravine came out onto a misty landscape, of white planes evaporating toward the horizon, where a band of moisture floated over a lake. Milky trunks. Long silvery leaves. Further on, a frail bridge, a small boat. White on white, a bamboo forest. The towers of a monastery.

As we went into the mist we discovered forms, colors appeared. In their burrows—velvety spheres, peaches—startled, ready to roll into a ball, armadillos hid. Among nearby branches, unable to keep their balance, pheasants flew before us, burdened with ornaments, slow in the thickness of the air. Noise among the rushes: it was a fleeing tiger, orange-striped and covered with black marks.

Making our way among the stalks which surrounded us by the thousands, road to the towers, we came upon a stone wall whose junctures were split by bramble-bush. We followed it until we found an opening: a winding road, passing over a bridge in the form of an arch, led to the door of the monastery crowned by a vignette of sealing wax with the inscription "Salut les copains!"

As we opened the door, the face of Buddha appeared before our eyes. His gold colors combined their reflections with those of the green clusters which gave him shade. The steps of a stone staircase and the base of pillars were covered with a moss smooth like cloth. From the back of the great room another staircase began, vertical like a wall, protected by a stone balustrade. This led to a terrace, facing the west: from here we saw an enormous rock more than twenty feet high, in the shape of a loaf of bread. A thin belt of bamboo decorated the base. Continuing to the west and then turning toward the north we went up a slanting corridor leading to the reception room, which consisted of three transoms and faced directly onto the great rock. At the foot of the rock was a fountain in the shape of a half-moon covered by thick bunches of a kind of watercress and fed by water from a spring. The sanctuary, properly speaking, was to the east of the reception room. It was dark and in ruins. A dark green coating, which at certain intervals thickened into yellowish, granular islands with white borders, shrouded the floor. A grey fuzz covered the stone of three of the walls; from the corners, filled with goiters of dark pulp, minute, purple flowers proliferated. Rust signs which seemed sketched in saffron striped the ceiling; drops hanging from these spots lingered a while, and finally fell to the green mold with a dry sound. In the center of the room were the ruins of the altar. The bas-relief of the foundation—a god dancing within a hoop of fire, upon a dwarfish devil; with one of his right hands (a cobra curled around the wrist) the dancer shook a tambourine, with one of his left he raised a torch—it was a nest of mollusks. On the crown mushrooms grew.

A large window sealed by great leaves in the shape of broken circles, like water lilies, filtered a whitish light; beside the window, along the wall, there lay a pond dug into the floor, also carpeted with moss. Swollen white roots were fixed to the bottom, with bony, shiny nodes injected with wine-colored veins.

Joining hands—we could barely walk on the slippery floor— we managed to draw near to the pond. The water was muddy, and in the shadow of the roots, duplicated by the reflection, ivory though deformed symmetries, lethargic and bulbous like the roots, slow fish traveled in a vegetal slumber, wrapped in jelly-like veils, in a tangle of fibers. They let themselves be touched. They did not flee.

We were leaving when TIGER slipped headlong into the pond. He banged the bottom with open hands. Slow, flat, lanceolated animals, open symmetrical leaves with tenuous nerves, hurry back and forth. Streaked with mercury. Mayan faces. Their glowing orange flagelli followed, entangled them.

We helped him up.

It was then that at the door, as if popped by a spring, a monk of the red hat sect appeared: "Do you want me to say a word, a syllable"—he threatened, with clenched fists, frowning—"and turn you into a bird? Do you want me to conjure up five thousand minor demons right this minute, to prick you, to poison your precious body fluids?"

"Make me a gin and tonic"—TIGER answered.

Eat Flowers!

I

Petals, filaments (Left foot over the right thigh.) : the body is inscribed in a net. (Right foot over the left thigh.) Six flowers mark the middle line. (I cross my arms behind my back.) From the flowers and in all directions forking, interweaving threads branch outward. (I grasp my left heel with the right hand; my right heel with the left.) The man is opaque; the skein is golden. (I lower my head; chin against my chest.) A dark fringe, a continuous black line borders the figure, which glowing fibers cross. Every one of his gestures, no matter how sudden or slight, reverberates in the entire texture, like the fright of a fish in its flagelli.

Wrapping myself around myself—ball of yarn, vulva—elbows against my stomach.

The room is white.

Black objects rush toward the walls, attracted by an external gravity.

The floor slopes.

The walls dilate.

The body, motionless, falls.

I was in a creaking enclosure, built upon rushes, over a cliff. It was raining. Below, among the rocks, a wooden building stood in darkness, at ground level, and beyond, a quiet river, meandering among feeble structures resembling fishermen's huts, burrowed a valley. Ribbons of foam crowned the rocks. At sea level and toward the woods, symmetrical paths became blurred as the vegetation, meager and scarce on the banks, thickened; later on the paths reappeared, sinuous, pursued by mule-drivers, border-ing slopes and peaks. At certain distances, successive waterfalls cleaved the landscape vertically, just like the grain of the paper does to the surface which unfolds from a roll.

Next to my cell's window, obstructed by a few chopped tree trunks, three enormous nests made of voluminous fibers hung from dry lianas.

On the other slope, less rocky and inclined, enveloped by sev-eral layers of humidity, ribbons of varying whites, one could see a pine forest.

Along with the sound of rain, I heard in the distance a con-stant, grave murmur, the uniform repetition of a single syllable; I heard the unceasing rotation of prayer mills, rattling of flustered children.

> Bull aboard
> a small boat
> down river
> across the rain of night.

The room is charred.

White objects come toward the center, toward the exact cross-ing of its diagonals, and there they remain suspended.

I bring my head down to my knees.

I slowly revolve upon myself.

Within a rolling barrel.

Sitting on a giant peacock—the bird's open tail formed a third halo, behind the red one which surrounded the triple head, and the amber one in which his entire body was inserted—a yellow god appeared. His middle face was calm; on the lateral ones, pro-truding fangs, irritated and globular eyes, nostrils fuming smoke. The middle hands together in prayer; the others brandished darts and daggers, bows and arrows. A vertical forefinger pointed to-ward heaven.

His opal jewels, the settings of which were repeated from the crown to the wide armlets and from there to the bracelets and rings, filled the room with an orange radiance.

On a wicker armchair, attracted, lethargized by that light, in slow flight a pheasant came to perch.

The king smiles, displays his weapons.

The peacock's claws, streaked with chalk, hold fast to the sand; the bird raises its sharp, ebony head.

The room is white / is charred / is white.

Wrapping myself around myself, elbows against my stomach. I await—has it happened already?—the crash, the white blackout, blindness, a second grasped only by the languor of memory.

Thick glass, sand falling, cracking clay.

Silence. Headlights in the distance.

Yellow plain that is crossed by the runway.

Discontinuous, a stripe vanishes into the horizon.

Arrows. The wind sketches and erases terraces upon the sand, strokes that go back and forth; breaches appear on the edges, darker palisades, sparking walls that wind like snakes. That stiff swelling wave—shrouded dunes, shuffled planes—covers the highway, blackens the gigantic yellow arrows which curve to the right and signal the name of a city—we walk over the letters—a cipher.

Wrapping myself around myself.

On this side of the fractures, on this side of the grooved screen, the body, motionless, falls.

SCORPION: He shakes his lion's mane, breaks a golden Tibetan necklace, takes out his phallus and pisses: "We had danced till dawn, they'd made us go round and round—the music just wouldn't stop, the hoarse howlers—; already we were drinking out of mugs without handles, the ones you hold with open hands, we were covered with the beads the musicians gave us and were smoking with them, too. Only then did we discover what their instruments were: the flutes: hollowed skin-bones; the loose, rotten teeth that hung in their alveoli resounded in their skulls; the skin that covered the drums was tattooed—blue dots— with eagles. Deathly party: we were dancing with the ugliest girl."

The shaved heads laughed, ran away—we lammed into them—their bones still resounding. Orange cloaks floated like flags.

I trampled on the instruments. Spat on them. I kicked holes into the skulls of the tambourines, went crazy on top of them and threw to the floor the funeral amulets in which, surrounded by amber beads, protected by two pieces of cut glass, little porous bones were heaped—baby teeth, bird cartilage—; I sprayed them with my cum.

A metal disk was left among the broken apophyses, a snail-shell among thorns; with his crest he flattened jingle bells, bone splinters.

TOTEM: "We masturbated: TIGER and TUNDRA; SCORPION and I. Each one came alone. Nobody touched the other guy's cum. We didn't look at each other."

TIGER: "It's snowing. I tell you it's snowing"—the first flakes fall immediately.

Like aluminum, in the distance, the lakes. Covered bridges go over them. On the shores, austere fortress towers, cedar palaces, tall dovecotes amidst cherry orchards, ruins of synagogues, truncated minarets.

"It's so cold in this country that not even the tea spills over!"

Checkered, identical compartments go by, regularly lighted by neon tubes, skyscrapers are separated by frozen canals, treeless avenues, aerial rails, superimposed turnpike loops.

On a magazine cover, TUNDRA appears on a motorscooter, seated like a yogi. The white smoke that comes out of the exhaust pipe forms a third halo behind the red one—a spotlight—which surround the head, and behind the silver halo—aluminum cylinders—in which his entire, nude body is inserted.

TO SCORPION

Afterwards, we shall read your bones.
With a burning metal rod we shall touch each shoulderblade:
on the fractures, omens.
With black ink
we shall write messages to your descendants on your skeleton,
your engraved frame will serve as our herald:

ciphers, dates, whom we were,
the age that befell us to live in.
Afterwards, we shall protect everything with lacquer.

TO TOTEM

Not the empty nets
but rather the support of all forms:
you wanted love—the dissolution—
Diamond's body.

You didn't know what you were asking for,
what ceremony you entered:
you invoked, you demanded
—the masters tried to discourage you—
you stopped drinking and eating
until, naturally, something possessed you.
You had convulsions,
you rolled on the floor, as if overcome by some poison;
bundle of discordant gestures, your body was escaping you,
you did somersaults,
you played a sitar that nobody saw.

What were you dancing?
Whom were you addressing,
disjointed pantomime, dispersed gestures?
What demon did you embody in an aphasic opera?

You were impervious to pain, to human presence.
You crawled over red hot steel sheets.
You slashed your skin with them,
and then,
lest you would ever repeat what you had seen,
you cut your own tongue from its root,
and threw it, in a stream of blood, among burning coals.
The ashes were gathered.
With petal ashes and honey we drank them.

Now,
dumb and mute,
in your limbo
—love is intolerable—
they keep you in a sanctuary, monster of public concern,
amidst incense burners, prayer mills,
red porcelain bull-dogs and great golden gongs
which the servants pound as you pass.

Fed daily with wild doves
—fed daily with butterflies—
bathed and dried daily
upon ladders according to their rank
the thousand prescribed snakes
which defend your abode
sleep in the whorls of altars
in the moldings of furniture
in drawers and in ritual cups,
and nest in your sleeves and hats
—at night you can hear them curling into knots,
searching for the moisture of the trees—.

There will you remain until your death
among statues and stupas
—God is intolerable—.
Until your death is paid by the State
—perhaps love is that—.
Taxes must be good for something.

TO TIGER

In the autumn you would come out of the forest
of the western highland
and raze the plain
—the constellations of the quadrant
rose in the night sky—.
You were white.
You had firm legs, excellent thighs,

that looked like elephant trunks; similar
and fleshy were
your knees.
You possessed all the signs:
your thick eyebrows were joined, and between them,
scarred, a circle.
You displayed the cranial protuberance.
Your neck was marked by three creases,
like a snail-shell:
When I saw you, I knew you were a god.

Like stars, men rise and fall.
Your guards will be of no use
of no use your flying horses.
All yin comes out in winter.
You can invoke.
You can conjure.
You will burn.

TO TUNDRA

Draw on your chest the dragons fighting.
Take care in your performance.
Watch out for the details.
Do not use either a hog's bristle brush
nor one of rabbit hair;
try the softest: mouse whiskers or children's hair.
The flaming heads will form a face:
The crests of the monsters will sketch the eyebrows,
the claws a smiling mouth.
Do not rush.
Do not squander.
Use black ink as though it were gold.
Invoke upon awakening.
Meditate each line.
Because you will see death with those very eyes.
After the report of gunfire: dirt in your eyes.
Headlights turned on at midday.

The air of hospitals,
of the dying and of white robes.
Of one who among forceps and red cotton,
pustules and screams
headbands and shrouds
stagnates, dense: I breathe.

On a green table, as narrow as a scaffold, head reclined on a stake, a gaping and toothless young man lay, his abdomen empty, his eyes swollen, small spheres divided by black grooves.

Next to the stretched body stood four girls equally grey and combed, wearing enormous lace hats punctuated by yellow flowers. One of them had folded down the wide brim of her hat—only her mouth could be seen; another had turned hers up and showed her face, proudly.

A chubby one, smaller than the previous two, holding on to a blue muslin embroidered with scales from a discarded snakeskin, was opening her mouth under her disproportionate pink algae hat, resting her chin on an open hand, and her elbow on the body.

Another girl was coming out of the basement. She was not covered by a hat, but rather, of course, by an open umbrella.

Useless are the skills of dissection,
the formaldehyded gloves,
the cough of the coroners,
the cotton balls in the mouth.
Useless are the exact pins of the shroud.
Cartesian, the dead always remain
looking
at their feet.

Our traveling companions were Mongols from the kingdom of Khartchin, who were repairing in pilgrimage to the Eternal Sanctuary; and who had with them their Grand Chaberon; that is to say, a Living Buddha, the superior of their Lamasery. The Chaberon was a young man of eighteen, whose manners were agreeable and gentlemanly, and whose face, full of ingenious candor, contrasted singularly with the part which he was constrained to enact. At the age of five he had been declared Buddha and Grand Lama of the Buddhists of Khartchin, and he was now about to pass a few years in one of the Grand Lamaseries of Lha-Ssa, in the study of prayers and of the other knowledge befitting his dignity. A brother of the King of Khartchin and several Lamas of quality were in attendance to escort and wait upon him.

. . . after following for several days a long series of valleys in which, at certain distances, black tents and great herds of buffaloes appeared, at last we camped near a great Tibetan village.

. . . it was not, however, a village properly speaking, but rather, one of several ample farms well-finished in terrazo, finely painted with whitewash. These were surrounded by great trees and crowned by a small tower in the shape of a dovecote where flags, of all colors and covered with Tibetan sentences, floated.

. . . shortly before arriving at the base of the mountain, the whole caravan halted on a level spot where there stood an Obo, or Buddhic monument, built with piled stones, surmounted by flags and bones covered with inscriptions.

. . . we bent over the edge of the plateau and saw beneath us an immense glacier jutting out tremendously, and bordered with frightful precipices. We could distinguish, under the light coating of snow, the greenish hue of ice. We took a stone from the Buddhic monument and threw it down the glacier. A loud noise was heard, and the stone, gliding down rapidly, left after it a broad green line.

. . . the flames were consuming the dry grass in their path with such fearful speed that they soon reached our camels. Their long thick manes were burning. We ran to them armed with our felt carpets, endeavoring to smother the flaming bodies.

Men and birds have their place here (I imagine concentric squares); stars and their orbits, the snows, blind stones, and those that support a temple, everything here will come to contemplate its own identity, everything will climb to its own center. (Those black lines support my thought, its diagram structures and clarifies it, it does not escape from that framework.) From the outside inward surge rivers, clouds, assemblies of demons, flights of the chosen, their enormous footprints and from the circle inserted in his forehead, between the joined eyebrows, the glow.

Surrounded by trees, white (In that blueprint I search for my body's own.) houses begin to appear in the inside squares; the cities are isolated, as on a map (web within another web). From Mount Meru, everything emanates, expansion of the void, succession of syllables (I repeat the syllable.), compact, firm, earthy double of the dark emblem, snowy on its peak, in one piece, pineapple thrust, stone, stupa, Buddha.

I was alone, in a carpeted apartment, with white walls and furniture. Sitting on the floor (outside it snowed) my legs folded like a yogi, naked.

On the wall an Albers.

II

The faithful are sitting under the great foot, doing their thing, as one would say. The smell of urine, among other smells—a poster of *The Wild One:* the bubble coming out of its mouth says MEN—detectable under that of hash, and take a good sniff, of the filth typical of taverns in the Malay archipelago, doesn't bother them.

A green neon light curves to form the heel, sketches the toe sinuously, the arch of the foot with a continuous line; the shadow of the sole is in chalk.

Through changing screens of uselessly mentholated smoke one can see, holding tight to their machines, pinball players; behind, a naked man tied to a post—the door to WOMEN.

The walls: blow-ups of women in transparent kimonos, racing cars, a Nepalese temple, Karel Appel, Che Guevara. Flowers.

Between records—the very same that's dropping under the needle—one can hear the rattling of the machines, thrusts against the wall; light bulbs flicker on the backboards; strawberries, clubs, lemons, cherries fall.

Without an electric eye and without anybody pushing it, the small peeling door to the Rembrandtsplein opens heavily, slowly: the guru has come.

"My head"—he declaims, adding one more gesture to those five ritual gestures with which he made his entrance, while the players fuss over the machines—"is a perfect oval, my eyes have the shape of lotus petals, my lips have the fullness of the mango and the arch of my eyebrows is an imitation of Krishna's. Fix me a tableful of rice. And, I beg you PLEASE, don't touch me"—he holds off the curious with a hand reeking of incense and the faithful with a shove. "Ask your questions from afar. Every man for himself. I care little for the human race. And enough sighs, please. I travel by jet, *not* by elephant. Holiness is so boring."

The Most High One takes off his orange hat, the rings—fake tiger teeth—he wears on each finger. He drops onto a bench, under the great neon foot, among torn cushions, knapsacks and shoes. In the dust cloud that rises, some longhairs grunt, startled, and push him; they turn around and go back to sleep. The Master pulls off his shoes—sandals in spite of the below-zero weather, scatters glass beads and tin rings. He chooses one of his kerchiefs for the night, and one of his blondest followers for lover. Hand in hand they cross the smoke screens, the rows of players, the barely opened door of MEN. The mustard-colored light reveals scribbled walls and two urinals ditched with thick, opalescent water. The guru touches his forehead: "You have been chosen from all the rest," he whispers in his ear; he fondles his navel and kisses it. The blond boy, erect, soon reaches ecstasy: "I am about to enter the isles of the blessed," and he grabs the sink faucet. "I can already see the Heaven of the West!"

Before the peeling mirror the Supreme One shoots up.

He comes back from the toilet most cryptic.

"I have not subverted anybody," he grumbles, eyes ablaze. "What a smell of burnt grass! Verily I say unto you that truth can be anything, that a true god cannot be distinguished from a madman or comedian. Let's have more ice. And would you please stop that music. Barbarism, your name is the Western World."

SCORPION: "What should I do to get rid of the reincarnation cycle?"

THE GURU: "Learn to breathe."

(Applause. Laughter. Silence.) (An Abyssinian athlete faints.)

(Four nude pin-ups, smeared with Ambre Solaire, slip in through a half-opened window, forefingers on their lips and carrying overnight bags. Coup de théâtre: as they reach the center of the room they draw out of their bags four newly starched Salvation Army uniforms and four giant money boxes. Buttoned from head to toe in a white coif, they shake the collection tray, starting with the guru and toward the four cardinal points: fracas of florins.)

TOTEM: "What's the best spiritual exercise?"

THE GURU: "Sit down. Place your left foot over the right thigh and the right over the left. Cross your arms behind your back. Grab your left heel with your right hand; the right heel with your left. Look at your navel. And then try to unravel . . ."

(A young Moroccan—pitch-black body, smooth and shiny, grape-colored pupils—dances to the rhythm of the numismatic quartet. A Dutchmen bathes the boy's head, thick Karakul tapestry, in dark beer which runs down his back and between his buttocks.) (Out of a chewing gum machine, Don Luis de Góngora emerges:

"Foam down his back:
on the ebony frost!"

TIGER: "What's the quickest way to liberation?"

THE GURU: "Don't think about it."

(Sighs. Interjections of approval.) (Shirley Temple comes out of the men's room.) (The narcotics squad comes in: polyurethane muskets, shields of expanded epoxy.) (A black man takes the backboard off a pinball machine: hides a kif ball in each light bulb and a syringe in the groove for the aluminum balls. Another black hides a diamond in the inside pump of the toilet and then swallows a list of Buddhist maxims, another one containing the names of the members of the Supreme Soviet—which he had previously copied in white ink, although translated into Swahili, upon the folds of his testicles—and still another, in color, containing top secret designs of the new winter fashions.)

TUNDRA: "What formula should I repeat so as not to be reincarnated as a pig?"

THE GURU:

Ubiquitous is the whiteness of heavenly purity and happiness; ubiquitous are the snowy, shadowless, immutable bodies of the divine. The silence and the unique gesture of zero are perfect.

Marine, invisible, forever blue, are the demi-gods that surround us, the weightless ones.

Neither word nor object, in his own yellow world of successive circles man is moving.

I suffer in it. Sunken under my feet are antelopes of grass, sparrows of sweet basil, snakes of mint, animals and birds.

What a commotion the elves cause against the red walls!

O Humanity, what demons and what a blackness befalls you, as night does, upon the plain.

He finished the prayer frantically scratching his head.

"Religion, my dears"—he added psalmodically—"is sound."

And he shook a small bell. From the back of the room one of the faithfuls answered him with a small bone flute.

"What a life!" he sighed. "I must travel east for the spring equinox, south for the summer solstice, to the heart of the west when fall arrives and to the far north in the dead of winter! I'm going then," and the peeling door opens by itself again. Before passing through it, the Unique One turns to the distracted crowd for the last time and states:

I RECOMMEND THE INGESTION OF PETALS

For the Birds

I

"O nobly born, COBRA,
the time has come for you to seek the Path.
Your breathing is about to cease.
Your instructor has set you face to face to the Clear Light;
and now you are about to experience it:
heaven empty things,
clear intelligence,
transparent void
without circumference or center.

Know thyself;
Lucidly.
I take you to the test."
                                        —BARDO THÖDOL

With Cobra's body over his shoulders—the perforated head
bleeds from the nose, against the nape of his neck, on his right
shoulder—here comes TOTEM; on his coat, down the leg of
his pants, to the cuffs, two scarlet stripes: cadet in his Sunday
best.

He shines phosphorescently: mint drivel, the dead man's green
drool bathes him; a cloying cloak of concentric humors covers
him. Hunched over, he presses onward: wooden Dutch beggar,
hunter bent under the excessive gifts of hunting; what he carries
is not a corpse, but coppery ducks instead, guts with holes and
flaccid necks; pelleted swans, claws, feathers.

They sound like nuts cracking, but actually he's stepping on
blind crabs who are desperately fleeing from the smell of death.

More daring still are the birds, who are pecking at the two
heads, savoring the ganglia cocktail.

THE BIRDS' COURSE

They pierce cellophane packages—dehydrated potato chips—on the tables of restaurant terraces, they take flight—concentric circles, the wider, the slower—they perch on corpses abandoned on nearby towers, they play, fight, eat, defecate over them; they take flight again—a spiral accelerating as it closes—spitting cartilage and toe-nails, teeth and hair over the conical roofs of temples, over trolleycars, into pools and courtyards, into barges filled with folly and the holy—long black hair, white tunics—with fakers and gods; the birds, pecking at eyes, vomiting bone-marrow, off to the terraces once more, chirping, without mistakes, without faults, guided by the river, by coal dusts, by the grey stains of ashes and by fistfuls of red petals scattered to the air; the birds, spitting skin over the steps that go down to the stinking water where children play among yellow-turbaned cachetic impostors.

TIGER, TUNDRA, and SCORPION had fled.

COBRA always had a liking for cheap shows: TOTEM recalled the initiation, the tin frog, the yogurt and the ketchup; so he entered the morgue howling, between showy fainting spells, drowning in saffron tears which he dried with his mournful cravat.

The night watchman was a faded and shaky Indonesian who held a small camphor bag in his fist. Before him and with effective vaudeville gestures, the mourner displayed his consternation.

They had already stored him in the cellar.

They went down a crippled and smelly staircase. Through scaffolds and rope-wheels, under a light-shaft soiled by pigeons, black ropes, strung from the highest supports at determined intervals, secured stairsteps, fastened beams, held wedges firm.

A greasy, sweetish odor rose from the lower chambers: "The sponge of intestines, opening"—explained the Asiatic custodian touching the tip of his nose while making a disgusted little face.

He recognized him among the repeated dissected bodies, in the blinking of an acetylene light—according to their custom, in a pool of formaldehyde, the drowned were spinning, adrift. He was still warm.

Posthumous homage: a friendly neighborhood theater effect: out of his pocket he pulled a dagger of gross dimensions, its sinuous blade engraved with the eight emblems of good fortune, and taking advantage of a yawn, he buried it to the handle in the watchman's mouth.

He fled with the body over his shoulders. The crushed head bled from the nose, against the nape of his neck, on his right shoulder.

He fled with a rainbow background of a mountain and seven circles of oceans separated by seven circles of golden hills.

He fled with a harbor background.

With a rainbow background of a mountain and seven circles of oceans separated by seven circles of golden hills.

On its peak, just opened, foamy and snowy, a bottle; two glasses with ice; lemon peels hanging on the rims.

With a harbor background: in the forefront buoys and masts were piled, Shell's wooden fences—a heart bordered by a thin red neon tube—empty spheres, of green glass, a giant tube, of tin, ejecting a white cylinder with fluorescent stripes. Motionless sea gulls. Hard flags.

Behind, and on the other side of the estuary, of the coal barges, a grey plain of grass spread out, squared off by the shiny lines of the canals; at certain distances, in the rectangular gardens bordered by the water, lamaist funeral piles rose, their golden white-striped needles pointing to the clouds. Distant red ochre. Upon the rooftops old cypress trees cast their shadows.

Further away, on the horizon, a windmill.

He shook his head. He came to. He was looking at a collage posted on the MEN's door—clippings from *Life*—in a shabby and weedy café in Rembrandt plaza.

He came in the kitchen door. He wiped the dining table with a rag dripping lye. He lay the corpse down. He covered it with a tablecloth.

Over the four straight, nickel-plated cylinders, in the middle of the black Bakelite sheet, shrouded to his mouth in oil cloth, CO-BRA was getting cold; his nose dripped into the silverware drawer.

"Don't anyone look at him," TOTEM ordered the first trembling arrivals. "Don't anyone say his name. Don't anyone touch his feet or he'll go straight to hell. Build a paper effigy with lots of arms around the trunk, like the spokes of a wheel. Paint an eye on each hand. Hang it up like a lamp over a table. Silence. Tell his instructor. Tell the people at Rembrandt's to come over, but let each bring his own food."

TIGER appeared: barefoot, shaven skull; wrapped in a yellow sheet, a red bonnet in his hand:

"Everybody out." —The new scabbed arrivals protested. The lama pushed them into the living room and slammed the door. He bolted the back screen door, closed the wickets which faced onto the canal, onto a row of brick façades with very high windows and, still further, away, onto a bridge.

He drank from the faucet. With the back of his hand he dried his mouth. He rolled a mat; he sat next to the dead man. He whispered something in his ear, then, parting his hair, examined the skull: he tore a lock out of the parietal joint.

He talked to him for an hour.

Running circles around the corpse—he stuck the head to the knees, heels to the buttocks—starting with the feet, he wrapped him in adhesive tape, girdling him, an innocent in glass clay.

Between the white bands, on his thighs, there remained fine watery adhesions, parallel spindles which were breaking off: a red seam, like an eyebrow; under the transparent skin, minute, black, capillar flowers burst open.

Thus wrapped—embryo and mummy—he left him in a corner, leaning against the refrigerator and contemplating an electric dishwasher.

For four days they received seedy condolences and fed the libbers from Rembrandtsplein. They would run, between Tibetan sighs, to the automat on the corner. They would bring back cold cuts, vegetable salad in boxes, apple turnovers and even dwarf mangoes imported from China.

Among butter lamps, conch shells and flageolets, tiny petal cups and five unfinished or worm-eaten statues—a portly Buddha pointing to the ground—there piled fruit peels, fluorescent teaspoons, paper plates smeared with rancid mayonnaise, flower-printed napkins and thermos cups which they passed around—hash brownies—from hand to hand.

While they officiated in the kitchen, TUNDRA and SCORPION took turns cleaning, and preparing the food which, in a big cup, the Instructor presented to the dead man and then renewed, once the subtle, invisible essence was extracted.

The mourners dozed off, stacked in corners, under faded or ragged banners of prayers, among books nobody knew how to read any longer, nor which could be preserved in a stupa, tambourines—yak-skin stretched over skull halves—amulets and mandalas. They cuddled up against discarded statues—cleared by antique dealers, auctioned as premium along with cargoes of Burgundian madonnas, Chichimec heads or copies of Murillo's *Ascension*—whose piety or anger had not been restored by the faith and constant offerings of the four lamas, far, as they were, from the pristine sources; crossed legs and lotus flower served as pillows to the filthy; to those lacking an earlobe or the cranial protuberance, thrones of Buddhas, or to those who had sawed off the tuft, or stolen the paste of glass eyes, or yielded to the perseverance of termites.

Drinking down Nescafé and cough pills, eating and pissing, the wailers spent the day in the shade, their eyes opaque, talking to themselves, far gone, exchanging, with lifeless gestures, wooden tablets they spent hours examining: in concentric circles of all colors, narrow-waisted and big-assed women, wrapped in red garments and flying—their black hair floats, from the same spiral as the clouds—thousands of pilgrims, titans and demons, palaces, rivers. In the center, a mountain.

On the fourth day, the knowledge factor abandoned COBRA's body.

Newly bathed and smelling of Maja, TOTEM, giving jocular slaps, went among the raving harlequins.

He uttered a rotund "That's all folks" which rendered the dinner guests compunctious and disgusted.

TIGER checked the corners of the mouth and eyelids, the orifices of the nose and the ears, of the penis and anus: they secreted a yellow sap, a thick and purulent humor.

With a chair and his clothes, he began to assemble the dead man's image. He slid pants on the front legs as well as a pair of boots; he dressed the back with a red sweater, he buckled a worn-out and dirty antelope jacket: on the back one could still see a vertical arch opened in the hide, dripping, soaked in by the plush, writhing like a mangled snake; then, like yesteryear, sketched in a single stroke by an expert penman with an angular style, the circle of Divination, twisted over itself and edgeless, the perfect hoop; stamped by a stone seal, beside the circle a square mark: BR; branded into the shoulder, an A.

On the neck he stuck a printed sheet of paper that revealed holes and threads when held up to the light; in the center, the figure of the deceased with his legs girdled, praying over a lotus flower and surrounded by things most pleasing to the senses:

> mirror
> conch-shell and lyre
> flower pot
> pastries in a chalice
> silk dresses, a canopy.

Beside the left shoulder, vertical arabesque, six phonetic symbols:

> god
> titan
> man
> beast
> unhappy spirit
> hell.

On the bottom, a prayer:

"I, who depart from this world"—here they sketched his name: TUNDRA the arch and the circle, SCORPION the monogram and final A—"COBRA, worship and take refuge in my lama director and in all the deities, both peaceful and wrathful."

"May the Great Pious One forgive all the sins I have accumulated and all the impurities of my former lives and may He lead me on the road to another good world."

TOTEM brought a black scarf, of fine wool, which the deceased himself had stolen from a drugstore; TIGER tied one of the ends to his neck.

"Eat what you want," he whispered to him, "from what we have given you. But bear in mind that you are dead, so don't come back to this house any more and don't start bothering the living. Remember my name, and with that help take the straight road, the white road. Right this way . . ."

He pulled the other end of the scarf, and began to lead the funeral procession while chanting a liturgy and jingling a bell. He was followed by TUNDRA, blowing into a sea-shell and by SCORPION, with cymbals which he banged against COBRA's body from time to time. In his left hand TOTEM carried a tambourine: he'd flip it over and a few metal balls hanging from ribbons would beat against the skin; TIGER himself, interrupting the liturgy, played a femur-flute.

Every once in a while the lama director would turn around to invite the dead man's spirit to join its body and to assure him that the route they were following was the right one. Behind him came the pall-bearers with the corpse and, along with candy and sodas, the rest of the grimy riff-raff. The ragged wiped their eyes, howling sporadically, sobbing between puffs of smoke.

When the funeral ended, the paper face was burned.

By the color of the flames and their manner of burning, they knew the departed was on the right road.

"With a derisive support," TUNDRA congratulated himself, "I have succeeded in visualizing the dead man's insides."

SCORPION, who had been examining a mandala for some time, abandoned his rigorous contemplation in order to listen to him.

"Yes"—the enlightened one added—"by these stains on the wall I have known it: black grass grows in COBRA's intestines! Want me to trace his curriculum mortis for you? Very well, at this moment he is contemplating the fifty-eight divinities, irritated hoarders of Knowledge, inserted in concentric hoops of fire. Wrathful and blood-sucking flames surround him. Four disheveled black demons make faces at him while they devour small bodies in large chunks. Surrounding these large-fanged monsters, beasts with pelican and frog heads, drooling blood and ganglia, scream upon a dark rainbow."

But, so many drawings had to have some use! The late-lamented knows: that hair-raising Cinerama is purely an emanation from the lower part of his brain.

The wheel will break.

He will reach safe harbor.

From the paper face
they gathered the ashes on a platter.
They mixed them with clay.
With that paste they modeled minute relics, letters and symbols.
They offered a few upon the altar of the house,
others, beneath trees and protruding rocks,
upon hills and cross-roads.
While they burned the page they undressed the chair.
They auctioned off the clothes among the ragpickers.

"With these florins," TOTEM warned, "we shall throw a party in his honor . . . in a year's time."

ANATOMY LESSON

You were diagonal, yellowing. You were a dead weight, a perfect, knotless wooden pole, a found object which the curious four examined.

They read you. Pointed at you. Confronted your body with a sketched body—a map of Man, opened—; they enumerated your parts, named your viscera, opened your eyelids—dimmed globes—taking notes, they turned the page.

Next to your calloused feet impregnated with brimstone, there was a book, unfolded like a musical score.

They sank their fingertips into your flesh: the imprints of the tips, the grooves of the nails, remained: you were made of wax, of paper, of soft marble, of clay.

They slashed your wrists with a scalpel; they tightened bindings around your arm, starting at the shoulder. From the wound gushed a black paste which they collected in a small case. In two others they kept samples of your urine and excrement.

Those three residues, dissolved in urine, sprayed the funeral banquet.

They wanted to throw him into a canal wrapped in a fiery-colored cloak so that once the water froze he would remain on the sandy bottom, the soles of his feet facing up, cloak opened, and the children would point at him beneath their ice skates, trapped in the glass;

they wanted to cremate him: ashes within a cobra of carved scales—its eyes two coarse emeralds, its tongue a ruby zig-zag—whose head uncurled;

they wanted to embalm him, seated and holding a swastika, to preserve him in the basement, surrounded by daggers with emblems and dried oranges.

Finally, a lama astrologer calculated the horoscope of death: at six o'clock they had to take him up to the hills.

They cut his skin into strips which they nailed to the rocks.

They crushed his bones.

They mixed this dust with barley flour. They scattered it to the wind.

They repeated the syllables for the last time.

They abandoned everything.

For the birds.

II

In hollow heads of benevolent Buddhas the five transformers received the coke balls which they'd extract by unscrewing pupils and then refine. The ninth sublimation would turn the curds into their white and light opposites. A resentful and irascible addict delivered the statues masqueraded as a diligent antiquarian and effeminate Tibetologist. He had given them this warehouse where several traders in Asian art accumulated their fraudulent junk in its front rooms.

They wrapped the distilled snow in small jute sacks—scent bags!—in thin packages without depth, adjustable to shoe soles; they hid it in small circular boxes of TJING LJANG YU, essential balm—with a sky-blue background, in relief, a turquoise pagoda of conical roofs: The Temple of Heaven—they concealed it in inflated condom balloons, they dyed it, red sugar.

All day long in artful, frantic enterprise, inflamed, feverish, poisoned by their own waste, infected by their own refuse: thus the fanatics survived.

They had deserted the too hot and crowded upstairs rooms of the warehouse; the refiner was at work in the condemned cellar which the stench of the nearby canal invaded. Outside and next to the counterfeit windows which yesteryear had been covered with thick stained-glass, from whose frames broken circles, dismounted shields and twisted iron flowers still survived, there accumulated—blankets of foam dragged by the drainage of the Garden's Indonesian laundries—scattered oil stains with spread-winged dead ducks floating on top of them; stale food, pecked at by the birds, fermented among pine-wood and empty tin cans.

From the deepest rooms—labyrinth of crumbled steps, irregular doors, and humid hallways on the other side of which one could sense the ditched water—the traders of white no longer emerged except to deliver the little bags and boxes among the sweet-toothed and punctual Rembrandtsplein "connections"; they'd choke themselves with smoked sardines on top of piled apple crates, they'd urinated hurriedly and in dark corners; seeking the delicate metamorphoses, sampling finer and finer sand, they'd drink sugar water, sleep sitting up.

To maintain themselves in that fever they would consume the product of their own gestures: on domestic trips they'd burn the most subtle part of their craftsmanship, the swiftest jewels, the neatest grooves.

They sank further and further; to deepen the dungeon, they'd dump rubbish into the canal, they advanced into the most humid places, perforated walls, dug the ground—the light became a pincushion and a sea-urchin; moles digging holes.

They slept wrapped in straw mats. Ears against the wall, they listened from the other side of their sleep to the sluggish flow of the water on the bed of the canal, its filtering between the stones, the dripping from the eaves over the thick oily sheet, slowly undulating on the surface, the festering of the sewers.

Once a week they had to abandon the coolness.

They ascended. Well into the night, they'd emerge, suffocated by heat and fear. In the crypt they'd armor themselves with small bags and metal boxes.

More congested and tinkling than a leaping dwarf wearing a vest of coins, COBRA climbed a column around which there still were remains of steps, hanging on like propellers. He'd raise a hatchway, inspect the warehouse through the crack, fling it wide open, whistle intermittently like a blind owl. Scarily looking everywhere at once, the four remaining heads, wrinkled and dark, began cropping up, one by one, on the white floor tiles. The hairy eyebrows turned right and left: their locks swept the tiles. When a bearded sphere, a giggle, would rise, the one below pushed up like a spring: on the lime background, among the depot's broken down statues, the fugitive distillers suddenly appeared: glazed carnivalesque demons, large oval eyes of transparent indigo, automatons from a cathedral clock striking five.

Behind the guide, tinted by the oblique veins of the earth, panting and layered turrets, TOTEM, TIGER and TUNDRA appeared. They gave another signal, a foot stamping on the hatchway, a scream: SCORPION germinated.

The five of them now in exile, they closed the entrance to the refined inferno, to Proserpine's underground estate. In single file, crocked, brimming with creaking paper wrappers, coated like glazed pineapples by a thin sugary layer, winter doves covered in snow, they crossed the nave.

Far off, they listened to the squeak of trolleycars, footsteps in the street, their metallic, empty repetition refracted by the naves, voices in summer's splendor—volumes, vessels—their muted reflection against the wooden gods.

Piling up on either side and, at some spots, even up to the concrete ceiling, the spiteful ancients: a smiling Maitreya displayed the hind-side of its unscrewed eyeballs: the convexity of the globes, both irises painted, fell from the hinge of the lower eyelids, like the open cover of a clock.

An Avalokitesvara mercifully showed the palm of his right hand supplied with a pupil: one of his own unscrewed ears was hanging from a forefinger; a blackish cornea, like the one in a magpie's beak, lined the inside of the skull-case. At certain intervals, on the petals of a jointed throne in the shape of a lotus flower—the prince lay face down—as if someone with a scissors' tip had torn off big lumps of the same dark rind—below, over red sealing wax, small sheets of gilt; the opaque crust, the nail pickings that clog bronchial tubes and drain pipes, had taken over everything, even the rear end of the dismounted statue.

All that remained among the displaced venerables were the intruders, who, though demolished, were worthy, worn down either by the sea or devout lips, their features faded—how pious hands rub!—proud and splintered: their cloaks restored, their hearts intact, the tin of daggers and crowns glittering; all pointed toward the beams on the ceiling, euphoric annunciators, relinquished Sevillian martyrs, worm-eaten mahogany madonnas, pious baroque women of jacaranda, contracted monks and fatuous archangels.

In order to pass between a solar quadrant and a player piano, a Flemish peasant lightly lifts his right foot and picks up his cloak to his knees; his hair and beard of identical whorls—Gothic flowers of cauliflower—fall to his waist. Straddling his shoulders, two chubby little legs fall in front of his chest, the small feet among the beard's snail shells: they are joined to a little boy's trunk and this, in turn, to an arm pierced by termites that raises a golden sphere—cross the north pole.

On a black rug scanned by a texture of tigers and white letters, a maiden hurls a wheel bristling with barbed wire.

To slide open a metal door, COBRA pushed aside a leprous beggar whose concentric sores were licked by hungry dogs.

They could barely stand the night's glare, the noises reverberated in their heads. There were motorcycles lying on the sidewalk. It was raining. In the square one could hear the distant guitar-strumming of the inns, far off. At the subway entrance a frightened woman appeared. She was wearing a red hat; its ribbons, falling from the brim to her black cape, hid the gold flowers on her face.

They walked against the walls, slipping through the crowd. They wanted to flee, return to the cloister, be someone else. They didn't look or talk to one another: they took different sidewalks, crestfallen.

"The itching rain of glances is making us soaking wet," hummed TOTEM and TIGER *a dúo*.

"Mocking eyes give us the once over. Fingers point at us, put asterisks on us," quoted sweaty TUNDRA.

Same slowness of gestures—they were walking on the bottom of an aquarium; they were floating over the same glass fiber, advancing over the same beard a few millimeters from the floor.

They saw the same colors, one word contained them all. Transparent spheres. An iris haloed things.

The same horizontal and fixed rictus stretched all their lips.

Between records—the very same that's dropping under the needle—one can hear the rattling of the machines, thrusts against the wall; light bulbs flicker on the backboards, strawberries, clubs, lemons, cherries fall.

Without an electric eye and without anybody pushing it, the small peeling door to the Rembrandtsplein opens heavily, slowly: Rosa, the seer, has come.

Her neckline plunges to her navel; a white flower fastens it between her breasts. She doesn't greet anybody—that's Rosa for you—she doesn't return anybody's greeting. A black bead necklace, funerary baroque showpiece, chokes her throat.

She settles at a purple table, next to the MEN's door. She immediately arranges her deck of cards in an arc. With a filed nail, polished in her very own scarlet, she points to the ace of hearts—a golden cobra curled around her forefinger; with the other hand she's holding the arm of her glasses: a green plastic snake bordering the eyes shapes the frame. She sticks out her tongue, fluted like a U, the most lucid lady, she turns her head: out of her hair, splinters of scorched mahogany, out of the wide-brim hat touching it, a pastel blue fox-tail leaps, its very tip opening near the cards into a tuft of turquoise feathers.

"Ask, gentlemen. About life and death. But remember I am nothing but a concretion of the primeval viscous chloride, a creature of the eternal and full truculence." —She sticks out her tongue again, touches up a beauty mark:—"We must dramatize the uselessness of everything!"—and she breaks into laughter.

People crowd around her. Under the great foot fringed by a fluorescent tube we take advantage of the mob to hand out red boxes. We glue ourselves to the customers from behind. Into pants' pockets we slide our right hand. On the bottom we leave a Temple of Eden. We glue ourselves in front of the customers. On the right, into our pants' pockets, we feel their sliding hands, warm against our thighs. On the bottom, a ticket is left behind.

Near the urinals, under the mustard light of the MEN, shrouded by smoke, by the greenish and lukewarm vapor of urine, the essential balm is propagated in circular cases which we tear from our bodies—poisoned talismans—; snow is scattered among black ideograms.

We distract the cardsharp:

SCORPION: What should I do in order to have a chest like Superman's?

ROSA: Learn to breathe.

Stuck to a convex base, a skull with frightened eyes looks up, imploringly, and shows a reddened tongue, opened in a U, like Rosa's. Over the skull—its claw scratches the bone—a stuffed crow displays a daisy beaded on a necklace.

COBRA: I'd like to be an acrobat in the *Palace of Wonders*. What should I do to loosen up my joints?

ROSA: Sit down. Place your left foot over the right thigh and the right over the left. Cross your arms behind your back. Grab your left heel with your right hand; the right heel with your left. Look at your navel. And then try to unravel . . .

Behind the card dealer, with a lilac background and glass eyes, three gentlemen peer over in unison. The patent leather bowler hat of the eldest—monocle, tidy goatee, hoary mustache—crowns the pyramid. A bald fellow, puff-cheeked, good-natured, and contrite, lowers his head; beside him the third examiner, who is cut off at his mouth by a green wall—the symmetrical spirals of his pitch-black mustache stand out—: sneaky eyes, straight red hair, arched eyebrows.

TOTEM: What should I do to keep it hard while I'm putting it in?
ROSA: Don't think about it.

On the door frame—a bilious and phosphorescent mummy with white eyelids watches us from the shadows—a Gypsy woman appears, smoking.

TIGER: What formula should I repeat so as not to be reincarnated as a pig?
Rosa sighs. She takes a tortoiseshell case with gold initials out of her purse. With her free hand she destroys an arc of clubs. She opens her vanity case—green glass—she touches up her beauty mark with Chinese ink—that's Rosa for you—she orders a high-ball with lots of ice . . .

The cobbler's children go without shoes: the decipherer didn't know she wouldn't get to drink it: through the Rembrandt's door, "on tiptoe stealing," the narcotics squad came in.
Turning toward Rosa the crowd held its breath. The five transformers disappeared into the MEN.

The urine vapor: emanation from an offering.
The urinals: oil flasks.
The sink: a fountain of petals.
Sitting on a white china peacock, a yellow god appeared. His middle face was calm; on the lateral ones, protruding fangs, irritated and globular eyes, noses fuming smoke. The middle hands together in prayer; the others brandished darts and daggers, bows and arrows.

Five refugee lamas from Nepal emerged sorrow-struck and devitaminized from the bathroom. The Indian summer was choking them. They recalled the rancid tea, the reflection of the copper pitchers in the snow, the barley flour, a wall of white stones, each inscribed in black with a maxim, the passing of a yak through the frame of a narrow widow, the hand-painted *tankas,* once so miraculous, abandoned in the outskirts of Lha-Ssa.

TUNDRA pointed to the ground.

SCORPION cursed the red demons, instigators of the Chinese invasion.

With metal helmets imitating heads of owls, of monkey-eating Philippine eagles, an officer of the peace approached COBRA:

"Documents . . ."

. . . .

"Drugs . . ."

. . . .

"Dollars . . ."

. . . .

"Detained . . ."

. . . .

He didn't lose a single effect:

he handed him a flower,

a Temple of Eden,

A florin;

he took out his penis and urinated on his feet.

Holding him by the shoulders, the cop cornered him against the wall.

He buried his claws in his neck.

With his iron beak he perforated his skull.

White

The room is white, the window square.

On the frame of an empty wall—Thought: glowing threads—bordered by lime, compact grey clarity of light rain—forking, interweaving: a fish's flagelli:—a square, now outlined, advances; its edges vibrate.

Further away it flees toward the background, it oscillates—disordered net, disjointed ciphers of fire—a black square is about to fall.

> wall
> open window rain
> far away a closed wicket
>   :
> a white square containing
> a grey square containing
> a black square.

Two rivers sprout from the penis—your skin is a map:—: one of them, impetuous, climbs the right side of the body, hoarse, dragging sand—I cover you with plaster, I draw upon you with black ink and the finest brush, climbing up the right side, in a torrent that swells with my breathing, the consonants mutually entwined;—; the other, tame, clear, goes up the left side, slow green spirals, algae upon the windings, murmur of falling pollen, transparency—I draw the vowels upon you.

The center of your body:

six corollas,

six knots,

six couples screwing.

Semen retained:

> syllables knotting syllables:
> anklets the ankles,
> letters the knees,
> sounds the wrists,
> mantras the neck.

Semen retained:

> snake that curls and climbs: rattles among the
> hinges of vertebrae: around the bones, hoops of
> scales and glistening skin: oiled cartilage glides,
> girds the marrow.
> Lotus that bursts on the top of the skull. Blank
> thought.

A black line borders the figure
furrowed by three channels
interrupted by flowers

the body
three axes
letters the petals.

They returned to the cellar by way of the port taverns, drinking beer and banging on the show windows—the knitters shrieked—. With the sale of the deceased's jacket they paid for several rounds, a steam bath, tea and marihuana.

They chose two Indonesian girls, newly arrived, who sprayed their beds with jasmine water, masturbated with their fingertips soaked in privet powder, and who attained dilations of the rear thanks to a breathing method of scanning with samsaric sighs.

Pawing and cackling they crossed the rows of Buddhas and other liberated hollow heads. They went down the unfinished steps. They closed the hatchway.

Inside a skull—in the background, in front of a blue oval, a red child, shining and polished, as if made of porphyry, his feet joined at the heels; surrounded him, among purple clouds, the Bodhisattvas—they gathered their victuals, mixed and kneaded them: foul-smelling guts, oozing a black grease from the inner membrane, bristles and eyelids covered by threads of fresh blood, kidneys and testicles, claws, livers. Greenish taint, bile and serum gushed over the bone.

They stripped laughing.
    They stuffed themselves with the skull.
    They fornicated over nails and blood-clots.

They garnished themselves with gross bone trappings.
    With an excess of condiments
    and willing brutality
    they ate the flesh of men
              of cows
              of elephants
              of horses
              of dogs.

In a tin cup they drank bhang, ground and dissolved in milk and almond juice.
    The *five ambrosias* crowned the banquet:

              COBRA's blood
              TIGER's urine
              TUNDRA's excrement
              SCORPION's saliva
              TOTEM's semen.

TO COBRA

TO TIGER

Circles (colors), igneous anagrams: you saw the skull upside down, overflowing: the viscera still breathing, the tissues palpitated, rhythmless. Yellow transparency: the humors were ditched in the empty alveoles, gushing over jaw bones, over deeply perforated eye sockets, to the occipital cone, leaving the forehead's fractures exposed, down to the floor, slow clam liquor. Density of pus, hyaline thread of drool, lymph dripping—out of the mouth—of—by the feet—the hanged man, syrup, vein of honey, urine.

From the void sprouted the syllable YAM and from this the blue circle of air.

RAM red circle

of fire

A   three blinking male heads gave you mocking side glances, opened their mouths, winked, stuck out their tongues at you: giggles, what were they whispering? Their flour-dredged skin was splitting.

Over that tripod, the skull, golden monstrance, *immense like space.*

Over the skull:

OM	white
A	red
HUM	blue

Rays flash from the syllables.
(The potion in the skull boils.)

You laughed to yourself.
"What'd you mix it with?"—the last of the Rembrandt potheads asked you.
The same record. The door that opens. The fluorescent foot.

They were tearing down the bar.

TO TUNDRA

Lie on your right side, your head resting on your open hand. Let your lion's mane fall, vertical to your body fixed in the fury of sleep. On your heart, an octagonal glass. A strong lotus. Colors assigned to each petal. An A on that throne, beast of glistening skin. From another white one, secure, on the top of the head, numerous *a*'s swarm toward the A of the glass: fall of swift signs, minute white birds, milky pebbles, dew returning to the summit.

A red A over your phallus. Burning coals, glare that climbs to the A of the glass, shredded hummingbirds; descent of bleeding arrows.

Swift hoops of frost, garnet atoms circumscribe your body.

When sleep lays siege—mandala of mute animals, slow wave of lava—absorb all the letters into the central letter.

Let the lotus close.

The white wall, the city blurred by rain, the distant wicket.

All the rest and your I: zero.

TO SCORPION

One dram of bhang drives a wild elephant mad. You knew this when the quiet travelers, cuddled amidst the bar's rubbish, passed you the small black stone. The pachyderm kicks and bellows, the trunk bleeds, he vomits a ton of grass. Ten Pakistani shrimpers hold him down when Ganesa, fuming, reaches the estuary. He sinks into the mud seeking coolness.

With a razor blade you scraped off the texture that was truffled by yellow grains, with your nails you tore off opaque scales. Sweetish papers. You hid them among the loose tobacco.

Nothing.

Yes. The stomach full of ice. Cramps in your feet. A rope that vibrates. A fetid breeze through the nose, quicksilver through the ears. You ran to the MEN. They had torn out the sink.

Dragged iron. The crack of cymbals shaking among flames is followed by that of pomegranates bursting on the ground. Pieces of glass over worn black tiles. Over bare feet, drops of blood. Cobrastilettos. Perforated tongues.

You were surrounded by the nude possessed, with hooks clamped on their backs and dragging tin shrines, carts gushing honey and puff pastries, hidden by flies, anointed porphyry phalluses.

Families of macaques played piccolos amid trays of figs, flowers, newly born gods waving rattles, their lips worm-eaten, cankerous giggles.

His straight black hair dropping to his feet over a currant-colored cloak, his forehead smeared with black signs—mice shriek as they devour the wheat—the officiant approached.

Into the fire, burnished with oil, glistening for a moment in the air filled with petals, corpses fell.

Scorpions nested in the ears.

Crows covered the frozen feet.

Mushrooms sprouted on the orbs.

Snakes came into their anuses.

With a teaspoon
they scraped their eyes,
obstinate oysters
gobbled by the monkeys.

TO TOTEM

Interlocked with one of the Indonesian girls, you were rolling on the ground.

The officiant penetrated the other girl in front of a hundred-handed god with a hundred popped-out pupils, one in each hand.

Along with the smell of his unctuous braided hair, that of burnt viscera also reached you.

Indian Journal

I

"Buildings the color of barely dry blood, domes black from the sun, the years, and the rains of the monsoon—others are marble and whiter than jasmine—fantasy-foliaged trees planted in meadows, as geometric as syllogisms, and, within the silence of the pools and of the enamel sky, the shrieks of crows and the silent circles of birds of prey. The rocketing flock of parrots, green stripes that appear and disappear in the quiet air, crosses with the dark grey wings of ceremonious bats. Some return, to go to sleep; others are just waking and fly heavily. It is now almost night and there is still a diffuse light. These tombs are neither of stone nor of gold: they are made of a vegetal and lunar material. Now only the cupolas are visible, great motionless magnolias. The sky falls into the pool. There is neither down nor up: the world has been concentrated into this serene rectangle. A space into which all fits and which contains only air and a few scattering images."

II

LA BOCA HABLA

La cobra
        fabla de la obra
en la boca del abra
                recobra
el habla:
        El Vocablo. *

—OCTAVIO PAZ

*The Mouth Speaks
The cobra/speaks of the labor/in the mouth of the break/recovers/
speech:/The Vocable. This anagram-poem, which is a play on the word,
or vocable, *cobra*, is, evidently, untranslatable. (Translator's Note.)

Among burning timber, the body. Beside the pyre, on the ash-covered ground, a dog licks a bloody white turban and tears it into linen bands. Further away, under an eave, another pile of tree-trunks. Fire technicians hurriedly gather around. A small elephant-god plays among flowers. Copper hand-bells. Death—the pause that refreshes—is part of life.

Carved on the wall, with strong, symmetrical wings, the Mazdean eagles; their prophets' heads crown the doors. Flocks of green parakeets repeat their circles in the sky. Gluttons for eyes, the crows, masters of the dense gardens, keep a watch over the palm-trees.

At dusk, satiated, lethargic, they will relinquish this silence. They will sleep on the barges, upon the red poincianas in the courtyards, amidst humid moldings.

The sentries will pick up the soiled shroud. The skeleton down the well; the bone chips down a drain, to the bay, where nocturnal crustaceans will nibble at them.

I wash. Strokes against the stone. In the small pools, white water. Purple water; the others wring out, lather, rinse, lay them out on the ground. A rancid smell flows from our bodies, steam of sweat and grease that rises to the bridge—the passersby turn their heads so as not to look at us: one's look can be stained. Hair falls into the ditched lye, feet in the dampness, cracks between the toes.

On the other side of the dunghill, behind the miasma, the train passes.

So much candy
   did the elephant-god eat
   that his stomach grew big.
   From his saddle fell—a mouse.
   The moon laughed.
   He threw a tusk at her.

I was born. One step. I am dying.

Joining thumb and forefinger in a circle—golden spheres stuck to their nose, celluloid beauty marks on their cheeks, red shadow on their eyelids—fifteen hoarse apsarases in battle formation, facing the smoking rooms, jump on those sleepers piled on the sidewalks, shredding the shirts of passersby. They're dancing, that's for sure: on the bodies, the three flexions.

In fluorescent saris, trapped in their superimposed cages, eating peanuts, the whores shriek. A grimy curtain allows one to glimpse the bed and the mats from the top of which the family appraises the panting.

On the window, crack in the glass, a creamy chameleon sleeps.

Rice on his feet, smeared in red dust, a little monkey-god, in his concrete temple, entertains the village—his eyes glass balls, petals stuck to his nose. Startled like storks hearing nocturnal sounds, three heads watch over him upon a neck: methylene blue, saffron, eggshell white.

Necklace of flowers, a mustard bull grazes.

A jolting from the turning water wheel. They're singing—purple turbans in the cloud of dust—; far away, a monkey's shriek. They flee: bells on ankles, heavy earrings, hoops on their nostrils. Black signs on their foreheads, the dogs bark differently.

The branches, fixed. Lianas covered by small purple flies.

Ashen sky. A pheasant.

He quarters a shriveled-up chicken smeared with bile, and bathes it in marmalade; he seasons pieces of raw lamb with onion, thyme, and mango; while counting the drams he weighs a handful of marihuana, in front of a display shelf of glittering bracelets, he offers a wooden fiddle.

(The wind scatters silk bands—net of gold threads—disperses the cotton piles in flakes, covers the pastry with dust.)

He cures the hide, inlays, haggles, resells.

He drinks out of a dark green puddle.

Thermos-bottles of tea, mandarin pullovers, the monks took over the cave. Yawning, wrapped in blankets, they delivered homage to the Smiling One. The Indians covered up their mouths, laughing behind the columns. Japanese tourists took pictures with a flash.

Frost, invisible crack in the clay: out of the voices, the lowest fell concave in the air; the children's: fragile piccolos, cartilage flageolets, blown tallow lamps.

The walls—scenes from the life of Diamond—restored the sullied hind-side of the mantras: resin, sweat from the tsampa pit.

Cough. Scratchy throat. Flow of phlegm in the bronchial tubes.

Following the imprints on the floor, worn down by devout feet, the pilgrims wandered around the *dagoba;* they stroked the polished figures with their hands.

Hollow is the urn, a blank white space facing the skeleton, the beggar, the old man; empty is the saddle of the one leaving on a horse, under the fig-tree nobody meditates, the blue-eyed girls in the park, gazelles, listen to nobody.

His arms, swift propellers, shaking the world, a peevish god dances. Beside him—her breasts, half-spheres, her waist, narrow, and wide hips—an undulating goddess in whose arms, perched upon a mouse, an elephant romps—with twisted bejeweled trunk he caresses her ear. At certain intervals, conch spirals, fossilized sea-horses, grooves from a yellowish rock where a peacock comes to perch, blossom in the carved stone.

In the purple of the cloths, silver lines. The copper dish where stalks burn glitters in the sun. Golden hoop, the light girds the wicker circle of the great bass drums.

Black faces. The reflection of the flutes undulates; raising their hands, the musicians shake cymbals as though they were branches loaded with fruit. Beneath his aluminum crown, the motionless one looks at his knees; strings of flowers fall down his ears, on both sides of his face, down to his arms, to his wrists fastened with trinkets and a watch.

On the ground, the flames slowly consume rice and oil, turrets of red dust, petals. A rancid smell impregnates the air, pink ashes stain the feet.

The tree-trunks, agglutinated roots; destroyed lianas embrace the ruins. The underbrush has invaded the fortresses of the abandoned capital. Birds nest in the brambles that gird the capitals, through the drains of reservoirs black squirrels flee. The monsoon and the drought have cracked the walls buried by dust. Furious monkeys demolish the minarets stone by stone, tearing out cartouches and letters.

Beneath the white dome of a mausoleum, its lantern blinded by the foliage, lime against lime, without stirring its wings, a pheasant moves in uniform circles.

Tied to the end of the baton, a bag of gun powder explodes on the ground: the drum major—a jaundiced, sunken-eyed fellow with polished finger nails—chases the foolish spirits from the streets. Banging great hoarse drums, the retinue arrives at the door not protected by a garland of dry seeds. In the hall, surrounded by a cheering crowd, covered with flowers and flies, the motionless one waits, in a wicker chair. Strings of black and blood and a purple drool fall from his lips which the mourners, upon arriving, touch.

THE INDIES[1]

It was covered with trees right down to the river and these were lovely and green and different from ours, and each bore its own fruit or flowers. There were many birds, large and small, which sang sweetly, and there were a great number of palms of a different kind from those of Guinea and from ours. They were of moderate height with no bark at the foot, and the Indians cover their houses with them. The land is very flat.

Their houses were very clean and well swept and their beds and blankets are like cotton nets, and looked like real tents, but without any streets, but rather one here and there, and well swept inside and their adornments very well ordered. All are made of very beautiful palm leaves . . . There were dogs that never barked, and there were nets of palm fiber and lines and horn fishhooks and bone harpoons and other fishing tackle . . . Trees and fruits of most marvellous flavor . . . Birds and the singing of crickets throughout the night, which everyone enjoyed: the sweet and

[1]Columbus' diary.

delicious winds of the entire night, neither hot nor cold . . . Great tree forests, which were very fresh, odorous, by which I have no doubt that there are scent trees in the islands.

All young, as I have said, and all of a good height, a very fine people: their hair is not curly, but straight and as coarse as horse hair, and all have very broad brows and heads, broader than those of any people I have seen before, and their eyes are very fine and not small, and they are not at all black, but the color of Canary Islanders.

A most tame people.

THE GALLANT INDIES

"Tonight," the doorman announces, "on this stage, a real god."

The scenery superimposes turrets whose windows—cellophane and wire—are lit from the inside by red light bulbs; before a leaning tower, the equestrian monument to Queen Victoria.

With a red circle between their eyes, four thick girls are smiling—golden dentures—dancing a Beckoning to Dawn on the proscenium; in the background, on a luminous float which climbs among celluloid clouds, the Sun God appears with a slicked mustache and golden circles on his cheekbones; at his feet, blinking spotlights of all colors, the throne of the maharajah, his favorite.

The mother of the prince—an exhausted, grey-haired transvestite—rushes around backstage, screaming and fanning herself with a feather fan, followed by a fat woman squeezed into a sari of emeralds and pearls, her nose perforated with tin jewels. The hammering of wooden pegs covers the orchestra's tremolos.

On his golden-pillared bed, under a satin mosquito net, the maharajah sleeps. Shifting shadows behind a screen: a violent mulatto with arched eyebrows, the enemy of the prince and of the Star, approaches. A whirlwind of electric fans ruffles his mane, a red spotlight illuminates him. Raving mad, the Mother appears on a swing, uttering threats and insults.

Rolling of drums. In the background the clouds roll toward the side entrances, revealing a starry sky which suddenly turns red. Clash of cymbals: from the ground, sitting upon a flying ox with bloodshot eyes, waggling his wings and ears, the Sun God appears. He raises his arm, points to the sky—lights blink—and belts out a war cry that makes the earth quake.

Titans and their mechanical cows push against each other: each with twelve arms and in their hands, darts and bows, they rush against each other clashing saddles and weapons.

The Malignant One attacks with a spear. Sun responds with a golden saber. Mother hurls a sharp-hooked cockatoo at the Intruder. Like a grasshopper with its own cocoon, the maharajah thumps away against the linen palisade that protects him: the servants, their feet and hands open—as if trying to prove that human extremities are the diagonals of a rectangle—have armored the palisades with swift tapestries around the throne.

The Dark One, like a giant electric fan, makes all his arms rotate—knives in his hands—to grind the Star to pieces. The chopping propeller is already nearing the Luminous One's neck when the latter, pushed by two apsarases who drop from the clouds above, leaps from his chariot, shakes the demon by the nose and throttles his neck. The Villain pops out his eyes, sticks out a plushy yellow tongue, kicks madly . . . and falls to the ground amidst brimstone flames, broken knives and unscrewed ears which leap toward the audience where the fanatics grab for them.

Indigo, saffron, white: silk strips over the ground; against the stone steps that go down to the river, the washerwomen slap their saris. Cow heads emerge from the water: on the tips of their horns, silver cones.

On the opposite shore, under a cliff and of the same yellow ochre, a village of huts with flattened dirt floors. From above, the monkeys, who plundered the forest, climb down clinging to the rocks with their nails, hungry for oranges. Entrenched on the roofs, they assail the pilgrims arriving in carts.

To keep the fat demons from entering, a pillar obstructs the temple door. Next to his copper pitcher, an ashen man, covered by his own scorched hair, strings a liana with red-lettered palm tablets.

Under the figs, old women weave. Into the dark green water of the pond, boys dive from the crown of a niche where a god, with half a mustache and one breast, receives purple flowers. The travelers, bare-chested, wash the bands of their white turbans.

In the cell's shadows, oil lamps sway. Caressed slowly with ointments, covered with fresh flowers, the basalt phallus shines in the center: a ciphered line marks the frenum. The thick cream with which the officiant bathes it remains on the polished plate that serves as its base.

Behind the reverberation of the dense air, Brahmans burn their offerings; in front, blurred by the smoke and standing beside a gate, others absent-mindedly intone the ritual words and give water to the devotees—who bring milky annona pyramids, split coconuts, small bananas, coins and petals—for them to drink and anoint their heads.

The forefinger anointed with oil, with red dust, swiftly traces the sign on the forehead.

Concentric imprints hollow out the descending floor, tilted like a roof. Upside down, fixed in their rolling toward the stream, the bases of the columns have remained among lifted slabs: the air is chipping sand off their edges. Superimposed strata of different veins shape the ruins: horizontal lines, parallel like the marks left on a wall by the flood.

Temple after temple—birds fly straight through them—corroded, lean.

From the niches where lizards nest, armless, marble children watch us, their eyes circled by golden lines. In a puddle of urine, alone in a cell, a lunatic repeats the twenty-four names.

Fig-trees on the frontispieces. Between the branches of a dry ashen tree, the moon.

The straight middle line, pure lime: the lateral curves, bloody: the trident marks the figures of the heaped gods, the stones on the wall surrounding the pool, the forehead of the great elephant that the Brahmans bathe and perfume all day long.

On the ground, after the ceremonies, crushed flowers, yellow rice, incense, walnuts, shit have remained. Only once a year does the sun light up the entire mustard mast.

Great plaster monkeys, peacocks with inlaid stones, three-headed gods and a golden-winged ox—the feathers chiseled like a bird's—all await the day of the feast, crammed into a stinking corridor.

Upon the pyramids of figures screwing, the Brahmans flourish brushstrokes of hot pink, pastel blue, canary yellow.

The mirroring of the fish-filled rectangle, untouched for millennia.

A naked boy, his skin impregnated with ashes and ciphered with red signs, sounding a receptacle of coins, crosses the street.

His bare feet, embroidered; his worm-eaten feet, golden threads; his hair, anointed with coconut oil. ·

Beside the sea, in the lower chamber you sleep, on your couch of cobras.

Sleeping among sacks one on top of the other, in a steam of rotten grapes, of milk, of excrement and vomit, playing, rolled inside burrows of hay, fornicating, waiting on the platform invaded in the morning by a coppery vapor, of burnt rubber, opening their mouth, digging in the garbage, walking.

Wrapped in white sheets, taking shelter from the rain, under the portals, upon the sidewalks covered with glass where the harbor birds, choking from the black air. DRINK KALI-COLA, come to fall.

Twisted tin statues support the domes stained by the clappings of crows' wings. In wax, the equestrian effigy of the donors fixed in a funereal smile. Big mother-of-pearl flowers: petals spill strings of water. Behind enameled gates, semi-nude officiants in the night await. Green mosaic fountains; around them, aluminum Venuses offer apples; amid glass peacocks, luminous, blue-eyed prophets with slicked mustaches examine marble books. Columns decorated with minute mirrors reflect the light of the morning sun.

Upon a wide pearl throne, a boy with a shaved skull smiles; his legs folded, the soles of his feet turned upwards, his enormous eyes bordered by black lines, on his forehead a bluish diamond.

Through the ambulatory—gallery of mirrors—the officiants

approach, balancing on their hands pyramids of copper dishes pierced through by a rod.

Nothing that grows on the ground. Nothing that contains blood. Nose and mouth covered by a thick cloth.

The floor is majolica: wild bellflowers, glazed fruits, butterflies. In order to worship the Whitest One, we rest our bare feet on the tiles' central rosettes where the reflections from stained-glass windows—red blots—vibrate. Hundreds of garlands surround him, birds that fly away when we open the door to the sanctuary, escaping toward the glare of the central courtyard where naked bricklayers whitewash arches that are crowned by needles, weather-cocks, golden bulbs.

Throughout the rainbow-saturated sky, upon embroidered barges—the prows are heads of animals, the sails, parasols—the worshipers spill petals over Mahavira, crown of a human pyramid lifted by twenty-four identical ascetics. With four arms in a swastika and on her shoulder a sitar, an ostrich-riding goddess follows them—a string of pearls in the bird's beak—; another goddess, upon a cockatoo with blazing feet, brandishes darts and pronged wheels with her eight arms.

Further away, two princes wearing Persian turbans, standing over the knot formed by their eel tails, cool the prophet with white fans. From the throne emerges a luminous ribbon which, undulating like the tail of a kite, climbs to the sky where its course repeats a caravan's: rounding the mountain, with harnessed elephants and banners, with a thousand trumpets and monkeys, King Shrenik approaches the alabaster domes.

In the cracks of the flagstone pavement, curly hair; red curds, like sealing wax. A smell of lukewarm viscera, blood clots and flowers impregnates the air: to placate her anger, to make her forget us, we offered sacrifices to the Terrible One.

Cries. Someone is blowing a conch shell. Your face is black, bloody are your fangs, your necklace is strung with skulls, your feet are cooled in the splatterings of slashed jugulars.

The city cracks under the shelter of your cloak. The salty wind corrodes stones and men.

In bamboo stretchers they carry them: their glassy eyes open, their foreheads tarnished, on their lips two white butterflies.

The soaked shroud; a vermilion dust, grain thrown in the air, the stain.

The hum of bazaars around the temple. On the walls red blemishes. Scribbled figures; Sanskrit signs written with coal. The glare from the factories brightens the muddy river water, the iron bridge.

Death is neither here nor there. She's always beside us, industrious, infinitesimal.

The elephants clasp trunks to greet each other imitating the handshake of men.

Bearded man with oval eyes; you, naked woman, are dancing to the rhythm of a triangle, with your arms arched you display an apple in front of your forehead.

Standing, naked, you write me a letter.

With a burnt wooden stick you stretch the corner of your eyelids, you lean your elbow upon the head of a servant.

You forget the thorn; you look at yourself in a circle of polished metal.

A monkey licks you.

A scorpion undresses you.

Two crowned *nagas* intertwine their tails: scale braid. One of them displays a bottle of perfume.

I with woman's hair, you, in front, bent over, the palms of your hands on the floor. My fingers leave imprints on your waist, where strings of pearls are knotted, your buttocks and breasts girded.

With his turban on, a whiskered warrior, laughing with his mouth wide open, penetrates a mare with a member as wide as a horse's; his companion, mounted on a bench, mockingly covers his face; another drinks wine from a conch-shell.

Head against the floor, feet up, each of my arms clasped by the legs of a naked woman: my ringed fingers penetrate them.

Seen from behind—her hairdo: a tower of jewels—a third one comes to sit between my thighs. I force her. Smiling, my sentries make her sink down. To let it further in, you bend your legs, raise your feet off the ground. Tiny servants come to help you and get sucked by maids who, at the same time, play with little monkeys.

Beside the river, to a cabin, you pulled me along by the tunic. With an andante step you glided through the rushes. Thin like a lioness's, your waist reminded me of the frame of a *dombori* drum. You arched your back. The bees buzzed in shiny circles around the lotus of your feet.

Your breasts are full spheres which my fingers stroke, a golden point on the corners lengthens your eyes, your straight nose, your eyebrows sketched in a single stroke. You carry a cymbal, I a flower.

So numerous and pretty are your ornaments that it seems as if a hundred thousand golden bees have lighted on your body, the music of hoops that repeat the fifth note of the scale on your ankles is as sweet as honey.

Dyed with lacquer, your big toes glitter in the sun.

I spent the whole night sipping a little gazelle, in whose eyes there was such a delicious languor that I could not go to sleep.

The guru sprinkles his face with flour, lights up his chilom, mumbles a salute to the pink apsarases of dawn; in the kitchen, behind a red steam of boiling pimientos, the disciples fondle a glass statue; like the master, obese, its hair in a bun.

Parasols of woven palm leaves, marked in red with Bengali writing, shade the lethargic ones. As the fog lifts, the praying men go down the steps, with copper pitchers.

Before a multi-armed celluloid doll in a dress of pink and purple satin, the chorus of faithfuls takes turns around the microphone so that the music doesn't stop; they've hung speakers on the poles so that people can hear it way on the other shore. A scarlet cloud, flowing from a blazing hill, perfumes the goddess; a frog-like dwarf moans at her feet.

Brahmans smear the temple columns with sealing wax; monkeys, hanging by their tails, swing on the bell clappers. Three immersions. Three times I drink water from my hands, which in silence I return to the river. A red disk burns the empty, sandy plain on the other side, and lights the motionless barges, the offerings—wicker trays dragged by the current—a circle of ashes which the dogs sniff.

Wooden balconies. Film posters carpet the façades. Gold sheath: the Nepalese towers of a temple. Two yellow tigers stand guard in front of the house of the man who collects the cremation taxes.

With a vanity case and a small stick he covers his body, already whitened, with what he copies out of a book: with sandalwood dust a yellow rectangle on his forehead, a red V on his arm, tridents on the hands, on a cinnabar background the repeated name on the sole of his foot. Shabby chambermaids bring him fresh flowers, sponge cake, a few coins; they sweep the floorboards, spruce up the fringes of the parasols. Two little boys show him, inside small earthenware vessels, lighted candles which they then place on the bank and push away with their hands like paper boats. He streaks his genitals in green, a silver ring circles his foreskin.

Brahmans will spray his shroud: stuck to the cachetic body, soaked drapery. They will roll him from the canvas stretcher onto trunks of wood. With a torch, through the mouth, his relatives will set him on fire. *You will leave Varanasi, but Varanasi will not easily leave you. Something somewhere inside you will not ever be the same again.*

The flood that draws near, dragging the sand on the bottom, will carry us to the delta, to the sea.

Beside potbellied dwarf-Vishnu, the worshiper—a key hangs from a white string crossing his chest—intones the prayer. He hums, murmurs, whispers names—the light through the branches lengthens the shadow of his body on the wall—; with his forefinger he touches the engraved letters.

In front of the temple, on the reverberating plain, two yoked oxen revolve around a well. An adolescent in a white turban drives and whips them. Earthenware jars draw the water and pour it into a gully; the ribbon follows the furrows, the edges of the village, the path which undulates through different greens, to the pools of the temple, where a blackish canal, amid cobra snares, pours out the milk of the offerings.

In the horizon, blurred, four minarets stand guard over the white mausoleum. Closer, among small handfuls of gold, a farmer pushes his plow; down the road go the muleteers, their reflections in a river framed by the dark arabesques of the Fortress.

Through the white latticework, the texture of stars piercing marble walls, white saris float in the wind; through perforated polygons—meeting of clear dots—turbans. The brick façade decomposes—minute red stains—seems to evaporate. Through empty light-shafts the sun penetrates to the lower chamber: a thick cloth, of black felt, conceals the Prophet's tomb; a repeated phrase glitters on the threshold.

Pigeons take flight in unison, as if they had heard a shot, and circle over the immense courtyard; they return to perch on the fountain, on the parallel mats where barefoot devotees kneel, and touch the ground with their foreheads. Beside a mimbar, an old man in a white beard and black turban balances his concave hands together, as if they contained a thick fluid, ready to filter between his fingers; another spells out a scroll with worn edges.

Outside, at the foot of the mosque, peddler stands, statue bazaars are crowded together; dealers auction off miniatures, tankas painted over with the wrong gods, coarse ivory deities, torn Tibetan banners. An enormous orange sun sinks between the minarets, in a spotted sky; the beckoning voice of the muezzin silences the hammering of the blacksmith shops, the shouts of the laundrymen, the tinkling of copper-filled tents. The ringing of bicycles and car horns mingles with radios' high, syrupy soprano voices, xylophones and harps. Rusty auto bodies, broken engines, tires are all pile to the porticos; rancid motor oil gushes from zinc; a pungent stench rises out of the scrap iron labyrinth.

The pigeons take flight again, extending their course to the bridge, to the brick fort from whose balconies, fringed by dark arabesques, one can see in the distance, where the furrows meet, the white mausoleum, and trembling as though behind a river of alcohol, the four minarets, the golden crescent.

The children stroll hand-in-hand through the garden centered around the tombs of princes; they climb up to the empty niches, remain embraced in silence, reading; they clamber to the terraces, race down, climb again, sing. One is biting into sugar cane, another throws oranges. They carry coloring books, chalk, cups, and little green plastic canteens.

Dry pools break up the lawn. Streaked with chisels, the vaults bear English nicknames, figures, dates which from afar are white with erasures. Splinters of the rim on the pediment.

Climbing stairways that lead nowhere, sloping walls, empty hemispheres. As they pass along numbered edges, shadows reproduce the Earth's curvature, cipher the stars' altitude, postulate a fixed Sun. On the stairs erased by the rain, each afternoon reconfirms these measurements. Bronze astrolabes have remained among the ruins, discarded, broken.

The exact time.

In your couch of intertwining cobras, upon an ocean of milk, you sleep, naked. A thousand scaly heads crown your head. You breathe slowly. Your body gives in to the soft rings; upon your open hands, the emblems rest.

Perhaps you are listening to the immense banyan trees that border the pool; the wind and the birds shake their thick black threads.

Through a covered bridge, the devotees come to anoint your feet, they drink from the orange water ditched between your legs, they touch the knots of the tails. Petals and *paisas* cover you; beside your head smeared with yellow dust, a copper jar shines.

From the far south pilgrims have come to sing to you. Two stone pigs stand guard beside the bell they ring in your honor.

Perpetual propellers, your arms have chopped up everything. Among the unwinding and flame-spitting cobras, your body has revolved. Serene, smiling, your gestures underlined by circles of fire disrupted by your own flight, assembled once more, swift, glowing borders of fine threads, lightning flashes of slow rainbows. A solar crown follows your body's undulations and repeats them in the space that curves around your arms, when they spin.

Your destructive dance has extinguished the Earth. Now, panting, you contemplate the devastated space. Your eyelids are heavy.

Your arms and legs give in to the tranquil reptiles. You rest your head. One by one your muscles relax. Your eyes half-opened, you see the winter sky. The night wind effaces the trees.

From your navel the lotus flower will emerge, and from her, the creator.

You will dance again.

Go back to sleep.

Behind the beet baskets, the rice heaps, the tarnished glass-case, in the warehouse mist, merchants weight the tea. Painted on the door, among parrots devouring flowers, the seven Bodhisattvas. Through the glass, beyond the roofs, and the carved beams, the EYES of a golden tower, the mountain.

They pass by on bicycles, thick bells sound upon the angles of pagodas, they touch their foreheads. The supports of the eaves are yellow goats with enormous phalluses. On the steps, vendors lay out tablets strung with red letters, in Pali, Sanskrit calendars, Nepalese berets, mandalas, maps.

To the goddess spearing a buffalo, we offer small bananas; over the blood-drooling skulls held in her multiple hands, we scatter petals; raw rice on the ground, which avid pigeons devour. With a harmonica, a fiddle and a triangle—a little boy sings—the old men of the neighborhood, sitting on a mat, regale the entrance; in the courtyard, candles light up a cup filled with flowers, a wheel, a swastika: among gold flags fouled by birds Buddha teaches. Mantra banners. The Liberated is surrounded by an eagle-god of shining metal, a Mongolian-eyed marshal who unfolds a scroll and two lions with red pupils.

Beneath conical roofs, demons open women by their legs, quartering them. So that the faithful can draw the prescribed signs on their foreheads we have installed small mirrors on all the walls.

A metal ribbon falls from the top of the pagoda, through the superimposed roofs, down to the lowest, which it touches.

Among the sculptures in the courtyard, sacred lambs are fornicating in a flock.

Smell of hashish and sandalwood.

Over a row of prayer wheels which spin with a metallic mur-mur—pilgrims are pushing them: the formulas unfold in the wind—in niches with broken doors, the Enlightened receive at their feet children who play; monkeys come to steal the offerings and greedily devour their clothes, then they clamber on top of the great golden scepter—one of them sucks an egg—they jump down to the white lump of the stupa, whose cement is stained by drippings, from the peak, of the yellow left by the rain; from there they contemplate the thirteen heavens—one by one—the crest, surrounded by lamps, ending in a lightning rod.

Upon shabby, parallel carpets, the pupils are reciting mantras. Surrounding Siddhartha, a thousand silvery statues; facing the shelf that contains them, atop a tall armchair, a lama wearing glasses and a red hat conducts the prayer. Piled on the seats, model temples of marzipan, yellowish cloaks, goblets of tsampa tea. An acolyte bangs the circular drum hanging at the entrance, another puffs his cheeks, turns red, manages to blow a horn and then a conch shell; a third one, under his cloak, opens a box of Ovaltine. They whisper, fling paper balls and planes, make signs and faces at each other, flawlessly repeating the Mani. One stands up, from the shelf takes a water flask and some pastries, opening a grimy awning he throws them into the courtyard; another falls asleep, bangs another with his head, urinates on his own cloak; his partner tickles his ears.

From the top of the hill we hear the stampede of cymbals, the only note from the great folding horns which the monks transport on skates, their voices, continuous and hoarse.

On the ceiling centered by a glass globe with a model plane from the Royal Nepal Airlines, the Great Mandala of the Irritated and Knowledge-Hoarding Deities; the walls are scenes from the life of Diamond. A little bird comes to bathe in one of the offer-ing chalices. The fresh air penetrates the windows sealed by metal-lic screens. With some effort a peasant spins a prayer wheel of his own size.

From the tower of the great stupa, the eyes of the Pious watch us—blue-dyed eyebrows, enameled eyelids; a red hoop girds the pupils. On the summit, colored banners flash in all directions from the golden parasol; the printed prayers float in the wind.

"Here I am, buckos, that is to say, your Grand Lama, and therefore chief of the world-famous stupa that we have before us. Yes, white shaggy monks, I am fulfilling my karma in this suburban hovel, selling the ancient tankas of the Order and trafficking in copper scepters, now rusted green, in order to support the last lamas of the Yellow Hat.

"With the tablets of the Canon, the portable instruments, a herd of yaks, a few ritual masks that we were able to collect in the haste of our departure and a collection of dies for printing banners, the Congregation, watched over by the Ancestors, crossed the coldest valleys, the highest mountains in the world. One of the dignitaries who precedes me was forced to emigrate; they display the other at the popular courts in those provinces of Outer Mongolia, so northerly and snowy that not even storks make it there in the summer."

TUNDRA: What should I do in order to convert to Buddhism?

THE GRAND LAMA: Shave your head. Ah, and please, if you really want to get into the "mainstream," stop all violence right now. The French ambassador came to see me this morning; in the afternoon his son killed a tiger in Rajahstan. From here they went to the Ashoka Club and drank rice beer. Verily I say unto you, kids of Holland, that it is Thirst that prevents you from seeing the uncomposed, the un-created, that which is neither permanent nor ephemeral. What do you think of this ancient painting, a gift from an incarnate lama in Bhutan?

SCORPION: I'm afraid of dying in an accident; what should I do?

DESIRED ANSWER: The aggregates that compose men, oh pale ones, are nothing but products lacking the least reality: to understand this produces a joy that ignores death.

REAL(ity's) ANSWER: Come on, man! That's what amulets are for! This one, for example—he takes from a table a dagger with four blades and emblems on the handle—sought after by several Western museums, envelops the body of its owner in an invulnerable halo. Or this one—he shakes a parchment rattle, two pellets beat it, on the end of a thread—which surely you have never seen: it protects and fortifies.

TOTEM: How can one eliminate anguish?

THE GRAND LAMA: Sit with your legs crossed—and, dropping his slippers, he crosses his own, which are squeezed into yellow suede pants—your back straight, your attention alerted. A circle. Inscribe a square inside it. In the center, a favorite deity of yours. Concentrate on it. Naturally, in order to start, a support is necessary, a painted mandala, like this one—and he evolves, over the carpet, a painted cloth with concentric geometries—so miraculous and ancient that for you, for such a noble task, I would give it up for a few dollars: rupees of this country could not come near it, and, of course, much less those of India.

TIGER: Which is the true road to Liberation?

THE GRAND LAMA remains silent. A silly giggle (in the next room, on a sofa, his children talk over a red telephone, made of plastic).

The smell of burnt sheets, the steam rising from the banks of the river: slowly, we breathe.

For three days we shall sleep under the eaves, beside the small tile platforms, looking at the water. We shall give alms to the crippled who crawl around with tin cans. On the fourth night we shall return home.

Inside a windowless dump—the sweetish smell of adjacent pyres and of curry stagnated—sitting near the frying pans, on the dirt floor, the yogis who have gone up north for today's celebration are reciting the morning precepts, and frying vegetables. With ashes from the coal stoves they smear their bodies; carefully they smooth out their hair, anointed with juniper oil. They allow people to look at them, but not with glasses.

The pilgrims scream at the temple doors, crowd along the river, break through the lines of soldiers and run toward the courtyard in order to touch the great golden Nandin—flowers on his claws, on his knees three white stripes. A silver trident and a tambourine stand out between the roofs.

As the sun climbs between the swollen trunks and the light filters through treetops, in the small corroded temples phalluses start appearing, in rows. The women who perfume them, the vermilion and gold of their dresses, interrupt at times, for an instant, the perfect succession of cylinders.

Monkeys steal and shred the clothes which the devotees have left on the shore. At the sound of three grimy musicians, a chubby little girl dances; her brother tells, in English, the story of the guru who blinded a hippie with a stone, he imitates the drowning of the holy man who, because of his wine-drinking, rolled into the river.

A Sherpian peasant displays in a basin the movement of a few river snails, and on a scale, handfuls of marihuana which four long-haired boys bargain for, in Dutch.

The women let the shiny bands of their saris float; the shadows of partridges crossing from one shore to the other are black arrows upon the stony bottom floor.

Stained by the cremation ashes, by the grime of the bath, and of spit, the thread of water follows its course down the valley, snaking between the rocks, sinking into the flats, digging a ravine in whose walls, sheltered in the crevices, the friends of the birds meditate, mutely.

Then it descends to the royal baths—two cobras feed the pond.

On the signboards, the first ideograms; on both sides of the road, successive terraces down to the dry stream—strips of shiny sand—like a swelling wave.

The farmers come down from the huts in single file, under the row of red trees; the wicker cabins are clear dots on the ochre slope. The morning wind unfolds the smoke from the pottery workshops into hazy layers. On the hills white banners float over piles of stones covered with black writing.

Where the road ends, on the other side of the bridge, the abrupt cliff of the mountains; frozen threads come down from the top.

A cement elephant, upon which a boy rides, hoisting a book, precedes the solid, parallel constructions covered by the black monograms of the March. Further up, between the peaks, maybe the wind will make the prayer wheels spin, aligned upon the walls of the abandoned monasteries, upon the altars buried by the snow.

The red-cloaked monks recite a greeting to Avalokitesvara. From left to right they follow with their forefingers the letters inscribed on the white tablets which they hold up to the outside and protect from the sun with a cloth.

A neon tube lights golden Gautama whose lips are stretched in a rictus. Silk banners embroidered with colors today carpet the columns and the roof. Beside dishes of pastries, pots of smoking tea, rattles and candies, the children hang white tulle bands from the garland that frames a giant poster, in acrylic colors, of a young haloed lama, and from vases decorated by myopic and prognathic kins, in profile.

At dawn we shall start out again, until upon the horizon, the peaceful and twilight-hoarding deities show their orange fingers. Then we shall contemplate silently the slowness of the sun sinking between the snowy valleys, on the other side of the mountains, beside the great and now empty stupas and the EYES clouded over the towers of the native land.

In the echo left by a cymbal, the deepest of the four voices will pronounce the syllables:

> May the lotus flower
> be by Diamond joined.

Maitreya

To Maitreya

To be reborn in the presence of Maitreya, the future Buddha, is the greatest wish of many Tibetans and Mongols, and the inscription "Come, Maitreya, come!" on the rocks of numerous mountains testifies to their longing.

—EDWARD CONZE, *Buddhist Scriptures*

Part I

At the Death of the Master

A wrinkled old lama, his robe hanging crookedly over his sweater and yak hairs entangled in his black locks, pressed his eye against the crack in the door as if he were peering into a grotto.

He pushed open the door: at the creaking of the splintered wooden planks the sleeper turned furiously and with his hands pulled up the blanket as if to protect himself from a sandstorm.

After the tangled hair and the bat radar, a hand appeared: the movement of the forefinger was as regular as if controlled by a string.

With acrobatic ease, sleepyhead did a somersault: was he evading the attack of some giant bird with a sharp beak, or tossing his head against an oncoming wave? He let out a menacing snore as he jumped beneath his sheet, followed by short grunts like those of a country cat enraged by an invasion of ethylic odors.

The jack-in-the-crack, wishing to transmit a message to the inert, to cipher scarabs in basalt, and to put off that persistent son et lumière, refused to cry out—the voice: a red, fragmented emanation of the body, a vessel of protection against violence. He merely clacked his slippers vulgarly, a double clap resounding in the cubicle like a shot.

All at once the lethargic monk was on his feet—the edge of sleep was the rim of an arrow, his body, a tin target—standing up stiffly. Hands joined in a reverent salute, he uttered a hurried *mani* not knowing if he was addressing a head lama befuddled by a nod in the midst of the Salute to Dawn, or a bloodthirsty monkey who grabbed and bit his finger or, shortly after death, the detested manifestation of Avalokitesvara, hot-tempered and myriapod, in a halo of black flames, wearing a necklace of heads sucking bloodclots.

A loose pair of underpants, clean only in spots, outlined his pointy hip-bones and, flabby under a starch stain, a resting member bent toward the left.

"What's the matter?" he articulated clearly, ready to look for pails of water to put out a fire, or to gather up the most valuable tankas, leaving only imitations to the invader as a final mockery and riddle, frogs instead of *Dakinis*, painted ad hoc to humiliate him.

"Hurry," the visitor prodded him: "he's about to give the wheel a quarter turn."

The awakened monk rubbed his eyes. From the top of a wooden casket the size of a salt trunk, seashells painted on the lid, he grabbed a long, mended rag, unevenly dyed crimson, which he threw on and tied to his waist with a hemp rope.

They didn't close the door.

They walked along a narrow, creaking corridor, past a large window facing the misty morning landscape. The passageway was supported over the void by black wooden beams and columns— from ancient palaces left to the winds or to the insatiable tinkering of monkeys—and by the ruins of forgettable statues, inserted into the rock. A hemp fiber awning, rolled up and tied with ropes, sheltered it from the snow, and from the birds during nesting season.

As bewildered as the first monk, two others joined the herald; they stumbled along after him, clicking their tongues disapprovingly, with abrupt gestures and even poorly concealed curses.

They climbed a few worn, irregular steps, dug into the rock, right up to a wooden door: two slanty eyes were watching under their thick gold eyebrows, symmetrically curved, drawn with the same rapid, irregular stroke. Indigo pupils, lighter around the edges. Over the eyebrows, and in the dent between, a hollowed red oval in the veins. Neither nose nor mouth, nor a lock on the door.

They pushed it open carefully, as if afraid to awaken the Lhasa Apso lying beside the threshold.

It was a warm, spacious room without furniture or any ornament. The dim light from a few oil lamps, trembling amid mounds of rice, tea bowls, a basin, an inkwell and a reed case, was too weak to dispel the gloom. Or rather, as one's eyes got used to the dark they could distinguish old furniture lacquered in black, piled in the corners as if on the eve of a move or an invasion of moths, shiny-threaded cushions and wooden figures heaped on top of one another, wrapped in rush mats or in Nepalese newspapers held together by bandages. The blinking lamps illuminated at moments the golden motifs of some tankas—lotus flowers, clouds, hexagons—not yet unfurled or flung hurriedly upon the furniture, loose and torn.

Painted images floated on the wall, like standards or banners for an enthronement, faded shreds inherited from ancient monasteries, which the monks passed down from guide to disciple for many generations, like the same repeated question from snowfall to snowfall. Beneath those banners and placed upon the remnants of others, were two tiny skulls set in silver mountings like large irregular pearls, a shiny femur, bronze bells and a thunderbolt. Over the silver-threaded white rags, among silks and bones, the dying light of the wicks gave off tenuous flashes, fleeting yellow streaks.

Secretive, huddled together like Chinese animals on the eve of an earthquake, the four monks entered the next room, where the master was dying.

His head resting on his own clasped hands, the guide, smiling, on a bed of stone, was breathing his last. His robe sprawled in regular folds, open waves, fusing with the gathered robes of the monks as if the same thick cloth, pleated cinnabar, enveloped the congregation beneath the moribund. A young lama gave him something to drink from a smooth jug, without handle or adornment; another kissed his feet.

One could hear in the distance, like thunder or an avalanche, the morning trumpets of another monastery, higher up in the mountains. Right before the rain or on clear days, one could see beside the blue cliffs the thick armor of the buildings, the wall enclosing them. The great white stupa fused with the snow.

The monks huddled beneath the drapery. Outside: birds and, further away, crossing the valley or climbing in search of pasture, a herd of yaks. One of the larger prayer wheels rotated. Someone was sobbing.

The dying man contemplated him, pretending to be angry. With restraint, as if solving a riddle or glimpsing the answer to an unformulated enigma suspended in mid-air, he declared firmly:

"I dreamt of the sea."

Silence pierced by the brief creakings of a giant tree, leaves shaken by the monkeys, in the Indian noon.

In a lower, breathless voice:

"Beside the crumbling geometries of a mandala devoured by two kinds of fungus, near a stream: there I will be reborn. You will find me in the water, with my eyes closed. I will be the Instructor. A rainbow of wide stripes will encircle my feet."

Muted vibrations fragmented by the edges of the high monastery: large drums were banging furiously, demanding that the pink protecting divinities spill hail in the path of the invaders.

To the black-browed lamenters:

"Why are you so contrite? I have seen clearly my new birth. Each day the Bardo is shorter. On the other hand, in your sorrow, it will not take you long to find me. The moment of the great move draws near. Burnt flags, red mortar over the ancient frescoes. They will make others believe that we raised our monasteries over those skulls of children, buried in the foundations, and that from them we drank semen, opium and blood. Death, little monkeys, does not form part of life but rather the reverse: we emerge from noncreation, and we return to it in the twinkling of an eye. The rest, on the other hand, are little sketches in silk and, without offending the pictorial proficiency of those present, always the same. You will not see the Korean screen fading much longer: you will not see the sun on the embossed supports of the eaves, nor herons and cranes, nor the red-tinted rice on the foreheads of the dancing girls. To the south, before the flustered northerners arrive!"

His breathing was slower now. The lama who kissed his feet felt it first, and with a nod as if he approved, he announced it to the others: a recognizable frost was gaining on him. The appropriate points confirmed its progress along his body, to the base of his nose, where a little bluish man perched.

Accompanied by a uniform sound—with a metal rod they traced the burnished edge of a bell—they shouted in the transient's ear the reading of the last counsels: he should know very clearly that everything he was going to see, the most intense colors, the most present and palpable and, if he reached the end of that interval, even a white, immaterial light, was only the beguiling projection of the lowest part of his brain, as meticulously false, as lacking in reality as whatever it is that serves as a screen to life.

"The void is the form. The form is the void . . . That ought to keep you busy for years." These were his last words for the mortified mourners, as well as his last breath. Without further ado, he entered stillness.

Two days later, exhausted by the noisy complexity of the rites, which they had followed scrupulously, beneath a vertical pennant sewn to a bulrush and with an identical red effigy stamped from top to bottom, they burned him near a precipice.

When the fire was consumed and the bones were left among the burning coals, naked and polished, they gathered them up carefully in a white wool carpet, without disturbing their order, as if afraid of breaking them.

This task over, they each held a corner as they suspended and began to swing the woven rectangle. First slowly, as if sifting or shaking. With twangy or atavistic voices, malevolent ancestors, masks of painted birds, they repeated tantric incantations. Then possessed or merely ostentatious, they waved the carpet three times, and hurled the bones into the void.

First the remains rose all together, rotating rapidly over themselves—white omoplate-boomerangs—to the height of a granary or a chorten of piled rocks; they hovered over the void for a moment, motionless, like a band of boreal birds sensing danger; then, from different heights, according to their weight, they began a slow descent. The head like a planet out of orbit which upon falling would turn back into lava, lime or mother-of-pearl, in a luminous, spiral unwinding, became a giant iridescent conch.

The head, like a planet torn from its course and which upon

falling would turn back into lava, lime or mother-of-pearl, in a luminous, spiral unwinding, became a giant iridescent conch which when blown by the wind emitted a muffled, unchanging sound, the charred vibration of a remote explosion. A sound that became deeper until, followed by a rain of tiny bones, a hoarse hailstorm, faded in the circle of an OM.

They returned hungry.

That same night they ceased to utter his name.

They hardly slept. After the vigil lamps had been revived, and the recitations reluctantly completed, someone began to knock before the animals could warn them, as if wanting to break down the front door with a sickle.

Not all of them ran to the door. The youngest, shy, preferred to spy from the windows; some, fearing cattle rustlers, bandits, armed Indians, salt thieves and even the *yeti*, fled wildly to the inner recesses, which nobody had opened since the fumigation parties and there they stayed, breathless and blockaded, among old harnesses, mended hats and ancient ceremonial costumes now faded and filthy which the monks, to obey the Sutra "may all animals be happy," offered annually to the moths.

They thought that some absent-minded novice, who had lost his way in the mountains looking for alpine flowers, had strayed at twilight.

Pondering excessive threats, like leprous or porcine incarnations, and mortifying reprimands, the eldest monk freed the door knockers:

Like them, he smelled of stale tsampa brew and was dressed in a filthy crimson robe. They flashed a lamp on his face: they didn't know him.

The blurry, oily light, shaken by the wind, spread fleeting stains over the dusty red robe, like fish beneath a beacon. A white, wide-open mouth. Mask with human eyebrows: he tried to articulate, uttering animal or taciturn sounds or—one of the indignant insisted—a dialect that wasn't Tibetan. He pointed to his feet.

They lowered the lantern to the floor. Filtered by the branches of a banyan, the moon blanches the rush mat where the turbaned plowmen of a canebreak sleep: the yellow light of the wicks through the ground glass covered the mute man's robe with ashes.

Lifting him by the arms they managed to carry him into the kitchen. They sat him on a birdseed bag. They gave him tea. With a Chinese flyswatter they began to fan him. They untied his boots: between the strings, bloodclots. The leather of the soles stuck, like a scab, to the cracked floor.

"The message of Sakyamuni," he burst out choking and wheezing, as they raised his feet to a chair, "has completed its orbit. As the night falls upon the mandala, so does the time of Maitreya draw near."

Panting asthmatically and clearly irreverent:

"I want to eat meat."

He pointed to the empty jug of tea.

"The ancients knew how to fly. They could strip naked: they felt so hot that they'd arrive sweating after crossing a frozen lake. They'd continue the same conversation through successive incarnations."

And, without a transition:

"Gather your trappings. They destroyed everything made of paper, carried off the metal things in a cart. They stuck notices on the walls. They acted out a secular passage: women and arms on stage. They set fire to the place."

From the high monastery—were they officiating at off-hours, celebrating sleepless divinities, meowing guardians of the temple? —brief explosions were heard, first dispersed, sifted by the wind, as if from beyond the jungle, but then clearer, planks falling, tree trunks rolling down the slope. No: the newcomer recognized them immediately: gunshots from Chinese rifles.

An hour later they cut short for the first time, and celebrated for the last, the Salute to the flying tutelary divinities of the morning. They all stood there scrutinizing their feet, afraid of moving, when the authoritarian cymbalist marked the end of the echo of mantras, coughs, throat clearings and rolling bells, the copper emanations becoming blurred, finally fading.

"Shall we say something," the youngest asked contritely, "or shall we say nothing?"

The lama at his side, in response, bent down to put a bundle on his back, placing around his forehead one of the bands that tied it together.

A subterranean hustle and bustle startled them: it was the war-hardened Trappists who, seeing that nothing was happening, were abandoning the third zone of the wheel—district of the fortunate animals—and, throwing open the floodgates at each new flow, they emerged joyously, sloths shaking off the frost.

They all dressed as mountain-climbers or as peasants. In wicker baskets they hurriedly piled the objects which for a long time they had kept in newspapers or bandages, or hidden between two rush mats. They resorted to divination to determine the precise moment and direction of the journey:

> dawn
> south
> seeking river
> toward the mountain

They picked up, in passing, some animals.

Three days through snow.

They found other refugees.

Tea. Fatigue. Sleep.

They were followed by a band of birds.

The Instructor

The two painted plaster tigers, with their onion eyes and large fangs, watched over the back entrance of the temple, hidden by a red-lacquered partition wall. A dark corridor, lined with ancient frescoes—slanty eyes, pennants and flyswatters, an orchid, the concentric folds of a chin—led to the patio surrounded by darkened rooms filled with wicker baskets and grey cracked clay urns. Bony old men, with straight shiny beards and dirty undershirts, meditated over tables covered with paint brushes and seals, heads between their hands. A jolly chubby Chinaman, in a chair leaning against the wall, was drinking a beer in a doorway. Next to him another laughed, pointing to a great cement prick beside a well.

Beyond the patio, at the end of a passageway with hanging clothes, a vast black-beamed nave opened out: from the ceiling hung large pink-paper lanterns printed with flower vases and conch shells, colored ribbons and engraved garlands. Outside, one could hear the bells of little bicycle-drawn carts. Among streamers and cellophane castles with boxes of incense sticks, cardboard towers and hare-faced guards, there was a grainy screen: perforated little shadows with feeble trembling feet waved their arms, leaped and stamped about like frightened pelicans. They had extremely long arms, bent at right angles, and moved their pointy little fingers; their noses were straight and narrow, and horns were engraved on their heads. A bunch of bursting cymbals and tambourines—which fit in the palm of a hand—announced the leaping black filigrees upon a foot nail, flying in profile between two rods, inserted into the nerves of a leaf.

Behind the screen and the overworked puppeteers, golden

scarlet-face convulsive gods awaited, brandishing enormous curved sabers, their female companions with eggshell white faces. Furious, mounted on mustached, toad-eyed animals, they were retouched by a pomaded acolyte with a rabbit-hair brush. The two tendinous old Leng sisters accompanied him, yellow with age like sulphuric sibyls. In a large plastic basin—seven fluorescent colors—purposely splashing the figures, they were bathing a little boy who squeezed his eyes shut so that soap wouldn't get in.

Then, in a corner of the nave, they smoothed out a wrapping of dirty sheets with a ruler, squinting, panting, expert like cats digging up bird bones. No: with knife-shaped sandalwood slabs they scraped the pockmarks off a corpse; they wore down its teeth with a file; they stuck metal circles with empty squares over the center of the hard eyelids: the skin swelled, spotted with greenish ideograms. Scabs fell to the floor and whitish sand from the teeth stained the mouth: the ashen halo, like rice powder around the lips, was scraped by the old women's bracelets, armadillo claw clasps.

Funereal little flutes could be heard from afar: the Aragón Cha-Cha Band.

The soapy infant stuck his right foot out of the basin: his hand was squeezing a spheric sponge with large pores; a thick liquid trickled so slowly that it reflected, like quicksilver, the elongated purple cloaks of the gods, their crowns of silvery fruit, and the old women's poisonous bracelets.

"Everything was going very well here," he recited, arms stuck to his thigh, closed fists, stiff like a savage before a camera, "until the men with hair on their body arrived."

And while the old women in their creamy tatters soaped him more, he added:

"I'm the one who bears a stupa on his head."

One of the women turned toward the back of the room with two empty pails. She carefully pushed open the door beside the altar with her right foot: along a vaulted gallery, identical statues on thrones extended as far as one could see: feeble long-eared Buddhas. A long slate interrupted the succession: upon a sketch of the human body seen as a tree of orthogonal branches and inscribed leaves, a monk in thick glasses and an orange robe indicated with a pointer the highest petals. From the pulpits a chanting chorus responded, spelling out Sanskrit names.

The old hag returned with full buckets, gave him one last rinse and began to rub him with a rag, as if she wanted to make him shine:

"You have made many offerings to the Buddha," he stated as they polished him, "parasols, banners, flags, perfumes, garlands and unguents, and on his altars placed sandalwood or saffron; you have given many gifts to those studious monks—robes, drink, food and medicine—and even to that missionary from Toulouse, always in his sweater and taking notes among them, in order to deserve being here and to hear me.

"In the beginning," and with a gesture he stopped the Lengs who, vexed, quit their rubbing, "I thought that astronomical news, that is, the surprise of the explosions, was enough to create in the mind, for the moment, the void, like those bearded Japs swinging canes and busting flower vases. Now I realize that such magnitudes, for a little bird head, are like the wind . . .

"They took me to the river. They put me headfirst in the water. With a firm hand upon my neck they pushed me under. I was drowning. Opening and closing my mouth like a fish on land. I flailed my arms. I no longer saw where my head was sinking. I was going to collapse; then they freed me: 'When you need to extinguish desire as you have needed air . . .'

"I will give neither questions nor answers, then, not any exercise; only indications, suggestions of staging, as if I were nailing in a banana tree little leather figures.

"This is the last time I shall be born. I will not return again but I shall go from here, in my purity, to nirvana."

Outlined by the black door of the passageway, a silvery grey storm sky mirroring over the patio—pierced by lightning and herons.

Beside the red partition wall, two girls with very black straight hair smiled on a motor scooter, a red dot on their foreheads.

It was night. In a wobbly cabin, enclosed by a bamboo fence, several boys in green uniforms ate fried vegetables, shrimp and noodles. They looked at us. They listened to the Javanese radio.

In the bramble, three palm-frond huts. Beside a small copper well, three naked hermits meditated. The main road behind them, a bus with people hanging out the windows, a car.

Along the beach, a man with a lantern was walking away. Yellow stain on the sand. Shadow of rapid feet. There were so many fireflies that, like the sky, the grass winked and blinked.

The exile's astrological search for traces of the master's reincarnation went on, day and night. Nostalgic for snow, the smell of yak shit, nocturnal pollutions and loose tea, they abused the moderate precepts of the Greater Vehicle, seizing the prophetic altarcloths and, for further efficiency, waving them as if shaking off breadcrumbs.

It's true that such mantic self-denial led them, inevitably, through some nightless nights and a day on a freight train, among amulet smugglers.

An architecture of concentric geometries—a mandala, seen from the air—served as a point of departure; in the middle of the jungle, in fact, the walls crumbled, devoured by fungi: a white bacteria—dried milk—as well as greenish and microscopic. Western experts, arriving by helicopter with anti-fungal powders, numbered the leprous stones one by one in order to reassemble them, once removing their crusts, within a century's time.

Regarding other traces of the master, the five self-appointed members of the Expert Commission on Metempsychosis lacked metaphoric audacity: having reached the temple reservation, amid wood scholars, behind a flea-bitten screen for Javanese shadows, they all wondered why there were so many shrill colors in one basin.

When they were finally fed up with elbowing and knocking figures down on the ground, they returned to the patio. From the far end of a damp, scribbled corridor, one of the old women appeared, holding a grey lock of hair and a handleless mug, inflamed and repulsive as always at that hour of the morning.

The commissioners set upon her so impetuously, opening a file so suddenly, that the hag replied: "It's useless, if you're trying to sell me some insurance policy. I know only too well the usuries of insurance men."

You live and learn: the next day, getting up at the crack of dawn, they undertook the material proof of the transmigration.

Seated around the presumed incarnate—whom they forced, who knows why, into a fainting fast—rubbing their eyes and yawning they offered from several pairs of hats, walking sticks and rosaries, to choose from—an object of each pair had belonged to the master. Then, upon an embroidered cloth—on colored threads a pig, a serpent and a cock were biting their own tails—

they spread twelve little bells and thunderbolts, so that he would indicate the pair with which he had officiated, in his previous command. Finally they recited to him, loud and clear, the beginning of the Four Noble Truths:

"Continue on your own," the vociferant suddenly stopped.

When they saw that the examinee didn't limit himself to responding, but rather anticipated in mockery the tests which he considered farces, and the questions, which he answered as if they were riddles, they handed over to him the sacred protective cord (sungdü) and the traditional scarf (khata), which he tied gaily, in the prescribed way, around the neck of the oldest examiner.

"Why harass me with more tests?" he protested. "I know only too well the fifty-one models of thought.

"I wish to take up again the interrupted conversation with my friend the supreme abbot of the Surmang monastery, and which we've been sustaining for eleven generations. He owes me two chickens."

"He will not be an ordinary Brahman," the learned men asserted, "or a lazy sacrificial official, an avaricious dealer in magic sayings, a conceited worthless orator, a wicked sly priest, or just a good stupid sheep amongst a large herd."

The Leng sisters attended the keen investigation, sheathed in their myopia and cylindrical grey linen skirts and, black-browed, the circles darkening under their eyes, they began to realize that this trashy dialogue destined the infant to occupy, in god knows what Tibetan wayside inn, a throne of three cushions covered with strips of brocade, before a collection of official seals and documents. It also destined the Lengs to wash piss-soaked robes, cook yellow rice for feasts, serve as witches in ritual dramatizations and gather dung to warm themselves in the winter, so they decided to have an emergency meeting in the cellar, to "consider with objectivity"—they separated this word into syllables—"the situation, and program the future in accordance with its secondary contradictions"—spelled out as well.

And so it was: in a few minutes of penetrating analysis they decided to pass on to praxis, to cause the immediate disappearance of the object of such greed, poisoning the harassing delegates, if necessary, with strychnine-sprinkled Alicante nougats. Varnishing their stiffened corpses with paste, silver-plating their lips and eyelids, they would then mix them in with the bound Arhats piled upon each other in the back of the temple, shielded by bows and broadswords.

They studded the doors. Survived two days on boiled potatoes. On the night of the third, disguised as Cantonese witch doctors, carrying elegant bundles of dried herbs on their heads, and mounted on strong wooden boots, they left the temple dragging between them a crippled child: they had fastened his knees with splints, coifed him in a scabby wig and lengthened his eyes with ink: a Mongol dolt. An overdose of valerian made him docile to all simulations.

Thus, they reached the train station.

They tried to mix in with the untouchables who slept in joined cardboard boxes—large cradles for sleepwalkers—on the nocturnal platforms traversed by feeble mice, and even upon broken rails.

Dragging the cripple with doleful faces they got on without tickets and changed cars three times, in a train that had crossed the monsoon with Pakistani refugees in white dhotis, perched on the roof and sticking out of the windows.

While that hulk sank toward the south, screeching throughout the damp and suffocating night, the old women, to compensate for the fatigue of the trip, gulped down greasy bags of fried plantains and open cans of hot beer. By dawn they were overwhelmed by uncontrollable cramps and vomiting.

They didn't know where they were. They were slobbering and dirty, their hair sticky and eyes watery; all that shaking had swelled their feet.

They took a last train, which for a whole day crossed cracked land.

The kidnapped one awoke crying.

They reached the sea.

The Island

To continue soaping him in peace and to see, in passing, if he said anything at all, the diligent Lengs founded a vegetarian hotel on the outskirts of Colombo.

There they could smell, after the rain, the rank dense air from the temple across the way and the greasy rations of rice—pyramids kneaded by patient hands and wrapped in plantain leaves—that a gaunt, buck-toothed Brahman in a ragged sarong was handing out to needy beggars beside a well covered with black raffia and roughly nailed zinc sheets—the landing strip of ravens—as he smoothed back his hair with cocoa butter.

At sunset, the insular initiates began to arrive parsimoniously, still sweating, their hands swollen or saffron-stained. Gathering at the lodge, they sniffed camphor and drank arak on the sly to attenuate dietetic erosions. They had been recruited by the old women and their opportune kinfolk—who, following them in exile, had journeyed to the island in third class with their thermos flasks. They had also recruited certain Tamil pilgrims who went from temple to temple in and around Madras, exhibiting a signed testimony of mystical solvency to raise donations, and shaven Parsis converts who were skillful makers of digestive spring rolls: flaky concentric pancakes filled with bits and pieces of meat and submerged in three pans of boiling oil.

They listened lethargically and reverently when the instructor came downstairs from his den—where disturbing demons were materializing in the form of perfidious fleas—to the little he had to say. There were those who ciphered with round, separate, loop-like letters, on wooden tablets that were still green, later to be bound, the newcomer's fleeting hyperboles.

Little is known, though the bamboo fan may be vast when unfolded, of those aporias and impulsive dinner conversations when,
heads bowed before black bowls, the listeners asked questions in
the misty gloom of the main room. Ravens came to perch on the
windowsills, escaping the rain, and even on the blocked blades of
an old English fan in the middle of the ceiling. A smell of dirt and
chewed betel accumulated in the air. From afar came the scratchy
voices of a phonograph.

Fearful of curses and lightning, the austere hags went around
the house removing cats from closets and covering mirrors.

Yellow cloths were draped over the wicker furniture. A streaked
creamy tulle, hanging from a rod with rings like a shower curtain,
protected a Buddha in immanent meditation from stares and
mosquitos, tenacious layers of paint plastering it with menacing
cosmetic signs from the Bombay movie theater.

Upon the arrival of the ever-bathed, the old women closed the
curtain with a furious yank, as if to hide a greasy kitchen from the
visitors or, in the niche of an electric meter, a giant cream-colored
rubber phallus.

Pale grey fringes, curved like frames, come out of a great almond on the meditator's back and extended, in dull ochre colors,
along the walls and simulated columns of the small temple to a
little worm-eaten door that led to a pink washroom where a lit
bulb swung slightly at the end of a black cord.

Beneath the lotus flower where the Too-Radiant One rested, in
a circular hole like an alluvial grotto among petals, with two entrances, the old women had hidden away and were nurturing two
dwarf tortoises. The would look for mosquitos to feed to them.

"Little is known," I said, "of what he said." But what is certain is
that he tried, in order to ruin the ancestral ceremony of the Buddha Tooth and to "push a riddle toward the real," to bite the precious fang right in front of the astounded guardians. The braided
red cord that, tracing a quick ideogram, follows the head movements of the six drummers—in silver bracelets and red sarongs—
who adorn the opening of the odontological couch every morning
with the same devotion and Japanese photographers, stopped for

a moment in mid-air and fell stiffly.

Over the sandalwood bannister—leading to an ambulatory on the first floor, with chapels filled with quartz Gautamas, ficus religiosus, golden lotuses and plated gold leaves—the usual plaintive, barefoot old women appeared, furiously covering with kitchen leftovers and giant white flowers the marble plaque in front of the canine.

A thin boy with straight black hair, wearing a University of Indiana sweatshirt, dropped on the floor a conch filled with yellow rice and pebbles.

At daybreak he crossed the lower rooms of the hotel, where two flat, stinking spirals, like burnt licorice, burned throughout the night between sandalwood rods to drive away mosquitos. From superimposed platforms the choral snores of the Leng sisters ascended in slow whorls opening onto the ceiling: checkered scarlet and ochre over a border with a thousand faded impressions of the same Buddha.

The warm stove still shone, like last night's bonfire on the open plains. From above, he took a barley cracker. He drank a whole jug of buffalo milk yogurt.

He noiselessly opened the frayed screen separating the cots. Facing a Victorian vanity as if posing for the unfolding of a box camera or its eye, Illuminated Leng appeared, dressed in pearly canary yellow silk and with a poinsettia in her ear. She seemed to be preparing to sell on the sidewalks, considering the hour and the little tortoiseshell purse hanging from her right shoulder, what exile and a month among rotten heads of lettuce in the floating markets of Hong Kong had taught her never to give away for nothing.

The old women's niece had adopted for this sarcastic exercise the white makeup worn by the ancient harlots of the Empire, though in her own revised, operatic version. She had plastered her face with eggshell powder, which she kept in a little spherical corked vial—as if for burying ants—and a bit of chalk, tracing a shaven, painted oval to outline better the border where, like a black hard shell, her hair sprouted. Her lips, which remained closed even when she laughed, were hidden. Orange eyebrows. A jet gem on her nose.

That's what he perceived, like a belch of yogurt, when opening the screen: Illuminated illuminating herself. Now, what she glimpsed in the vanity mirror, framed in a threadbare landscape, was less verisimilar and—worse for me—describable: a roguish fat cat, occupying the place and size of the passerby, dancing on one paw, proudly showing off the sole of the other.

So he danced—and nervously bit into a sesame seed nougat—without music, but with a tower of grimacing heads arranged according to size on top of his head: red, laughing, greenish, crowned heads with big curved fangs and, between their eyebrows, vertical bloodshot eyes. There were so many arms that there seemed to be a hundred: swiftly slicing the air with mechanical, helicoidal movements, waving a whistling conch, sistrums, sceptres, darts, double-skinned tambourines, a lotus flower, a little leg that had been bitten off, black flames and a triple head with locks of straight hair, the mane of a horse whose neck sprouted black blood.

That thing stepped on, crushed slow fleshy mollusks with little pink antennas, or dwarf demons with protruding, fleeting, mercurious eyes. With a right hand he nonchalantly caressed the chin of a juicy girl with her legs opened, she looking at herself in a tiny oval mirror and licking her upper lip as if she'd just eaten a sweet crème caramel.

Illuminated couldn't describe what she saw in the mirror and broke down when trying to face it, but she could describe, with details, what she heard since it lasted briefly beyond the vision, the floor vibrating from the jumping, like a military dais upon an elephant's passing; that dull boom was interrupted by the jingling bells of his ankles, crashing knuckles, bloodclots spurting upon the rush mats, and finally a lubricated rubbing embolus going in and out: yes, because what he held in his arms without squeezing—his fingers separated and curved—was his white partner, wearing heavy crowns and dull stone bracelets, legs opened and facing him, big breasts and a narrow waist, wide hips moving slowly as she let him thrust into her a huge red phallus without veins, right up to his hard spheres, as she murmured, in the moaning midst of oohs and ahs, giggles multiplying in the echo of superimposed hands, something like "ooh, yummy, give it to me honey," in oral Sanskrit or ancient Tibetan.

Illuminated rubbed her eyes and then leaned her head upon her fingertips. She lit up a mentholated Camel. And looked at herself again in the mirror.

"It's the laudanum infusions," she said to herself. "I'll have to dilute them a bit more."

She wet the tip of a black pencil with saliva and furiously retouched, over the right side of her upper lip, a discreet beauty mark, pendant to the jet gem on her nose.

Careful not to make the hinges creak, the wakeful wanderer had closed the screen, and left the streetwalker's cubicle.

He crossed the sleeping city, the dense night air: a smell of urine and iodine rose from the port. In black baskets on the sidewalks, dripping a watery drivel—enameled spatterings—among dried fibers, lichen or algae, there were piles and piles of oysters. Ravenous yellow dogs emerged from the dark depths of patios to lick them.

A stamp-cutter opened the folding windows of his store. Leaving aside his caskets lacquered with winter cherry trees and filled with cinnabar powder, his wrinkly white screens, and paintbrushes made of baby hair, as if impelled by the sulphurous breath of a demon, he appeared before the passerby, ceremoniously bowing:

"I knew you were the guide," he said. "For days the animals have been lying on the ground. The silverware suddenly rusted."

He walked on by. In the suburbs, along the banks of Dutch canals, horses hauled, under the shade of palm trees, slow grey boats loaded with pineapples. A damp, sweetish vapor, smelling of rotten fruit, stagnated in the air.

He walked along the beach. One could hear, close at times, according to the direction of the wind, or fading in the distance, the muted cornets of a fox-trot, a piano, clinking glasses, conversation, laughter. A man in a white drill suit, hat in hand, walked out of an American hotel toward the water, bent over, vomited on the foam, looked toward the horizon.

Enormous tortoises were returning from the setting sun, leaving in the ochre sand a slimy, silvery, awkward trace, traveling from the hole filled with oil or amber-colored translucid fat eggs, to the moving line of the water. The tide was rising. The birds, fleeing. Near the edge, grey air, glittering terraces.

Wrapped in a brick red sarong, a stiff adolescent suddenly appeared, his arms crossed, his face opaque: with a brief gesture he pointed to a promontory out to sea, covered with luxuriant trees, ceibas and royal poincianas, moving red spots linked together by a thick net of vines.

They walked a long time in silence, reached some sculpted rocks inhabited by tiny crabs; among them, dug into the rock, they discovered, sandy and deep, some worn old stone steps.

Pushing aside vines, startling small birds, they climbed up to a wooden house. The nails of the roof were becoming loose: among dry branches, through which they could see the supports, a peacock nested.

The door opened without their knocking.

"How dare you interrupt?" they were scolded furiously by an emaciated old monk in a frayed robe, his pupils fogged by mist. "I am meditating on the thirty-four components of the body: nails"—and he opened before their eyes his scrawny, tendinous hands—"the flesh, which is rotting, toenails, eyes, with their whites, the sex and what it secretes."

And, tired of cataloguing:

"Give something for the building of the temple."

It was a dark and dirty little room: on the floor, bunches of green coconuts, a guano leaf; cracked walls. Rice on a plate with scattered petals, before a small pink plaster Buddha in Samadhi.

"Why such a fuss?" the newcomer dryly began, "over the elements of the body? Thinking about one hair is enough to get you to nirvana."

And without further to-do:

"I want coconut milk."

With one machete slice, the waiter from the beach cut one of the green, woody fruits from the floor. The thirsty one drank it in one gulp as if it were a glass of snails with ketchup. He asked him to cut it again. With his hands he ate the slippery white meat. He left the hovel without saying good-bye. The empty halves of the

coconut rolled down the slope: a brief, fibrous sound, crumbling
stones that frightened snakes, breaking against the red reefs.

A little further up the promontory black bricklayers, in bathing
trunks and large purple turbans, busy and sweating, were preparing to finish the temple: a tollbooth with latticed windows, a zinc
roof and a little altar inside. They plastered the cracks between the
bricks, with rapid little touches, like woodpeckers. With high-
pitched voices they sang songs from Madras, and between two
edifying trowel blows, pretending to be overheated and wiping
false drops of sweat off their brows, they ran to the shade of a banyan where, in a little sand barrel, a bottle of rye whiskey was cool-
ing among ice cubes. They passed it around, drying their mouths
with neckerchiefs. Singing louder, they went back to work.
Laughing, they scratched and adjusted their genitals constantly, as
if the trunks were too tight.

"Where did we come from?" asked the youngest worker as he
leveled a brick, "when the universe began?"

"Come on, man!" he answered. "If a warrior is pierced in the
sole of his foot by a poison arrow, should he look for the one who
shot it, where it came from, what curare was used, or try to get it
out immediately?"

And saying this, he turned around and started down the promontory. Alone: his morning companion, enlightened by the bricklayers, had accumulated comforting tricks beneath the tree, and
was reeling amid the debris, disoriented by the expansion of ethylic stars in his blood. He was trying in vain, in order to be afloat
again, to squeeze a piece of ice, melting in his awkward hands,
against the sandy scar between his legs.

Was it that centenary vapor which duplicated images for him,
or a mirage in the sand, beneath the dense, grey air of the monsoon?

He called to the other bricklayers: along the beach two identical boys were walking away slowly, embracing.

No, they weren't jiving. Nor was it a reflection in the sand:
they walked hand in hand, separate, moving evenly, symmetrically.

He disappeared along a path of pebbles.

At each bend the sea seemed more vast and uniform: near the edge, sunken stones traced the outline of former docks.

For three days, a grey, harsh landscape. In a wicker basket, white fuzz: newborn kittens. Further on, a horse.

An old man with a straight beard, under an eave covered with dark, silent pigeons, read as he leaned on a twisted, knotty cane. He did not raise his hand to greet him. A dog slept at his feet.

The next day he found himself in front of the buildings: sloping stone patios, diverse wooden balconies among fallen scaffolds, ruins.

In the dark, windowless, abandoned hall, an iron hoop, with prods for hanging lamps or men, occupied the whole space: the hoop oscillated slightly: rusty chains with engravings suspended it from the ceiling.

Along the top of the walls, though faded and interrupted by cracks, crossed wings appeared, eyes linking them together like nailed feet; long white bands with black rectangles were lined up in a row and in their center, like stains absorbed by the stone, stood tall, emaciated saints, the bands tied to their necks. Smooth, uniform purple robes contained their bodies. They went barefoot. Pale hands with long fingers held books with burnt pages tightly to their chests. Their eyes: empty or retouched.

Concluding the succession of figures, and covered by one of them—the most clearly and brightly outlined—a man-sized door, neither truncated nor cracked but with visible vertical joints, was silhouetted on the wall.

He was about to leave the room when the creaking of hinges stopped him. Behind the door, identical to the image covering it, and as if displacing it forward and turning it around to show its other, wooden side, a monk appeared embracing a mongoose.

He stepped forward until forming part of the row. There he remained a moment, concluding the series:

"We were waiting for you."

They ate beans, always poorly heated, and herring, in a clay dish. A fibrous tablecloth covered the sanded wood.

They lived in silence. Dusty gowns, unbuttoned boots. The day gave each one his rhythm. They didn't touch each other. Beside the deep, plain windows, over the spillways—urine veins in the ochre stones—they'd listen at night to the roar of the waves.

They'd arrive in flimsy boats, covered with canvas. Early in the morning they'd skirt the island, yawning in the coves. Some went out in wide canoes, dodging flying fish. They'd read in the prows. Rapid, silvery needlefish traveled in schools, always in unison and near the bottom.

On the buffaloes and horses they'd clamber up to the cloddy, uneven cultivated lands which each one, followed by his cats, would plow. They slept during midday under the eaves. Then toward sunset they'd contemplate, over the mountains, the passing fog.

He didn't sleep the whole night. He couldn't because of the constant rattling, as if reeds were rustling or leather belts were being shaken to frighten away bats. Without further incentive than nocturnal contemplation he scrutinized the changing landscape, reduced it to words, to pure shadows, to overlapping circles of different blues. Thus geometrized, he used it as a support for meditation on the mission to which he had been assigned.

Confused by the noisy bells, he understood later that he was meditating without any support whatsoever.

And then: neither with or without support.

He perceived the thick promontories as one more attribute of the void, as arbitrary in their form and devoid of consistency as the mist that blanched them.

It is not known how long he was among them.

When he returned, everything had changed. He didn't recognize the Lengs' hotel nor its seasoned vegetarians.

Without dialectic modesty or even a limit to her arrogant exercise of contradiction, as if wishing to advance abruptly the backward thrusts she gave the Wheel each night, or perhaps pulled along by a Zen undertow, Illuminated had begun, visibly roused by the ascetic new look of her fellow diners or by the old women's eagerness to impart peaceful vibrations, the structural reforms to which everyone, in the flophouse's meditative quietism, aspired.

Not without binary residues: she had divided, following functional or animistic criteria, with an ambitious gesture marking in the air a fuchsia-painted nail, the ashram into two orthogonal zones.

"Upstairs," and she pointed reluctantly to the creaking, crumbling spiral staircase upon which the supposed little Buddha would ascend to his rooms, "*Misty Mountains*, and downstairs," she reflected for a moment, "*Roaring Waves*," as she proudly surveyed the surface of the room whose floor would be carpeted from wall to wall with fresh green rush matting. "The walls will be covered," she expounded with a symbolist lilt, "by sixteen moving panels with discreet gold locks, on which a single roaring crest of foam will rise at the far right, advance all along the shinden over a changing turquoise blue background, and finally break against the reefs, in the left corner."

Having determined the themes, Illuminated abandoned her productive evening walks as ostentatiously as she had begun them, without the least concern over her Karmic incoherence and without losing sleep, in order to dedicate herself completely to her Work.

In the company of a benevolent meditator, a former mandarin cook now converted to the message by the old women, and known among the catechumens as Honey Boy, she surrendered wholeheartedly to the sketching of stylized landscapes.

They left, in mid-winter, for the northern end of the island, to descend a coastline laid waste by storms and cold spells.

"If I choose to paint the sea first," Illuminated explained upon her return, "it's because in winter the waves are stronger and the colors austere; on the other hand, in summer the mountains are more picturesque, covered by a luxurious vegetation over which the fog glitters."

After several days of climbing and surveying they finally discovered, upon crossing a cloudy peak, the mystery-filled landscape that responded to her inspiration.

The sketches they had done at every full moon, armed with notebook, snack baskets and thermos, and which they brought back from their journey, allowed them to decide the general composition of the frescoes: soon the blue lines—powdered azurite—and green lines—powdered malachite—of a majestic landscape appeared on top, on thick hemp-fiber paper, glazed by an alum and glue varnish, copied from a large sheet with wood charcoal powder: light clouds rose from a serene valley to the mist-enveloped mountains, and then they extended toward the horizon, fusing with a white space—burnt, pulverized oyster shells—shaded by a pigment of pure blue, with a drop of ivory black.

"If we obtain the ideal doses," Illuminated specified expertly, "of glue in the proper proportion of water, aided by care and a speedy hand, these oceans and mountains will overwhelm the seminarians with the solemn severity of nature, but they will also notice"—and to exhale a puff of smoke she abandoned for an instant the bamboo stick with which, in a wooden vessel, she was dissolving the pigments—"the profound compassion that emanates from these infinite horizons."

In this gorgeous setting, followed by his constant cipherers—a clatter of loose planks, punches and brushes on the meditating mats would announce his descent—the young master scattered throughout his lengthy dinner talks his questioning silences and lunatic responses. He kicked and struck the floor with his cane, raised a finger wet with saliva, threw celadon against the floor and a hat soaked in black ink against a silk record of the mystical visions of the fifth Dalai Lama.

He handed out fermented drinks.

He responded to every koan with a belch, a hoot or the easy aphorism "Samsara is nirvana."

When the elders, who in his absence had begun to charge entrance fees, to diminish the rations of chicken, to give preference to curious aristocrats or influential people and to fill the vacillating trays with boiled flour and avocados—they were contriving, besides, an order that "would take his message to the west"—became aware that he was beginning to take his mission lightly and was drinking double martinis in the kitchen, without caring a fig about dharmas, they turned sour and grumpy.

One night, by this time outraged, slapping and dragging him up to his room, they gave him, effortlessly, a piece of their mind:

"So, wise guy, you've come to this island, dutifully abandoning the Paradise of Amitabha east of the mandala, to liberate all living beings, and we shall not let you return, whatever it takes, until the last ant enters nirvana. You are going to squander your teachings upon the autistic, waiting over the waves, and you're going to learn English on records so that everybody can understand you."

"What macrobiotic dive?" the other Leng scolded, distancing her anger, her mouth wide open beside the ear of the accused, and staring insultingly at his auricle, "or what spiritist center do you think this is, that, ever since you went up to the hills, you have thrust aside and abandoned the congregation, pissing in the sink and replying to everything 'what, me worry?' In order to undertake spatial redistributions," she continued, less ruffled now, "and to give these quarters the configuration of cosmic base which today serves as your context, not to mention Illuminated's pictorial travels, we're up to here," the other Leng raised her trembling hand to her forehead, "in abusive mortgages and loans. Where are we going to find the cash to maintain these sliding waves and to protect from moths the bamboo tablets on which the few statements you make are engraved?"

In response, he looked at them one at a time and up and down, not without some sarcasm. Without flexing, like a sick cat or a boneless body, he dropped onto a very low bed, Japanese industrial renaissance-style, which the old women had made with wooden planks and red cushions.

Then, he abruptly sat up erect from the waist, like a victorious athlete at a Turkish bath, though not to touch his toes with his fingers, exhaling dead air, but to pull from the corners, up to the head of the bed, a fat, cottony blanket of glass foam which the old women had folded at the foot of the bed. Thus he covered himself, like a giant chrysalis, pretending to drift toward stillness or sleep.

He pulled too hard, in his calisthenic zeal, on the isolating blanket. The old women contemplated him in his cocoon, solemnly indignant and offended. They were about to go down to the Zend, to entertain the tautological with new stories of former lives when, uncovered by his yank, the soles of his feet came into view.

They looked more depressed and deranged than if they had seen a hairy spider on the mat, or three thorns at the base of a

plank: on the upper part of each sole, near the toes, perfectly outlined like a birthmark or a colorless tattoo, was a wheel.

"With its center," one of the old women clarified rigorously.

"And its spokes," retorted the other, also transmitting the spectacular discovery to those inferior subjects, hungry for more details, and for the ginseng with which they had begun to marinate
the boiled cabbage salad, sure that the sole-man, with his invigo-
rating powers, would chase away the astral anorexia that troubled
them.

"He has walked barefoot," they said to one another, coming
out of their marred mutism, "on burning round irons. He surely
went to the festival of Kataragama. That's where he picked up
those manners."

"We should look carefully at his cheeks, to see if he's pierced
them with some prod, and look for tacks and glass among his fe-
ces."

They came downstairs with lips pressed and eyes grim and hair
greyer, a trident of wrinkles on their brow.

On the staircase, whose spirals seemed exaggeratedly uneven
and dizzying to them, they let loose.

"Something," they confessed, digging their yellow nails into
the bannister, "is taking the wrong turn."

He waited for the dissatisfied addicts to retire in resignation,
and for the modular snores of the Lengs to warn him that the
Zend had unbolted its moving walls to lay behind the waves, now
mute piles, brief mats for the sleepers. Then, as if obeying the laws
of sleep, barely touching the spiral steps, he abandoned the immutable zone of the mountains and, with a curved knife joined to
a scepter, which he held in his right hand, he appeared stealthily
among the resounding speechless subjects.

"This is the way!" he raised them by the hairs one by one, as if
digging up a bunch of radishes, cutting off locks with a blade, and
dropping them again, softened and sleepless, flaccid like wrung-
out old tablecloths, piles of dirty clothes flattened lifelessly against
the mats.

"Excellent!" the tonsured ones responded between head butts.
They turned around, listening close to the rising tide, naked on
the sand in the insular night, the water advancing over the rolling

pebbles, at the foot of the mountain; they went back to sleep.

Into the ears of those who after the trim remained standing and alert, and who didn't display excessive contentment, metaphysical conceit and surprise, he blew a brief sound, a syllable whose deep vibrations made them shake their heads, as if they had water in their ears which they covered with their fingers.

He gave them a slap on the buttocks to calm them down.

Now without academic pretexts, Illuminated had to renounce her rural tours with Honey Boy. She wandered in a daze, day and night between sea and mountain, cooking frozen shrimps or going up and down the exasperating staircase without rhyme or reason. She missed the scenographic incentives of mysticism and also, it's fair to say, the escape and twilight surprises of her peripatetic past when, in cream-colored cars, official emerald engravers and even managers of arable terraces would come looking for her, their steam baths with persistent rubdowns and imported cologne from London failing to rid them of the bitter smell of toasted tea.

One sleepless night she returned, without knowing why, to the Victorian vanity, which the austerity of the mats had relegated to the cellar. In the drawer, inside a large felt pincushion—black-beaded brooches, diamond salamanders, lockets with faded portraits—she found the hidden laudanum potion.

She looked at herself in the mirror.

She quickly drank a little, with her eyes closed. The sound of the bottle on the glass of the vanity pierced her like the cracking of a large fishbowl.

She began to hum a Billie Holiday song.

She felt someone staring at her. She turned around suddenly: in the dim light from downstairs she recognized, peeking through the crack of the half-opened door, Honey Boy's sexy eyes. In a two-toned sarong, a dark handkerchief tied around his head, he was shirtless, perhaps barefoot.

As to be expected, Illuminated received him with a gesture of disgust.

"I have not come," announced the intruder without stepping forward but opening the door a bit more until the light from downstairs framed him in his rectangle, like a courtier standing beside a mirror, "to quarrel, nor to beg for new picnics: I grieve for those happy nights now past. If I had known that our sea safaris were going to lead to such airs and pompous silences and that, for a few rupis tied in handkerchiefs, the old hags would switch analgesic sandalwood basins, I never would have withstood so many privations beneath the shade of guao trees nor would I have let a wild pig stampede over me. I'm leaving this island, even if I have to be tied to a pine tree truck, which the tide will carry north."

And with the exasperated gesture of a cheap broad he untied his sarong in the front, shook it as if to fan himself and tightened it again with a furious knot on his right hip.

Illuminated looked at him in the mirror. The cellar light turning grey blurred the border between the wall and the floor: Honey Boy seemed as if suspended by the caracoling of his own gown.

"The disciples already have enough worries with these stage settings," Illuminated replied haughtily, "which will have to be mortgaged off. So why persist with those tiresome slogans?"

From the velvet heart, as if cutting a thread with her teeth, she tore out an onyx peacock, which she fastened to the right shoulder of her negligee with which she disguised her wasteful hours. The funerary sparkles from the big ugly bird streaked for a moment the bottle green silk:

"Who says that an instructor, if he's the real thing, cannot renounce teaching, eat spicy rice and curry and, initiating voluntary work, break the vow of poverty? As far as I'm concerned," she sent him piercing glances in the mirror, "you'd better not count on me to behave improperly."

But that's not how it went.

One afternoon they wandered away from the building, hand in hand and distracted as usual by their discussions of divine matters; they followed an embankment along the curve of the coast, past a row of white wooden English hotels. Boys in short striped pants, berets and bow-ties were flying enormous, vibrant, red paper-silk kites which each gust of wind seemed to lift off the earth; other boys, in sailor suits and holding little copper rods, were playing with hoops or walking black and white spotted long-eared dogs.

Upon reaching the dock, caught up as always in their arduous liturgical protocol, they were surprised by a brig coming into port, banners and masts stained with saltpeter, in a great confusion of ropes, tangled sails—dark, mended sacks—shouting and, on deck, bright lanterns.

A fandango was agitating the busy port mob.

With great packs of thatching palm on their shoulders, amid whose swollen and parallel ropes the brown nerves of tobacco leaves appeared, green-eyed, barefoot mulattos, with golden earrings and kinky curls, bumped into each other or, like ants, bumped their loads slightly as they circulated among berths filled with trunks, sacks of sugar with purple-printed letters, green and glassy bunches of mashed anis and empty cages—ornate black architectures.

The music of dizzy guitars, rusty cowbells, güiros and maracas from the taverns adorned that thronging moorage, accompanied by the smell of crushed medlar, rotten mangos, stale sapodilla and sour cherries bursting from the coves and thickening the air, inebriating passersby and birds.

That hidden cornucopia, and the little sugar-coated glasses with which the sailors, now in guayaberas, toasted to the visitors, drew to the boarding ladder, as if magnetized, Illuminated and Honey Boy.

They never came down.

They subverted unreservedly, and all the way across the seas to Matanzas, the centenary canons of Cuban cooking, mixing, on juicy spectacular platters, their incompatible and basic ingredients: pork marinated in pineapple slices, chicken in sweet and sour sauce, duck à l'orange, and other even more perverse variations which gastronomic modesty forbids me to mention.

As the bay came into view, a cabin boy, fed up with enforced dictatorship, threw at Honey Boy, who did not yield in his culinary ideocracy, tyrannical when it came to the dessert soup and other saucy concepts, a ringdove croquette with ginger juice:

"Enough presumption," he fired forth. "I want to eat like a Christian, and besides," he added, emboldened by his victim's poker face, "when you set foot on the island, take off that skirt, because our men don't wear them, or sandals either. And one doesn't belch in public."

Illuminated stood there stiff and flustered, holding out a pan. Into which an Egg Foo Young fell crumbling.

The War of Relics

This is as far as the "accommodating" account of Illuminated's versions goes: how could one explain, otherwise, the luxury of her brooches, the apparent pertinence of her gaudy clichés, the perfume of her suitors and above all her impeccable appearance despite the deplorable hoity-toity housecoat she'd wear in the morning, wax flowers stuck behind her ears, painting her face like a tramp and drinking down a bottle of opium-spiked wine or whatever the hell she'd find among her rags when the monkey nipped her neck?

After she was gone they tracked her for a week with hounds equipped with the smell of her panties but, as Honey Boy didn't give any sign of life either, the sour, hostile hags declared them traitors to the faith, charisma pushers, embezzlers and paper tigers.

What follows, reconstructed from tablets which given their scarcity soon became canons, is choppy and contradictory. The young man's neglect to clear up conceptual double-talk opened the door to more than one revision:

"What I have taught—to be deciphered on an illustration—is like the leaves of a tree; the revelations which I have not yet taught are like the leaves of a whole forest."

Upon the incarnate's total indifference—if indeed he was still among them—the greedy, opportunistic old women indulged in the most outrageous mystical meanderings, contradicting each morning, with obstinate gestures, what they asserted just as stubbornly the day before—urgently scribbling and tacking some *dazibaos* on the moveable landscapes—as they expelled those do-

dos who were still spelling out yesterday's slogans.

Between the two of them, muddles and discrepancies were always cropping up, which the asslickers, always ready to pour it on thick, to slavishly obey the bossy hags, shoved to the hilt.

They dedicated themselves spitefully to self-humiliation: without warning they began to drink repugnant substances: saliva and urine.

In a spasm of punk ecstasy, wanting to show her disgust, one vomited on the other's feet, pierced her lips with a pin, burned her arms, and finished it off by entangling two bloody chicken necks in her bright green saffron hair which she rubbed with henna.

Her booties splashed with gastric filaments, smooth and golden like the fibers of a Philippine mango, the offended one tried to pacify her in the name of the Congregation's proverbial serenity; nonplussed by this unpleasant loss of self-control, she tried to calm her by showing her the punctured pages of a book, unfolding before her eyes—which she rolled upwards—pleated like a lacework marble fan.

"I'd like you to know," replied the ecstatic, snatching the scriptures away from her in one fell swoop, as if tearing the veil off a Muslim woman, and throwing them furiously to the ground like a pack of doctored playing-cards—which explains the shuffling of many aphorisms—"that apart from thought, there is nothing," and she stared disdainfully at the dried palm-leaf sheets at her feet, "absolutely nothing: neither subject, merit nor fault. Nobody commits nor causes evil. Karma bears no fruit."

"The cobra poison," argued the vanquished, recoiling step by step over the rush mats, without taking her eyes off the ill-treated leaves, "that you sneak into my mamey sauce every day, and those spells you invoke to make lusty demons appear before me every evening, have lost their strength. Though ciphered fitfully in Pali, these feeble tubes, gathered in a triple basket, will bear witness to the little our supposed guide has coughed up when not responding to everything with a repellent 'no!' I will collect more: hair, teeth, skin, flesh, bones, nerves, marrow, brain."

It wasn't ginseng that one of the wrinkled hags had distributed among the needy but dark, gritty, striped mushrooms: little men in painted hats, weird doughy paste peasants. At every full moon the old women went to look for them in the coolest part of the cellar.

Thinking her end was near, for she fell frequently into livid swoons with hints of a breakdown, or perhaps as an artful trick to intimidate the other and chill her blood, she decided to reveal to her the power of the "dear little revelers who come hopping along," as she called her grumpled mushrooms.

That night, gathered with the last candidates for extinction, she hummed as she handed out and also ate the little things that told her what to say, and how to sing.

In a hoarse voice she cast spells in a dark, windowless room, surrounded by believers, puppies, irritated turtles and children of all ages who clung to her skirt standing, with her chants resounding in their ears.

All alike perceived, in the warm silence of the island night, a few minutes after swallowing the little saints in a vervain brew, the one who was respectfully called the Most Noble Infant: a vigorous, athletic young man, naked, slant-eyes, surrounded by a white transparency like a milky halo, leaping from a shining basin with his arms raised. Very slowly, soaking wet: one by one the drops rose, flew into the air, scattered and fell. Little bluish threads radiated from his gestures.

He was emerging from adolescence: though still beardless, his features were more defined, his voice lower; he laughed less.

The initiates flocked to the ashram seeking instruction, but seeing that he refused to elucidate, through evasive subterfuges or simply by pulling their legs, what in their eyes was essential—the origin and end of the universe, the reality of reincarnation, the existence of an individual soul, etc.—or perhaps in pursuit of pointless miracles, blessings, auspices, vulgar communications with the dead, their intercessions little by little veered away from the astral plane to charlatanism, fortune-telling and horoscopes.

One afternoon, weary of this spiritual Stakhanovism, picking up the gift basket where his clientele placed his kickbacks—betel to clean his teeth, incense, silks, topazes—he called off the next day's appointments and fled upstairs to take refuge with the old women.

It was useless: they too begged for instruction, fasting techniques, secret signs and dogmas.

"If for one moment," he said to them breathlessly—he had bounded up the stairs—"I appeared to you in my true nature, the self which in everything that exists, you would be so terrified and thunderstruck that you would lose your lives or your sanity. I am ending this benevolent dispensary which has become a spiritist center for retrieving unfaithful husbands, exorcising morons and relieving women in labor. Whatever *is*, cannot be recaptured by the intellect or by the senses, nor can it be the object of devotion or patience. It is useless to resort to sacrifice or to the brutal pedagogy of the koan, like the story of the drowning pupil. Approaching things negatively doesn't make any difference."

Black-browed, paralyzed by his aporias, the surly old women contemplated him like two cats looking at a bell that's imitating the squeak of a mouse.

"To become, effortlessly, what is," he added, "all exercise, no matter how astute it may be, is, more than vain, stupefying.

"And with this, pious sisters, I fulfill my function in the story, and my last cycle in this kalpa. Don't talk about me. I didn't squander knowledge: I marked its empty nomadic place."

They heard, across the way, squawking and cymbals: rations were being distributed in the Indian temple.

"This very night, once the football scores are out, I will enter nirvana forever."

The old women covered their mouths and noses. They began to sob.

He sat in the meditating position, near a red and orange mandala whose central figure was Avalokitesvara.

He imagined a tree: its purple leaves shimmered in the transparent heat of the Indian noon.

Smiling and serene, he gradually slowed down the rhythm of his breathing until it stopped altogether.

Seeing his stillness, the old women broke into howls and ripped their clothing, insulting the nocturnal divinities; later, aided by their responsibilities and by Sebain—a sedative but not a depressant—they abandoned jeremiads so as not to alert any professional mourners, and began efficiently, almost mechanically, the repulsive posthumous preparations.

They took off his white robe and underpants. They laid him down carefully as though trying not to hurt him or as if something inside him would spill out, centering him on a mat.

The bolder of the two injected corrosive sublimate deep into his carotid artery.

On his face: cream of milk, to prevent dehydration and to serve as a base for some discreet makeup, Tropical Satisfaction, which hides the unbearable yellowing of the skin.

Face powder, a tone that harmonized his natural skin color with the demands of artificial lighting, muted the shine of the cream.

The eyes received particular attention: they washed them with soap and water, rubbed the lids with the appropriate Vaseline to prevent desiccation; to keep them closed—the illusion of sleep—they slipped below the eyelids little plastic shells, rough on the convex side.

They left him till the next day.

In a brocade suit of geometric design—golden lotuses—they seated him upon a purple throne inlaid with excessive pearls, crowned with a heavy diadem, and with the thunderbolt and the little bell in his stiff hands as if he were about to shake them.

On the floor, on a saffron-yellow carpet, they scattered lamps, prayer wheels, bronze figures, silver goblets and two Tantric daggers.

The frescoes were covered with a monumental tanka, its topology radiant with the peaceful divinities, cerulean blue and green.

Hanging from the ceilings were snowy banners, their grids embroidered with a motif of pink pupils or buttons.

They tossed yellow flowers over the rush mats, like a sudden, violent rainstorm.

One of them tiptoed, so as not to rumple her clothes, downstairs to the entrance where, as on every morning, fans and devotees were waiting, wretched and footloose.

She propped the door ajar.

Before the crowd poured in, she ran back upstairs to the funeral chamber, she sat on the floor, respectful of symmetry.

On either side of the Godsend, in his last earthly representation, they contemplated him for a moment, as the front door opened and the hasty steps of sandaled feet resounded on the rush mats below.

The thanatos-practitioners had dressed pastel blue with red scarves, their hair in a single braid. They wore new earrings with gold galloons hanging like lace over their chests. Mourning masks, white with titanium: soft, symmetrical cotyledons separated their lips. They had outlined them in black. Around the eyes: brick red, clotted blood.

They topped it all off with topsy-turvy tousled hats, a babel of buzzards, crowns of burnt feathers.

On their necks, driveling muzzles "to underline the incongruity of everything."

They reviewed his whole life, like a flash of lightning in fleeting images, from the basin they had bathed him in after finding him stiff with cold and hunger, abandoned in the temple turnstile, up to the moment he stopped breathing before their very eyes.

Two large tears streaked their masks.

When they had regained their self-control, they shouted downstairs, "You can come up."

A steely, opaque light streamed diagonally from the four grainy-paned windows onto his stiff body; a straight white shroud grazed the flagstones, hard, marbled, in parallel pleats like a newly folded tablecloth; a deaf, toneless light fleeing from the walls, as if the funeral chamber were underwater, was magnetically drawn by the edges of the table, by his metallic body shining with the unguents they had rubbed on, smooth as the shroud, and by his hair which the old women had smeared in silver, flowing over the headrest in enamelled threads like a sick flower, and by his sightless gaze turning back empty into his blind eyes. The old women threw themselves onto the corpse with the voracity of two vultures.

They tore out locks of hair, eyebrows, lashes, nails which they wrapped in streaming cloths soaking in a greenish eucalyptus or green basil resin; they ran off to hide them among little esparto pincushions, in fresh-smelling, double-locked cupboards.

When they had left him hairless and bald like a mannequin or burn victims, and scabby bloodclots closed his eyes and fingers, then with fussy precautions and periphrastic bombast they announced his death to the followers waiting downstairs and on the sidewalks, lying on the ground, devouring anxious pirouettes, impervious to sleep, to resignation.

The helicoidal hags descended, pulling their hair with a heart-rending "life is nothing" which they alternated with shrieking ohs and piercing guttural groans.

They wrapped the body in thousands of cotton strips, strewed white flowers in the corners, covered landscapes and mirrors with rough drapes. The two floors were filled with parasols.

The multitudinous faithfuls carried out the litter. After passing north of the river they filled the catafalque with perfumed oils. They gathered sweet-smelling wood, set it on fire.

Both the cotton wrapping against his skin and the one furthest from it didn't burn.

The old women snatched them up at once: wrapped in paper napkins, like pieces of cake smuggled out of a birthday party, they hid them in cunning pasteboard pocketbooks which they never took off their shoulders.

They handed out, stingily, the other relics.

(Nails and hair remained intact.)

When they lowered the golden sarcophagus from the litter and piled up the perfumed wood to burn the body, the fire refused to start. On this spot, as a memorial to the reticence of the flames, a white monument was erected, with six tiered roofs and the proportions of the great pagoda of the Wild Goose.

They cut him into a hundred pieces, one by one, following the joints carefully: without spilling fluids or blood. When splintered ends and protuberances were sanded down, the cleaned and polished bones were set in baroque mountings. Isles of uncut emeralds, lotuses of unmatched opals, onyx disks, splintered quartz like empty eggs harbored vertebrae and cartilage bones.

Hanging in a cylinder of ground crystal, like a neon light between grooved supports that allowed it to rotate—with opaque little light bulbs at either end—was an imprisoned hand, preserved by the old women. As if pulling the lever of a one-armed bandit, they made it revolve every afternoon.

They emptied out the head: salted meticulously and wrapped in silk cloths separated by fine layers of quicklime, it was locked away in a sandalwood chest with four elephants and a wheel carved on the lid, flanked by reverent gazelles.

When the remains, minted into jewels, keeping the order in which they had been mounted in the body—now a row of chalices and boxes—were exposed among the hidden peaks like a prehistoric giant in a snowy tomb, and the old women could contemplate them without witnesses, reuniting them into a single image, then, as if this metallized dispersion were the true death, they gazed incredulously into each other's eyes and broke into hysterical tears:

"Here lies the body of the fragmented man," they moaned, in plaintive disgust.

And toward the shielded bones they turned the palms of their hands anointed in vinegar, on which, among the wrinkles, was written in mastic the word END.

"Here lies the cause of desire."

And so on and so forth, with rhythmic and strophic variations, for three days.

Until the mourners, still fasting silently on the ground floor and meditating on the notion of impermanence, noticed that the Great Lament had ended, and decided to rush upstairs to share the spoils.

The upper floor was silent. From afar, or muffled by the air vent fans behind the windows, and by the dying afternoon light, came the contentious voices of Cantonese cooks, footsteps in the street, a woman's cry and, even further away, a shrill, nasal voice, perhaps recorded in the early days of the phonograph, singing over and over the threads of a tango.

The old women were sitting in profile on two rolled-up mats on either side of the head, nostalgic weavers gazing into the void.

And having hot chocolate with crullers.

Dressed in coarse tunics, stingy and disgruntled, they handed out all night long, with feigned equity, jewelry settings and amulets.

At dawn, after a few uncomfortable intervals interrupted by the first street cries and distant sounds of foghorns, or flocks of parakeets and ravens, a huge fuss arose over the possession of the big pieces, bringing to a close entreaties, hysterics and even a proposal, furiously vetoed, not to scatter the remains.

In a matter of minutes, passionately covetous of the bones, haggling over eyeteeth, they splintered caskets and femurs.

In the midst of the brawl the butchers, beaten, crushed and outflanked on the left, were screaming for QUIET—the ruling principle of the order—and in complete arthrological delirium were promising to give out, in pairs, the central supports of the skeleton.

They ended up losing not only their heads but *the* head.

The last of the vandals fled with the panels of mountain or sea scenes folded under their arms, or on their shoulders like river rafts.

They auctioned them off, with gilded hinges, as Burmese screens in the antique shops of Kandy.

Mantelpieces went, as did exotic wardrobe doors and even oval chinoiseries with angular medallions in the rococo Versailles style. A misted cusp of dried plum-wood with mannered branches was a persistent motif in the riddled canvas tapestry embroidered by apocryphal princesses of the Austrian Court. The oriental collection at the Boston Museum of Fine Arts conserves one wave—with the addition of a dragon—dated 1244 and attributed to Ch'en Jung: at Sotheby's there's another.

Three generations later, when the teachings were distorted to total oblivion, and neither faith nor bidders remained, the heirs of the last authenticated bones ended up chucking them into a charnel heap.

This is where they found the knee bone, which some Jesuit missionaries took for one of Saint Jehoshaphat's, now worshiped in a tiled niche under the main altar of the Cathedral of Cuenca, contained in a monstrance of American gold, the contribution of a crafty West Indian.

When the flames died, the disjointed bones lay in disarray over the trickle of ashes which the morning wind had not dispersed, under the shade of big, grey, leafy, motionless trees. Then silently, neither abrupt nor hasty, the last faithful disciples, ready to comply with the posthumous instructions, went about picking them up in their hands as carefully as if they were protecting wounded partridges; they raised them to their lips and blew slowly: a warm, misty breath enveloped them. Their tears fell on the joints. They seemed to be rubbing their eyes to wake up, or to remove snow from their lids after a storm. Cautiously they wrapped the relics in embroidered cloths: on a black background, gold sashes: Moroccan bridegroom belts. They hid them under their robes like stolen toys.

Then, with the bones, a copper bowl and an umbrella as their sole belongings, they took off to beg along the coastal roads, showing off their filth and thirst from temple to temple.

They covered the island from east to west, alone or in small peasant bands, sure of harboring a truth without violence, which could liberate instantly even a pariah or a pig.

If by night they took over wine cellars and rice barns, they did so without violating the precepts: they left more well-worn rupees than the worth of what they devoured.

They resorted more and more, alas, to short cuts—arguing smilingly, stroking with long, gentle gestures the pates they no longer shaved—to obtain donations with which to build imposing white tumuli to enshrine the relics forever, and besides which they would retire to meditate, compassionate and vegetarian, once they had implanted their message.

In an outburst of summary appropriations, and always under cover of the most benign premises, cloaked in pious speeches and moderate admonishments that barely disguised the underlying threats, they reached the point of confiscating the most salable belongings of any potentates on the island who had reservations about their mission: without bothering with petitions or red tape, they took for themselves the terraced tea plantations and the mansions with English verandas filled with other people's betel supplies.

"Sapphires," they cajoled docile jewelers, in cracked and ostensibly mystical voices, "suffer outside of the orifice to which they are destined in the pristine diagram of the universe, imprinted on the forehead, between the eyebrows of the Peaceful One. There, enclosed in the center of each tomb, free from the harmful air, they are happy, and await the end of time without regrets."

With these reasonings, and with others less tortuous but no more plausible, scattered randomly before diamond merchants and usurers—they teasingly showed them, in the complicity of back rooms, among sloping blue tables covered with coffers, crude coral dealers and jewelry assayers, some dilapidated little bone that would crumble at the slightest puff—they managed to get hold of a case of newly carved amethysts which they exchanged that very night, to avoid the opprobrium of illegal possession, for the circular scaffolding of the first mausoleum.

To build the second, they had to continue inventing pious frauds, detaching themselves, upon each act of plunder, from the repugnance of impure words and thoughts—as if, for a purgative, they were eating bitter grass. Rarely did they resort to force; they always relied on their wits.

They authorized incestuous marriages, commerce in leather goods, menstruating women in kitchens, and even the eating of animals slaughtered with more than one blow. They went so far as to attend posthumous revels and banquets, dressed in borrowed lay cassocks. Warmed by heavy red liqueurs, one talked loudly and danced in public; another, wrapped in a brick red sarong, his arms crossed to suggest indifference but his face darkened with desire, waited on the beach for a young man.

They bought and resold drugs.

Regaling regalias, they created the abridged initiation ceremony for neophytes: they sprinkled them five times, and five times they invited them to drink a syrup: sugar and water stirred with the tip of a sword. Then, they had the right to add to their names the suffix *Singh*—lion—and were obliged to wear the five ritual *b*'s on their persons: blade, bloomers—silk underwear—braid—tied in a knot on top of the head—bracelets—steel—and brush.

The old women were trying to spruce up, with acryllic-painted screens garnished with profane motifs—they corrected them by adding tambourines and lotuses left and right—the Colombian den, now a suburban museum for pious scholars and tedious Sunday courtships. When they found out that, in the name of the congregation, gorging orgies and robberies were proliferating throughout the island, they set out on exemplary crusades against the dissidents,whom they accused of theft and insanity. Sprinkling saltwater on their names written on the ground, and reciting black mantras with their faces turned toward them, they condemned them to one irreversible jump backwards on the creaking wheel of incarnations.

To purify the beds where the schismatics had slept, they washed them in milk.

With the tenacity of hatred, the Mother's followers, incited and, gods forgive me, even rewarded by the above, devoted themselves to profaning or razing, on lightning night raids, the stupas which the relic bearers, nicknamed bloodhounds or caretakers, arduously built by day.

Around each foundation, the builders and their shadowy adversaries met punctually, in confrontation, pulling down pillars and stones.

But the Sisters' mandate did not last long.

Driven back by bellicose believers and offended vassals and, toward the coast, equally fanatic plundering pirates, scoundrels or intruders, the scaffold demolishers soon capitulated.

They returned arrogantly to the duplex, recounting epic details, hiding big scars and pustules beneath opulent overcoats. The old women received them as conquering heroes, with the music of lutes and a tea party.

The mausoleum builders allowed themselves no further respite. Soon, "like one more relic in a pearl dome," the island was encircled by whitewashed stupas, each one enshrining a legitimate remnant, though sometimes—a tooth, a hair—it was so small it could not be seen against the cement.

The believers would gather round the vaults at the close of the day. Red saris in procession across the sand.

The architects expired one by one beside the ossuaries. So as not to arouse envy, nor give the unfaithful a clue as to what it contained, the donor of the head saved for the last cupola, feigning incredulity and ennui, abandoned to the birds and the newly built dome which hid, behind a conch inlaid in the tower like fancy heraldry, "death's head."

The chapels near the sea, assimilated to the cult of avatars or ephemeral coastal divinities, received more and more pilgrims and monkeys who defecated generously and gobbled bananas and cyprus vines.

So as not to crowd together in the narrow doorway of the sanctuary—an obstacle to keep out fat demons—the travelers circled the monuments, leaving them always on the right, grazing them with their hands and repeating—though thinking of something else—the familiar formulas until they were emptied of all meaning.

Rarely did they achieve concentration and silence: they were followed by slobbering charlatans, lepers and dogs, begging for crumbs and affection.

When the message faded away, and nothing remained of the Instructor, builders and old women except distorted allegories, local legends, gossip and anecdotes, the relics contained in all the tumuli on the island fled of their accord one night to the north, to Tibet.

Over a snowy abyss near two empty monasteries whose tiered roofs hidden beneath zinc sheets revealed Chinese barracks, they took the shape of a body about to fall apart, about to be scattered like a handful of jacks thrown into the air.

They hovered over the void for a moment, motionless, like a band of boreal birds sensing danger; then, from different heights, according to their weight they began a slow descent.

The head, like a planet out of orbit that upon falling would turn back into lava, lime or mother-of-pearl, in a luminous, spiral unwinding, became a giant, iridescent conch which when blown by the wind, emitted a muffled, unchanging sound, the charred vibration of a remote explosion.

A sound that became deeper until, followed by a rain of tiny bones, a hoarse hailstorm, faded in the circle of an OM.

Part II

The Double

I

They were born together. One had almost popped out after one easy push when the war-hardened Chinese midwife, beating her brow, let out a speckled cry as if at an explosion of rockets turning into parakeets. What she saw shocked her more than a cold shower after sweating over a hot iron: a firm, reddish little hand was grabbing the newborn by the left ankle, as if trying to keep her from leaving the tunnel or as if pulling herself up toward the air like an exhausted swimmer. The other hand, fist closed, remained between her legs.

After three yanks and a spray of Afro-Cuban prayers, the midwife hauled out the infant-in-tow who assailed her with screams and menacing grimaces, as if she had been startled from her siesta.

The midwife separated them, opening the hand around the ankle, finger by finger. Then, with a rusty knife, respecting ancestral maieutic traditions, she sliced with one blow their common umbilical cord, dumped them into a basin of warm water, and pressed her fingertips into their cheeks "so that they'd have dimples when they laughed."

She wrapped them up in the same bedcover. They were so identical and cried so much that they had to be marked with colored dots on their foreheads, to distinguish the one who had suckled already and the one who needed two spoonfuls of mint infusion or two little slaps on the fanny to make her fall asleep.

They grew up looking into each other's eyes, amazed by the symmetry.

One day, by pure chance—they were playing ring-around-a-rosy—they discovered that if they passed their hand or jumped three times over a cripple or a person in pain, the paralysis or shooting pain would instantly disappear.

Mantónica Wilson, the shaman, called them frequently for consultations.

A pineapple, a mango and seven red apples—cut down the middle— shone in the center of a table with a long tablecloth, illuminated by an oil lamp. Hypnotized beside the fruit, its eye fixed on the white line at the end of its beak, a pigeon fluttered slightly.

The witch doctor's godson had painted all the walls, except the one next to the table, a dry, brownish red—rupestrian blood. On the wall near the table were thick charcoal or dense grainy ink lines: among vines, sugarcanes like flattened bones with jointed tubes, and leaves with prominent nerves, a warrior appeared, stepping toward the fruit with a massive, cuneiform foot, rigid like an onyx Egyptian chancellor. In his double ibis or gnome owl head, startled eyes devoured space.

Two flower-lines lances, or perhaps two reeds, crossed over his sex. Black orchids, stuck together, dripped a white, gummy milk down their pistils. Long spatulate fingers on his chest, with oval nails, held a perforated güiro, or a big striped half-maraca, filled with tuberoses and little ochre figures: spinning tops, *claves*, kinky laughing heads with goat horns, mouths with pointy fangs, among crane beaks and paws.

Facing the warrior, the therapeutic twins jumped crisscross over the sufferer lying face up, between chalk marks drawn in hurried legal style by Mantónica; as they leaped, they gathered up their legs and opened their little hands as if they were falling from a canal.

The grateful complainers gave them crullers. The more strides the twins made as healers, the more prosperous and plump, in their sugary gluttony, they became. Because of their analgesic gifts, which they calmly confirmed in the bouncing sessions every noontide, and because they were bold and blue-eyed, they were the living goddesses of all Sagua la Grande for a whole decade.

They had to be hidden away.

They lived in a colonial wooden palace, with wrought partition walls and curved balconies—filled with armillary spheres, anchors and ropes—which faced onto a closed patio of pavement stones, with an artesian well.

On Sundays, the building was opened to pilgrims. As they arrived they'd first see the office, the black servants' room, the coal bin and the bathroom; beside the well, the gigs. Upstairs they'd discover a tiled gallery leading to the spacious drawing room where they could see tables, chaise longues, embroidered cushions, bamboo chairs and a sofa. A blue and white silk muslin curtain separated this room from a smaller one where the twins resided, with beautiful furniture: a Gothic dressing table, a mahogany desk, a marble centerpiece and a console, mirrors, green and gold wallpaper. The floors were marbled, the ceiling beams, a pale blue mahogany. The windows were sealed by cedar lattices with tiny pierced stars.

They were accompanied in their games and whims by their *meninas*, nannies and relatives as well as by a Victrola, a collection of white pheasants and a dwarf—a former model for Carreño's *Dressed Monsters* in the School of Fine Arts. Fed up with stiff poses, one afternoon he decided to take over the easels and brushes. He managed to join the twins' entourage "to leave a graphic historical record of such eurhythmic models."

The chubby Chinese mulattas stripped naked in the summer and sipped sugarcane juice with crushed ice. Seated on low chairs, wearing pearly silk turbans, they'd organize tortoise races. The phonograph played a tinkling, persistent marimba music.

They sang quiet duets.

Along a closely watched corridor, connecting the lower rooms—filled with old worm-eaten or covered Spanish furniture—to Mantónica's chamber, they'd make their way to the warrior's room at siesta time, leaving behind the ophidian marathon and the chilling cackling of big birds.

Upon finding their next patient, and listening to the weepy enumeration of his sciatic sufferings, they'd look at one another before undertaking the palliative floggings and, both crafty and compassionate, they'd raise their now painted eyebrows, fan themselves with large palm leaves and murmur:

"C'est ça . . . oui."

They brought a president back to life whom the Mayo brothers had rejected, who returned with the brim of his black bowler bent downward; they unfettered a crippled rumba dancer, ankylosed by a delayed reaction to a spell that devastated her during a verbena festival in the gardens of the Tropical Club.

They jumped faster and faster, now mechanically or cynically, playing jump rope over the incredulous patients, who now lay face down as if they were going to be douched, in order to surrender without fear to the sarcastic gymnastics.

Their crisscrossing magnetism ending up by surprising even them, and they went as far as making fun of the vulgar efficiency and punctual performance of their own miracles.

Once a year, the day of Saints Cosmas and Damian, the *ibeyes* (as the yoruba witch doctors called the twins) would come out on the balconies.

They appeared holding hands, wearing showy makeup, linked amid crowns and jewels, a pheasant perched on each one's shoulder. In broad daylight they lit up hundreds of lamps. Bringing paper lanterns, honeycombs, little rice statues and cypress vines, pilgrims flocked from all over the island.

The natives of Sagua were celebrating their great feast.

They had their first menstruation suddenly and in unison.

They didn't know what was happening to them and began to scream that crushed glass had been put in their sugarcane juice.

That very same day they lost all their powers.

In vain Mantónica insulted the *orishas*, trying to revive them. They fell flat on their asses upon the spongy vertebrae of a stiff old man with such aplomb that the hinged curve clattered from top to bottom and the old fart turned mushy, like a cudgeled Cuban boa, spread over the chalk signatures.

They abandoned the palace and its display of ugly birds.

They tried to cure by following the directions in a homeopathic primer, but it was useless: the sick preferred Clavelito's magic water, which hypnotized people on radio, for free.

They returned everything they had bought in installments.

They had to take in laundry.

A lost gift implies the emergence of another, or rather: what disappears in the symbolic order reappears in the real to hallucinate us: soon the needy twins discovered that their voices, sustained by the puffy expansion of their diaphragms, and by the substantial calories of sugarcane juice, reached powerful soprano tessituras.

They ceased to sing quietly. Arrogantly and without the phonograph, they belted at the top of their lungs the marimba duets of former noontides.

With curved metallic bars that made little round hammers resound, and beaded bronze keys, a palm-fiber flute, a bamboo zither and hundreds of tiny cymbals placed in wooden frames, they undertook, to the joy of Sagua's Chinese community, the first performance of the opera; the outmoded choreography was done by Cheng-Ching, an exiled widow and the author of five musical comedies; the wardrobe was imported directly from Formosa.

The revived twins didn't appear, as was expected, playing the double golden phoenix of the Empire, nor mounted on a caracoling dragon in the Festival of the Thousand Lanterns. They were not followed by unicorns: they toe-danced, dressed in olive green overalls. Graceful like bacchantes bearing baskets of grapes, they'd raise in their closed fists a sombre submachine-gun and a luminous primer, with stiff pages, opened to the middle.

On a pink twilight with fluffy gold clouds in the background, over the tiered roofs of the Temple of Heaven, simplified by the ignorance of the dwarf—the hurried set designer—red ribbons in arabesques, kites and balloons ascended gravely, like a colony of flamingos filmed in slow motion. The lights, whose crepuscular effects were applauded, concentrated their colors on a spot moving around the trigger and the book.

The dwarf had sketched more sensibly the next drop curtain, though he couldn't get it to move between vertical rollers at the opportune moment. The Symmetrical Girls crossed, always in uniform and with a single sustained C, a vast, industrialized city: they had to be mounted on roller skates and pushed by four stage-hands, as far as the wheels went, from behind the wings.

Holding hands stiffly, they traveled to a snowy, mountainous region with towers on the peaks and white banners. A chorus of bouncing extras received them benevolently—this was the final dance—in orange robes and bald wigs. Joyously they handed them pennants and scrolls. They tried to open the big blue doors with golden eyes on top so that the lady messengers could pass through, but there was no feasible way to make the stuck curtain—which contained the props—roll.

For the widow, and for the three other organizers of that concealed divertissement, the sisters dramatized "The Peace That Exalts Socialist Nations" and "Solidarity among Struggling Sister Countries"; for the sassy Sagua citizens, addicted to the sumptuous fannies and lascivious faces of the Fatties, these were, forever, Ladies Divine and Tremendous.

Louis Leng came to congratulate them one evening, euphoric after observing the rotundities of Solidarity and the Sunday ritual of "down-the-hatch."

He'd praise and toast them once a day. He'd wait for the twins at the stage door, and invite them to his own restaurant; the mulatto Juan Izquierdo would prepare for them a birds'-nest soup which the skaters savored slurping their spoons, throwing back their heads and rolling their eyes.

They celebrated the tenth performance with a special dish of one-hundred-year-old eggs which the scullion seasoned—to "produce a shock"—with red peppers à la façon cubaine.

Fearless Miss Peace brushed the knee of the "Filipino john" under the table. He bewitched the two of them equally with his Ceylonese ancestors' anecdotes, his adolescence in Sagua and his rise to "chef" at the Cuban Embassy in Paris, and then in North Carolina, before returning with earnings accumulated from thousands of hand-beaten crab omelettes. With the money he rented that ramshackle establishment—where his father, Honey Boy, had consumed his first oyster cocktail—modernizing it with pink circular neon lights and a three-door refrigerator.

Each time they came, Juan Izquierdo sat them further away from the entrance, at the most secluded and sinful tables. They finally appropriated, in their enthusiasm for chiaroscuro, subordinating the institution's profit-making arguments to the foggiest lyricism, the only reserved room in the joint. Soon the dessert soup was being served in Leng's bachelor flat in the mezzanine, which had not yet been turned into a banquet salon.

The Geminis who, upon a now definitely unmoveable but retouched backdrop, excelled in a pas de deux on roller skates with arabesques and pirouettes, as well as in the spicy, native interpretation they gave to the sung passages—they wiggled sexily, as if they were singing that old song *María la O*—were again adored by all of Sagua. To the daily acclaim, and voluminous arrival of bouquets and delicacies, they would now respond with exalted and fatuous conceit:

"Flowers, flowers, they last a day and we have to thank them for the rest of our lives!"

Lady Divine's convulsive horselaughs at the Chinaman's tricks or lechery could be heard from the mezzanine all the way down to the restaurant, where Izquierdo had to put up with the customers' furious and censorious looks, especially since they could only hear the soundtrack of those hilarious love feasts.

The protagonists of these ostentatious soirées didn't see much more: the only lighting in the pied-à-terre—the only furniture was the little round table where the debauchers savored the hot, substantial dessert, and a settee whose springs had by now been defeated by the weight of the fallen fatties, and some hangers with Leng's freshly ironed suits—was what remained of a firefly green square neon lamp hung on the back wall: its lit or loose corners vibrated almost imperceptibly: a sound of summer crickets, or of a Jew's harp in the mouth of lost shepherds, could be heard in the cubicle when the two-toned laughter of the twins died down.

What also remained, behind the settee over a pipeless washbasin with high nickel-plated faucets in front of the blinking square light, were the vestiges of ancient mantelpieces or decorations: wooden figures: the traditional characters of the burlesque theater or opera: two old witches in front of the neon light, a little boy leaping out of a basin, a monkey.

Accompanied by the background buzz of the glassy phosphorescent light, when the saucy ado was over and done with, the twins sank down into the settee and slept, stone-deaf and steeped in soup.

Then Leng began to approach stealthily, barefoot, camouflaged in wool: he advanced on tiptoe behind a blanket which he held up high, tightly stretched.

The sleepy duo glimpsed, in front of the neon square whose green clarity outlined its four edges, the gradual advance of a velvety black screen.

As the dark thing moved forward, the halo clarified even better its contours: two bent forefingers held it like paper clips by the upper corners; under the lower line his large yellow feet alternately appeared.

When the floating bedspread was already nearing the sleepers' divan, Leng suddenly dropped it on them like a falling curtain or the collapsing cloth wall of a Japanese house: the poker faces squeezed each other's hands, simulating livid swoons.

Protected by the landslide or by the sudden intervention of invisibility, like a hawk at nightfall, Leng, his lance erect, stripped naked.

He threw his clothes, as if alone or absent-minded—as if not in drunken ardor—over the blanket which swelled from time to time, slow waves, sea of black oil. The breathless lasses were covered again by raw, ironed fabrics and then by other, lighter, wrinkled warm materials.

The smooth body was silhouetted, like a wooden statue jutting out of its niche, against the far, grey wall where the neon light blinked.

Enveloped in what was a double opacity for the twins, facing their sleepless, buried bodies, Louis began to caress himself.

He squeezed, joining thumb and forefinger as if indicating zero, the member's corpulent base which, swollen, barely fit in such a harsh hoop. He licked his fingers, formed the closed circle again, slid it from the head until touching the spheres. He rubbed the lingam with devotion, like a Tridentine Shivaist convoking the galactic spill over the yoni. When he felt that the germinating spark was beginning to rise from the ball-shaped distilleries, he drew near the blanket enveloping the symmetrical bulks. Amid his sweaty clothes, like a boar in his cave, he slid in lightly.

The shakers, lying one against the other, inserted him between their volumes of flesh. Through the black, undulating thickness in front and behind him, Leng felt their identical breath and heat.

When sighs and panting ceased, they fell, still entangled, into a stupor.

They were awakened late in the morning, not by the light—always shaky and blinky like a firefly—but by gauche Izquierdo's urgent bustle. Overworked, he was opening shutters and dusty little curtains; as he flew by, he threw forks and fruit on tables in front of the open windows at midday.

For the dock workers' frugal breakfast, on a creaky old slicer, he was preparing the first sandwiches.

II

Lady Tremendous landed or rather dived into a pool across the street from the Caridad Church, in the outskirts of Miami, among dolphins who received her with indignant cries.

The dwarf, without abandoning his tilted beret and palette, was waiting for her with open bathrobe and a cup of hot milk and cinnamon in his hand: he led her down a carpeted hallway, comforting her along the way.

Fatso was still dumbfounded and bumped against the walls leaving figure-shaped stains. She opened her big hands to balance herself as if advancing along the gangway of a drifting ship, or as if blank bullets had been sprayed into the labyrinth of her ear. Her little dip had slowed her down more than a pitcher of papaya wine or the wrong acupuncture.

The dwarf preceded her, shaking a little copper bell as if announcing in a marketplace a leper's rosy passing, or the public burning of an infidel who had refused baptism: reddish sparks spurted onto the mural lining the hallway.

Yes, the tiny fellow had enhanced his first afternoons in Florida by creating a luscious botanical summa with hyperrealist conceits and dense rural allegories. After those Tibetan backdrops, he again exercised here the skill he had disseminated in luminous frescoes and screens for French-styled interiors and discreet dens of iniquity.

Because of his tenacious hold on Cuban customs and the

pleated guayabera he wore to debutante balls, the frozen generations of southwest Miami would later call him a "Slice of
Cuba."

Slippery Slice—pronouncing the *c* as if hissing to an accomplice waiter from behind the red curtain of a private room in a
seedy Sagua boarding house—wanted the fresco to reflect, backwards, History. He nibbled with gusto on a guava jam sandwich
that had more layers than the Grand Canyon—his favorite snack.

All along the walls and days he had painted on the background
in folkloric fury, disregarding good taste, all that he could copy
from a *Zoological Golden Album* that ended in *cubensis*.

Side by side and even overlapping in the most mannered symmetry were flamboyant trees and tortoises, ceibas and black dragonflies, giant ferns, lianas, moss-covered guasimas, forest, plain
and mountain trees, sapodillas, caimitos, purslanes and rodents,
all of it saturated, of course, with mangos, glazed pineapples and
royal palms.

A rainbow-hued hummingbird, a big-headed snake with fiery
eyes and a little spider frolicked in the midst of the tangled
thicket. He was missing a few nuts, though, as well as strawberries—to break the monotony of the greens—a red squirrel, a mar-
supial cat and, last but not least, a kangaroo-mouse from the
Sonora Sierra.

As a finishing touch on this masterpiece he had placed in the
obsessive jungle, though in a corner and near the plug, two cautious bearded men lost in the underbrush, advancing along a
natural pool brimming with fish: among them, moving its caudal
fins rapidly, was—Slice's masterstroke—a sleepy, archaic mana-
tee.

The rebels could barely be seen, stuck in the background amid
intertwining rattan plants, miniature initials, enormous daisies
sprouting over leaves rough and fractured like rocks, stems and
papyruses with straight golden stalks—slender spears—which
crossed the whole wall.

In the foreground: giant chestnuts, centipedes, seashells and
sea urchins.

Their faces seemed slightly deformed, primitive and sharp-
edged, with large, flaring, oblong nostrils, as if seen on the con-

cave surface of a mirror; the beards also seemed distorted, as well as the minute details of the green hats, and even the damp, patched uniforms.

Not far from a reef crowned with dry reeds, the dwarf had found him on the sand, holding onto a pine trunk. Was he a giant from the ocean, who had drifted with the equinoctial tides, too close to land, like those lashlike intestinal worms that always extend beyond their ends? From what shipwreck had he escaped? Was he a god making fun of them by appearing with his arms around the wooden dolphin? Was he a spy?

In any case, the dwarf stood petrified on tiptoe, in a fawnlike pose, as if he had seen a tarantula. Then, with Dionysian movements, he approached the outstretched figure. He touched him. He shook him by the shoulders. He turned him over.

The stranded swimmer spit out a mouthful of thick water, which left on the sand a transparent, gelatinous stain, like punctured jellyfish.

Seeing no reaction, the dwarf dragged him—without telling anyone so they wouldn't steal his find—by his extremities to the next pergola where after fishing her out he had installed Lady Tremendous.

He wrapped him in the first thing he found in the closet: a queen-sized sheet. Like a big ant hauling a dead canary, he managed to carry him to the jungle's edge.

"It doesn't move," he exclaimed euphorically: "It'll be the perfect gift for Fatso."

"Surprise! Surprise!" vociferated the dwarf, his little legs bent under the strain as he advanced along the Trans-Amazon, the name he now gave the lush hallway.

His arms backwards as if he had been sewn inside out, he dragged a big, starched, rectangular linen sheet as best he could—aided by the smooth plush floors—its creases still visible as if it had been folded a long time. Over that rolling shroud, still battered and unconscious, lay the hair-raising, naked macho, mouth agape, arms and legs opened as if floating on the cloth.

Nothing's perfect: his feet were cracked, his hands were stained with big bloodclots, his lips and eyelids were swollen.

"Guess what!" he shouted to Lady Tremendous (taking her siesta with ice bags on her forehead) as his sweaty little face peered
through the crack of the door with a sardonic grimace.

"Oh, I know," answered Fatty, wallowing in her bedcovers,
"brown sugar."

"Take a good look," he said, pushing open the door to her den
with one of his big orthopedic shoes and taking a giant step forward.

Lady Tremendous perceived, in the tones of the dream she was
abandoning, first the cracked feet, then the strong legs with big
knees, then a thick though dormant dong and, over it, his large
scratched hands. The lips were swollen but not the eyelids: he was
Louis Leng.

The exhausted dwarf, his Herculean task completed, could advance no further and fell gasping on a lambskin rug at the foot of
the bed.

Lady Tremendous sat up her eyes like two flashlights, more incredulous and confused than a cat before a Vicks inhaler.

She was the one who finished pulling the sheet, and with such
force—as if opening a drawer filled with cookies—that macho
man raised his head as if emerging from a drunken spree, or a siesta after roast pig in guava leaves. Seeing the futility of his sur-
roundings he turned around, rested his head on his right arm,
closed his eyes and, with a gentle snore, returned to nirvana.

(The marks of his wound remained on the checkered linen
rectangle: blackish streaks, red stamps.)

She, on the contrary, upon seeing him close up, felt so stimulated and happy that the garters of her panties broke:

"I believe," she said, soft and wet, her eyes like the Virgin's in
the church across the street, "that I have an immortal soul."

Nobody knows to what mockery they submitted the
Chinaman, shamelessly taking advantage of his contusions and
nudity.

When he was able to sit up, he shoved aside Lady Tremendous
who, stuffed into an elastic red girdle, was bending over him and
caressing her breasts; he kicked away the dwarf who was drawing
near with raised arms and a plastic phallus between his hands.

He fled along the Jungle, still a virgin, bumping and tumbling.

The lechers couldn't catch him: a sound of propellers, followed by crashing glass, sudden like an earthquake in Santiago de Cuba, deafened and paralyzed them: smashing through the art-nouveau roof of the pergola, wrecking the delicate, vegetal, iridescent crystal and iron structures—a misfired bomb—fell Lady Divine.

Lady Tremendous received her with indignant cries.

The Fist

I

Lady Tremendous lay sprawling as if she'd been poured from above: a pink soufflé. On the floor a bold volunteer—wearing contact lenses and a nurse's uniform—with fleshpot's face between her legs as if giving birth to her, *sans douleur*, buried her heels in the carpet as she pulled on Colossal's black garters: the stockings rose like a glove around the rolls of pulp, dilated like a boa devouring a lamb.

She hooked onto the bloated blubber's earlobes Balinese seashells with different red stripes copied from Italian candies; to gather up her double pigeon chin and to put an end to the collapse of her face she pulled her hair up and knotted it in a quick bun on the top of her skull; with a tight sash, like that of an Attic hero, she gathered the cellulitic folds over her forehead: an African look hid the dam of flesh. A lethargic dolt, Roly-Poly laughed to herself, saliva shining on her lips; she looked amiably at her hands, twin turtles, mouth agape like a moron.

To revive her—such was a limbo into which the "lack" had submerged her—the assistant gave her a couple of slaps, choked her on a Dexedrine with a gin tonic poured between her false teeth. Making her vivacious, all smiles as if she had just popped a coin into the slot of a photomaton, she stuck into her artery a syringe that shot a sudden white spurt in two strokes, like an Arab's ejaculation. Roly-Poly's eyes sparkled: like a mouse fleeing along a tunnel after a banquet of rat poison.

"It's a wonderful life!" sighed the Monumental Miss, now helping her stockings to sheath her doughy thighs.

"Stand as straight as you can, dearies, there's another plump lass who has to be made up to look just like you."

Bacon Fat got up, walked over to the window and stood there beside the grey night, stony and leaden, contemplating the undulating, quicksilver reflections of the skyscrapers.

Right eyebrow pitched upward, the dwarf continued to scrutinize reluctantly the jewels which were so overwhelming, so voluminous that they separated his fingers: like the five in a primer. Among these gems he absent-mindedly laid his eyes upon a worn yellowish silk scroll: he unfolded it as best he could: a scrawny, baggy-eyed Chinaman appeared, powder and lipstick on his face, dressed as an official wearing a golden pheasant hat and several belts studded with precious stones: he was displaying with his right hand a light green jade ring with two battling dragons, as if it were an ancient hollowed coin or an astronomical lens; his left hand opened the black silk of his baggy trousers to let out a soft, perfectly cylindrical member with a fat head and foreskin: at the base, on either side of the fly, two thick spheres strained against the fabric.

On the scroll, seen from above, two naked, corpulent women with outlandish hairdos, hard as helmets, were superimposed upon an embroidered eiderdown, framed by the black pillars of a bed. A round mirror, the easy ruse of those mannered painters stimulated by the despotic academicism of the last rulers of the Sung Dynasty, repeated them with such excessive details that the real couple seemed a dim reflection of what the polished copper inscribed concisely in miniature.

Lady Tremendous returned to the center of the room accompanied. On roller skates.

She was followed, or rather duplicated, by Lady Divine, her eyebrows as shaven, eyelids as thickly coated with strass and mouth as crackling as hers. (Though exaggerated, they were disciples of the little Indonesian tramp who had been found in a basin. In passing he had disseminated the technique of illumination through shock.) The two of them stiff and always facing forward, we'll soon see why, skated as fast as their wheels would allow: without pushing off they crossed the room diagonally, as if there were propellers on their heels.

A wire crinoline spread their gowns into starched, glittering bellflowers: peasant girls from an ideological ballet: out of their front pockets, sewn with flowers, two lazy tomcats with white whiskers peered, their irises dilated. Knotted in front like shoelaces, the corsets containing the supple supplements opened on top into fringed low-cut necklines: separated by white lace, four taut, frozen spheres overflowed.

The second-born's knees remained bent as if she were initiating a courtly curtsy, a little lower than her model's: her right arm disappeared into Lady Tremendous' hoopskirt and the left sustained her balance as well as a dish with a Velazquezian bowl: together they looked like an intelligence test of interlaced nails, the two-cornered figure of dancing couples weaving the sashes tied to the maypole in the phony choreography of a highland festival. The dwarf, that screaming fag, danced with one leg raised and arms backwards as if being pulled by the hands. He had drunk three Nepalese rice beers, whose effect is in inverse proportion to the volume they irrigate. With little hoarse cries he proclaimed himself to be a "Hellenistic lady dwarf rattling her castanets."

The speeding Colossals, bending their legs slightly, did a quick turn as skillfully as Soviet ice-skaters.

Lady Tremendous' whale girdle split down the back. The loosened hooks grasped her puffy gluteal hemispheres between which Fat Number Two's hand sank to the wrist. A very tight, wide silver trinket, like the bracelet of an Abyssian slave or of an arthritic, bordered the dilated pinkhoop.

The second-born was as buoyant as if she had stolen a doubloon from a casket or had rummaged in a trunk of dirty clothes or pulled out a cat caught inside an oven.

Three tiny erect letters on the bracelet—très Bauhaus—revealed Chubby's and therefore her model's collusive membership in the up-and-coming sex sect "F.F.A.": Fist Fuckers of America.

II

Reviled, pestiferous, feared—ergo: portrayed—Lady Tremendous, Divine and the other clean-shaven "girls" in the retinue, the dwarf among them, flew off like a shot, choking on gin and estrogen, to the Garden of the Sung Dynasty. Were they returning from a war party, fed up? Were they preparing for a crusade? Fanatic butterfly collectors, members of a defense committee, possessed medieval children, they quoted off the cuff the ten commandments of the sect.

Catching the slightest slip, always the alert bloodhounds of internal enemies, they informed on one another, sending each other off to rehabilitation farms. They sniffed and drooled like dogs, like addicted private eyes searching for a case of opium on a Neapolitan ship. They wanted to broadcast the slogans on the telephone, on the radio, over large loudspeakers in the street, even on trains. Shaken with lysergic fervor they'd shout: model guerrillas!

When they'd take off their synthetic leopard-skin maxi-coats and put them in the front closet, they'd look like transvestites in the most unpredictable way. They'd enter the restaurant and occupy their places at the back table where the maître d' Louis Leng had hidden them amid paper balloons shit on by flies, cockroachy light bulbs and sour soup vapors, after trying to repress, expel and keep them at all costs on the outside or in the realm of the unconscious. In the most unpredictable way: beneath their synthetic leopard-skin maxis all of them wore real leopard skins. On their wrists some of them had tattoos copied from Japanese terrorists, still dripping blood and green ink; others wore Yoruba bracelets; freckly, scurvied skin bracelets; branded, runaway slave skin bracelets; wrinkled but childlike skin—senilita praecox—and other variations on dermic jewelry. Across their chests they wore the canvas straps of those practical, World War II pocketbooks: thus they were called The Commandos. Those who had something left kept it in woven guano penis sheaths with batik motifs.

To escape the militiamen and avant-garde workers, they'd hide in subway urinals, and sleep over the grills on steaming sidewalks; they'd change clothes in the morgue: their blood froze until they had a scurvied pallor like chameleons. Paco Rabanne's pineapple extract poorly disguised the equally sweetish stench of overripe muscles steeped in formol.

Lady Tremendous, drunk on Cuba Libres, undertook the exegesis of the fist. The others followed, bellowing, multiplying anathemas, hurling forth—as a harpooned octopus spouts black ink—the Obese One's commandments and intolerant remarks.

"The universe," recited the dwarf as if he were in a hexagonal white room, caressing a pelican choking on a wiggling salmon, "is the work of a hurried and clumsy god." His pretensions carried him to the conception of sublime and rosy things, with layers like an ice cream cake. "He also produced," he added, pointing to Lady Tremendous with a wagging forefinger, phalanxes swollen like tubes, making a repugnant grimace as if a ripe sliced papaya were stuck to his face, "tacky horrors such as this piece of flesh with Maybelline on its eyes. Our goal is," he concluded exaltedly, "total chaos. Let's be done with this uproar which is reminiscent of everything, from the aurora borealis to Dominican Dykes." The Chinamen arrived, petrified at the sight of the fanatics. But then they began to recover in pale tones the slow, diffuse movements of Cantonese opera finales. A sluggish hostess in a damp apron passed by, her hair tied with garters in two bunches, handing out white ceramic ashtrays with a brandy label on the bottom, turning around tablecloths stained with seeded hot peppers and taking away those with black spatterings. Making visible rectangular folds she piled them near the entrance in a soft heap, like bloody sheets under an operating table. Two raggedy hags smoothed them out with a ruler.

Behind the tablecloths and the old women, against a reddish wall, a machine with low levers dropped a dark, muddy broth. A yellow spotlight lit up a fishtank. Two fishes—egg-white fins—sucked on the swollen, milky head of the same bamboo shoot.

Louis Leng entered the dining room, bags under his eyes—he had always been jaundiced—his hair slicked back, his manners rough and gruff as if he had lost his temper; he was serving, spilling the now warm beers ordered an hour ago.

Upon seeing him close up, Lady Tremendous felt so stimulated and happy that the garters of her panties broke.

"I believe," she said, soft and wet, her eyes like the Virgin's in the church across the street, "that I have an immortal soul."

And at the same time, to avoid a predictable rivalry, she dumped on Lady Divine over a cosmetic controversy, and deflated her forever with a pinprick, accusing her, to get her out of the story, of oral eroticism, penis need, revisionism, Mozartian fickleness, and a tad of frolicsome Confucianism.

The dwarf initiated the applause.

Meanwhile, Louis Leng, after depicting her to the last detail in a hyperrealist close-up, came flying out furiously—did he remember those Floridian affronts?—so fast that he overturned the sauce of Chinese and fresh shrimp, a stubborn variation invented by him, that he was carrying out on a tray in order to season an okra casserole.

(To his ancient and refined cooking, he added the mastery of confection while he loafed around the Cuban Embassy in Paris. Later he worked in North Carolina, with lots of pastry and young turkey breasts. Back in Cuba he trained the mulatto Juan Izquierdo, who added to the tradition an arrogant dash of Spanish cooking and the rich surprises of Cuban cuisine, which may seem Spanish but declared its independence in 1868.[1] Upon the triumph of the revolution, and more because of the lack of materials to make mutton stew in five ways than out of conviction or disappointment, the Chinaman and his pupil had emigrated to the Cuban eateries of Eighth Avenue. But disgusted with the demagogical abuse of soy sauce and the officious syrups and batters with which the Cuban cuisine tried to maintain its exuberance in exile, they had returned to Paris where their mutual skill in marinating shrimp had found well-deserved respect.)

He cursed in several dialects, sprinkled with caustic Havanisms from the fifties. Then, as he had seasoned his Cantonese dynastic modesty with crude Cuban caprices, he scratched his balls in irritation and dedicated to Lady Tremendous a Taoist grimace of offended disgust, as if a rotten duck had been placed under his nose.

---

[1]José Lezama Lima, *Paradiso*, trans. Gregory Rabassa (New York: Farrar, Straus and Giroux, 1974), 13.

He returned swiftly to the stove. He kicked a cat out of the way. He threw with gusto "globs of fat" into the frying pan along with some garlic cloves. An orange spark lit up the kitchen for a second, like a battle tent awaiting the enemy.

Seeing him vanish, Lady Monumental was suddenly choked with emotion. She swallowed a Valium with jasmine tea, pricked her finger with the crane's beak hanging over her shoulder, tried to be hungry, to sleep, to recite to herself "You will pass through my life without knowing that you did," to think of something else. But it was hopeless. She surprised herself: she went from repose to slow motion, without an initial push, floating almost like a blimp moved by four propellers.

The dwarf and the other powerhouses, seeing their maximum leader disappear down the Forking Paths of the Garden, rushed to the last room to pay—extracting money from a mesh bag—for the "spring rolls" they had ordered as an appetizer. Knowing that with the eclipse of the Massive Miss the party would be over, they exited one by one with dismal sighs, flourishing their cigarette holders as they passed, over the pile of tablecloths at the entrance.

Lady Tremendous first saw him from afar, blurred as if behind a fiberglass screen or behind the Cambodian October rain. Was it her irises, obscured by a barbituric homage to Greta Garbo, or the smoke of frying crayfish flowing from the kitchen in Vermeerian vapors, almost asphyxiating a panting canary in a cage full of shit, and leaving on their coats that smell of fried grease that reveals the economy of Mandarin cooking?

There he was: a big black spot, furious pitch-black, rapid brushstrokes like the shirt of a man executed—tousled hair, lacquer streaks; stiff white slash below—his vest, hands stuck to his body, big buttons, grease stains, black stitches.

He was in the first room. A green wristwatch printed the sheet and the gloom with fluorescent figures, almost invisible phosphorus needles like a fleeting school of sardines over the moving background.

Lady Tremendous approached. The Chinese mulatto's tarnished hands flipped open the fringes of the curtain before her like the sonorous pages of the novel on the air. By the width and length of his third finger which she immediately calculated, bent over the palm of his wide hand, she joyously divined: a tremendous dong.

She entered the room with such a flamboyant greeting that the fringes clattered as they closed from bottom to top—like a Vietnamese rattle to drive away intrusive spirits.

Macho man was waiting for her, caressing his bulk with his right hand: he stuck his fingers between the buttons of his fly and even between his legs, nice and easy: he made a sound with his teeth as if sucking a wine-dipped sugarcane.

Beside an old-fashioned telephone pasted on the wall—bug-ridden wallpaper, flowers and phoenix—a little white neon tube formed a square. Within that blinking frame, in a niche dug into the wall, two wooden statuettes: slant-eyed, grey-haired old women giggling toothlessly, dressed like lepers or Korean witches wielding, in the same sandalwood, knife-shaped tablets. They were separated by a vase.[1]

A low door, embellished with emblems of good omens, was hidden by a double-paneled, thick-hinged screen. On one of the panels, sketched with acrylic dots, an obese singer with green cheeks and bright vermilion on the corneas of her eyes, was looking at the spectator: she lifted her full skirt with her left hand, revealing a fleshy salmon-pink knee, leaning grey outlines. The tip of her raised shoe occupied the foreground. At wrist level the right hand, tightly clasped by a silver trinket, was cut off by the crack.

She appeared on the other panel, fingers tightly joined like a mallet before the greenish, spreading gluteals (à la Botero) of an obese twin also looking at the spectator though standing with her back turned, legs apart, full skirt raised defiantly as if she were finishing a Pyrrhic dance and not the French cancan.

Lady Tremendous pushed aside the screen, touched the emblems on the door. A king-sized wooden bed occupied nearly the whole room. A purple curtain—four embroidered dogs—hid a Venetian

---

[1]Louis Leng was the caretaker of that little altar.

blind between the bedposts.

On a mantelpiece in the room: two polished bronze circles with handles on the back, a paintbrush, three open powder boxes with unguents and different yellow powders. The radiance of hot coals warming the bed and perfuming it with incense burst from a fine grid between the pillows. Over the thick eiderdown with black trigraphs a fat-cheeked, white, almost mother-of-pearl Chinese girl lay dozing: silvery pins crossed her black hair, gathered in a compact bun crowned by a tuft of large pale flowers. Another naked Chinese girl, equally coiffed and robust, lay on top and caressed her. Their pussies touched, squeezed, rubbed against each other until the lips opened like the mouths of two fishes devouring water weeds.

Carefully closing the screen, Louis Leng entered the room. He opened the curtain. Cautiously he kneeled between the thighs of the women caressing each other. When they were about to come, he separated their pussies with his hands, sticking in his prick between them. The two were thus receiving the jade scepter when Leng pushed it abruptly forward and then withdrew it slowly. They opened to trap the same white, swollen, milky head, like gluttonous fish mouths absorbing clear water and then spitting muddy water at the same bamboo shoot.

A jade ring—in relief, two dragons—fit tightly around the base of the member. The animals' tongues curled within each other, forming a protruding spiral. A white silk ribbon stained black as if it had been boiled in medicine, penetrated the orifice left open by the tails: passing between the legs it would be tied at the waist.

And thus they passed the time needed to make lesbian love. They played, touched each other in silence or muffling their giggles in front of Lady Tremendous, who followed their movements fascinated, mouth agape, nodding her head and joining the soles of her feet. The illusory rattling of her coif—yes, she was now naked and had placed on her head a frame of tin flowers: glazed raspberries and cigar vignettes found inside a lacquered casket— was interrupted by the ringing of the bell in the restaurant announcing that the dishes were ready and demanding, futilely, Leng's distributory skills. Again behind the screen, he imbibed daiquiri after daiquiri. His liberal morality was distancing him, as usual, from Cantonese rituality which organizes pleasure like a cyclical feast or hunting party. Thus he regressed to his Santiago life as a bon vivant when in the company of Chinese mulattos and other half-breeds he deciphered his insomnias in Lebanese port brothels, provoked by the lashes of the Leibnizian crown of Bacardi.

Lady Tremendous' capillary little cymbals were interrupted by gastronomical clinking, in turn interrupted by the sustained, deep-throated tones—like a Caucasian bass voice—of a wall clock responding punctually to the tolling of Saint Sulpice.

The sonorous summa of such dissimilar metals: like Sicilian hardware when the earth shakes or a Javanese gamelan when behind a black-and-white checkered curtain a giant she-monkey is about to appear, biting her own tit.

After the Carta Oro rum cocktails and mouthfuls of vital candy which he sucked with ancestral parsimony, as if glimpsing the solution to some koan, he carefully modeled—hand anointed with snake lard—the jade stalk. He returned slowly to the imperial bed where the three houris crouched over the mirror, vainly contemplating their little cracks as they painted their nipples scarlet and perfumed the genitals with after-shave.

When he reappeared from his side of the screen posing as a falconer, he already had in mind, high on the minor spirits of Bacardi, the whole mise-en-scène of his pedagogical theater. As he nibbled on the orange slices hooked onto the sugared edge of the glass, and scratched the seam between the two spherules as if to make sure it was still in its place, he had conceived reality as an empty place, a mirage of appearances reduced to the myth of its interchangeable representations.

He removed the bedspread. He lay face up, hands on the back of his neck. In the copper mirror on the mantelpiece he contemplated himself contemplating the three women who scrutinized their interstices in the other mirror.

His stake kept growing: the frenum pulled it until, becoming harder and more erect, it reached its most towering position. From the mantelpiece, beside the mirror, he took a pot of cream.

After sticking his fingers into it and smearing them, he began to rub his glans. He marked on the orifice a thick, translucid drop: the Chinese girls were reflected concave and miniaturized as they picked up the bedspread.

The watched over Leng's body as if to envelop him in a shroud. One of the yellow girls, arms opened, spread the ends of the cloth beside his feet, the other, beside his head. Placed over the besmeared macho, the net of black trigraphs covered the projections of that topography of brief valleys: a Meru raised in the middle like the main support of a circus canvas. The fabric indicated, upon falling, the first forms, the plateaus: sketching, chiseling him like the body of a slave carved in marble: the slightest inflections were underlined: the jade ring with its dragons. An oily stain extended in concentric circles outward from the mast, whose throbs shook the tent with brief seismic seizures. When the linen finally shaped him without residues, a double void imprinted by the body in which he breathed rhythmic and slowly as if enveloped in algae, then the supine looked steadfastly at the symmetrical Chinese girls, discreetly signaling with his head like a circus dancer ready to perform the shocking variations of the saucer whirling over the bamboo stick:

"Make waves," he quietly ordered them.

The big yellow gals, still at the head and feet of the River, grabbed the tips of the bedspread with their fingertips, excessively cautious—were they performing a senseless rite, repeated until it was a simulacrum? Had the obsessive protocol of revisionism penetrated these back rooms? They began to move it from bottom to top, first timidly, secretively uncovering a statue, then stronger as if to bounce a Goyesque dummy on a blanket: finally it was a raging typhoon sea, waves as high as lake houses and abysses that swept sargasso over the sand.

At each low tide the cloth perched on the merlon: the friction of the rough trigraphs hardened and dilated the burnished cupola. Lady Tremendous was all eyes, or rather, deposited her gaze, as if surrendering it to the paintbrush, upon the descending cloth: the untouchable fascinated her, like the dragon in Vietnamese festivals. She followed the undulations of the Tao, flabbergasted by that torturous up-and-down—the Asiatic transmutation of the

Fort-Da, of the now you see it, now you don't.

"Grab it with your mouth, without touching it," Leng then ordered her.

The shakers shook harder. Lady Tremendous approached the floating tent. She opened her mouth. She wanted to catch it but caught nothing. She stuck out her tongue. The women were laughing, waving their arms as if to divest themselves of the beings who hold one back with invisible red kerchiefs. Lady Tremendous drooled on all fours: the linen dust made her cough. She was choking. Opening and closing her mouth like a fish on land. Flailing her arms. Whining. She no longer saw where her head was sinking. Exhausted she tried here, then there. The capillary hulk jingled and jangled.

She was about to collapse when the column sank into her mouth.

The jade dragons oppressed her lips.

The Double

I

Even when in prison the witches managed to go to the "Sabbath," as a girl of fifteen or sixteen called "Dojartzabal" from Azcaín revealed. The same girl declared that when the Devil wanted to take young girls to the "Sabbath" he placed an image of them in their mother's arms as a substitute. This had happened in the girl's own case since she had found her double with her mother when she had returned on one occasion.

—PIERRE DE LANCRE, *Tableau de l'inconstance des mauvais anges et démons ou il est amplement Traicté de la Sorcelerie* (Paris, 1612), in Julio Caro Baroja, *The World of the Witches,* trans. O.N.U. Glendinning (Chicago: Univ. of Chicago Press, 1964), 163.

Following a Chinese chanteuse from Havana and an ugly little big-headed Spaniard with coins on his chest, Lady Tremendous came out on stage dressed as a sickly flower: her lips were corseted in a bright green sawtoothed chalice: withering weeds and tinted cloth petals covered her uneven skirts of pied pink.

At each "I" in the lyrics, her knockers crashed against each other, she tore off her pearl necklaces, flashed piercing glances at the pianist when his straddling hands failed to capture the petulant juxtaposition of leitmotifs, and even knocked her head against the wall.

These were not, as to be expected, Olga Guillot's songs of blast and bombast, nor Lupe's hysterical psychodramas: what she was shrieking, with as many veils as emphatic stresses, were the enraptured roars of frenzied fat divas from the repertoire of Richard Wagner. During intermissions she would dance with a big strong Colombian mulatto.

More and more addicts of her orthophonic screams filled the Yes, But of Course!* as did the reticent though persevering tearful music fans of Lady Foster Jenkins who dressed as an angel with unfolding wings.

"The public," she pontificated pompously, praising the high notes she pitched from the depths of her kidneys, callously comparing herself with Callas, "is up to its neck in kitsch, lately . . ."

After those German vociferations, a little regressive music—the guitars and güayos of Camagüeyan sunsets—again resounded upon the platforms: the obsequious manager of that downtown dance club for Latin fags uttered in affected French, ". . . et à présent . . . place à la danse." A sea breeze blew in from port.

Shining behind the bar, over colonial volutes and blue glass panes, were the plumes of three gold-illustrated palms, spread like the tail of a peacock. Orchids in the moonlight sucked up the sap of the tree trunks. In an old grey stone fountain, among silver flamencos and an illuminated spray of water, greenish ducks with orange beaks and rainbow necks dipped and then glided away, ruffling their iridescent feathers.

The provincial chords chased Charming Chubby down a long hallway of greyish skylights, a Puerto Rican hunting scene on the ceiling. Synthetic areca palms, always a fresh equatorial green, with dewdrops and even fluttering, iridescent drones, put the finishing touches on its tropical look: on both sides, full oval-backed woven wicker chairs of fibrous geometries, varnished white, glazed tables covered with Hungarian vases, immersed in black light.

Lady Tremendous flopped, or rather crumbled, upon a divan.

Staring at her nails, she decided to put an end to her warblings.

"I've had enough cleaning and caulking," she said to herself as in the spoken part of an aria, "they've nearly beaten me: enough of eating lukewarm tamales and reading *Vanidades* in the cockroachy dens of Yes, But of Course!"

Leaving her double in her place, she'd escape to the most arid mountains, with a goat and a straw basket: fruit juices, fresh

*¡Sí, cómo no!—a gay bar in San Juan (Translator's note).

vegetables. She'd grow her own carrots. At night, before a red landscape, she would think about the struggle between good and evil. She would return transformed: no chicken feet or bags under her eyes, her hair naturally gold, her hands no longer trembling.

With the impetus needed to overcome the force of her inertia as she yanked out her bristly eyelashes—her eyelids stretched, green and wrinkled: a Basque witch's frog—she ran to the refrigerator, took out a bottle, gulped down a last swig of vodka with beef broth, spilling the rest into the sink.

The Texan living room, à la Kienholz, was lined with washable calfskin.

On top of the big television that was always on with the sound off there were, poor things, three little stuffed crocodiles.

In Lady Tremendous' boudoir haven a dark-paned window faced the skyscrapers. Two symmetrical fleur-de-lis sashes, on either side of the frame, gathered the creamy tulle curtain: singed little circles, black edges.

Lady Tremendous rested her feet on big cloth fish, with chrome-plated, pearl-dotted scales. She was meditating. The light from the setting sun lengthened the shadow of the vases over the tables.

She imagined herself facing snowy hills in a tilted, black felt hat, wearing coarse cool clothing, a cane under her arm. She bit into a piece of goat cheese. The music of cowbells scattered the tinkling of bells tolling through the night, surrounded by coppery halos. Her long blonde hair fell to her waist in even waves, beaded with loops and little wild flowers. She sighed. Articulating the vowels—her lips, perfect circles—moving her arms gently as if waving invisible pink veils, she began the *Liebestod.*

It was then that the proud lady impresario of the boîte appeared in boots at the threshold of the entranceway, branches in the background and a curler across her forehead: a glass trembled in her hand, in full effervescence: two enormous white tablets were circling, crashing against each other. At the sight of the puffing pain-killer Lady Tremendous swallowed a scream:

"I thought it was a cat."

And she came down from her cloud.

"Macrobiotic terror," the patroness intoned immutably, "and

that bleary-eyed man who visits you for a fee on Sundays, has made you more demented than a ruminating flounder. If you get one sty from so much straining at twilight, you'll get seven, which will have to be cauterized with yellow oxide. Besides, dearie, that chiseled, fleshy mouth you once had, à la Bardot in black leather on a Japanese motor scooter, is turning into a sloppy circumflex. You drag around abominable slippers."

Pointing to her with a blue-dotted finger:

"Back to bellowing!"

With ritual or exasperating languor, Lady Tremendous moonlanded on the dark stage: more or less Wagnerian sets, recovered from the theater's stock room and taped together, shifted tautly between the two palm trees: the crude cabin of a Pyrenean hermit woodsman fled toward the left, and from the right a Temple of Solomon advanced, trembling: it was such a realistic trompe-l'oeil that at the end of the performance the infidels came near to touch the twisted columns and pale marquetry.

As she went up a ladder lengthened by the stagehand's cruelty—ducks fled in fright, hiding among the volutes—the Diva stretched, adopting fiery positions—the steps creaked—and her throat rose: a bristly blowfish, she duplicated her volume swallowing air, dilating her eyes, and in an archaic, surly German, tainted by Mephistophelian accents, she embraced the most Parsiphonic tessituras.

Severe in her tailored suit, the manager, that art-deco bulldyke, her horizontal curl rolled over her forehead like a diploma, intoned aria entries with a deep, comatose voice, and stamped her heel like an expressionist corporal as if performing a Uzbekistan dance with knives hanging from her heels. The cumin alcohol and an inhaler filled with Peruvian coke, along with the effervescent wafers, had reduced her voice to the lowest chords and had festooned her eyes with forking wrinkles, plastered on with a wad of dark makeup.

The Prima thundered before the backdrop panels, surrounded by tables topped with matching lamps and luminous flowers which the expansion of the "locale" and the audience's Sunday curiosity demanded: her listeners were enraptured Puerto Rican boys, their hair parted down the middle, Peruvian maids improving their lot on their day off, Havanans nostalgic for the Pro-Arte recitals at the Carmelo restaurant—such exquisite inter-missions—and even some Mexican maids, shouldering their Weltanshauung and little tortoiseshell purses.

Having squeaked out her last note Lady Tremendous wel-comed their applause with belched *dankes* and cold sweats. Con-vulsed with nausea, a handkerchief pressed to her lips, she again rushed along the hothouse hallway, pushed open the door to her room and collapsed on the divan.

She bit her cloth fish. Ripped off their pearls with her teeth.

Yes: The Mucha-Mass was falling. At the aria's most tempestu-ous peak an ominous swoon came over her, internal groundswells of "Why am I living alone?", Teutonic depressions which altered her, painting her plaster white with a glaze, a layer of varnish.

Sometimes the poor wretch crumbled between areca palms, staring at some high point: the greasy, curved skylights of the hall-way. A winter rain fogged the metal-framed windowpanes and the greenish ironwork.

In the Puerto Rican hunting scene, the pretext of animal paint-ers, her eyes rested wearily like a black butterfly with wet wings, on a protruding hoof or on the mannered relief of a knee.

She remained, as if ravished or dumbstruck, pondering centrifu-gal seraphim. The manager, always so human, slapped and snapped her fingers at her to see if she'd return to her vast senses. It was no use: her face was falling: crumbling cellulitic terraces, fatty wrinkled love handles from forehead to double chin, no longer sus-tained by the taut bandages under her wig nor her continuous look of amazement, followed by an attack of shivers as well as digital tremblings and defeatist little phrases like "life is over, the rest is a post-mortem" that she had heard in God knows what Mexican movie, to the rhythm of Hesychastic sighs.

Her hands swollen and rosy, like a dropsical child's, she opened the tulle curtain with little burnt holes, vestiges of lyrical fainting spells and of the Colombian grass that served as bait to the pimp on duty.

There she stood beside the grey night, contemplating the un-dulating, quicksilver reflections of the skyscrapers.

She doesn't know how long. She does know that she didn't return to the Texan living room, nor the hall of impeccable areca palms. When she moved away from the window she found herself in a drawing room: low furniture, or rather amorphous piles of silver-covered sand. She was rigid, a quartz mass. An orange vibration, like a tenuous spluttering against the night, bordered half of her body from her eyebrows upward, around the sphere of her hair, following her back, down to her feet. Lights and sounds crossed her in slow, olive oil waves, shining terraces.

A worn-down rug covered the floor with nomad motifs, symmetrical black and white herons, knotty like coat-of-arms initials: they were framed by pale red arabesques, loose threads.

The dwarf, plastered in vermilion, wearing earrings and a gold dot between his eyebrows, gravely unfolded a scroll: identical bodies like zodiac twins, holding hands, streaked by Sanskrit inscriptions which the bejeweled gnome translated with care, squinting his eyes as if deciphering the message of the ancestors engraved on a femur, or a recipe of Nitza Villapol, the Julia Child of Cuba.

Like a dexterous blindman, the customary nurse followed his indications: from an inflated doll on the verge of bursting, she had achieved a reproduction, indistinguishable from the original, of Lady Tremendous who, punctured and petrified in her socialist village maid's costume, returned from the window.

It was then that amid muffled cries and curses the Gloomy Gals entered the salon, all barefoot in quicksilver silk: on the soles of their feet and the palms of their hands, scribblings in grease. Silver-lined and amorphous, they fell into the sandbag seats. They bit their lips, pinched one another, split their sides with horse-laughs, trembling in unison like a colony of birds, brazen, blazing and aphasic.

"Look how we pulled the wool over Fatso's eyes!"

And they pinched each other again, wringing their skinny, tendinous fingers until they creaked.

To calm them down, the nurse handed them in clay bowls a potion they adored, like very thick milk with ground watercress.

"Her greatest strategy," asserted one of the convulsives, holding the bowl with her pinky raised, "is to make us believe she doesn't exist."

And she let out a discreet Draculesque laugh.

"Now the girls can go fresh and buoyantly to the devil's sabbath," the other responded. "Now we'll leave their mothers with an inflatable copy."

She was very pale. She belched. She had on red contact lenses. She was shaken by an apoplectic giggle, mixed with sobs.

In the midst of the chorus, stiff Lady Tremendous kissed her double with the amazement of a circus twin finding the other on top of charred monkeys after a fire.

They put on her skates.

With the rubber doll tied to her waist, Lady Tremendous began skidding gratingly from one side of the room to the other: she leaned over in a curtsey or a tango step: the obedient replica also bent forward. They zigzagged, tripping: the carpet left threads between the wheels.

Lady Tremendous turned around. A rubbery arm sank its pink, cold hand without nails beneath her bustle; the other, holding a plate and a bowl of potion, remained extended, as if offering broth to those present.

Frozen in a friendly little grimace, Lady Tremendous held her saucy Sosie with excessive precaution, as if she foresaw an air leak or pinprick.

Swearing and grunting the Gloomy Gals applauded each turn:

"Look how the silly goose imitates or kisses her."

And they exploded into horselaughs of hoarse vowels, larded with beastly howls.

As if adding to her a lace handkerchief or a little kicking kangaroo, the nurse thrust into Lady Tremendous's wide, round, busdriver style front pocket, to finish off her outfit, a greyish, faded cat with scabby stains, as if he had received sulfurious spurts— that's how he was: the Gloomy Gals nibbled him in their furies, to calm down.

"They've danced gracefully," the hospital nurse declared mockingly.

And, uncovering a red ceramic platter whose fumes rose to Lady Tremendous's flaring nostrils:

"Rabbit stew!"

The Gloomy Gals had to race to the bathroom with their hands pressed between their legs, goaded by itching secretions.

Between the brief fates, the guest at the devil's dance gluttonously inhaled the smoking spirals: masked by a peppery steam a dark green whiff of parsley ascended; a mustard sauce smothering the oniony stew flowed over the red cracks of the enamel in successive layers, withered terraces over the Indian plain.

The Obese One closed her heavy shining eyelids, breathed in the seasoned volutes which she then submitted to her simile's impassive sense of smell, exulting in gluttony. The Gloomy Gals whinnied, and out of pure mischief sank their teeth into the Gaudiesque phalanxes of their twisted thumbs.

"Eat it fast, and give a little to the other!" they shrieked, their little eyes blood-red with mustard-green rims, "and then you'll see what's good!"

"And don't forget that pill," added the dwarf. "It performs miracles on the digestion."

He thrust into her pocket a flat, porous wafer.

And thus Lady Delirium and her rubber bosom buddy sniffed and sniffed, enjoying vicariously the heavenly pudding. The softer Miss Molly lavished a little smile à la Jackie Kennedy, both sweet and sexy, her sole expression which the nominal mammoth took as a sign of gastronomic delight.

They danced with the platter. They played with it, like a cat with his grub before gobbling it down. Already ulcerated and fed up with all that fuss, the austere male nurse uttered a scream which scared them shitless:

"Eat, damn it!"

Like an anteater, Lady Tremendous sucked up all the sauce so quickly that the crisp little shrimps which pleased her so passed into her gullet unharmed; with the skill of a monkey, and in a twinkling of the same monkey's eye, she gulped down the best onion bits and crammed into her silly, laughing crack branches of yellowish parsley riddled with caterpillars.

From the round of piss-soaked cushions the Gloomy Gals feigned verisimile voracity as if they were broken-hearted taxi weepers: they sucked their fingers, licked their lips, exhaled moans and gluttonous gurgles:

"Um, how divine, it's good enough to eat!"

With these incentives and with the well-known hunger that Snow White induces, Lady Tremendous laid her hands on a piece and sucked it. She was going to bite into it when she thrust it fitfully from her mouth which remained open in a grimace worthy of the witch in a rural drama. She threw it on the platter with a ripping spit followed by cirrose vomit. The bilious gall spurted over the dunes and the glaring get-ups of the Gloomy Gals: it was a rubber tatter with painted hair and eyes, the amorphous wrapping of a flayed body dripping sauce: Lady Divine reduced to a grotesque prop, so emptied and so identical to herself that it was horrifying. With the same greedy little smile.

Divine swelled up with air until bursting, dilated her eyes as if seeing inside a grotto, stepped back, the back of her hand against her lips, counted mentally to three . . . and uttered an indescribable scream that turned the earth upside down. She staggered. Leaned against the door. Raised her arms. She began rotating her head and hands, synchronized, clockwise.

The Gloomy Gals, a silvery whirling of vultures, ran from one side of the living room to the other, screaming hilariously, glittering scaredy-cats. The greasy soles of their feet stretched the mustard stain over the black and white herons: the satiny reflections of their clothes traced scribblings in the air: their hoarse voices chanted spells backwards.

Lady Tremendous frightened them away with Latinate hails and signs of the cross.

She shook her head like a Luciferian Basque renouncing that Sabbath. She stuck her hand into her front pocket, looking in vain for the kicking little tomcat they had thrust upon her: all she found, in drips and drabs, were short locks of grey feline hair. She got up as best she could and skated straight past the furies who had begun boastful choruses and Brownian movements, into the elevator.

In tears, on skates she reached the avenue.

The night blanched the high façades of dark glass: a dense, viscous night, saturated with carbonic snow, stagnated among the trees.

Suddenly she clicked her heels together and stuck her arms

against her body like a square corporal, and with her hands opened against her thighs, without taking a breath or a headstart, she let herself fly off, an Egyptian sarcophagus, down the street.

The pavement and background moved as if pulled by giant rollers but not her: she hummed timidly, a faint gramophone voice, a dropsical Shirley Temple. The cars saw her coming and turned on their headlights: polyhedral lights on her eyelids, Tunisian strass arches on the curved cupola of her hair, a wire dome.

Drunks. Drugged blacks. Children shedding light on themselves with bottles filled with fireflies. Motorcycles mounted by naked machos. She heard sirens as if a sea urchin were rotating in her ear. Horns, the American anthem, cracks in the macadam. The steam from the sewers enveloped her in a pillar of gas: she skated downtown diffuse, formless, a soft saffron seraph.

She was slowing down as if the hot puffs of smoke and the streets she crossed resisted her with fine veils: the traffic lights speckled her with whirling shiny lights.

She reached Washington Square. The aluminized warm mist blurred the forms of the square. She kept losing speed as if sand were blowing against her wheels. She stopped beside the fountain. She raised her arms away from her body. Took a deep breath. Relaxed. Looking at the water she automatically put her hands in her front pocket. She had forgotten, but there it was, at the bottom, the wretched antacid.

She took it out. Looked at it with disgust. Furiously she threw it into the fountain.

The surface glittered for a second. A muezzin voice from the water began to sing, reading the sura "Only God Wins": the voice rose on the open vowels, vacillating, scratchy, breathless as if spelling, and then gravely whirled, before taking on the gutturals, beginning again, with a dry cough.

A brief circle formed, widening until breaking against the edges, while another and yet another emerged, expanding from the same center.

Bubbles. Boiling briefly. Gushing foam. Geyser. Light mother-of-pearl lava. Then, like a drowned man returning to the surface, a dark stain ascended, a lock of black hair opening into shining waves, splashed with hot luscious weeds.

The forehead emerged,
black, luxuriant, arched eyebrows,
big eyes staring in amazement,
straight nose, high cheekbones, mustache,
hard, unlaughing mouth
beard
thick veiny bull neck
shoulders
hairy chest black specks around the nipples
dry brushstrokes
wide wrists big hands
smooth waist
hair shaved off
erect sex tendons purple head shining drop
swollen balls full spheres
thighs
knees
legs
feet on a rosette of slow waves
Two black asterisks: Lady Tremendous's eyes.

And he, fresh as a cucumber, with an aloof little lilt that didn't suit the situation at all, as the Koranic shivaree ceased:

"I'm Iranian."

She, crushed and listless:

"Oh . . ." And thinking to herself: "Since I don't have a Chinaman . . ."

"Profession," announced the divine macho man with mucho cool: "Chauffeur."

II

The pointed parapets of the castle faced the bar. In the golden mist, a sinuous path descended from the rocks to the valley as far as the distant hills. Shining toy swans dangling on nylon threads hovered in the pastel blue sky. Over the river, a wooden rainbow.

The orchestra's first chords—yes, there was an orchestra: Cuban virtuosos down on their luck, mestizo opera singers from the

Conservatory, and even a couple of Philharmonic Germans whose faces had been redone, a swastika in their past—drew forth the rosy orb of Lady Tremendous, one mass attracting another. The haughty Hottentot appeared in vaporous crêpe, wearing a winged helmet. But, the majesty of the conceited pachydermic goddess didn't last long: at the first trumpet blasts she plunged into a state of Germanic stress: tidal marshes in her head, as if crammed with crabs, uric acid lightning bolts in her jaw, piss lashes in her uvula, vocal knots and burning embers in her throat, ashes blocking the canals of her labyrinth.

Overcome by an itching yeast, she gave into gargles and liniments during fleeting backstage changes. The itch pricked her in the midst of her most razor-sharp notes. She alternated cauterizing compresses with cortisoned inhalations. She cried in profile.

She sectarianized her diet. Resorted to mint leaves. She futilely exhausted, in inscrutable ethnic downtown zones, Cuban santería, macrobiotic Maoism and acupuncture. Suddenly she realized, rolling her big eyes from side to side as if seeking a transparent enemy, that the Gloomy Gals had entered the Yes, But of Course! posing as posthumous fans of Maria Callas, organized in lyrical, hysterical commandos. They hid in cameras, in a lady's bun or even in a miniature orchid thrown on stage as the curtain rose, micro-transmitters of waves whose immediate effect, aside from the smarting in the part of the body where their rays were concentrated, disturbed the perfect vocal curves radiated by a diva.

With these diabolical artifacts—and not with the mental powers that dolts or cowardly idealists attribute to them—they had destroyed at La Scala more than one vocal résumé, expelled without further ado a bellowing French fishwife from the Opéra de Paris reluctant to invest in half-hearted hurrahs and bravos from the gods, and had also sown panic on the musical yacht of a Hellenic shipowner, filling the lifeboats with similar Mephistophelian electronics.

But the greatest havoc they wrought was, without a doubt, the annihilation of the golden career of Florence Foster Jenkins,[1] whose recital at Carnegie Hall took place amid a seedbed of

[1] *The Glory of the Human Voice?*, RCA 901031.

gadgets hidden in the neo-classical volutes, in the prompter's box and even, thanks to a bribable maid's complicity, in the pyramidal heel of the prima donna herself. The devices were tuned with such skill that instead of structured Mozartian arpeggios, only discordant cackles, convulsive hiccups and scratchy creakings interspersed with unbearable asthmatic panting reached the eardrums of her devotees.

The Callous Gals had made their first appearance years ago, provided with long, foldable telescope- or bazooka-like contraptions, which they aimed toward a vulnerable part of the victim's body, targeted thanks to a millimetric range finder.

Once the bull's-eye was pinpointed, they'd thrust toward it ultrasonic beams, raising the temperature of the bombarded region, provoking an unbearable itch and destroying cells: concentrating on the vocal chords, the rays stretched them irrevocably, generating delirious, intermittent cries instead of well-projected notes, in decibels fortunately inaudible to man but no less real for that: the hall would be flooded with bats.

With this decade's technological advances and the Nipponization of electronics, they had managed to miniaturize equipment whose obvious size would have made them impracticable. They now possessed tiny (though no less malignant) artifacts which they could hide in a wart or in any gold element, lodged in the crown of an eyetooth thanks to the heavy-handed technique of Andrija Puharich, the parapsychologist mentor of Uri Geller whom they had met in a televised session of key twisting.[1]

---

[1]See the diagram of his radio receiver, supposedly in Uri Geller's tooth, in *La Recherche,* vol. 6, no. 53 (February 1975), p. 184:

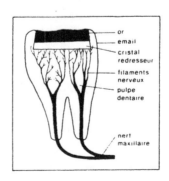

Night after night the quiet effects of the morbid laser were felt in that downtown den with its Bayreuthian airs: concentrated in the gullet they deformed the grain of her voice to the point of cacophonic dyspnea.

Lady Tremendous was emaciated and aphonic: in the neon-flushed rings under her eyes one could already see the synthetic areca palms of that garish Puerto Rican boîte.

She began banging the floor with her lead toes; soon she broke into a kicking fit, her nails bared and tears oily as a black tide:

"God or Big Bang," she pleaded hysterically, while battering the boards with her taps, "if with operetta props and queer ducks in the background I've re-created Wagner's least accessible gam-uts, if I've covered my right eye with feathers torn from the necks of bleeding pheasants and if I wore a flowery helmet and opened my mouth à la Flagstad in slow motion with a hawk perched on my forefinger, it was only to praise your supershow cinerama . . . Why?" and she pitched her tantrum on a higher note, "have you made me so vulnerable, a defenseless target of these rays, and why do you let them revile the design of that voice that sings in praise of you, with such mangy gadgets?"

She stopped kicking, took a swig of "barroco"—coconut milk with aguardiente—and calmed down:

"I have taken," she asserted prophetically, in front of a mirror and with a comb in her hand, "realer than real measures." The impresaria who—it is not time to state—was listening expression-lessly to this trashy monologue, lit a cigar. She blew three bluish rings into the air, muttering an "il y en a, je vous jure," and quickly left.

The door of the envied diva closed in slow bangs.

That same night, with her eyes like this—I'm forming two zeros with my fingers—Lady Tremendous came up with the trickiest solutions to demolish the enemy and zap him at his very founda-tions:

I) She would dress up, in Gilles Larrain's studio, like another idol: wearing the Coquettes' poisoned jewels, little Klimtian eyes all over her. She would unfold under her arms three overlapping panels of a very fine skin, like bat wings. Thus they would leave her alone, confused by the excess: mounted on a scaffolding of invisible threads, she would feign total stillness and death: a thick varnish, like honey, hardening on contact with air, would achieve the morbid, silvery camouflage of the final prostration. She would be an opulent butterfly, a glassy ephemerid caught in her own crystallized saliva, of no interest to those twelve-tone rays.

II) No: painted on a corpse. Sketched over the stretched, damp skin of an inflated stiff.

"Inflated?" inquired the Patroness.

"Yes," added the Expansive Sister, "because in order to reproduce myself over a carcass without residues it would be necessary first to increase its volume with starch paste douches that swell up inside."

III) "Plus vraie que nature!"

Quoting the Manager, Lady Tremendous pushed open the door of John de Andrea's studio on the ground floor of an old loft in the Bowery. To enter she had to jump over, of course, three winos hugging empty bottles, lying among cardboard boxes and piss-soaked newspapers.

Covering her nose and wearing a rabbit smile, she advanced among jointed wooden arms, broken death masks, and sleeping naked machos leafing through girlie magazines, in tanks of liquid plaster.

Yes, as a last artifice to stun the Callous Gals, she had resorted to the manual skills of a maker of doubles, similes, Sosies and other naked dolls lying face up, recently set aside and gasping after the act, so realistic that they could easily replace the original, called in the sculptor's slang "the breathing version."

She presented herself wrapped in vaporous pale pink satins with cloth flowers: the petals fell in yellow bunches to the floor. She had allowed herself a couple of Mickey Finns and looked with feverish irises at the bluish shiny edge of things.

"Let them take me," she asserted, completely doped up, with the nebulous majesty of Candy Darling entering the Factory, "for my deadbeat double, for my self-denying substitute working with benign Asiatic flu and a fever of 104."

"Yes," she burst out, rinsing her eyes amid the immobilized dullards, "the fatuous fabrication of what I have come to order, is to replace me, opening her lips properly, in my most resplendent and vulnerable appearances in the *Ring* cycle while I, behind the front curtain, protected by the thick Bordeaux fabric of gold galloons, will achieve the purest forms of the highest tessituras. If I manage to trick them with this transformation, I will escape electronic cruelty."

. . . And she broke into disjointed sobs, interspersed with friendly giggles.

She had to be gathered up: she had softened from her hilarious shakes and had spread all over the place. They put her on a circular sofa to jell, supported by cushions.

In the plaster tanks, though drowsy, the *Playgirl* sloths squeezed their noses so as not to laugh: they filled their ears with putty, counted the beams on the ceiling: a laugh, a start or a sneeze could split the mold.

"To obtain precise and empty figures"—this was John speaking before a display of knees—"mute, molded statues sheathing the body without residues, or merely plausible prostheses, the sole secret is the *immobile soaking* of the model, the prolonged immersion in a coagulating substance after the absorption of sleeping pills: impatience and trembling are ruinous. Thus"—and he displayed an overflowing plate—"this anxious consumption of mushrooms, leading to mental sloth and stillness."

It was a wide corridor, or rather a gallery: filled with plastic palms painted a tropical, ever-bright light green with the tears of night's dew and even buzzing, iridescent bumblebees. Trembling among the branches, on pedestals, were gold-illustrated mechanical princesses, all their hinges creaking, or glistening hydraulic dwarfs with oval pupils: more than seasoned robots they seemed like fragments of live Pygmies completed through prosthesis. In front of them were emaciated girls on their best behavior, hands and feet trapped in volumes of plaster: they faced little fluorescent plates filled with mushrooms. A deformed, big-headed model, circumspect as a bishop, contemplated in her right hand a great red felt pincushion. The little dishes were divided like bowls for dogs, the mushrooms in slices: white, fleshy stalks covered with fine sand; a pink bulb, bright blue grooves, glassy fibers. Their Jewish nannies and cats, also weak and anemic, followed the enraptured models. A cavernous light—as if in the Palermo catacombs—blurred damp, filtered through dirty bull's-eyes, bathing the hallway of the plastered lasses, clouded at the end by a poisonous vapor of boiled mushrooms.

The kitchen furniture was of white formica and nickel-plated tubes. A dirty ivory vein-streaked paper covered the walls: it was interrupted by lighter rectangles: the marks of torn-off landscapes. The pantry, imitation marble, exposed the gap of a drawer; four little basins of water protected its legs. In front of the cupboard, two slant-eyed old women with straight grey hair and a yellowish complexion, Indonesian witch doctors dressed in black oilskin, shook with lazy but inhuman gestures as if regulated by washers, a checkered tablecloth, or rather a very fine, raffialike net. A white, volatile dust, like penicillin, fell over the thick-painted cardboard tiles.

Lady Tremendous swayed her head: she followed the hags' movements like a cat watching a windshield wiper.

"Damp nights will come," muttered one of the crones, without ceasing to shake the fabric, "when the milky light will be reflected on the skyscrapers: the full moon, that dwarf of tempered magnetism, will call to the hallucinatory mushroom and impart to him her lethargic power."

And she went on to wash a pile of mushrooms with fermented wine. At the other end of the table, the other veteran was acidulating a pile of truffles on a luminous platter, as if made of ground bones or fish eyes.

The sound of the acid-scorched moss was accompanied by the metallic sound of little knives with which the old women cut them in sections; the joints of the hydrostatic midgets creaked in the distance alternating with the snoring of the narcotized ninnies.

The hags were preparing for the monthly descent: starting at the cellar, in the clay stratum of the island, they had dug narrow galleries extending in a straight line, sinking slightly until reaching the damp, greenish, stagnant mud of the nearby river.

"The dark and the miry," stated the wrinkled, spidery Sumatrans, "favors the budding of these pocket parasols, lending a bitter edge to their flesh and filling their fine edible leaves with the sleepy, thick flow of water."

At each full moon they'd descend to the cool underground like sick scorpions, their shiny, compound eyes black-dotted pineapples. They'd wear artificial plush and glass fibers; they'd avoid eating animal products on the days preceding the transplant. With disembodied voices they'd intone a lethargic song before inserting the mossy, infernal offerings in the soft earth.

They'd murmur incantations invoking the salamander forms in threaded sheets of bamboo.

At each lunation they'd return to the surface with the previous descent's harvest. To sample the soporific effects of the little umbrellas, they'd dine that night on a big omelette fortified with the fleshiest fungi. Prepared with the greatest care. They'd shake them in a sieve: sticky, sandy piles would fall to the floor: a white halo would expand beneath the moving fiber. They'd wash them with vinegar water, cut them in fine slices with a Gillette. Thus they would present them, in small compartmentalized trays, to the sculptor.

For the girls they'd season some morels with crushed garlic and sweet-and-sour sauce. They'd mix them with noodles and vegetables browned in sizzling oil. They'd pop open cans of beer. They'd eat with chopsticks.

When, mildewy from soaking in plaster and fed up with truffles, she finally obtained her goal, the threatened Diva dedicated herself, secretly reversing her proclaimed plans, to the imitation of her double.

She placed the biological robot, completed through the addition of electrical organs, in a reclinable chair; she sat facing the big doll, its porcelain mask skillfully made up or clean, and plugged her in carefully. The facsimile started to function: she moved her eyelids gracefully, her lips forming German vowels; she raised her boneless arms, opened her hand, cried, and even dropped her big head forward to bow for the final ovation and the poisoned flowers of the Callous Gals. Lady Tremendous, as if obeying audio-visual stimuli, reproduced the slightest eyelid flutterings and romantic grimaces of her simile. She could verify, in a mirror behind the chair, the progress of her repertory of mechanical gestures, of her expanding ma non troppo automation.

Seeing the involuntary advances of her mimicry and in her muscles the echo of successive, interspersed movements, as if she were a polyhedral, multicolored cyclist or an ochre nude descending a staircase, she decided to resume, without further misgivings, the obscure sevenths of the *Twilight of the Gods.*

More corpulent and compact than a cetacean, and never without the bulldyke in black tie who, after announcing his rentrée, snorted at each appoggiatura, Lady Tremendous came out on the stage of the Yes, But of Course! packed with nostalgic fans, already bellowing her Celtic warblings.

A Bavarian castle—shades of Disneyland—faced the bar: glaring streaks of gold paper, confusing the queer ducks, mirrored a vast, slow river. Through the cracks of the joined panels one could guess the volume of the verisimilar copy.

Against her, and not against Lady Tremendous, now changed into a coarse, vociferating doll, the malevolent villains directed their disturbing rays. They insisted so much, upon seeing how little they affected the sublime Brünnhildildoings of the soprano and her fine chromatic replay, that they provoked in the sculptural rubber black and blue rashes like festering pimples.

They found the rubbery twin all scalded, as if she'd been sprayed with boiling water. Swollen cankers of parched celluloid enveloped her, a morbid necklace.

Mad with envy, the Callous Gals threw the microtransmitters to the floor and crushed them under the lighted heels they wore on festive nights. They cursed. They scraped with their nails the inside of their mouths to spit out bloody phlegm. They uttered electro-acoustical blasphemies and tore out their transistorized eyeteeth. From the hole in their gums a little green thread streamed over the gold lamé.

Upon the last hurrahs and an "Uf!" in minor key, Lady Tremendous fled down the hallway kissing a ruby and the portrait, in a cameo, of Ludwig II of Bavaria. Dazed with happiness she opened the dressing room. She looked for a moment toward the night and fell, not on the Texan divan, but into a bathtub of hot water.

Thus Botero painted her, quoting Bonnard and in homage to the history of the bel canto. Glossy and expanded, reflections of water on her rosy skin. Coral red mouth. Little feet. Her red hair in lacquered waves. Her cunt: a piggy bank crack in a little black triangle. White background.

The Fist

I

Hurling zeros and suras, swiftly brushing past other Mercedes, they cross the city. The concave front windows reflect, with excessive clarity, passersby, trees, store windows—neon Arabic letters, fig boxes—fleeing toward the windshield that duplicates the opposite sidewalk: a man in shirt and tie who looks to the right, squinting his eyes, and on the yellow stripes of the pavement an old man in a white beard is about to rest his heels. Dome in the distance, brick minarets, cluster of loudspeakers.

They—who?—: Lady Tremendous, goddess or queen, ibis or kiss; the dwarf, and a local cat, disguised as emirs from the Persian Gulf, in Moorish cloaks, black braids around their foreheads, English accents and green sunglasses. And then there's the chauffeur: lowered to fucker-by-the-hour who, to revenge the duo's tortuosities, sets free the backseat amplifiers: a vile and Andaloose music drills the right eardrum and mini-labyrinth of the left. They bite their hides, beg for earplugs, swallow furious lysergic raspberries:

"To the desert, to the desert," they rant and rave, adamant. Through the scanty windows formed by the slabs of that blue then copied by the Chinese, one could see, beyond the red minarets, the snowy mountains. On the tile floor, in tin washbowls and polished pitchers, a dense and creamy water settled, with which the dwarf rubbed the clients. From the bones of the feet, which he stretched one by one till they cracked, to the scalp, the brief assistant greased the gentlemen with that ointment. In a gray felt hat like a helmet, he came in and out, drawing open an opaque curtain; he couldn't manage with the pails: his arms trembled.

Fed up with boredom and petrodollars, the turbaned magnates ran from the ever-inflamed towers—and even some, emerald yokes, from Maracaibo—rosaries of big amber beads, Koran in hand.

Stretched out among prophylactic vapors, on a fringed tapestry of nomad motifs, Lady Tremendous underwent the apotheosis of the fist. She divided infinitely divisible branches, she censured, for their impurities, other contacts. She was surrounded by the chauffeur with his old buddies, persistent like her, big mustachioed machos with big bellies, shirts and flies opened. They were having Bloody Marys.

A galaxy of light bulbs yellowed the small living room. Among piles of rolled tapestries the binary initiates left their bicycles. In the next chamber gifts accumulated: wrought dishes, lamps, candelabra, hookahs, a mannerist Toledan apostle, and a portrait of Kennedy, in canvas and bas-relief. After making their offerings, they'd go up a spiral staircase until disappearing into the soffit of stalactites, among burnt flags. They'd order yogurt with effervescent water. They'd go out drunk into the street. The wind was blowing so, that it drove you crazy.

They catechized among scaffolds, in the ruins of a mosque. Among the riggings which supported the dome, pigeons nested. Thirsty silk merchants arrived in caravans. The wind raised red sand, frozen drops.

A hawk perched on her forefinger, the wealthy and robust Lady Tremendous widened her pupils, arched her eyebrows, looked to the left to indicate "forbidden." The dwarf dragged himself convulsively to her feet, screaming like a newborn rabbit being devoured by a red-haired dog. They ate dried fruit.

The faithful swiftly crossed the patio. A big eye. Covered in black rags. Reflected in one another, cracked polygons formed blue buildings, walls which decomposed into other walls, rotating domes, palm trees.

From a marble serving dish with geometric designs—the name of the prophet, stylized—Lady Tremendous scooped out with a big spoon thick glazed syrup with lumps of caramel and sugar candy, which she served to the initiates. The potion started putting them to sleep. Sluggishly they circled the Great White Lady.

Yes, they adored her for being fat and creamy. Fists raised high,
the idolators asked her to bless the scrofulous and the virulent, to
guide disputes or to save lambs. In little blue lamps, the tip
crushed by fingers, hemp burned in oil.

In the distance one could see the lights of a toy-filled bazaar. A
tomb in the middle of a pool. Carvers of turquoise and white forehead stones labored in nearby porticoes.

Back to the baths—there the stereophonic chauffeur awaited
them—they gave in to prescribed infamies: in translucent grey
nylon baggy trousers, tightened with elastic at the thighs, they
played with dirty water. The dwarf, sporting an Austrian midwife's apron and a protruding gold dental plate, brought over,
on a metal cart for serving hors d'oeuvres, a douche jug with a fat
spout and a Pompeian nozzle. With solid Vaseline and in the
presence of the chauffeur and other confused fans—sniffing dirty
old men, stinky truck drivers, masseurs and masturbators—he
impaled the Overwhelming Lady, clumsily, with the porcelain
prick filled with a gluey water that swelled up inside.

They played with excrement and coins. They drank fermented
palm juice. Splattered with urine, they painted black masks.

First he put his joined fingertips into the anus, as if to close a
flower or caress the snout of a tapir; then, the hand already inside
up to the wrist, he turned it slowly, with precaution, from one
side to the other, as if waiting for the slight sound that opens a
strongbox.

In the tiles Lady Tremendous saw the reflection of the hand
sinking in, as if into another body, between her rosy, rather soft,
buttocks. Luminous, it went in and out; a thin glove, the lubri-
cant seemed to envelop it like a piston.

Then the chauffeur appeared with an unfolded screen on his
head, as if protecting himself from a gale wind. Right in front of
the gasping actants he extended, with false modesty, the tense
screen joined by thick hinges. Behind it, he placed on the floor
two large lamps.

Through one of the panels the obese lady was lifting the cloak
with her left hand, revealing a neatly formed fleshy knee. The tip
of her shoe brushed the fabric. A little hand with its fingers tightly

joined, as if in a mallet, appeared before her spread gluteals. At wrist level it was cut off by the crack.

The expansion of Islam and/or petroleum had unchained in that country, as in many others, an Ayatollesque mania of "seeing everything big." Soon it was deduced, though never uttered among the megalomaniac businessmen of the steamy establishment, that a talkative and crooked runt, planted in the midst of that set of satraps in bloom, was, and don't feel hurt, an intolerable buffoonery to the imperial vanity.

With the rise of the flaming petrodollar, the new breed rushed to the tidy blue tiles of the house of ablutions—reflections of jewels and newly coined dinars crossed the resinous vapors of the sauna; with the rising class the dissipating dwarf arrived at the perversion of his handlings. In a mutilated pyramidal cap like an Assyrian hunter's, and on his wrists many trinkets with phrases ciphered like groped and grateful impresarios, he staggered up the tin stepladder. The plated soles of his orthopedic bootees resounded against the steps, coins falling on an aluminum drum. His little hands reached table level: the stiff customer lay wrapped in a cloth dampened in camphorated oil as if in a greenish shroud. With the remedial fluctuation began the clinking of the offered bracelets and the racket of the nodding stepladder. The ointment of boiled nettles was seasoning beneath the chaste towel the bulky or swollen body.

He reached, and that was his loss, such spare and speedy methods that, now without basis or caution, his hands repeated on their own the prophylactic movements, like a swimmer on dry land. The sassy whorehopper would crumble onto the couch and, ipso facto, the showy ding-a-ling would resound, without further introduction than the Vaselined hand: deepening pleasure, he also deepened without further ado the gloved and shiny embalmed fingers into the loosened sphincters of the despots.

His mannered manipulations contaminated his muffled clientele: there were those who went to be humiliated by an Abyssinian swimmer, a vulgar braggart deliberately contracted by the house, in simulated gymnastic classes.

The mild-mannered stretched awkward bellows between their

arms, provoked punching bags, rowed out of rhythm or leaped hydropically upon a cork mattress as the Master sardonically giggled, inviting the eventual knuckle-blows of his pretended irritation.

Behind a thick colored glass door, where the screen of a giant television was reflected, one could imagine the creeps on pedals, obediently imitating the oiled, half-naked leader ready to correct the slightest fault.

Others, more tortuous, required programmed furies: every Tuesday, under the promotional impetus of leather and rock—which the ticket-seller, to drown out ays and whip-snappings, turned on full blast—several solvent and mild old men assembled for belt lashings, slaps and burns, with their remunerated chastisers.

"And click and clack!" the dwarf hummed mockingly, leaping like a grasshopper amid the morbid cubicle.

And, according to the reception of his digital assaults, he continued cataloguing *s*'s and *m*'s for the next session.

Until one day.

A potentate from Oman arrived at the dump, drunk and drowsy after ethylic jiving—the vodka's reflection divided, over a red platter, grayish piles of Caspian caviar—chubby with innocence and perspiring aspirations.

No sooner had the jolly drunk crossed the horseshoe doorway, bordered in gold by Koranic precepts, than the maieutic dwarf was straightening his lubricated gloves and, with a grimace of disgust, preparing to wriggle his rotary hardware.

When the soused Omanite perched big bellied upon the powdered massage table, the pygmy's knotting little fingers were waiting for him, erect and bundled in rubber, like sickly asparagus in green cellophane.

The phalanxed pyramid penetrated abruptly, a lusty fairy, between the dripping gluteals. The great magnate felt a burning stake, a thousand dazzled formic little seraphim, or rather the assault of drilling darts escaping a smoked wasp's nest. With the grunt of a Hittite mask and closed fists, he jumped from the table, pushed from behind by a cleft-footed demon. After a somersault upon plush cloths, beneath an uneven cloud of talcum, he bounced cursing onto the chessboard floor.

The dexterous dwarf began to kick and broke into a comatose giggle, as if amused by the gambol of a big squeezable toy. Senselessly he tried to applaud, but his concave palms couldn't coincide to produce the explosive clash. Fanning himself with his little hands outstretched like stork paws he blurred the precise shapes of the halo: the besmeared gloves left in the expanding dust broken, black stripes, the droppings of charred birds in an atomic mushroom.

He coughed from the dust.

A deformed bishop, the potentate slid with rectilinear decreasing speed past blue, burnished squares. Suprarenal shots of rage yellowed his joints.

Above him, also duplicated by the floor but further away, diffuse, with fuzzier colors, a chemical twilight spread in cumulus clouds and even further up, whitish basins in the reflection, Alhambra cupolas where, sheltered by stucco, the medicinal vapors of the baths accumulated.

The dwarf, dealing knuckle blows to the mist and waving a wet towel as if to make his way through a cluster of locusts or frighten away flying witches with a holy shawl, followed him in his diagonal displacement, as if through a range finder, until the slippery saphead ended in profile, after a final complex caracole, against a copper basin and a giant jug filled with snake lard, piled in a corner along with three vinyl-handled brooms.

Upon the purple noise little oval soaps fell from a shelf, and ten tiny plastic packets of shampoo bounced twice against the tile, like jacks tossed by a furious winner.

The sheik stood up, swollen and staggering. With his trembling forefinger—his emeralds: dancing little lights in the steam—he pointed at the dwarf:

"Cat vomit," he addressed him while wrapping himself, like a judo wrestler leaving the mat, in the plush robe a fearful attendant handed him, and putting on wooden clogs with striped platforms, "you are the mangy and sickly inversion of the expansion."

He was shaken by biliary seaquakes: his thick eyebrows joined—porcupine bristles—a straight crack on his white face;

white lips. He dragged his *r*'s like barrels filled with stones. The last bewildering sparks of vodka traced around his head an orange flash:

"Shameful scarecrow," and the crack spread as if pulled apart by two hands until becoming blubbering liverlips or a horn, "without awaiting a telegram, appear before the authorities with your pajamas and toothbrush. In less time than it takes for a monkey to scratch his eye, you're going to disappear from this shady establishment, from the city . . . and off the face of the earth. You have abused caliphal tolerance, allowing yourself backroom backhanded handlings, violating the annals of the Empire. Now you're going to hear the wind raising sand."

The executor's voice resounded in the chamber and was re-peated three times without fading, amplified by the cupolas. The Squirt barely managed to shut his eyes tightly and cover his ears with his fingertips. He bent over, shrinking, until his elbows met his knees.

He spent the day running to the urgent call of his kidneys, the whole night awake. He listened and counted the taped, nasal sup-plications of the muezzin from the loudspeakers on the large minaret. He heard birds pass, the reactors of a Boeing, saw the blinking lights of a luminous El Al jet.

Though starched and bleary-eyed, he appeared the next day, as usual, at the baths. With excessive caution he dispatched his morning clients. At twelve o'clock sharp he ate a dish of cu-cumbers and yogurt, tried some skewered beef and mint tea. He managed to take a brief siesta. At two, he was as good as new. He took his time, singing and handling with care the dropsical three o'clock client. He had a beer with him. He was going to have a second, ice cold, when the telephone rang. Jumping like an elec-trocuted rabbit, he landed on the wobbly bench where he reached for the phone. His little teeth were chattering. He picked it up ipso facto. There was nobody.

The impertinent ringing was repeated at four.

At six, dragging his clogs and shedding amber beads, the old man from the ticket office came to get him.

He abandoned the dark little room where he had regaled so

much digital comfort and entered the swimming pool room feigning great cool.

Behind the pool, coinciding with the pink pillars of two arches, impressive mulattos were waiting for him in green patent-leather shoes and silver-plated shades.

The reflections of the water fractured their black canvas suits into big white stitches and veneered buttons: reflections in their dark glasses traced divergent dotted lines.

As soon as he caught sight of them, the dwarf bolted like a shot. He was running zigzag between the grooved columns as if pursued by a recently castrated boar or a gunshot. He slammed behind him shutters and doors, unfolded double screens, opened boiling showers full blast, unfurled steam pipes, sprayed on the floor hot resins and burning stones, razor blades and soaps, advancing at different speeds like an automatic miniature, hopping like a frightened hummingbird. When accelerating, he tripped and bumped his head. He fled rapidly, almost blindly, toward the back of the baths. Chanting a little battle song.

But he heard behind him, sounding like an approaching chain of fractures and cave-ins, the protective stockades falling like walls of sand, one by one, with the same innocence and agility with which he had raised them.

Like a shot he entered the back room and double-locked the door. Behind which he piled an exercise bicycle for motionless pedalers, Charles Atlas dumbbells, two oars and some steel wool. He climbed up rusty, porous pipes that sweated cold water, grabbing onto the faucets like a monkey spider; panting and disheveled, he lay down upon a red tank, near the roof. He clasped his hands and rested his head on them. He gathered up his legs. He was lying on a hill, over an underground river. He was listening to the flow of the water in the earth, of the blood through his hands. The friendly murmur shielded him. He thought of a leafy tree, vines and rope ladders hanging down from the top.

He fell asleep.

The ruffians broke in, knocking down the door. They brought with them a big net as if for fishing salmon or hunting giant butterflies, and a pole for knocking cats off trees. They brought concentric walls of poisonous gases. Slogans and work songs. They were communicating to each other with walkie-talkies. The old ticket-seller was pandering to them with fawning, cloying gestures.

They attacked the pipes, helter-skelter, and then with the fury of a blindman tried to dent the tank. The dwarf jumped at each cane blow as if the earth were quaking.

They placed bets on who would knock him down. They laughed. Threw a bottle of napthalene against the ceiling.

"We're going to fry you," they hummed.

They perforated the barrel. Ripped the pipes on either side, leaving it maimed, like a heart ready for a transplant. Rusty water gushed out, a fermented curtain against the wall. When it had stopped spouting, with the pole as their lever they picked him off in one fell swoop. Preceded by the tank and by a clattering of nuts and bolts, the dwarf fell on his ass like a ripe coconut, amid the hearty laughter of the killers.

Before the jesters could bend down to pick him up, he shot out between their knees, separating them like an automatic door. He threw a bottle of beer at them which broke into pieces in a puddle of foam. One of the agents tried catching him with the net, the other threw a hot stone at him.

Though dopey, the tiny one slipped away. He bumped, fell and bounced; he crossed their traps like a jutia streaking through the jungle. The agents of the law jumped, threw themselves upon him but the jack-in-the-box evaded their grasp, like a greased piglet at a country fair.

They got fired up. Started chasing him with lassos: a wild colt. The circles of the rope marked symmetrical, braided wounds on his skin, like leech suckings, bloody imprints and emblems of tenuous threads, bloodclot rosettes. The dwarf refreshed them with a sponge, continued running, rolling down the stairs: reciting Yoruba spells that paralyze poisonous vermin and enclose them in circles of fire. He cried. Spit blood. The glass from his missiles, bouncing back like sharp boomerangs, tore his feet.

The ruffians saw he was a loser, but still weren't content. They pursued him sneakily from room to room, amid jumbled platforms, throwing coins at him for amusement, and on his wounds spurts of detergent.

They grabbed a thick plush giant towel. Each with his arms opened, shook it from two corners. The radio scattered a blur of music, screeching marionettes and marimbas. The walkie-talkies exchanged giggles.

In a laundry room he hid among dirty sheets, baskets of clothes, soapy gloves and aprons. He stopped breathing. Turned white, rumpled, sketching on his skin the initials of the sauna. A hole in the wall? Had myriapod gods transported him to a safe place? Blinded the henchmen to his image? Or, according to the logic of the place, had he evaporated?

"Where is the traitor?" demanded the apparatchiks in unison.

The ruffians paused, snapped their tongues, punched their left palm with their right hand. They spat. Wiped clean their soiled dark glasses.

The ticket-seller detected him: a tremor in the pile of dirty clothes. The malevolent goons threw him the towel with a wide and contemptuous gesture, like drunken fishermen throwing a net. The plush engulfed him. The cloth bulged on all sides from his kicking: his little hands molded five rounded tips.

(Thanks to a system of hand-numbered cards which he distributed as gratuities, the ticket-seller—pierced ear and a cigar in his mouth—named himself "owner of the numbers game." He treated the Shah's constant companions as upstarts, to provoke megalomaniac bonuses as a rejection. Social climbers, hustlers and promoters from Dubai were welcomed with arrogance and calculated insults: the compulsion to humiliate him tempted those big bosses of the future to disproportionate compensations. The police—he said to himself upon seeing the ruffians—should have meaner, more rentable techniques of submission. "Here I am," he spit with excessive poise two dark streams of saliva at them, spilling from between his teeth like spurts of venom, "to help my country to the best of my ability." His trembling fingers, with rings and nicotine stains, hoisted a cigar with a slobbering tip.)

After pillowy leaps, tracing at full speed the diagonal lines of the towel, the fugitive crossed the borders before the bailiffs could grab him. Buried at each leap under a wool landslide, a hundred fiberglass earthworms on his back, he suddenly skidded, falling into a fluorescent plastic basin left by the old charwomen each morning, filled with soaking sackcloths and sponges. A soapy, itchy solution entered all of his orifices. He coughed and shook, invoking Mohammedan mercy, when a new flood inundated his ears. He tried to escape. He slipped down the slope. A cloud of fluff closed over him.

He sniffed and snorted like a stray Lhasa Apso, rubbing his eyes with his fist. The fuzzy wave was choking him. His pursuers tied the towel to the edge of the basin with a rope: thus they carried him out on the street, like a hothouse tree in a flowerpot. The atlantes held up the hooded captive by the base. The loyal ticket-seller followed, shedding fateful comments like "it was written" or "that's the way the cookie crumbles," an Andalusian mourner pitching pious ejaculations to a penitent. Now on the sidewalk with their package, they threw the basin into the gutter and tied the rope around his feet. All packed. A hole for him to breathe. Into the trunk of the Cadillac!

It was evening. Through his wrapping he heard the sound of the city slowly fading. Two blasting loudspeakers exploded on either side of the trunk, one into each ear, to lacerate his labyrinths and slice his Eustachian tubes into pieces with sadistic decibels: a bombardment of flamenco particles. He was able to detect, none-theless, because of its Moorish meows, the presence in the back seat of a local cat.

The packaged gnome gnaws his paws, misses his earplugs: he is disoriented by the flamenco tap-dancing. When it finally stops he doesn't know where he is or how much time has passed. He does know, however, that the car is moving fast, leaving the city—he recognizes the murmur of pigeons nesting in the dome of a mosque in ruins, and then, the drone of stone carvers in a bazaar filled with toys.

For long hours sand laps against the curve of the trunk.

They stop at an inhabited place: running trickles of water. He makes out the wheels of a mill and, duplicating its constant mur-mur, the hum of a prayer wheel.

Crackling cranes.

Pulley wheels, ropes, pails lowered, the brutal voices of nomads.

They're on their way again. It's night. Cold in the trunk. Whistling wind. They're rolling along in a straight line at a steady speed, tearing through the sand.

He awoke beside the sea. It was a modern beach hotel, or a *medersa*. Three floors: different woods, arches with different curves. Along the top of the walls, star-studded blue tiles. Meticulously carved and varnished balconies, ancient fretwork, face an inner patio.

He felt as if a mocking crowd were going to peer down at him on the ground, a yellow background of orthogonal pavement stones whose joints were enameled by saltpeter.

Neither the smell of the sea nor the sound of waves. As if the arches were sealed off by thin steel sheets, the exterior was only a painted, masterly mirage.

Coastal silence: no birds.

He was alone, sweating.

Neither a trompe-l'oeil nor windows: in the water, steady audible splashes: a naked swimmer emerged.

He was a local superstud, sporting mustache and beard. Black spiral specks radiating whirling tufts of hair joined at the middle line of his chest. Big purple prick. Tendinous heels.

"I've had it hanging around these beaches," he said to him, passing smoothly under the arches without breaking anything: while drying himself with his hands, he splashed him with saltwater:

"It's a shame there's so much poverty in a country that has defeated an invincible enemy."

"On behalf of a lovely obese and albino woman," he added without a break, as if repeating the preceding statement, "I am looking for animals with human faces."

"What you need are dwarves."

II

They all resurfaced at the Grand Hôtel de France: Lady Tremendous "somewhat heavier, no?" she said in front of the dressing table mirror, suffocating in a metallic whalebone girdle, a giant comb in her hand, the chauffeur, each day sassier and sexier, the dwarf, a fugitive from the pioneers of the fatherland, and the Persian cat, now a wicked scoundrel, too spoiled to eat canned food.

They had been lodged formally for one night only, by two filthy overworked old women whose foreheads were riddled with faded blue tattoos, the last stronghold of native servitude: catering to the requirements of colonial splendor, they scrubbed with enzymatic and perfumed detergents the peeling porcelain of the urinals and, on all fours, the tarnished tiles of the reception hall.

"For Madame"—they adopted the traditional distance of overwrought managers—"we have reserved the pink room. For the chauffeur, a cot in the shared bedroom in the cellar. The dwarf and the cat will have to settle for the broom closet. There are no mice."

And they continued distributing mothballs frenetically, to all the empty, broken-down wardrobes, scrubbing with Tidy Bowl the dry bidets—traces of blackish foul-smelling urine and chlorine—the nickel-plated faucets with dents and grease stains, the clogged and rusty drainpipes.

The next night they met for a hermetic session in the middle of the oasis, hiding in a white marabout, with deep windows and carpeted with mats. No one could guide them to the appointed place. Separately, dressed in dark rags, they had crossed the palm grove. They were oriented by the wind, the direction of the air current in the furrows, the different date trees, and, closer, the copper crescent and the star, a lime dome, a nailed green door.

They had drunk fermented palm juice. Beside the funerary tumulus, sweating, bored, they touched one another in silence. Aided by faith, which sensitizes the devoted and dulls the ear of sentinels and thieves, they had mocked the vigilance of property owners and the observant eyes of thugs, crossing, unharmed the beats of watchdogs.

They didn't startle ringdoves. Or tear out pomegranates as they passed.

They wanted to vomit.

They undressed.

Lady Tremendous did three passes with a black kerchief, a camphor ball tied to its tip. She turned around in circles, spraying a white lily incense with her atomizer. A long bell-shaped dress pressed snugly against her body—the dwarf had reinforced it with three borders of embroidered inscriptions.

Standing at the head of the tomb like a Parsi guardian welcoming birds, the recompensed chauffeur, a glass of fermented juice in his hand and shaking with pyloric tremors from Zoroastrian hiccups, scratched his black, now copper beard which Lady Tremendous had painted with henna. His eyes were light, the color of beer or of dull opal, his cheeks smooth. He was still naked. Or almost: with linen dampened in anis, the dwarf had braided him a giant turban with an overripe dome, incrusted with gold threads like those of a Mongol mausoleum. His large feet with filed nails rested on the edge of the tomb. From under the turban his thick hair stuck out, burnt and disheveled. No rings on his fingers.

He drank down in one gulp the dregs of the lekmi, as if swallowing a shrimp cocktail. Sweating.

The four were about to fall into a striped dream when they were distracted, from the far end of the marabout, by a slight, steady fluttering of wings, barely audible. The cat raised his head suddenly and dilated his irises like two flaming hoops.

Upon the enameled majolica floor of the mihrab, coinciding with the footsteps turned magnetically toward Mecca, in a slow descent, a pheasant came to perch, its neck and wings very white, ending in mother-of-pearl feathers.

Suddenly, the mihrab shone with the splendor of a frosted urn, as if illuminated by a boreal halo or a great invisible neon light. From the prophet's name silvery letters sparked like a blowtorch, live blue coals lighting the whole retreat.

They remained still, with the stupefied stiffness such miracles require. They did change colors, however. Lady Tremendous seemed to turn to marble. Her breasts, becoming exposed in her rapture, were taut, puffy spheres. She thought she was rising, in a swirling spiral, toward the skylight, drawn up toward the Koranic heavens. The pleats and planes of her dress were projected in a helix around her body. Three borders of Kufic inscriptions surrounded her in a fan.

She was actually dense, thickened by fear, anchored to the floor. She shone, of course, like the rest of the miracle-struck mihrab; she had the ease and majesty of an elephant seal slithering into position for intercourse.

The chauffeur: red, also hard, without veins: like porphyry. Closed fists, stiff arms. Staring at the burning name, as if the letters called to him. He entered into erection. They no longer knew, those gathered under the vault, which miracle to praise more, the incandescent arabesques or the massive musculature that throbbed—the only thing moving in that wax museum— touching in its diastole, with the proverbial knot, his belly.

Small Fry only managed to close his eyes tightly and cover his ears with his fingertips. He bent over, shrinking, until his elbows met his knees. Thus he fell to the floor, as if about to walk on all fours; he looked back and upward, a little sulfureous face, prenatal with amazement.

The cat jumped over to the tomb and after having sniffed meticulously the black velvet covering it, as if dividing it into squares, he began a baritonal purr, festooned with familiar scales, as if seeking at the bottom of a closet a newborn babe.

Thus they stayed for a long time till the splendor of the letters diminished, fading until gloom spread from the windows through the green flags and again took over the place.

The moon blanched the mats.

One could hear the howling of the dogs closer now: the night watch was approaching the marabout.

The old women, at first reticent, then softened by the dwarf's servile cajoleries, had allowed them to settle in, though only until the end of the month, on an abandoned floor of the Grand Hôtel— bug-ridden remnant of the colony—whose tile floors conserved intact the former fleur-de-lis.

The dwarf, more roguish and rascally than ever, was in charge of collecting cheap furniture, taken from poorhouses, and the burnt clothes of beggars or madmen, full of rough seams and knots, that he went looking for in leprosariums and even at the morgue and which, to distinguish them from insipid garments bought firsthand, he qualified as "lived in" or "rich in history."

Lady Tremendous and her mangy manager had taken lodgings in a former "blue suite," now requisitioned by the government and the cockroaches, which they had refurnished to flatter the chauffeur's petulant taste and the cat's plush demands.

With its creaking noise, advertising misty puff of smoke—when, in auspicious constellation, the water and the electric current coincided to feed it—a humidifier the size of an embalmed gorilla turned the room into a second-class Indian platform during monsoon.

Facing the fan, suspended from the soffit with garlands of crepe paper, the cat swayed in a wicker basket, surrounded by little dishes of fresh salmon and cushions of the same black cloth that covered the tomb in the marabout.

They had placed around the room frayed flags and unfolded mats and scriptures. A wooden buddha dozed among withering tuberoses.

The next room had been compartmentalized into two scanty cells for the women, the partitions made of closet doors, Napoleonic desk-drawers and even the shell of a car—the hurried work of the chauffeur.

They carpeted it with a worn-down rug with nomad motifs, symmetrical black and white herons, knotty like coat-of-arms initials, all bordered by pale red arabesques with loose threads.

A lamp, a Bauhaus vestige made of disks and triangular supports, shed an anemic light on a giant tree—the dwarf's find—an ornament with two braided, polyester trunks and varnished, elastic leaves, always a fresh equatorial green, with dewdrops and even hovering iridescent hornets.

An American atomizer, which had to be kept upright and away from your eyes, sprinkled the unmistakable scent of Algerian oases when the frozen drizzle looms at sunset and after the Ramadan.

They went a bit too far with the birdies: too many and too warbly. What's more: they had to be wound up every morning.

Lady Tremendous entered that cloister secretively.

The dwarf preceded her, smoking marijuana, in a red plush dressing gown, his pockets bulging like panniers. Repoussé pigskin gloves and deformed slippers.

The bluish silhouettes of the sleeping old women dissolved in the smoke: breathing bulks stretched face down like long animals: they were covered by horizontal undulations, their own hairs. Large black jointed rings crossed by shiny lines: caterpillar or centipede segments.

In the midst of that calm witches' sabbath—slow tumblings on the platforms—in a silence barely interrupted by the archings of Lady Tremendous and her continuous clumsiness, the dwarf took out of his pocket a glass vial with a big glass stopper, carved like a diamond. He opened it swiftly. Lady Tremendous drank with gestures of vomiting: a light yellow unstable liquid, sedimented gold; at the bottom, dense, muddy dregs. When she had absorbed the last drop from the opalescent bottle, panting and containing her nausea, then, exalted by the furies of the philter, they went off to get the chauffeur, who, roused by abstinence—they had seasoned his food immoderately; a jade green ring oppressed the base of his member—was prepared for the act.

In the shade of the creamy sheets falling from the berth at different heights according to the twisting and turning of the lethargic, like frayed banners in the dim light of a nomad feast, Lady Tremendous thundered, naked and painted pink. A continuous gold line marked exactly the halfway line of her body, from her head, where it coincided with the part in her hair, to the black, curly triangle of her pubis; there it sank in, to reappear between her buttocks and rise along her back, following the curve of her spine and neck until reaching her head again.

Infuriated by the early rising and by the follicular pricks of continence, the macho man came in yawning, his eyes irritated; between two insults he scratched lecherously where it itched most.

As if flying on his slippers, the dwarf jumped from a berth

with a small cymbal in either hand. He pretended to clash the disks up high: he stopped them before the crash.

The performers looked each other in the eye as if revealing themselves in the silence of a nocturnal tent. The Iranian began to undress. Still drowsy, he lazily took off a Mohammed Ali sweatshirt, which must have once been white. He threw it on one of the cots. From amid unbraided tangled hair a grunt burst forth.

He was barefoot. When he lowered his pants he wasn't wearing underpants but horizontally-striped light Japanese green and cinnabar red bathing trunks. One would have said—if one didn't know him of course—that he was bluffing: what stood out on him, my friend, pressed tight by the stripes, as if the complementary Oriental colors were serving to sheathe such a generous and touchable contribution, was . . . let's not beat about the bush . . . a big basket.

Lady Tremendous looked him up and down and, resting her eyes for a moment, like a stunned hummingbird, on the taut and rounded frontage amid the fresh grass and prehistoric blood, she let escape a muffled "it would be madness."

To take off his trunks Superman stretched the elastic of the waist like the string of a bow. The vibrant dart leapt out rapidly, like a Chinese squirrel set free from a trap. With his right hand the chauffeur tried to smooth it but his attentions and caresses, instead of imparting peace, stimulated vigor.

The dwarf disappeared for a few moments entangled in the mosquito net; he returned carrying on his head a copper platter. The atlas's stature invites us to a description from the top:

Surrounding the center, occupied by a pyramidal display of floured pastries, were regular depressions, like little concave mirrors, for tiny cups of mint tea and, toward the outside, wrought geometries: a border interrupted symmetrically, on each side, by four little gloved fingers. Below, on a background of herons and arabesques, two tiny frozen yellowish feet advanced, in black canoas.

In silence, looking at the floor, the performers ate from the dish; they exchanged saliva-drenched delicacies which they inserted between each other's lips with their fingertips.

Then, at a signal from the dwarf, the chauffeur, whose body sparkled, surrounded by white halo, touched the Obese One's forehead, as if to imprint a red dot between her eyebrows. Careful, fearful of separation, he followed the gold line with his forefinger. Over her nose, over her lips; he put it in her mouth.

Lady Tremendous parted her teeth, felt it penetrate her, stiff, still syrupy from the pastries, to the back of her tongue. There the signaller stopped him for a moment. Then, still looking at the floor, he slowly withdrew it, until it was again on her lips, shining with saliva, again touching, lightly, the gold line.

He moved it down her chin, and, falling from terrace to terrace, like an overturned sled, down the white double chin that made Lady Tremendous' neck Rubensian. It disappeared in the narrow path between two twin peaks, whitewashed and smooth like stupas. It then sank into the little well with a wrinkled bottom and, further below, into the wet fault with slippery walls.

It came out.

The dwarf simulated another clash of cymbals.

Lady Tremendous turned around slowly.

The finger, vacillating acrobat over the gold thread, began to scale the other slope.

It entered the rough passage, drier and more direct than the preceding. It made a mock retreat. The dwarf assented with a nod. Then the Iranian, spitting into his hand, his fingers joined in a cone, sank it as far as the phalanxes, into the tunnel that dilated as he passed.

It didn't slide in smoothly, like an oiled embolus, but rather forcing rings, unrhythmically, with abrupt pushes. The dilated hoop, pink elastic, squeezed the protuberance of little bones like a ligament soaked in reddish ointments.

Lady Tremendous lent herself meekly to that obsessive diversion. With her fingers she parted the whitish and gravitating masses of her gluteals—iridescent reflections—magnetic spheres: they wanted to fuse together. Her nails marked on her skin violet blotches, streaks, slight slashes that grew with the pressure of the fingers: the compact hand, wet with saliva, advanced, sinking toward the Obese One's gummy center.

After the ligament, the first hairs, then the lines of his palm disappeared—thus the dwarf saw it, from below. It then pen-etrated gradually, going as far as the narrow wrist; there a silver bracelet detained it, engraved with three letters, like the signal agreed on to suspend the digital advances, or the handkerchief knotted at the middle of a penis judged too large for a deflowering.

The dwarf had located a Moroccan mirror on the carpet, and in the oval mercury among cranes, like a winter lake, he contem-plated upside down the giant's entrance into the grotto.

Out of ritual excess or sarcasm he had donned a big hat like a Ghardaian tower with its four imploring fingers.

The chauffeur got as far as the initialed trinket. The officiating dwarf raised his right hand, as if to detain or to bless him. Squat-ting, squinting his eyes, he had examined the threshold of pen-etration in the mirror. When he saw that it had gone the required length—the complete disappearance of the hand—making a racket with his joint springs he stood up and murmured into the ear of the sweaty penetrator a contrite "enough."

The hand withdrew in the dark, hoop by hoop until liberating the fingers.

Rusty lay aside the mozabite tower and raised the mirror.

The overlapping digits separated with a slight snap, intertwin-ing pieces of a riddle of nails, Siamese twins, or figures fornicating on a painted screen when, upon the arrival of a rude visitor, the gates are suddenly closed.

Lady Tremendous awoke the next morning with a song in her heart.

When after lunch she found the chauffeur already up to his twentieth can of Carlsberg as usual, and, amid beer belches and pissing foam, he ran off with his buddies to the hammam of the Medina, she feigned an oval-shaped yawn and lowered her eyes.

That very night she began to swell.

She ate brown sugar straight.

She raised her legs on a little wooden chair with painted fish.

Disturbed by her weakness and swelling, the old women made her get up in the afternoon. They bathed her in sweet basil. They shook squeaky bells in her ear and told her dirty jokes to revive her. They gave her a whole glass of eggnog, with lots of rum.

Feigning an interest in high fashion, to kill time, they busied themselves in dressing her up. Beneath the more and more rounded curve of her belly, they fit her into a full-length black and white skirt, stiff like a marble cylinder or a column with split circles, loops and sashes; a large embossed belt, with inlaid black stones like domino pieces, sustained it over her dome.

They had gathered her hair in a voluminous, shiny onion bun crowned with a braided coif, of silver circles and grey rhombuses, both dazzling and severe, like that of an Austrian queen.

They didn't finish adorning her.

As they were adjusting pins, she was assaulted by the first pains. The old women undressed her rapidly; with persistent or stubborn gestures they recited hoarse exorcisms; they bent over to examine her.

They compared the anal opening with a coin and began to race ostentatiously down the corridors of the Grand Hôtel, looking for mustard compresses and Muslim amulets that had been rubbed against the marabout wall, which they stuck, while invoking the planter of the first date palm, on her ears with tribal emblems, on her ankles and wrists and, as much as possible, on the dropsical fingers of the Obese One squared. The dilation increased from dinar to five, and then to fifty.

(The dwarf was trying to feed very sugary, warm Quaker Oats to the cat who vomited every spoonful, squeezing his lips together and whining for Fatso.)

The old women clattered their slippers about the bug-ridden dens, tied up in knots; they dried their tears with mopping rags. They prayed hidden, turned toward Mecca.

Grabbing onto the plastic tree filled with diverse glazed fruit and warbling birds, Lady Tremendous gave one big push. Upon a black and white-threaded bedspread—remnants of an Iranian tapestry—appeared the runt hatched by the dwarf, falling on his feet as if upon a lotus flower, his right hand raised and opened, his face smiling and red as if from fresh blood or porphyry.

He beheld a "lion's view" of the whole space and took seven steps: to the right, to the left, to the north, to the south.

Uttering sharp, intermittent cries—they touched their lips with their fingers as if to announce a kabila tribal wedding—the old women managed to catch him. He was fleeting and slippery, as if he were covered in oil. They put him into a wash basin. The jack-in-the-box was shaking and wanted to break loose, flee toward the tree. With a cloak of seven stripes they wrapped his feet. Lady Tremendous then looked at him:

His skull displayed a protuberance. His hair, braided on the right, was bluish. Wide, smooth forehead; between his eyebrows, a small circle of silvery hairs. His eyes, protected by heifer-like lashes, were big and shiny. His earlobes, three times longer than normal. Forty solid, even teeth protected a long, pointy tongue: excellent sense of taste. Strong jaw. Delicate, golden skin. A body both flexible and firm like an arum stalk; wide torso, the chest of a bull, rounded shoulders, full thighs, the legs of a gazelle. His arms, hanging, touched his knees. A thin membrane joined his toes and fingers.

From the sand, a rapid, jet black snake leapt at the neck of the Saharan leading the caravan. And struck him down, poisoned.

Twice the earth shook.

In the mountains, among the ruins of a snowy fort, a lamb was born with a human face.

All night along the wall the muezzin blew grating, monochordal brass trumpets. He was followed by dogs masked in muzzles, and two hooded acolytes in white wool burnooses, whose lanterns traced rapid lines sloping like *l*s or lances on the wall. At their passing, pigeons and whitish lizards fled, hiding in the hollows of the ancient supports.

Disposing of lanterns and flutes, illuminated by the first quarter moon, the retinue of heralds was a procession of Zurbaranesque monks wearing white voluminous robes against a dark green sloping background.

Sleepwalkers and dogs joined the procession.

The watchdogs were licking the copper doors.

When they concluded their tour of the citadel—passing fireflies intertwining with the towers ending in tips like imploring fingers—the sky clear now, they lingered briefly in the patio of an ancient *medersa*.

They contemplated, in the motionless pool, the reflection of perforated windows, green borders, a declining succession of arches and, further away, the white, uniform rectangle of the sky.

"No one shall eat or drink from dawn to twilight; no one shall smoke or fornicate until the return of the first quarter moon. The right side of the body must be washed first. Alcohol is proscribed forever."

"The night must be spent in vigil: religion is living upside down."

Two days later the fanatics tore up the vineyards and fired upon a wine delivery truck.

They condemned an infidel to a salty well, having been caught in the baths with a youth.

The fasters denounced those whose breath was clouded with a beer, or whom they suspected of secretly listening to Libyan broadcasts.

Friends beat each other up.

They fainted over piles of saffron in the marketplace.

To observe Lent, not without ostentation, the old women veiled themselves in Prussian blue; they darkened the tattoos on their foreheads with henna and indigo.

They turned the mirrors to the wall.

To these self-imposed deprivations they added silence.

They assigned the yellowish dwarf, who was deteriorating, his eyelids all wrinkled, to be the household magnet of sickly or sinister emanations: they stripped him bare, wrapping him in white cloths.

They locked him in the cellar, surrounded by anis branches.

They fed him only milk and garlic.

They all faded, plunged into sorrow and aphasia, confined to a sluggish attic amid dented copper pots and pans, three piles of dirty tablecloths and a withered carpet with dog-bitten herons.

Already declining toward true ascesis, the old women sold their last goods wholesale. One morning, needy, soaked, and bedraggled, they went off singing the Koran, as if insane or blind, to beg for their daily sustenance along the narrow paths of the Medina, among the tanners and tripe-sellers.

Now in the last stages of Lent, the Iranian, having withstood without relief the restrictions of abstinence, multiplied his customary doses of kif for the night, mixing it with even more violent herbs, in order to recover the strength lost in fasting, and escaped, though just for a while, from the dingy dens and the old women's vigilance.

He didn't see zebra-striped colors nor hear tense strings buzzing in his ears; he didn't cross concave, phosphorescent geometries.

After a few hours, when he thought the effect of the little fibers was over or now innocuous, seated in front of the television—discordant violins, sleepwalking choruses—a black demon with tentacles blew on his chest.

He jumped out of his chair, as if freed by a spring. He threw himself against the glass of the windows.

With a bloody undershirt and his kinky hair coiled, in tweed pants and a pair of broken dark glasses, he ran the whole night, calm and menacing, talking to himself and laughing out loud, along the muddy, stinking streets of the citadel.

He was never heard from again.

Neither was Lady Tremendous.

Some thought they recognized her dancing Berber folk dances with a skinny shrew, and exhibiting her webfoot as a circus curiosity or a miracle, in the annual festival of a mineral spring.

They were singing with twangy voices and wiggling to the rhythm of a fiddle and a piano on a platform, in front of a cracked store-window filled with Orangina.

It was also said that she hung around the discreet cathouses of Tetuán.

But surely it wasn't she.

We find them again in a purple house with rolled up awnings blackened by filth.

The dwarf was leafing through a manuscript: white geometries.

The old women were weaving under dried willows, among sad dogs whose ears had been devoured by wolves.

Further and further south: they settled in a mill whose wheels were pushed by the forking waters of a stream.

A *santon* in rags whitened by the flour, an opal necklace in his hand, gave them oil and wine. He was followed by the Koranic cat—little owl face—who was always inquiring if there was any danger.

The sound of the prayers duplicate that of the wheels.

They asked questions day and night. Early in the morning Lady Tremendous went out to eat grass.

Far away, in the middle of the desert, one could see among steep rocks, brick and terracotta mausoleums. They were topped by meticulous constructions, revised year after year: stork nests.

Every afternoon they contemplated the low disk, the last reflection on the horizon. They dressed in jute jackets.

Mangy Afghans followed Lady Tremendous. The women bit their veils. Madmen and dervishes recited the suras backwards. Nougat vendors—horizontal trays in their right hand—guarded the catafalque enveloped in black velvet. Mustached men with little cuneiform eyes brandished lances which they rested on their strong feet.

The patio was vast—twisted creamy trees, ravens.

Lady Tremendous stamped her two-toned high-heeled shoes over the grave, so that it sinks. She lay down on a white carpet and rolled back and forth, until the mound was flattened out. She stood up, humming.

Embalmed Islamic twins: thus, beneath minarets, lay the dwarf and Lady Tremendous' anal son. Koranic saints joined together, buried between oil wells, listening to the sound of the pigeons, their feet ciphered in gold letters.

They adopted other gods, eagles. They indulged in rites until they were bored or stupefied. To prove the impermanence and the emptiness of everything.

Dalkey Archive Paperbacks

FICTION: AMERICAN

DALKEY ARCHIVE PAPERBACKS

FICTION: BRITISH

BROOKE-ROSE, CHRISTINE. *Amalgamemnon*	9.95
CHARTERIS, HUGO. *The Tide Is Right*	9.95
FIRBANK, RONALD. *Complete Short Stories*	9.95
GALLOWAY, JANICE. *The Trick Is to Keep Breathing*	11.95
MOSLEY, NICHOLAS. *Accident*	9.95
MOSLEY, NICHOLAS. *Impossible Object*	9.95
MOSLEY, NICHOLAS. *Judith*	10.95

FICTION: FRENCH

CREVEL, RENÉ. *Putting My Foot in It*	9.95
ERNAUX, ANNIE. *Cleaned Out*	9.95
GRAINVILLE, PATRICK. *The Cave of Heaven*	10.95
NAVARRE, YVES. *Our Share of Time*	9.95
QUENEAU, RAYMOND. *The Last Days*	9.95
QUENEAU, RAYMOND. *Pierrot Mon Ami*	9.95
ROUBAUD, JACQUES. *The Great Fire of London*	12.95
ROUBAUD, JACQUES. *The Plurality of Worlds of Lewis*	9.95
ROUBAUD, JACQUES. *The Princess Hoppy*	9.95
SIMON, CLAUDE. *The Invitation*	9.95

FICTION: IRISH

CUSACK, RALPH. *Cadenza*	7.95
MACLOCHLAINN, ALF. *Out of Focus*	5.95
O'BRIEN, FLANN. *The Dalkey Archive*	9.95
O'BRIEN, FLANN. *The Hard Life*	9.95

FICTION: LATIN AMERICAN and SPANISH

CAMPOS, JULIETA. *The Fear of Losing Eurydice*	8.95
LINS, OSMAN. *The Queen of the Prisons of Greece*	12.95
SARDUY, SEVERO. *Cobra* and *Maitreya*	13.95
TUSQUETS, ESTHER. *Stranded*	9.95
VALENZUELA, LUISA. *He Who Searches*	8.00

DALKEY ARCHIVE PAPERBACKS

POETRY

ANSEN, ALAN. *Contact Highs: Selected Poems 1957-1987*	11.95
BURNS, GERALD. *Shorter Poems*	9.95
FAIRBANKS, LAUREN. *Muzzle Thyself*	9.95
GISCOMBE, C. S. *Here*	9.95
MARKSON, DAVID. *Collected Poems*	9.95
THEROUX, ALEXANDER. *The Lollipop Trollops*	10.95

NONFICTION

FORD, FORD MADOX. *The March of Literature*	16.95
GAZARIAN, MARIE-LISE. *Interviews with Latin American Writers*	14.95
GAZARIAN, MARIE-LISE. *Interviews with Spanish Writers*	14.95
GREEN, GEOFFREY, ET AL. *The Vineland Papers*	14.95
MATHEWS, HARRY. *20 Lines a Day*	8.95
ROUDIEZ, LEON S. *French Fiction Revisited*	14.95
SHKLOVSKY, VIKTOR. *Theory of Prose*	14.95
WEST, PAUL. *Words for a Deaf Daughter* and *Gala*	12.95
YOUNG, MARGUERITE. *Angel in the Forest*	13.95

For a complete catalog of our titles, or to order any of these books, write to Dalkey Archive Press, Illinois State University, Campus Box 4241, Normal, IL 61790-4241. One book, 10% off; two books or more, 20% off; add $3.00 postage and handling. Phone orders: (309) 438-7555.